The Darkest Side of the Moon

M.C. RYDER

WARRINGTON
PUBLISHING

DANBURY, CONNECTICUT

The Darkest Side of the Moon
Copyright © 2025 by M.C. Ryder

Published by Warrington Publishing
Danbury, CT
www.warringtonpublishing.com

Printed in the United States of America
First Edition
ISBN: 978-1-944972-71-4 (paperback)
978-1-944972-70-7 (ebook)
978-1-944972-72-1 (hardcover)

Book cover designed by Getcovers
Edited by Mike Waitz at Stick & Stones

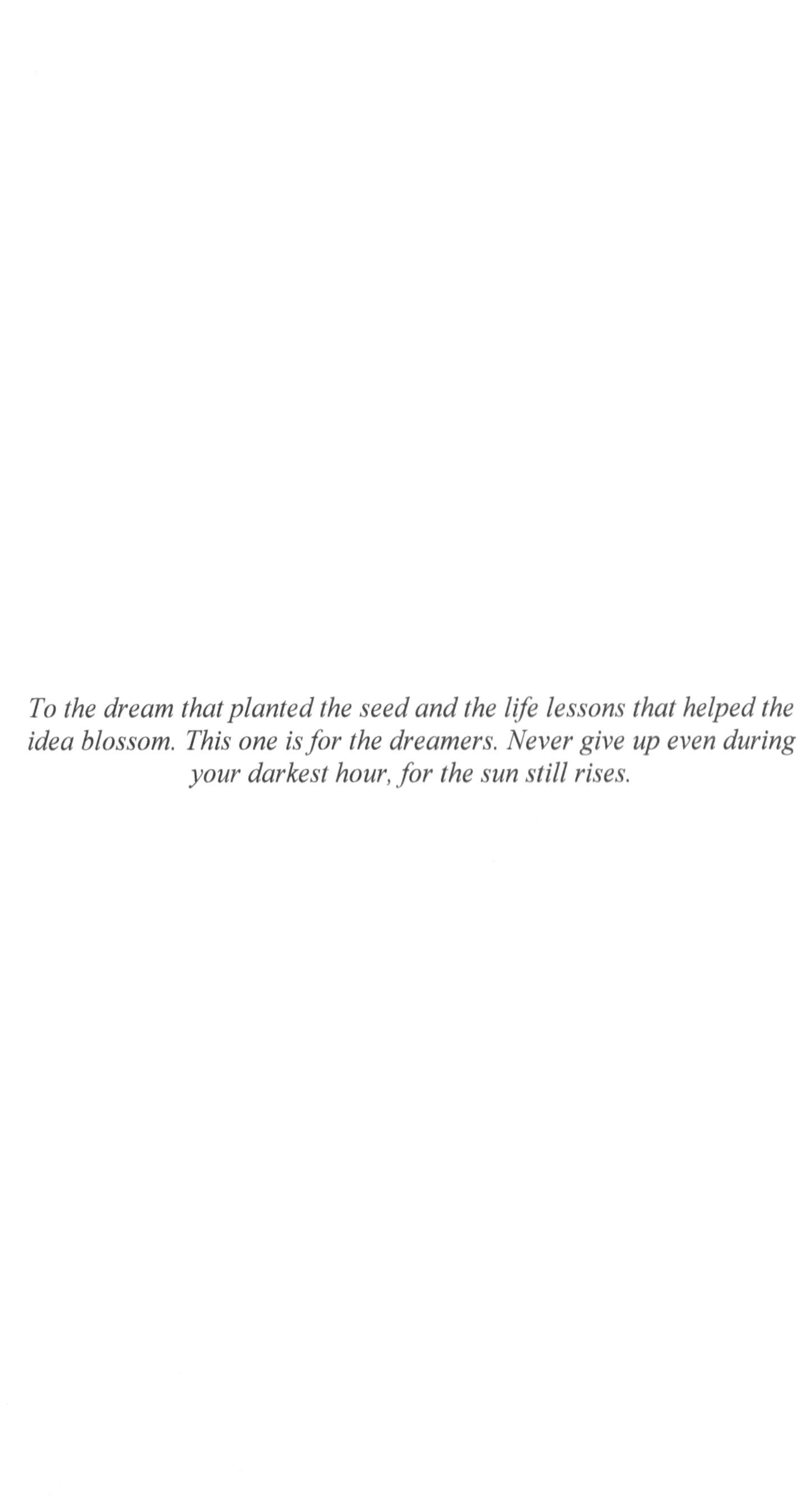

To the dream that planted the seed and the life lessons that helped the idea blossom. This one is for the dreamers. Never give up even during your darkest hour, for the sun still rises.

Part 1
DARKNESS COMES

Chapter 1

You smell stagnant air inside an unknown house. Feel in total isolation. From a distance, you see the distorted face of a young girl around your age facing you. Two males are completely attentive to her. The girl gasps while both males turn their attention in your direction, only they look beyond you. One male's face is veiled in shadow, while the other has one distinction you are able to perceive.

Blue eyes.

Suddenly, you are one with the girl. Feeling her fear as you watch both guys vanish into the unknown. Where are they going? Will they be seen again? What are you going to do if they don't return? How will you survive in this forsaken world?

Beep. Beep. Beep.

You groggily reach over to silence the deafening ringing in your ears as the image lingers in your mind's eye. You want to slip back into that dream world to get answers, but it's already too late. The image has faded. You feel cheated. The only way for you to have any closure is to allow your imagination to fill the gaps. However, you know there will be no satisfaction. It already haunts your mind.

The honking of a car horn announcing the arrival of your ride snaps you back into reality. You look down with confusion and wonder when you get dressed without realizing your movements.

"Good morning," your best friend, Camille, cheerfully greets.

"Morning," you mumble as you click your seat belt into place.

"Late night reading again?"

"No, got caught in a REM cycle this morning."

"Did any tall, dark, and handsome guys make an appearance?" She flashes a grin.

"Ugh," you moan with dismay.

"That's a yes," she squeals. "Do spill. I never get those kinds of dreams."

"Cam, I don't remember."

"What color were his eyes?" she brushes you off. "Did he have baby blue eyes?"

You roll your eyes and direct your attention to the scene outside the window. You know how Camille can go on and on. Mostly about the man of her dreams that she lacks to dream about. Camille has an obsession whenever you report having random dreams. You have been having a lot more lately. None of them make sense. Most of the time, it feels like you are being transported back in time, but this one was different. You sense it hasn't happened yet.

You snap to attention when hearing the screeching of tires. Your focus drifts over to the green Ford Focus that slammed on the brakes hard at the stop sign.

"I love my car." Camille shares a smirk before proceeding.

Camille's father, a police officer, bought an outdated white Dodge Charger for her sweet sixteen birthday. The unmarked Charger had once been used heavily around town until the police department invested in an upgrade. However, the locals are still on edge whenever they see it. You both enjoy parking at random spots on the side of the road, in plain view, and watch people driving by panic and stop hard when nearly running a red light or stop sign. Whenever either one of you has a bad day, it always boosts your spirits.

Camille pulls into the school parking lot and circles until she finds a spot in the back. While she touches up her mascara, you grab your tan canvas messenger bag from the floor and ease out of the passenger door. You swing your bag over your left shoulder before proceeding to the back of the car. As you're rounding the corner, you're caught off-guard when you collide with an unfamiliar male student. The strap on your shoulder slips off and smacks against the ground.

"Oh, sorry." You reach down to grab the strap.

"You should be. Watch where you're going," the male student remarks before stepping beyond you.

"Excuse me?" You whip around with daggers in your eyes.

"For what?" he mocks, meeting your stare.

You freeze momentarily as your blood turns to ice. It has to be just a figment of your imagination. Only a coincidence that he has the same blue eyes as the guy from your dream. Camille must be getting into your head. "You got some nerve. Who do you think you are?" you clap back, the spell broken.

"Vinson Weber, but I go by Vince." He stands with arrogance.

"Well, hello, Vince." Camille steps in between you, extending her hand. "I'm Camille Epler, and this here is my best friend, Nadine Drexel. It's nice to make your acquaintance."

You stand, flabbergasted, with raised eyebrows and mouth agape, staring at Camille's back.

"Pleasure's all mine." He takes her hand, turns it over, and plants a kiss before looking up with a grin.

Disgusted, you push Camille to the side. "Well, now that we all had the pleasure," you drawl, "of introducing ourselves, we must get to class."

"You know, I would expect a sophisticated lady such as you to be courteous enough to show a novel student like me to the main office."

"You know, a gentleman such as you would be chivalrous enough to pick up the bag he knocked off a lady's shoulder," you fire back.

He raises his eyebrows without comment.

"Nadine, don't be crude. It was just an accident." You look over at Camille before she links her arm around his. "I'd be delighted to escort you to the main office."

"Cam!"

"I'll see you later." She waves before tugging on Vince's arm to follow.

You wrinkle your nose in disgust. You are in disbelief at how Camille would fawn over some guy she just met—a guy she knows nothing about—and kick you to the curb. Not only has this Vince guy disrespected you, but Camille has as well. You are livid.

You head to first-period class. Before the bell rings, you feel your phone vibrate in your vest pocket. You debate whether you want to take a look at the incoming message, knowing it's most likely from Camille.

Hot! Hot! Hot!

You huff with displeasure. What a fool you were, half expecting an apology. Camille is oblivious and probably doesn't even realize what she did. With a shake of your head, you switch your phone to silent.

When lunchtime comes, you grab a turkey sandwich and a bottle of diet green tea before slipping back out. You head to your haven, the auditorium. It's a nice isolated place where you can escape from all the noise and high school drama. Before selecting a seat, you adjust the lighting to your liking. Just enough light so you aren't in complete darkness and can hide in the shadows if unexpected visitors drop by. Like stars in the night sky.

Unwrapping your sandwich, you chew over the thoughts swirling in your mind. You try to resist temptation, but you can't and succumb to your mind's desire.

You pull out your phone and note eleven missed text messages from Camille. She must be going out of her mind right about now. She hates it when you don't respond promptly.

Hello? Are you seriously mad at me?

You shake your head slightly with a puff of air rushing out of your nose while you read the latest message. Was it not obvious?

You close out of your text messages and open Facebook to perform a search. After entering several names, you are a little discouraged to come up empty on Vinson Weber. It doesn't mean he doesn't have some kind of social media under a different profile name. Some people, like you, don't like using full names and would rather use a nickname or middle name as a last name.

You're not proud of yourself for trying to dig up dirt. It's a cop-out trying to find information on a person you don't know. You tried to stay above that but caved.

Even though you suspect it's a waste of time, you try Twitter, followed by every other popular social media site out there. Again, you come up with absolutely nothing.

You sigh when you hear the bell ring. You are dreading this part of the day.

History.

You share the class with Camille. Ignoring her texts is one thing, but ignoring her in person is another. Your zipped lips are about to break. You know Camille can be persistent until she gets her way.

"Hello." You pause in the hallway, just before the open classroom door, approaching at the same time as Camille from the opposite direction.

You drop your eyes and proceed into the classroom. What is Camille doing here already? She's a social butterfly. Normally, she arrives at the last minute.

"Are you really going to be selfish enough to let some guy ruin six years of friendship?"

"Selfish?" You whip around.

"Finally, she speaks." Camille grins.

You huff, irritated that you fell for Camille's jest, before heading to your assigned desk. She always has a way of saying or doing something that causes you to break your oath of silence.

"Come on, Nad. You really think I'd let some guy come between us?"

"Well, you kind of already did," you protest.

"Wow, really?"

"Yes, really."

"Lighten up a little. You've got to stop taking things so seriously. I was trying to de-escalate the situation."

You look away and say nothing. You want to stay mad at Camille, but as you flash back to the scene in the parking lot, you see it from her point of view. You can let your temper get the best of you. It still doesn't make Vince's actions right, but you shouldn't have engaged. You know better. "Okay, maybe I overacted a little."

"A little?" Camille arches her brows.

"That's all you're getting from me." You stare her down.

"Well, it's progress, I'll take it." Camille flings against you in a bear hug.

You stand there stiffly before relaxing a little while patting her on the back. Hugging was something you had to get used to after meeting Camille. You're not the hands-on type of person. You learned to accept it when it concerned Camille and her family. They are all hands-on. At first, you were completely uncomfortable, but it was second nature to the Epler family.

The bell rings, signaling the end of class. You can't recall anything that was gone over. You were too distracted, lost in thought, and watching Camille scribbling in her notebook. You can only guess what was on her mind. However, you are not about to bring it up.

When you walk into English class, you want to walk right back out. Not only is Vince in your class, but he is also sitting in your assigned seat. You feel the steam rise to your collar.

You take a deep breath before strutting over to the desk. Without a word, you grab his books and plop them down on the desk that has a card with his name on it. "You might want to get your eyes checked." You stand firm before him with your arms crossed and your head angled to the right.

"Feisty one, aren't you?" he states in his deep voice as he towers an inch over you.

It takes all your willpower not to comment back as you pierce his sky-blue eyes with your glare. You take him in. Tousled dirty-blonde hair with a sturdy physique, he wears a button-down light blue shirt with sleeves a quarter pushed back, dark blue jeans, and brown lace-up canvas sneakers. A total charmer. Only you're not charmed. Not one bit. You're not like the other girls who would melt at the sight of a guy like him.

Without another word, Vince sidesteps past you and proceeds to his assigned seat. You follow his movement out of the corner of your eye until he is out of view. Once out of sight, you don't dare look over your shoulder at him.

You catch yourself rubbing the upper part of your left arm during the middle of class. Early that morning, when in the ladies' bathroom, you pulled down your long-sleeved shirt to reveal a nice black and blue mark. You know you are prone to bruising easily. However, you have never bumped into another human being before and received such a deep bruise.

Chapter 2

Camille saunters up to you at your locker after chatting with a group of girls. "So, are we still on for Lexton?"

"Why wouldn't we go to Lexton? It's Monday. An espresso and a bagel are what I look forward to that gets me through school."

"Okay, okay," Camille laughs. "Wasn't sure if you would still be too upset with me."

"I'm over it, as long as you don't bring it up or talk my ear off about the new guy," you say and roll your eyes.

"I'll try my best not to." Camille crosses her heart. However, you notice she hides her other hand behind her back.

"I guess that's good enough. Let's go." You shut your locker.

As Camille navigates the roads, you drift, unaware, into your own subconscious. Another school day has come to an end, which also means graduation is one day closer. You don't have big plans to rush off to college. Before you can even think of attending, you have to save up enough money for it, and the money you have set aside isn't nearly enough yet. You know your mother, for a fact, can't afford to pay another loan since she has her own to pay off from nursing school. It's just the two of you, and you know your mother is tight, just living day by day as it is.

"Why do you keep rubbing your arm?"

"Hmm?" You jolt as your attention snaps onto Camille.

"You've been rubbing your arm for like the last five minutes."

You look down at your right hand that's resting on your upper left arm and immediately remove it. "I wasn't even aware."

"Is something wrong?"

"It's fine," you dismiss.

"If you say so." Camille pulls into a parking spot.

Until she mentioned it, you hadn't given your arm a second thought. Now, it's all you can think about. It's sore. Like someone punched you.

"I can't believe we got slammed with so much homework on the first day back." Camille takes a bite from her blueberry bagel with a crunch after you find an open table.

"Did you really expect anything less? It's our senior year. It's not meant to be easy." You sip on your custom-made decaf caramel espresso.

"I'm so ready to have my diploma in hand and kiss high school goodbye."

"Be careful what you wish for. From what I hear, college isn't a picnic. Speaking of which, have you submitted your applications yet?"

"Ugh, do you have to nag about it with me, too?" Camille sips her French dark roast coffee, avoiding the question.

"Have you at least written your essay?"

Camille looks away.

"Cam, you don't have much time left before the deadline. You shouldn't wait until the last minute."

"Save the lecture." Camille puts up her hand before sighing. "My parents are already harping on me about it. It would be easier to make a decision if you were going, too."

"I've told you before that you can't base your decision on mine." You bite into your cinnamon raisin bagel once you've picked off all the raisins.

"I don't know if I can survive college without you being there with me." She bites her lower lip.

"Cam, I know it will be an adjustment, but no matter where life takes us, we will always be friends."

"Best friends," Camille corrects.

"Yes," you revise and smile, "best friends."

"Although," she prolongs, "it would be a little harder to have each other's six." She smirks.

"Through thick and thin, no matter the distance." You wink.

Automatically, you both reach for your necklaces and burst out laughing. Your necklaces represent your friendship. When you first met, you tried pushing her away. Expressed how opposite you were from each other. As a gift for your twelfth birthday, Camille gave you a non-traditional "best friends forever" necklace. The necklaces represent yin and yang, light and darkness, good and evil – opposites. A perfect symbol of your friendship.

Camille kept the dark half for herself and gifted you with the light portion. Neither one of you removed it from your neck since that day.

A year later, after seeing the military commercials advertising the meaning of "I've got your six" and adopting the phrase, you found the number six on a silver charm and gave it to Camille for her thirteenth birthday. You both added the charms to your necklaces, making them unique. Whenever either one of you reached a low point in your friendship or just needed reassurance, you uttered the phrase and, in time, expanded upon it, making it your own.

"What are you doing?" you ask when you notice her scribbling in her notebook.

"Nothing." Camille is quick to close it.

You fold your arms against your chest and stare her down.

Camille sighs before opening it back up.

"You can't be serious." You scrunch up your nose in aversion when you see a heart shaded in with Camille's initials and what you presume are Vince's initials.

"A girl can dream, can't she?"

"It's not even been one day."

"I know, but he's just so dreamy." Camille bats her eyes.

"It's lust. You know absolutely nothing about Vince other than he's obnoxious."

"That's your opinion. I refuse to believe every guy has a hidden agenda. Aren't you always telling me, 'Don't judge a book by its cover?' How can you dislike him so much in one day?"

"He's rude and arrogant. Qualities I detest."

"But his eyes. How can you not melt before them?"

"Looks are deceiving."

"Don't worry, I don't stand a chance anyway compared to all the other girls vying for his attention."

"Don't sell yourself short."

"Come on, Nad, I'm not blind. A guy like him would never go for a girl like me."

"Any guy would be lucky to have a girl like you in his life. You don't go around breaking hearts just because you can."

"Yeah, well, the guys always go for the heartbreakers." Camille shrugs as she downs the last remnants of her coffee.

You sigh with a shake of your head as Camille rises and pulls on her blue plaid jacket. You rise as well, zipping up your silver puffer vest before slipping on your black quilted jacket.

Just as you reach the door, you stop in your tracks in confusion as the door swings open.

"Allow me," utters a deep voice from the other side of the door.

"Vince!" Camille exclaims with delight before walking out the door. "Why, thank you. That was very kind."

"The pleasure is all mine." He smiles with a twinkle in his eyes before they land on yours.

"Why are you here?" You don't blink, and you cross your arms.

"Pardon me?"

"You heard me."

"Nadine," Camille pleads in a semi-whine.

"I heard this is the place to go after school that has the best coffee in town."

"Of course you did."

"Do you beg to differ?"

"I'm perfectly capable of opening the door myself." You proceed to the other door and push your way out.

"Bravo." He props the open door with his foot while clapping his hands with a light smack.

"Nadine, he's just being a gentleman," Camille hisses.

"Oh, is that so? You should stop. It's not a good look for you." You pause, standing face-to-face with him.

He smirks, which irritates you even more.

"We'd better go." Camille latches onto your arm and pulls with force. "It was nice seeing you again, Vince." She waves as she continues to steer you to her car. She slams the door. "Seriously, Nadine?"

"What?"

"'You should stop. It's not a good look for you?'" she mocks while starting the engine.

"Where were his manners this morning when he bumped into me?"

"Are you seriously holding a grudge?"

"I'm entitled."

"So much for me having even the slightest chance. You just tossed my opportunity out the window." Camille pulls out.

"I did you a favor."

"One day, that tongue of yours is going to get you into trouble."

"I can take care of myself." You look out the window and watch the traffic.

"You can't always fight with your words."

"All guys have the same weakness."

"You know, just because you don't like him doesn't mean I have to dislike him."

"Well, I can only frown upon it if you want to be spellbound by some jerk."

"You do realize he's not here to hear your insults, so you can stop."

"Sorry, I just can't help it. He irritates me to no end."

"Well, I would appreciate you trying for my sake."

You look over at her, hearing the hurt in her voice. She is serious, and nothing you say will let you win the battle. You are going to have to let Camille's fascination with Vince ride itself out. She will lose interest eventually, you hope. You peg Vince as the type of guy who won't stay single for long. "Okay, I'll try to tone it down."

"Thank you. Now, was that so hard?" Camille grins after parking alongside the white fence in the front yard of your house.

"Yes, dreadfully," you tease.

"Get out of my car." Camille shoves at your left arm.

You wince as pain fires up the length of your arm. You're quick to cover it by dropping your head and grabbing your bag before climbing out. With a smile planted on your face, you turn back to wave goodbye before Camille drives off. Once she's out of sight, you head up the path and enter through the front door. As soon as you walk in, your orange tabby cat, Leo, greets you. You reach down and pat the top of his head. He purrs with glee.

"Hungry?"

He perks up before racing into the kitchen.

You chuckle and drop your bag by the coat rack before removing your jacket. You slip your phone from your vest pocket and pull up the text message from your mother while heading toward the kitchen. As usual, she is working late.

Leo rubs against your legs as you open a three-ounce can. You scoop half of the pate contents into his dish. Smile as he meows with impatience. Slowly, you walk over to his placemat while he follows and stumbles over your feet. As soon as you set the dish down, he devours his dinner.

While he eats, you prepare your own dinner. First, you pop a CD in and let music play before you grab all the ingredients you need to make butternut squash chili. You dump all the ingredients into a pan and let it cook on high heat.

When you finish with dinner, you curl up on the beige sofa with Leo and the novel you just started rereading. You smile to yourself, thinking how it would dismay Camille that you are reading *The Search* by Iris Johanse again. Camille can't fathom how someone could read a book more than once.

Setting aside reality, you become engrossed in the fictional world the characters live in while Leo purrs with glee, cozying up next to you. You love the sharp stance of the main female character. She's stable on her two feet and doesn't need some macho guy like the main male character in her life. Your guilty pleasure is the heated bickering whenever they are in the same space together.

Chapter 3

You hate gym class. Hate running laps. You don't look forward to suffering the remainder of senior year with the extracurricular activity. To add salt to the wound, it aggravated you that you can't roll up the sleeves of your T-shirt since you want to conceal your bruise. Until it disappears, you have to be mindful of it, especially when you're at home. You know that if your mother ever caught sight of it, she would put you on the stand. You hate being drilled.

When you walk out onto the gymnasium floor, you want to walk right back into the locker room. You're not amused when you see a particular face, Vince. When his eyes land on yours, he flashes a grin. Promptly, you turn your head, ignoring him, and focus on the teachers.

"All right, class, let's form lines," Mrs. Morton announces after blowing the whistle.

Alphabetically, you're directed by Mr. Gibson to divide between girls and guys, forming lines of five across the court. Mrs. Morton doesn't waste time making everyone stretch their muscles before running five laps around the perimeter of the gym.

"You run slow." Vince matches your pace after completing a lap.

"Can't all be overachievers." You pick up your pace.

He closes the gap, running alongside you.

"Hi, Vince." Julie waves when she passes by.

You take the opportunity to back off your speed. When he looks over, he realizes right away you are missing and looks over his shoulder. He smirks before taking off.

You're glad to be rid of him. Before, he was simply being rude. Now, he is being deliberate.

"We meet again," he comments.

You bite your tongue. Vince is definitely egging you on, and you're not going to play his little game. You wait for another opportunity to lose him. He'll be done with his laps in no time at his pace.

Halfway through your laps, you feel winded. You breathe heavily and try to get your breathing back under control by breathing in through your nose and releasing through your mouth. Surely, Vince is to blame for breaking your concentration.

"I get that reaction a lot," he remarks.

"What?" you gasp. When you're able to comprehend what Vince meant, you're aggravated at giving him the satisfaction.

He chuckles as he puts on a burst of speed and finishes out his laps. You relax as you watch him move into the middle of the floor. Now that you don't have him to distract you, you can finish your last two laps.

You can't help spying as the girls gather around him, including Julie. Your eyes roll. The sight makes you sick. They are all in competition with each other, trying to be the one who wins the prize, Vince.

You're more than thrilled when dismissed to the locker room to change back into your regular clothing. The only good thing to follow gym class is having the same lunch period as Camille. Unfortunately, you only luck out to share the same lunch every other day. Even though you are friendly to a handful of your classmates, you don't share the same bond with them as you do with Camille. You're okay with that and like avoiding drama. Sometimes, Camille is more than enough.

You proceed to an unattended round table in the corner on the other side of the cafeteria. You drop your bag in the chair as Camille approaches, mirroring you.

"Hello." You half smile.

"Hi, Vince," Camille exclaims with a wave. "You're welcome to sit with us."

You whirl around and see him walking in your direction.

"Is that so?" He pauses with an arched eyebrow, meeting your eyes.

"What do you want?" you hiss.

"Well, am I invited or not invited?"

"Not invited." You scowl.

"Ignore her." Camille ducks between the two of you. "She's always grumpy after gym."

"Oh, really? Well, good to know it's not me." He shares a laugh with her.

"Excuse me, but I am standing right here," you fire off.

"Thank you for the invitation, Camille, but I've got something to take care of. Maybe some other time?" The nerve of him to ignore you.

"Absolutely." She bats her eyelashes. "The invitation always remains open for you."

"Have a good lunch, ladies," he beams before proceeding.

"Seriously, Cam?"

"I was just trying to make him feel welcome." She walks off, but you heard the tone in her voice.

You huff with annoyance. Camille is fawning over him, just like the girls from gym. Are you the only one not spellbound by his charm? He checks most of the bad boy boxes; tall, blue eyes, and leather jacket. However, his hair is not dark. He wears a brown leather jacket, not black. You are going to have to find something on Vince to paint a picture that he is nothing but bad news.

You flop down into the chair, your appetite gone. You narrow your eyes and catch sight of Vince moments before he disappears around the lockers. What is he up to?

You look over your shoulder. Camille is oblivious that you didn't follow, and is making conversation with a classmate. Curiosity getting the best of you, you slip out of the cafeteria as well. You round the row of lockers, only to be met with disappointment and see no sign of Vince or anyone else.

With a sigh, you head back. As you sit, you pull out your phone. This time, you enter his name into the search engine.

"Where's your lunch?" Camille sets her tray down.

"I'm not hungry," you proclaim without making eye contact.

"What are you doing?" She takes a seat across from you.

"Nothing." You scroll through the page of results.

"If you're trying to dig up dirt on Vince, don't bother."

"So, you've already looked?" You look up.

"Maybe." Camille takes a bite of her mashed potatoes.

"Who doesn't have social media these days? Don't you find that a bit suspicious?"

"No, especially if it's to keep nosy people from prying into their business."

You stare at her in dismay. When did Camille become the voice of reason? How the roles have reversed. Until now, you hadn't realized how obsessed you have become.

You look off at nothing in particular, feeling defeated. You note Gregory Pierce casually exiting the cafeteria. He walks past Tommy, a freshman, who is standing at his locker with the door open. As soon as Greg walks away from him, Tommy drops his head before closing the locker and following.

Greg is a classic bully. He is capable of intimidating others with his sandy brown hair, almond brown eyes, and lean build. Everyone except you. There was a time when he teased and tormented you when you were younger. Until the day you stood up to him. When he realized he had lost his hold on you, he never bothered you again.

"I'll see you later." You quickly grab your bag.

"Where are you going?" you hear Camille's faint voice call after you as you duck out after them. You don't take the time to answer. You know something is up and want to be there to intervene. It wouldn't be the first time you put a stop to Greg's goading.

"You got my college essay?" You hear Greg's voice.

"Yeah," Tommy's voice mumbles as he unzips his bag.

"Don't give it to him, Tommy." You walk around the corner.

"Stay out of this, Drexel," Greg barks.

"Make me."

"Maybe I will." He takes a step forward.

"Here." Tommy sticks out his hand. In his grasp are crisp white papers with neatly typed text.

"Lost this time, Drexel." Greg grabs them with a smug grin before walking away.

You sigh.

"I'm sorry, I just couldn't."

You tried encouraging Tommy to stand up to Greg the last time you witnessed a similar scene. Gave him a few different methods to try. He seemed motivated, and you thought he would stick up for himself, but the same scared stick-skinny pale-white kid can't even look you in the eyes now. "When's it going to be enough, Tommy?"

He lowers his head even more in shame as his oversized glasses slide down the bridge of his nose.

"You can't let fear strike you down."

"I'm not like you."

"You're just giving him power over you. The only way to take that power away is for you to stand up to him."

"Or I can just endure it until he's gone."

"You'll never be free." You shake your head.

"What do you mean?" He looks up, cocking his head.

"There will always be someone to take Greg's place, no matter where you go, as long as you don't stand up for yourself."

He drops his head once more, but the bell saves him. He rushes off as students pour into the quiet hallway. You heave a sigh of disappointment.

Mindlessly, you drift back to your last year of elementary school as you head to your next class. You were not the prettiest…or thinnest…or smartest girl at your school, and you were definitely not popular. You kept to yourself. No one ever included you during recess. The one friend you had had moved away the year prior. You were a lone wolf and an easy target.

Since the beginning of your school days, you could recall being a victim of bullying. It didn't matter if it was physical or mental. Bullying was bullying. A way for someone else to feel superior to another.

You got pushed around a lot, tripped, or shoved. You endured it because you felt there was nothing you could do. You accepted it the way it was. If you told a teacher, you got called a tattletale. Half the time, telling made no difference. It just meant the bully came back harder.

One day, it all changed. You had been walking the perimeter of the playground, lost in thought when you came upon Kaylin and Greg.

"Please, give me my ball back," Kaylin whined.

"No, I found it. It's mine now," Greg sneered, holding the blue soccer ball away from her.

"My parents will be mad at me if I lose it."

"Not my problem." He turned away.

"Give Kaylin her ball back," you demanded, shocked the words had left your mouth. Something had ignited within you. An instinct to fight back. You had never had that desire before for yourself, but something about standing up for someone else instead of sitting on the sideline burst forth that day.

"No," Greg fired back with confidence as he stepped toward you.

"I'm not going to ask you nicely again. Give Kaylin her ball back," you said as you inch forward.

"And just what are you going to do about it if I don't?" he taunted, dangling it in front of you.

For the first time in your life, Greg didn't intimidate you. What you did next hadn't been planned. In fact, your actions took you by complete surprise.

One minute, he was standing in front of you, and the next, you were staring down at him sitting in the grass, stunned. Your mouth wide, you looked at your hands. You had just pushed him hard enough to knock him down.

"I'm going to tell the teacher what you just did." He jumped back to his feet, shouting in a high, uneven, squeaky voice.

"Go ahead, be a tattletale," you threw his words back into his face.

"You're going to be sorry for what you did." He stormed off, leaving the ball behind.

You walked over, plucked the ball from the ground, and handed it to Kaylin.

"Thank you," she said, standing there in astonishment.

You continued on your way, trying to process what had just happened. You felt exhilarated. For so long, you had been rendered powerless. You had taken the hit time after time. That day was the start of something new. You were no longer that lonely, voiceless girl, allowing others to knock you down. You had found your confidence, and with that, the power had shifted into your hands.

From then on, Greg never bothered you again. He tried a few times after to regain his hold over you, but he wasn't successful.

You had learned how to go your own way and got used to doing things alone. Suddenly, others wanted to follow you. You started to find yourself included more by the other students. It was strange. Something you weren't used to. Something you didn't care for. You were too used to being on your own. Now, it started to feel crowded. After you continually declined inclusion in activities both at school and outside of school, your classmates started to lose interest.

The following school year, you tried shielding away from Camille when she introduced herself. Cam was wild and carefree, while you were down to earth and reserved. You were complete opposites, yet a true friendship managed to blossom once you gave in. A friendship that made you two inseparable.

Chapter 4

A dusting of snow is on the grass come Thursday morning, when you look out your bedroom window. It isn't enough to stick to the roads or cause a two-hour delay at school. So far, winter has been mild.

"What's wrong?" You read Camille's expression like an open book as soon as you slide into the passenger seat.

"I overheard my parents arguing last night about a threatening letter."

"What?"

"Turns out there have been more than one addressed to my father left in the mailbox."

"What do they say?" You frown.

"I don't know. They sound pretty vague."

"Does your dad have any idea who it might be?"

"He's not even taking it seriously."

"How many more letters have there been?"

"I don't know. My mom didn't say, but she's worried. She said she usually finds them on Friday with the mail."

"Well, if your dad is not worried about it, neither should the two of you be."

"You know that's easier said than done."

You sigh. You don't know what else to say. Finding out about the threatening letters is going to weigh heavily on Camille's mind. It's going to weigh heavily on yours as well.

During your morning classes, all you can think about is the letters found. You feel like you are underwater. Every sound is inaudible. You have no recollection of what was gone over in each of your classes. When you feel your phone vibrate in your vest pocket, you immediately pull it out and look at the display.

OMG!

You sit up straighter on high alert when you read the first message from Camille.

Vince just picked up my pen cap!

You slump back down in your seat, annoyed. You immediately slip your phone back into your pocket without responding. Other than having to see Vince's obnoxious face in English class, Wednesday had been a good day. Camille hadn't mentioned him, and he hadn't bugged you. The way it should be.

You are not overjoyed walking out of the locker room after changing and having to see his unpleasant face. Until Camille texted you, you had forgotten he shared the class with you. Gym is bad enough. You can't stand running in circles surrounded by sweaty people. Your type of extracurricular activity is hiking in a natural setting away from social interactions.

"So, I hear you've been trying to look me up." Vince matches your pace.

"What?" You whip your head, baffled.

"On social media."

You fail to respond, and you look forward. Did Camille tell him?

"I'm flattered."

"Don't be." You wrinkle your nose and put on a burst of speed.

"The faster you go in the beginning, the more tired you'll be by the end, like last time." He matches your speed with ease.

"I didn't ask for your advice." You stop dead in your tracks.

"Hey!" Amanda shouts as she maneuvers around you in the nick of time to avoid a collision.

You back up against the wall as a few more students run by before you get back out onto the floor.

"That was a foolish move. Someone could have gotten hurt." Vince matches your pace once more in a matter of seconds.

You ignore him. You are not going to allow him to egg you on anymore. You focus on the path before you, one stride at a time, while keeping your breathing in control.

You hear his one chuckle before he speeds off. It annoys you, but you refuse to give him what he wants. Attention. He is being deliberate in getting under your skin, and you will not allow it by giving him a reaction. Now that you're aware, you're not going to encourage it anymore. Would you slip up from time to time? Absolutely, but eventually, you hope, he'll lose interest, just like the rest before him.

"Hi, Vince." Julie runs up next to him.

You roll your eyes.

"Did you run track at your old school? You're a natural."

You stifle a gag.

"What are you guys talking about?" Greg inserts himself between them.

Annoyed, Julie runs ahead. She's a typical blonde-haired and blue-eyed girl every guy is infatuated with, including Greg.

"She's off limits," Greg growls out.

"Is she? Funny, I didn't see your name stamped anywhere." Vince picks up speed.

"Do you know who I am?" Greg matches him.

"Does it look like I care?"

"I can make your life miserable."

"Oh, I doubt that."

"You're asking for it now."

"Am I?"

You watch Greg elbow Vince, only he maintains his balance while Greg takes off. Greg looks over his shoulder with disappointment and rubs at his elbow.

You're surprised at Greg's actions. He has never physically done anything before. Normally, he's all bark, no bite. You can't stop replaying the scene in your mind afterward.

You hear Camille groan as she opens her locker. "I thought geometry was going to be easy."

"What made you think that?" You raise an eyebrow, your mind back in the present.

"Calculations of shapes."

You toss back your head and laugh.

"It's not funny." Camille scowls as she takes out her geometry textbook.

"Hey!" you yell with annoyance as someone bumps into you.

You turn your head and narrow your eyes. Several students seem to be in a hurry as they rush out of the building.

"What was that all about?" Camille asks.

"I don't know." You feel a force pulling you in the direction everyone seems to be gathering.

"What's going on?" Camille asks as you approach a crowd out in the school parking lot. You push your way through the sea of students and hear some chanting that encourages a fight.

"You think you can waltz into my school like you own it?" Greg stands with Dillon and Cory banked behind him, facing Vince, who stands alone.

"I don't recall waltzing in," Vince retorts.

"Are you trying to be funny?"

"I need to borrow this." You grab Camille's textbook.

"Nadine, don't," Camille whispers, trying to tighten her grip, but she isn't fast enough.

You walk out into the open and let the book slam against the blacktop with force. All heads turn to you, stunned.

"Show is over, folks." You move to the middle, inserting yourself between the two with blazing eyes directed at Greg.

"Go home, Drexel." Greg clenches his jaw.

"You first, Gregory."

You see him stiffen. No one calls him by that name.

He looks beyond you. "Pathetic that you need some girl to come to your rescue and fight your battles. Let's go." You hear moans as Greg turns and stomps away with Dillon and Cory close to his heels. The crowd disperses at once with disappointment.

"Vince, are you okay?" Camille rushes to his side.

"Never been better," he mutters.

You roll your eyes as you pick up the textbook.

"I'd like to express my gratitude." He approaches from behind.

You pause halfway down before grabbing the book.

"You're the last person I expected to come to my defense. It's an admirable quality to face a fire head-on."

"I wasn't trying to impress you," you hiss with the book wrapped in your left arm. "I don't like bullying. That's the only reason I intervened."

"Regardless, I am indebted to you. How about I buy you lunch?"

"I don't accept charity." You march over, grab Camille's arm, and steer her away. "Let's go."

Chapter 5

You stand by the window and scratch beneath Leo's chin when you see Camille pull up. You press your lips to the top of his head before setting him on the couch.

"What's the matter?" you ask Camille when she doesn't pull off right away. You note her hair is pulled back in a low ponytail. She always makes an effort to look her best everywhere she goes.

"Well…" Camille delays.

"Just spit it out already." You despise when people stall before getting to the point.

"Do you really want to go to school?"

"Want to? No. Should we? Yes."

"But wouldn't it be more exciting to do a stakeout?"

"A stakeout?" You raise an eyebrow.

"Yeah. My mom mentioned she found the threatening notes when she got home from work on Fridays. Maybe we could keep a lookout and catch the culprit."

"Absolutely not!"

"Oh, come on."

"Do you know how reckless that is?"

"For once, would you just not think rationally?"

"Someone has to."

"Why?"

"Cam, our parents think we're at school. If something went wrong…."

"I didn't say we were going to try to catch the person. Just observe," she cuts you off.

"Still, if we're detected, who knows how they would react?"

"Fine, I'll take you to school, but I'm skipping."

You sigh. "Are you guilting me now?"

"No, I'm telling you what I'm doing."

"You're not really giving me a choice."

"Yes, I am. Go to school or come with me. You know, I'm surprised you're not jumping at the opportunity."

"Just how are you planning on defending yourself if things go south?"

She offers a little shrug. "I have like a four-thousand-pound car."

"I believe that's manslaughter."

"No, I believe that's called self-defense."

"Only if you can prove it in a court of law."

"Maybe you should become a lawyer."

"Seriously, this again?"

Camille sighs.

You look away, thinking over the matter. Do you really want to face another day at school? No. Is it reckless to monitor Camille's house all day? Yes. Would Camille be bold enough to go at it alone? You look back over and study her. "I'll go with you on one condition."

Camille starts squealing with delight, clapping her hands.

"First sign of trouble, we leave on my command."

"Done." Camille nods as she hits the gas and drives over the two blocks.

Your stomach begins to knot. You are already regretting your decision.

"Here." Camille reaches into her glove box and grabs one of the many canisters of mace. "This should make you feel more secure."

"Really? I already have one in my bag."

"Just take it. You can never be too prepared."

You roll your eyes with annoyance, snatch the mace from her hand, and stuff it into your vest pocket. Cam's father is always giving her mace, so she has some at all times, if the need ever arises. "Don't you think you're parked a little too close?"

"We're a house away, and besides, two teenage girls won't get a second glance."

"Depends on who's around. Besides, your car does tend to get a double-take."

"Would you stop over-analyzing?"

You sigh. It's useless to say anything else. When Camille's mind is set, there is no changing it.

"Oh my gosh, this is my favorite song." Camille turns up the volume and begins to sing along to Ed Sheeran's *Perfect*.

"Lovely," you mumble to yourself.

"I can't believe you don't like this song," Camille pauses to comment.

"That's because they overplay it."

"Well, he's kind of a big deal."

"Overrated is more like it."

"Here comes my favorite part," she squeals, adjusting the volume even louder as she belts out the verse.

You grumble as you suffer through Camille's dramatized singing. You can't stand hearing the sappy love song, or any for that matter, that plays on the radio.

"Okay, *Miss Independence*, I'm pretty sure Kelly Clarkson was overplayed, yet you still enjoy hearing her song," Camille comments once the song ends.

"Yes, I agree, it was overplayed, but I don't know, I can relate to it more."

"Well, maybe if there was someone you were interested in, you could connect with my song."

"Ugh," you say as your eyes roll.

"Hey, it could happen if you didn't push every guy remotely interested away."

"And who do you believe is remotely interested?"

"Vince."

"You can't be serious." You scrunch up your nose in aversion.

"You should have seen the look on his face yesterday."

"I'm glad I didn't. Are you going to keep your car running the whole time?"

"Yeah, what if we need a fast getaway?"

"Don't you think it's too obvious?"

"Fine." She cuts the engine.

You both sit in silence for several minutes, watching out the window. You're repulsed at just the thought of Vince having any kind of interest in you. You're also on edge being here when you should be in school. What if you miss something important in one of your classes? This is completely irresponsible of you. You hate how Camille really gave you no option.

"Truth or dare?"

"Huh?" You look over.

"Truth or dare?"

"Ugh. You know I don't like this game."

"We have to pass the time somehow. Unless you want to continue to sit here in awkward silence."

You sigh. You know what's coming. You derailed it earlier, but you knew you wouldn't avoid it indefinitely. "Why don't we just cut to the chase instead of playing some silly kid's game."

"Oh, come on, you're going to rain on my parade."

"No, I am not interested in Vince. If you want to date a jerk like him, there is nothing I can do about it except disapprove."

"Wow, Nad, you're being a bit harsh, don't you think? You don't even know the guy—"

"You don't either," you say, cutting her off.

"You're being a little judgmental just because he was rude one time."

"How did he find out I was looking into his background?"

Camille drops her head.

"Why?"

"I just wanted a reason to talk to him, sorry," she mumbles.

"Cam, I don't like that you're obsessed with him."

She looks back over. "Maybe you should get to know him."

"I don't want to know him."

"I do."

You cross your arms. "It's very suspicious that Vince has no social media."

"What does that have to do with anything?"

"He could be a serial killer for all we know."

"He is not a serial killer," Camille says, her voice rising an octave.

"How do you know? They can start at a young age."

"You know what I think. I think you read too many books that tarnish your mind."

"I bruised after he bumped me," you spit out, regretting the words as they leave your mouth.

"Huh?"

"Never mind." You look out your window.

"Well, sometimes you bruise easily."

"Easy enough to leave such a deep purple bruise?"

You look back as Cam contemplates an answer.

"Maybe he works out a lot."

"I've noticed his arms in gym class. They're not that muscular."

"So, what exactly are you trying to say?"

"He could be dangerous."

"Nad, do you think maybe you're overreacting? Why defend him yesterday if you're so concerned about him?"

You open the glove box and take out a can of mace. "You should keep this on you at all times, especially if you are going to be around Vince."

"Oh, my gosh, now you're starting to sound like my dad. You sure you don't want to pursue a career in criminal justice?" She pushes your hand away.

"You know I don't like violence."

"There are other jobs in the field that don't require the use of a weapon, you know."

"Not the ones that would interest me."

"What about a private investigator?"

"I couldn't imagine doing this every day. I would go half insane."

"You're good at being attentive to details, and you're an excellent observer."

"How did this get turned around on me? I'm not going to college, end of story. Have you decided where you are going to pursue a degree in fashion design?"

"No." Camille huffs as she looks out the driver's side window.

You have to admit, at least to yourself, that you're intrigued by the thought of being a professional investigator. To know certain information about a person, at times, is an advantage. However, it could also be dangerous, and you like to avoid putting yourself in those kinds of situations. You don't like violence. You just want to live a safe and peaceful life. Not a life where you would feel compelled to always look over your shoulder. Even now, you feel jittery.

The hours stretch on with a mixture of silence and small talk that steers away from the future or Vince.

"Well, looks like this was a bust." Camille sighs.

"I hope you don't plan on skipping school every Friday because this was a one-time thing for me."

"No, I'll have to figure out another way."

"Or leave it to your father, who is a cop."

Camille doesn't respond.

"Cam, promise me you won't do anything irrational."

"I'll run it by you first." She grins.

"I mean it."

"Okay, I promise."

Chapter 6

The night is clear, crisp, and silent. Perfect conditions for star gazing. You sit on the back porch, snuggled up with a blanket draped around your shoulders. Leo is curled in your lap, purring while you massage the top of his head. You are able to spot Orion instantly by the distinct three stars in his belt. You stare, feeling a sense of peace before your gaze travels downward to the shape of Lepus. You smile and transport back in time.

Astronomy was your absolutely favorite class. You aced it with flying colors. During the final test, connecting dots, naming shapes, and scientific names of the stars, you went out of your way to name ones not even required. Amazing how natural something could be when you were interested in the subject.

You loved reading up on the myths. There were some fascinating ones, but you don't truly believe in any of them. They are, in fact, myths. Just stories made up. Some had different stories, like Orion, the hunter. You prefer the mild ones.

In an ever-changing world, no matter what, the one thing that's always constant is the stars shining brightly in the night sky. When you feel like everything is spinning out of control, you rely on the stars to make time stand still. For a moment, you can get sucked into something bigger than you and forget all your worries. Sometimes, you wonder what's written in the stars about you.

You have to be honest with yourself. Camille struck a nerve. Her constant badgering about what you should do for the rest of your life has you facing the harsh truth that you are trying to avoid. You have absolutely no idea. You don't like routines. Don't like it when doing something becomes mindless and loses purpose. Don't want to set a course on a straight path. You like uncharted territory. Changing it up like the seasons. Want each day to be a new adventure. The one thing you know for certain is you don't want to stay in the banking world for the rest of your life. You work after school on Thursdays and Fridays and every Saturday morning. You hate it. It is a means to save up some money, but it's not nearly enough for college tuition. Especially when you are indecisive. How are you supposed to decide on one career for the rest of your life? How are you supposed to know if you pick the right path? Of course, you have possibilities in mind, but it also discourages you from being stuck in one place forever. What if you end up not being as passionate about it later? What would you do then?

You wish you could know if everything would turn out all right in the end. You want to do something worthy. You also want to be able to give back to your mother, who has sacrificed so much to make your life good. You don't want to fail her.

Leo tenses. Instantly, you tighten your hold on him and study him in the starlight. His head slightly bobs up and down as he takes in the night air. You know that stray cats tend to roam the area. Did he pick up on one of their scents?

A deep rumble comes from the back of his throat. A sound you're not accustomed to him making. You're on edge at once before he hisses. You follow his line of sight but see nothing.

Uncertain what's lurking in the dark, you rise from the chair and head in through the back door. You lock it before setting Leo on the floor and watch him promptly sit in front of the door, guarding it. Leo is a mellow cat who doesn't scare easily, so if he's alarmed, you certainly are, too. Just another strange occurrence to add to the first week of the second semester.

When he relaxes, you retire to bed and dread the morning.

"You will never guess who's going to mentor me in geometry during study hall," Camille squeals as you take a seat in history.

"Mentor?"

"Yeah."

"Since when are you failing?" you ask, bewildered. Camille may not be an Einstein, but she's above average. You can't recall a time she brought home a failing grade.

"I'm not, but that's not what's important. What's important is Vince is going to help me!" she shrieks.

"Vince?" A few weeks have gone by with nothing dramatic happening. You thought things had gone back to normal. How wrong you were.

"What's that supposed to mean?"

"Are you deliberately falling behind as a ploy?" You narrow your eyes, studying her.

Camille looks away and refuses to make direct eye contact.

"Camille! Now is not the time to goof off. Your grades still matter."

"College isn't going to base their decision on one class. I'm not that naïve to make myself fail on purpose."

"I don't know, Camille. It seems like you would do just about anything to be noticed by some guy."

"It's harmless. I'm sorry I even told you."

"Did you really expect my approval?"

"Whatever." Camille shrugs.

You inhale deeply and release it slowly. You hate when Camille acts this way, spinning it around on you. It's Camille's life, and if she wants to do something so foolish, that's on her. All you can do is disapprove, knowing you wouldn't take a risk like that.

The bell rings. The student body hustles to their last class of the day as you drag your feet. Your English class isn't far from history, but you don't feel like arriving early and sitting there impassively, so you take a lap around the perimeter of the first floor.

"You put down the wrong answers," you hear someone shout.

As the surrounding students make a beeline in the opposite direction, you march forward.

"What?" Tommy squeaks.

"Don't you dare stand there pretending you don't know what I'm talking about," Greg threatens as he has Tommy cornered against the wall.

"Greg, I think you should back away from Tommy." You speak calmly, hoping to defuse the situation. You have never seen Greg so angry before.

"You! You put him up to this, didn't you?" Greg's vein pops out, his neck scarlet red.

"I didn't put him up to anything." The bell rings.

Greg crumples up the piece of paper in his hands, throws it on the ground, and spits on it.

"Next time you do a stunt like that, it's going to be your head I stomp on." Greg marches away, punching a nearby locker.

"It's okay, Tommy, he's gone." You approach while he stands frozen in place, "I'm proud you stood up to him."

He shakes his head. "I don't understand."

"Understand what?"

He reaches down, grabs the trampled piece of paper, and spreads it out. "I don't remember doing this."

You glance at the equations.

"This is my handwriting. The work is accurate, but the answers are random."

"Maybe you blocked out the memory in fear?" you suggest.

"I wouldn't intentionally put down the wrong answers."

An arctic chill runs up the length of your spine. You want to believe Tommy found the courage to stand up to Greg, but you know deep down his anxiety would have interfered. However, you can't fathom any other logical explanation.

"I'm late for class." He hurries away.

You try to clear your mind. This has to be some kind of dream you're having trouble waking from. You don't even notice or care when all eyes are directed onto you when you walk into class late. Don't even comprehend anything that Mrs. Robbins goes over.

Your attention snaps forward. Was your name called? You listen as other names are rattled off, as well as literature assignments. What was your assignment? And who is your partner?

The bell rings.

"Looks like we're partners." You turn and see Vince grinning.

"Partners?"

"Yeah, reenacting a scene from *Romeo and Juliet*."

You freeze. This has to be a nightmare. Partners with Vince reenacting a Shakespeare play about lovers?

Chapter 7

Snow is falling outside your window, but it's light and only makes the roads wet. You're glad it's Friday, but you still have to get through one more day of school before the weekend.

You find your book lying on the floor, next to your bed, upside down. You pick it up, mark the last page you read, and set it on your nightstand.

You drag your feet through your morning ritual. Your mother has already gone off to work, so you find yourself alone. Not interested in making a fresh breakfast, you opt for granola cereal. As you wash down the last bite with some orange juice, you hear Camille's horn announcing her arrival.

You pause at the door and sigh before feeling something brush up against your right pant leg. You look down and see Leo. He meows when his yellow-green eyes meet yours. An unconditional love. You bend down, pick him up, hug him tightly, and kiss the top of his head. You don't want to let go. "I'll see you later, buddy."

"What took you so long?" Camille complains.

"Sorry, tired, I guess." You take in Camille's appearance. Her natural, straight bronze hair, a little past shoulder-length, is curled into waves, partially pulled back with a few face-framing strands.

"Is everything okay?"

"Yeah, everything's fine." You look away.

"Doesn't sound like it."

"What are you, my mother?" you snap, looking back.

"Geez, Nad. You don't have to bite my head off."

"Sorry."

"You know you can talk to me."

"Yeah, I know, but I'm fine, honest." You force a half smile.

"Okay." She takes off. Halfway into the drive, she bursts out in an uncontrolled laugh.

"What are you laughing at?" You raise an eyebrow, bemused.

"O Romeo, Romeo, wherefore art thou Romeo?"

You groan.

"I can't believe you are going to be reenacting a scene with the so-called serial killer." Camille slaps her leg after parking.

"I'll see you later." You quickly open the door and rush off.

Why did you even tell Camille? You were irritated when you found out, and you vented, which you're now regretting. Cam will never let this down.

The first half of school goes faster than you like. Thankfully, Vince keeps to himself during gym. However, you are not looking forward to lunch with Camille. All morning, she has been sending hearts or kissing lip emojis.

You are quick to dodge over to your normal table, place your bag down, and go up to get food. After paying, you drag your feet back. You are not in the mood to make conversation. You have a desire to disappear to the auditorium.

"Hello, Nadine." Vince appears, smiling alongside Camille as he sets his tray down.

"Uh, did I miss something?" You glance over at Camille, perplexed.

"Sorry, I meant to tell you this morning, but you were a bit distracted." Camille blushes as she sets down her tray. More like Camille was distracted. Now you understand why she wore a burgundy cashmere V-neck sweater with navy blue slacks.

"If it's a problem, I can go somewhere else." Vince grabs his tray.

"Vince, no, you can stay, right, Nad?" Camille lays a hand on his arm while giving you a pleading look.

"Fine." You sigh. Only it's not fine. You know perfectly well that Camille failed to mention it on purpose. "A salad?" You raise your eyebrows. Camille hates anything considered healthy. She even goes to the length of pulling out tiny pieces of lettuce from cheeseburgers.

"So, how was gym class?" Camille ignores you and asks Vince as she pours two packets of ranch salad dressing over her small salad, closes the lid, and shakes it.

"Same old." He shrugs.

"You know that defeats the purpose if you're trying to eat healthier," you comment while stirring your mashed potatoes.

"It's salad dressing. How bad could it be?"

"Maybe you should read the label."

"Just so you know, I decided to eat healthier for myself." Camille stabs some lettuce.

"If you say so." You fork some asparagus.

Camille huffs. "How can you eat that?"

"I've told you before, don't watch if it grosses you out." You lean closer to her. "You know, for someone who wants to eat healthier options, you're going to have to actually like the stuff you eat."

"I like plenty of vegetables, thank you very much."

"Not nearly enough," you mumble under your breath while cutting into your Salisbury steak.

"So, you like asparagus?" Vince slips in.

You both look over at him.

"Is there a problem with that?" you challenge.

"Just making note." He shrugs a shoulder and plays with the food on his plate, the same lunch special.

"Do you have anything else in your wardrobe besides button-down shirts and blue jeans?" you fire back.

"Nadine," Camille whispers.

"What? It's just an observation."

"Maybe he was making polite conversation to change the subject since we were bickering," Camille remarks.

"Oh, is that what you call it?" You refocus your attention and pierce his eyes with yours.

"You know, you may want to play a little nicer since the two of you have a school assignment to work on. Maybe this is a good time for both of you to get to know each other a little better," Camille suggests.

You sit back and fold your arms. "Yes, I like asparagus. How about you?"

"Afraid I'm not big on veggies." He glances over and shares a smile with Camille.

"Who's holding back now? Isn't there one vegetable you can tolerate? Come on, I thought it was, 'get to know you' hour." You flash air quotes.

"If you insist, I guess I'll go with tomatoes."

"You know, botanically, tomatoes are actually considered a fruit since they produce seeds."

"Oh, no, here we go with the food expert again." Camille rolls her eyes.

"Really? I've been misinformed this whole time?" Vince mocks.

"Amazing how misinformed the Internet can be sometimes." You smirk before taking a sip from your diet sweet tea.

"You know, diet tea isn't the best alternative as it contains sugar substitutes," Vince remarks.

"Oh, really? You think I didn't know that, Mr. Know-It-All?"

"She reads like everything and usually is the one to spread the knowledge," Camille cuts in with another eye roll.

"Well, nothing wrong with learning and growing."

You purse your lips, insulted by the compliment.

"Vince just complimented you. What do you say?" Camille elbows you.

"I don't have to say anything." You fork at some asparagus.

"So, Camille, I was wondering if you're busy this weekend," Vince redirects his attention.

"Me?" She puts her hand over her chest in surprise.

He nods.

"No, why do you ask?" Camille blinks twice.

"I've been told that Pink Caddy has excellent food. Have you been there?"

"Of course! They have the best food in town."

"I'd be honored if a regular would show me around town."

"Does that mean like a date?" She blinks several times.

"If that's what you would like to call it." He flashes a grin.

You cough as the last piece of asparagus slides down before you are ready to swallow. You quickly grab your tea and take a sip to cover it.

"I'd love to." Camille does her best to contain her excitement.

"Great. What time should I pick you up?"

"So, where did you move from, Vinson?" you cut in with a stern voice and stare him down.

"West Virginia," he answers with no hesitation.

"What part of West Virginia?"

"Weston."

"Any siblings?"

"Not that I'm aware of."

You narrow your eyes, studying him. "Did you practice these answers?"

"Nad," Camille warns.

"It's okay, Cam. She just wants to make sure I'm not a serial killer." He smirks.

You whip your head toward Camille. Her cheeks are flushed as she casually sips from her water bottle. You're not sure what makes you angrier. The fact that Camille told him what you said, or that he used Camille's nickname. You look back. "Are you?"

"No, but I think we both know even if I was, I wouldn't tell you, Nadia."

Your eyes widen as everything inside constricts. "That's not my name," you manage through clenched teeth.

"Close enough," he comments with a Cheshire Cat grin.

Camille gasps.

The boiling water inside is ready to combust as you slowly look over at Camille. She has a hand over her mouth and shakes her head. It's hard to believe Camille would be that cruel and tell him your history. You thought that hatchet was buried a long time ago, and yet, a single word makes the painful memories resurface. You have to get out of here before you do something you'll regret.

Chapter 8

You look at your pale complexion in the bathroom mirror through your hazel eyes.

Nadia.

Exactly what your father uttered in his pickup truck the last time you ever saw him. He had come into your life when you were ten years old and tried to bond with you, but the man was a stranger. He hugged you once, but you felt no connection. Biologically, he was your father, but emotionally, he was nothing to you. You were doing just fine without him.

He had been in your life, taking you fishing every other weekend for seven months, until that day in the pickup when he called you by the wrong name. Furious, you demanded to go home, and he disappeared from your life altogether. No Christmas cards. No birthday cards. No phone calls. Nothing.

You hadn't been upset. Relieved was more like it. You hated fishing. You liked your life just as it was. You enjoyed your independence, just like your mother.

The recollection of your father makes you angry, and you loathe the name he called you. You might have been young, but you could tell he was trying too hard to make some kind of connection. You rejected him every time. He taught you how to fish as a way of bonding. You did not like touching dirty worms. Did not enjoy hooking a fish by its mouth as it flopped around in a panic. It was cruel. He told you it didn't hurt the fish, but you didn't believe him. After he caught them, he released them back into the water. What was the point? Spending hours with someone you hardly knew was agonizing.

"Nadine?" Camille whispers, slowly entering the bathroom.

"You told him?" you spit with fury.

"No, I swear I didn't."

"How do you expect me to believe you when you've told him other things about me?" you spout off.

"I'm sorry. I swear I didn't tell him. You know me. I would never intentionally want to hurt you."

"Do I?" The bell rings.

"Of course you do. Through thick and thin, I always have your six, remember?"

"How could he possibly know then?"

"He doesn't. He asked me what it was he said to make you upset."

"So, now you've told him?"

"No, I left."

"Whatever happened to not letting some guy come between us?"

"You want me to cancel the date?"

You look away without comment. Being angry is easy. You wanted to stay angry, but you could hear the sincerity in Camille's voice. Being vulnerable is a hard pill to swallow. Do you want Camille to cancel her date with Vince? Absolutely, but that's the selfish side talking. If she listened, then a part of Camille would resent you. You would resent a part of yourself as well.

"I did tell him, jokingly, about the serial killer part." Camille hangs her head. "I'm sorry."

"I can't stop you if you want to do foolish things to get him to notice you, but don't drag me into it."

"Okay." Camille nods somberly.

"Besides, I can't have your six if I'm mad at you," you say in a lighter tone.

Camille perks up with a bright smile before rushing over and crushing you into a hug. "I hate when we fight," Camille whispers in your ear.

"Me too. We'd better get to class." You embrace the hug for a few more seconds before pushing away.

"Or we could skip." Camille grins.

"Cam," you warn.

"Fine." You walk out with Camille before you head your separate ways.

All through class, you can't shake the flashbacks, and before you know it, English arrives. You want absolutely nothing to do with Vince and don't want to see the sight of him, but you are stuck in the same class as him. With your eyes cast down, you make a beeline to your desk as the bell rings.

"All right, class, you will get with your partner and discuss your reading assignment. Use this time wisely," Mrs. Robbins announces.

Your stomach twists at the worst-possible scenario. You are not ready to face him, not yet.

"Mrs. Robbins, may I go to the bathroom, please?" you ask before heading out of the classroom with an urgency.

Once you reach the safety of the ladies' room, you lean against the wall, close your eyes, and inhale. You know you are going to have to face him sooner or later, but you had not expected it to be so soon.

"Nadine?" You jump when you hear a deep, soft voice.

"This is the girls' bathroom, Vinson," you exclaim when you see him standing by the entryway. Does he not know boundaries?

"You didn't give me any other option. I want to apologize for upsetting you at lunch."

You stare. You're not accustomed to him being sincere.

"There's a history. It was not my intention to hurt you."

"Just aggravate me, right?" you fire back.

He says nothing.

"I don't know what game you're playing, but if you hurt my best friend, you'll have to answer to me." You step forward, shaking a finger in his face.

"I take it that means 'apology not accepted.'"

"No, it most certainly is not." You slip past him.

He follows you in silence.

"Let's get one thing squared away: We are not doing the balcony scene," you turn and state firmly.

"Well, glad we addressed that elephant in the room," he comments before you turn back and march onward.

You walk down the hallway, the echoes of footsteps the only sound.

"So, what were your thoughts on Act 1, Scene 1?" Vince breaks the silence.

You pause mid-step, taken off guard. "What were your thoughts?"

"Ladies first."

"I'm not the one you need to be impressing." You spin to face him, only you whirl around too fast and stumble forward. Your hands reach out to break your fall and smack up against his chest. At the same time, his hands grasp your arms to stabilize you.

"You should work on your balance." You hear irritation in his voice.

You lift your head and meet his blue eyes. Realization dawns on how close you are to him. You scrunch up your nose in revulsion as you wiggle free. "Get your hands off me."

"Well, I do need to impress you. You are the best friend of the girl I made plans to take out on a date," he glosses over.

"You disgust me," you toss over your shoulder.

"Touché."

You open the door, step into the classroom, and become aware that all eyes are on you and Vince. It infuriates you, predicting what the other students may be thinking. With a huff, you head over to your desk.

"The beginning is about a bunch of guys having an all-talk brawling match before moving on to Romeo wailing about some girl who doesn't have the same feelings as him." You take a seat, crossing your arms.

"That's a bit harsh." He sits down, scraping the desk as he moves closer to you.

Your eye twitches. You feel curious eyes on you again. You lift a hand and admire your nails, disinterested. "Maybe to you, since you're a guy. What did you take away?"

"Rival families taught to despise each other for generations, and a guy helplessly in love with a girl who does not reciprocate the feelings. I feel sorry for him."

"Why? She made it clear she was not interested in him. Guys can never get the hint."

"Well, maybe if girls didn't play games."

"Like guys don't play games, too?" Your eyes narrow as you divert them.

"Seems we've come to an impasse."

"And then suddenly, he forgets all about Rosaline and falls madly in love with a girl he doesn't even know. It's absurd."

"I thought we weren't supposed to read ahead."

"Like you don't know how it ends."

He smirks. "Why is knowing that someone is the one absurd?"

"Love doesn't work that way."

"Why not?"

"Two people don't magically just know they are meant to be together."

"Maybe one day, someone will change your mind."

"I doubt it."

The bell rings. As you grab your bag, you realize you actually had a civilized conversation with Vince. You huff. You can't wait for this assignment to be over and are dismayed that it's only day one.

Chapter 9

You slide into the passenger side of your mother's '97 white Jeep Grand Cherokee with a pout.

"What's wrong?" your mother, Leanne, asks.

"I was twenty cents short."

"Oh, no, it's the end of the world." She chuckles.

You grumble, instantly regretting mentioning it. You wave to your supervisor, Terry, as your mother drives off. Terry didn't even blink an eye when you reported being short. Twenty cents isn't a big deal. Not to the bank, but it is to you. You are a perfectionist and hate writing up a slip to offset your drawer. However, the fault was yours. You knew better than to open a roll of coins a customer exchanged for bills to put in your coin tray. You had the same occurrence happen before. A rookie mistake you vowed never to make again. Only you did because you were distracted.

Camille talked nonstop about her upcoming date with Vince. The entire ride to the bank, she babbled about what outfit to wear. The car ride had never felt so long before.

"Can I borrow the Jeep tonight?" you ask after supper.

"Sure, where are you planning to go?" your mother asks.

"The quarry." You shrug.

"Is everything all right?"

"Yeah, just need some fresh air."

"Okay, well, don't stay out too late. I got an early shift tomorrow, so I might be in bed when you get back."

You know your mother senses something is amiss, but she doesn't push. At five feet eight inches, your mother is an inch taller. You have the same brown hair and hazel eyes, except yours are greener. There is no mistaking that you're related. Sometimes, people you meet tend to think you are sisters rather than mother and daughter.

You fire up the Jeep. You need some peace and tranquility. Some time to clear your mind. Watching mindless television or reading isn't the distraction you need right now.

You drive up to the quarry on the outskirts of town, past the construction site, and stop at your secret spot positioned at the highest elevation. There are no lights up here or loud noises, just a calm and peaceful place.

You climb out of the Jeep, put your hands in your jacket pocket, and wait for the light to dim before tossing your head back and taking in the stars. The night is clear, with no interference from town lights. You stand in the pitch-black night with the only light coming from the stars while the moon is barely a sliver.

You spin slowly in a circle, taking all the stars in before stopping and smiling when your eyes land on Orion. Time stands still as you let go of all your worries.

A strong gale cuts through your layers, chilling you to the bone. You shiver as your mind is brought back to reality. The blissful moment comes to an end as the realization sets in that you are freezing. You climb back into the Jeep and note the time. You were standing outside for thirty-five minutes in below-freezing weather. You blast on the heat and sit there while the Jeep reheats.

As you drive back home, you decide to swing by Lexton for a cup of hot chocolate to warm your soul. You are thrilled when you find a spot across the street right down from the coffee shop. As you climb out and start to close the door, you freeze. Camille walks out the front door of the café, followed by Vince, who tucks a lock of her hair behind her ear. You quickly climb back in and duck in the seat as you watch them walk down the sidewalk before crossing. They pause at a maroon Impala. You crinkle your nose as you watch Vince open the door for Camille.

You're not sure what compels you, but quickly start the engine and pull out after the Impala. They travel a short distance down the one-way street before turning left around the loop onto the street leading in the opposite direction. They continue to travel several blocks down the one-way until they reach the end. You keep your distance, but soon know exactly where they are heading. He's taking Camille home.

You take a calculated risk. Instead of following them completely to Camille's place, you take a left down the street that connects to Camille's street. Unless he turns and goes in the opposite direction, Vince should travel down and pass the intersection.

You park along the sidewalk as far down as you can at the end of the yellow paint, turn off the headlights, and wait patiently. You have no idea what possesses you to want to follow Vince.

You're not sure how long it takes. It seems to drag agonizingly slowly, waiting for a maroon Impala to appear at the intersection. You start doubting he will come the way you hoped, but you keep pushing yourself to wait a little longer.

Finally, headlights pierce the night. You slide down in your seat as a car pauses at the stop sign. When it drives on, you crane your neck to make out the make of the car.

Impala.

You flip on your headlights and look in your rearview mirror before turning down the road behind the Impala. You keep his car in your sights but stay back a distance.

You travel straight for a little over two blocks before the Impala's left signal starts flashing. It takes all your willpower not to put your own signal on as you turn down the street after him. You don't know why you are worried about signaling when there are no other cars around. Obeying traffic laws is just a habit.

About a block into the drive, you soon realize he is gaining speed. Is he on to you? You step on the gas. You don't want to be too far behind him when he approaches Main Street.

He stops at the red light and puts on his right signal. You are still lagging a bit, and glad he's delayed so you can catch up. However, the light turns sooner than you hope. You step on it even more. As you get to the intersection, the light turns yellow. Normally, you would have stopped, but you floor it and turn right just in time before it turns red.

You inhale deeply, checking your rearview mirror for any flashing lights. All you need is to get pulled over. You exhale when you see no sign of a cop.

When you refocus your mind on the light traffic in front of you, you are quick to realize there is no maroon Impala in sight. He couldn't have gotten that far. You look into the parking lot of the business you pass by. There are no side streets for a block. How could he have disappeared? You look back in your rearview mirror at the parked cars on the street behind you. It's hard to make them out where you are now.

You huff, annoyed. You lost him. Everything you did was for nothing. Thought you had been careful, but somehow, he knew he was being tailed. Guess Camille was wrong about you becoming a private investigator. A professional would not have gotten caught.

You travel the one-way until you have the opportunity to make a left and travel back the way you came. You lost the desire for hot chocolate, and with nothing left to do, you head for home. You still can't believe you lost him.

While you are passing the street Camille lives on, brake lights blind you from in front. You slam on your brakes, coming to a hard stop behind the car. Where did it come from? You watch the car door swing open. Only now do you notice the color and make of the car sitting in front of you.

Maroon. Impala.

Vince emerges and strolls up to the driver's side before leaning down to eye level with a muffled voice. "Why were you following me?"

You react without thinking and thrust the car door open with everything you have. You don't like the fact that he has you cornered or how close he is to you. To your surprise, the action does not throw off his balance. He doesn't even budge an inch. Instead, it feels like you hit a concrete wall. Before the thought crosses your mind to shut the door, his hand reaches out and prevents you from closing it.

"What do you want?" you shout with fury as you reach over with your right hand and feel for the glove box.

"I want to know why you were following me," he says calmly.

"I don't know what you're talking about."

"Listen to me very carefully. It would be in your best interest not to follow me again." He releases his hold on the door, turns, and walks away.

This is a different side of Vince. One you've never seen before. He is very serious and seems a bit angry. You shiver, and not from the cold.

You should back down and not further engage, but you step out anyway. "And what if I don't listen?"

"There are some cans of worms not meant to be opened," he tosses over his shoulder.

"You know, you're only reinforcing the desire to find out whatever it is you're hiding."

"Good night, Nadine." He turns with a lighter tone, meeting your eyes before slipping into the driver's seat.

You watch him drive off. You're confused. What just happened? He was trying to mask his fury one minute, and then the next, his anger dissipated.

With a sigh, you start to climb back in. Only something nags in the back of your mind. The lighting is not good, so you reach in and grab your phone from the cup holder. You turn on the flashlight before your mouth drops. There is a nice indentation right in the center of the car door. You replay his gait in your mind as he walked away. He seemed to walk normally. He didn't even flinch when you slammed the car door into him. Now that you're thinking about it, you recall the moment you fell into him. You didn't comprehend it then, but you're starting to now. It felt like you had fallen up against a concrete wall. Not skin and bones. Who is Vinson Weber? Or what exactly is he?

Chapter 10

You lie in bed pretending to be asleep while your mother gets ready for work. You neglected to mention the dent in the driver's side door and couldn't think up a good enough excuse that would be believable. When it comes to lying to your mother, you score poorly.

You hold your breath, waiting for your mother to barge back in and demand answers, but she doesn't. You hear the Jeep start and pull away. You exhale.

You're relieved but, at the same time, confused. There's no way your mother would have missed seeing that huge dent. She wasn't running late. You expected the worst this morning, and now you have to go all day dreading when evening comes.

You feel a weight added to your bed. Leo walks up the length of your side until he pauses at your shoulder and butts his head against your cheek, purring. You reach out and scratch the side of his face. To think such a loving cat used to be a stray for who knows how long, roaming the streets covered in filth and fleas. Someone must have dumped him. You don't know why he could still be so trusting. You read a story once about how some guy took his dog to the shelter because the dog was too affectionate. You have to wonder if Leo was left to fend for himself because he was too loving as well. Some people don't deserve pets. Some search endlessly for that one loyal companion.

When Camille arrives, you're not ready to face her. You know what she is going to talk about the entire drive – her date with Vince.

"Best date ever!" Camille squeals.

"Cam, it's too early to be so shrill." You wince, covering your left ear with your hand.

"I can't believe how long it's been since I've been to Pink Caddy."

"How romantic." You roll your eyes.

The diner isn't the fanciest place in town, but has the best food with a 1950s vintage decked out in everything pink.

"Hope you didn't pass on their pecan pie."

Camille falls silent.

"Really, Cam?" You frown.

"I'm just being mindful of what I eat."

"For a guy?"

"Anyway, so we went bowling afterward."

"Bowling?"

"I know, but it was worth every second I got to spend with him."

You snort with amusement. Camille hates bowling. You wonder if she was even able to knock down a pin.

"He's so sweet. He held the door for me everywhere we went, pulled out the chair for me, and even held my purse when I went to the ladies' room. He did everything right."

"Or it was all an act."

"Maybe you should get to know him instead of focusing on all the negatives."

"Cam, I…." You stop yourself. There are so many things you want to say. Mainly that Vince might be dangerous. Only you know Camille would want concrete proof.

"Nad, I know you're always suspicious about everyone, but trust me," Camille parks the car and turns to look you in the eyes. "Vince is different from the other guys. I can feel it. I trust him."

"That alarms me because I don't." You open the door and slip out.

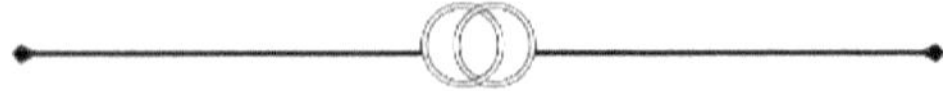

Saturday morning is busy as usual. As soon as the door is unlocked and the drive-thru lights lit, it is non-stop until near closing.

"You want a lift?" Terry asks as you walk out.

"Sure," you agree.

Once home, alone with only Leo, you can't stand the silence or the thoughts eating away at you. Reading doesn't settle your mind. Pacing around would only wear out the carpet. The only distraction you can think of is to cook.

You pop in your Skillet CD and turn the volume up as loud as you can bear. You bop to the music as you look through your recipes until you come across one that you found online and made about three months ago.

It's easy to make and to modify. Definitely enough of a distraction to keep your mind occupied for the duration.

You belt out about feeling invincible along with the chorus as you grab the extra spaghetti squash you have on hand and cut it in half before putting it in the oven for thirty minutes. Meanwhile, you look around the refrigerator for whatever vegetables are there that you can add to the mixture of eggs.

You hum along as you chop up some peppers and spinach. As you rinse off the knife, your timer goes off. You pull the squash out of the oven and let it sit to cool before you tackle an onion.

Once the squash is cooled enough to be able to handle it, you grab a fork and separate the spaghetti-like strings into a bowl. Once it's seasoned, you dump the squash into two separate pans, patting them down and forming into a crust.

You mix the eggs and vegetables, stirring them all together, before pouring evenly between the two crusts and then sticking them in the oven.

You are just pulling dinner out of the oven when your mother walks through the door. You cringe and wait to be berated.

"Something smells delicious." She walks into the kitchen in her scrubs.

You study her.

"What?"

"Nothing." You shake your head. "I made spaghetti squash quiche. Well, an improvised version of it."

"What's the occasion?"

"No occasion. I just felt energetic." You smile.

"Well, I won't argue."

"Help yourself. I forgot to grab the mail. I'll be right back." You duck out of the kitchen and walk down the front sidewalk, staring at the Jeep the whole way to the mailbox. After you grab the mail, you head over and stare, perplexed, using your phone flashlight. There is no dent to be seen. Did you imagine it? No, you saw it with your own eyes last night. So, where did it go? How could it have magically disappeared?

The only thing you can think about for the rest of the weekend is the disappearing dent. Every chance you have, you go out and look at the door, but don't stay for long to avoid your mother asking questions. Even when the start of the school week comes, you are still in disbelief at how a dent could just disappear. It just doesn't make sense. There has to be a logical explanation. You just can't think of one.

"What? You didn't do it?" You pause while making your way to the auditorium with your lunch.

"No." You see Tommy drop his head.

"Why not?" Greg spits out with Tommy backed up against the wall.

You instantly fume inside.

"I don't know."

"Unacceptable." Greg grasps his shirt.

"Hey," you shout and march forward.

"Stay out of this, Drexel," Greg growls with annoyance.

"Let him go."

"Or what?" He releases Tommy, takes a step forward, and stands upright face-to-face with you.

You take a step back with uncertainty. When did he get so confident?

"That's right, back off." He starts to turn away from you.

You duck past him and put yourself in front of Tommy. "If you want Tommy, you'll have to go through me."

You see both his hands clench into fists by his sides. Anger in his eyes. The image of him punching the locker enters your mind. Would he hit you? What would you do if he did?

"If you touch her, it will be the last thing you ever do." Greg whips his head over. You do as well. Vince stands there with a look that could kill. His approach was soundless.

Greg shifts his gaze back and forth before turning on his heel and walking away without a word.

"I had it under control," you snap.

"Looks like we're even now," Vince utters before strolling away.

You watch him disappear around the corner. The stone look on his face was terrifying. Like he wanted to rip Greg to shreds.

"Nadine, are you okay?" Tommy reaches out and gently touches your shoulder.

You shrug him off and turn. "I'm okay."

"I'm sorry. None of this would have happened if I had done his homework. I don't even know why I didn't." He hangs his head.

"Don't think like that."

"You could have gotten hurt because of me." His eyes rise over the rim of his glasses.

"You rattled his cage, and he's losing control. Seems he will do anything to gain it back."

"You shouldn't have gotten involved. This is my fault."

"It's not your fault."

"How do you do it?" He lifts his head.

"Do what?" You tilt yours.

"Stand up to him?"

"He's not used to others calling his bluff."

"I wish I could be brave like you, but I'm not. Everything will be better once I'm out of school." He looks away.

"No, it won't."

"What do you mean?" He looks back and studies you through his glasses.

"Nothing will ever change, no matter where you go, as long as you cower."

Tommy drops his head again.

"You only give others the power to influence you. When's it going to be enough for you before you stand up for yourself? Because when you do, no one can knock you down without your permission."

"I should get going." He quickly rushes off.

You sigh as you watch him retreat. He's skinny as a twig with sandy brown hair and smaller than average at 5'3". However, size doesn't matter. Heart does. If only he believed in himself.

Only, you're afraid the advice you gave Tommy doesn't ring true anymore. Greg isn't the physical type, but after witnessing him punching that locker, you have no idea what he might do next. You've known him since you were in elementary school. He is a classic bully; all talk but never physical, other than the occasional tripping. He's reaching a breaking point. Now, he is becoming a loose cannon. It's only a matter of time until he figures out what he is capable of.

It's hard for you to wrap your mind around the fact that Tommy isn't intentionally being disobedient. You have no idea what is going on. There is a rippling effect transpiring. You don't want to get mixed up in the crossfire, but you fear you already have and have no idea how to pull yourself out.

You look down at your hand. It trembles. You make a fist and continue on your way.

Chapter 11

"He's ghosting me." Camille whines as she slips her cell phone into her jacket pocket.

"Maybe it's for the best," you suggest as you both walk out into the parking lot.

"I haven't even seen Vince all week. Have you?"

"No," you answer with a shrug. You're not upset about it either. In fact, you are relieved after the incident with Greg. You're glad it's Friday. All you have left to do is get through work.

When you walk in, you are ecstatic when you find yourself listed for drive-thru on the schedule. You don't have the added pressure of seeing a line and hearing comments from people in the lobby to go faster with each transaction since it's payday Friday.

"Are you sure you don't want me to give you a lift home?" Terry asks as she locks the bank doors.

"No, I can walk. It's only a few blocks. Besides, I'm going to get some takeout at Franz," you insist.

"Okay," she sighs, displeased, "but I'm going to keep watch to make sure no one follows you."

You don't argue. You know Terry is uncomfortable with the idea that you would be alone in the dark.

Once you are off bank property, you hear Terry shift her white Ford Focus into gear. You don't look back as you keep walking forward.

As you open the door to the pizzeria, the bell chimes against the door. It's busy, as usual, but you don't mind. You only have an empty house to go home to anyway, since your mother is working late.

You focus on the menu for several seconds while slowly inching forward, debating. When it's your place next in line, you order a tuna sub and a ham and cheese for your mother before finding an empty place to stand and wait. Your eyes begin to wander around until they land on a blue pair. Vince.

Just as quickly as your eyes lock with him, his divert away. What is he doing here? You haven't seen a hair of him since the incident with Greg. You're not complaining. Yet, you have questions.

"Why are you obnoxiously present everywhere I go?" You approach the table.

"I'm sorry. Should I know you?"

You reel back with a frown. Why is Vince acting as if he doesn't know you?

"And who might this charming young lady be, Vinson?"

You look over, realizing Vince isn't alone, as you meet the cold, dark chocolate-brown eyes of an unfamiliar guy. He reeks of bergamot.

"Nadine," you answer in a hesitant voice and narrow your eyes. "I don't recall seeing you around town before, and you are?"

"Jomar. And I'm just passing through."

"Oh, how do you know Vince?" You spy a glance and notice he seems stiff with a neutral expression. You're getting a bad vibe that's worse than the one you got with Vince.

"I don't believe we have enough time to go down that road. How do you know him?"

"School, obviously. Share a few classes." You hide your anxiety behind a half smile.

"I believe that's your order," Vince interrupts.

"What?" You jolt.

"They just called out order ninety-three." He glances at the receipt in your hand before motioning with his eyes to leave.

"Oh, yes, yes, it is. Well, it was nice meeting you, uh, Jomar."

"Pleasure was all mine." His smile appears sinister.

Maybe you should have accepted the ride from Terry and not stopped at Franz. The night seems darker. The walk home feels longer. Every noise you hear spooks you, sending shivers up your spine.

You're glad when you make it through the front and lock it immediately behind you. You jump when Leo rubs up against your leg in the dark house. You wait, keeping on high alert, ensuring you were not followed before relaxing and turning on the light. You feel more at ease with Leo acting like his normal self. Leo would act defensively if there were something dangerous lurking outside. You pick him up and hug him closely. Tomorrow is a new day. All you have to do is sleep the night away, and everything will be fine.

You're not looking forward to working in the lobby Saturday morning as you put your belongings in the back and pick up your drawer from the vault. You enjoy working the drive-thru. People are more obnoxious coming into the lobby. You hate how they lean over the counter while you count out the money and log it into the system. You are always more on guard. The bank has a procedure in place in case someone comes in to rob it, but you can never be truly prepared. At least with the drive-thru, you have a nice glass barrier between you and the customer. And generally, the customer wants in and out as fast as possible.

As you count the money in your drawer to balance it, your eyes glance up to see a gentleman walk up to the door and pull, only to realize the door is still locked. You divert your eyes with a slight roll. They are like vultures circling and jumping at the first opportunity to get in to do their transactions, expecting to be serviced before eight, when the bank opens.

You flick your eyes over to Terry, who approaches the front door, unlocks it for the man, and apologizes. Customer service at its finest. If you were in charge, there is no way you would open three minutes before opening time and apologize for the inconvenience. It clearly states on the front door what time the bank opens.

You smile with eye contact as the man approaches. You take care of him promptly. You lose track of how many come in and out afterward as you take check after check and put money in and out of your drawer. You keep a smile planted on your face even at the obnoxious requests. Have to keep from rolling your eyes or shaking your head, especially when young individuals come in and ask what their balance is. If they kept track of their own finances, they would know and not have to ask or pay an overage fee. You don't understand how irresponsible people can be.

Your smile falters when you see the next person walk through the door.

Jomar.

What is he doing here? It's nearly closing time. Didn't he say he was just passing through? He couldn't have an account here.

"Hello, Nadine, right?" There's an alluring presence in his smile.

"Yes. What can I do for you, sir?" You remain professional.

"Sir? So formal. I haven't been called that in a very long time," he chuckles.

You just keep smiling, waiting for him to make his next move.

"This is a nice little town. Have you lived here your whole life?"

"What can I help you with?" You hope he gets the hint when you flick your eyes at the next person standing in line waiting for service.

"Well, I was thinking of investing in some real estate here. Any advice?"

"I'm sorry, sir, you'll have to speak to Terry, our service representative. If you take a seat over there," you say and point to a section cornered off from the lobby, "she'll be with you in a few minutes."

"So official. Very well, then." He turns away and heads to the seating area.

You smile at the next customer in line and motion for the couple to step forward. As you take care of their transaction, counting out the money they want back, you keep glancing over at Jomar. You watch as Terry approaches and extends her hand for a handshake; however, he refuses. You think it's odd that he is looking to invest in real estate. He doesn't appear much older than you. Can he be that financially stable?

As soon as the clock strikes one, you head gracefully toward the front doors and immediately lock them before anyone else has a chance to come in at the last minute. Just as you are turning to walk away, Terry emerges from her office with Jomar.

"Thank you very much. You were very helpful," Jomar states in a bittersweet manner.

"It was my pleasure. Please stay in touch. I gave you one of my cards, right?"

"Yes, have it right here." He flashes the business card.

You unlock the door and hold it open for him.

"Have a good day." He pauses next to you. "It was nice to make your acquaintance again, Nadine."

He walks out the door. You promptly lock the door behind him.

"Well, he was an unusual character," Terry comments.

"So, you thought he was a bit odd, too?"

"Odd is putting it nicely."

"What all did he ask about?"

"He asked very general questions like mortgage rates. Seemed pretty disinterested, too. I won't complain if I never see him again."

You're on edge as you exit the bank with Terry. You look around the parking lot on high alert and frown when you spot Camille's Charger rather than your mother's Jeep. What is she doing here?

"Surprise!" she exclaims.

"Why are you here?" You lean down with the door open.

"Well, I thought I'd take you to lunch and then go to the mall."

"Cam, I'm really not in the mood."

"Not even for some apple pie at Pink Caddy? I brought along some cinnamon." She flashes a small container.

You contemplate. "Only if you are getting pecan pie."

"Exactly why we are going." She grins.

You reluctantly agree as you climb into the passenger seat.

"How was work?" Camille eases out into the traffic.

"The norm," you say with a nonchalant shrug.

"Is everything okay?"

"Yeah, just tired," you wave off.

You raise an eyebrow, once seated in a pink booth that's trimmed with baby blue stripes, as Camille places her order, a Philly cheese steak substituting onion rings. You settle on a veggie burger with sweet potato fries. You don't know how Camille can splurge so much and stay so thin. Just looking at her food will probably make you gain five pounds. Clearly, you have a slower metabolism. You're not obsessed with trying to become stick-skinny like some girls; you just get annoyed at times. You stopped caring what other people think about your body a long time ago. Like making better food choices for yourself, but you still slip off the wagon, especially when stressed.

"This is my last splurge for a while," Camille comments after the waitress leaves.

"Oh, how come?" You sip your water.

"Hello? Prom."

"Oh."

"So, aren't you going to ask why we're going to the mall?"

"I figured you'd keep me in suspense until we got there."

"Always have to burst my bubble."

"You know it." You smirk.

"We're going prom dress shopping!" Cam bursts out.

"We?" you ask as your eyebrows arch.

"You're going to prom."

"We've discussed this before. No, I'm not."

"Prom only happens once in your lifetime. You'll regret it if you don't go."

"No, I won't."

"Maybe you will change your mind when you try on some dresses."

"I'm not trying on any dresses. I'll help you shop for one, but I'm not getting one."

"We'll see."

"Cam, I mean it." The orders come.

"You are insufferable." Camille munches on an onion ring.

"I know." You grin before taking a bite from your burger.

"You're really going to make me go to prom all alone?"

"There's still plenty of time for a guy to ask, you know."

"Doubt it. Vince won't even text me back."

"You have his number?" You're surprised as you pop in a sweet potato fry.

"Yeah." Camille stuffs the end of her Philly cheesesteak into her mouth and takes a huge bite.

"There are other guys at our school, you know."

"Umm," she mumbles as she chews. When she finishes and swallows, she answers, "But I'm only interested in one."

"So, if someone else asked you to the dance, you would turn them down?"

"How is everything?" the waitress interrupts.

"Good," you both answer in unison.

"I don't know, depends on who'd ask," Camille answers once the waitress walks away.

"You know, instead of waiting around for someone to ask you, you could ask someone."

"Like Vince."

You put your foot in your mouth on that one.

"So, if I worked up the courage to ask Vince, who you despise, would you come with then? You know, to keep an eye on me since he's so dangerous."

"No, you have a father for that."

"That's just cruel."

You beam with a smug grin.

"Well, you don't have to lose any sleep over the matter since he seems to have dropped off the face of the Earth," she sighs.

You don't know what to say to that, so you say nothing. You're not the only one who notices.

"Anyone up for dessert?" The waitress returns.
You both happily place your orders.

Chapter 12

When you walk into the mall, you want to run right back out. You hate crowds. Hate being surrounded by a sea of people. Hate feeling claustrophobic.

You follow Camille and hope it doesn't take very long for her to find a dress, but you know Camille. She will probably take a few hours to find the perfect one.

"I got to go look." Camille makes a beeline for Kay Jewelers.

"Cam, you can't afford any of that jewelry."

"I can still look."

Camille stares for countless minutes at the jewelry on display.

"I love this oval one. So simple yet elegant. They just need to have it in blue," Camille comments.

"Definitely not in your price range." You scrunch up your nose at the price tag. You don't understand why women always have to have such expensive things when there is beauty in something that is a fraction of the cost.

You both walk down the right side of the mall, navigating around people coming and going. Start to lose your patience with people who just stop and stand in the middle of the floor, blocking the way, like no one else is around.

"Bingo." Camille bolts toward a store that has nothing but fancy dresses for every occasion.

You groan before following.

"There's so many to choose from!" Camille declares.

"Guess you'll have to try on every single one," you mock.

"What do you think of this one?" Camille asks as she walks over to a white sleeveless dress with sequins around the upper part of the body.

"It's very white."

"Yeah, you're right. Too wedding-like."

"Here, try this one." You pick up a blue dress that's closest to you. Anything blue, Camille won't argue about.

"Okay." She grabs it and heads to the dressing room, but ends up feeling like it's not the one.

Camille tries on several different types of blue dresses after that, before changing to different colors, including a green, a pink, and a purple one. However, none make her happy.

"I need a break. I'm exhausted." Camille sits down beside you outside the dressing room.

"Maybe we should call it a day and come back another time?" you encourage as you really just want to go home.

Camille gasps and rushes off before coming back with a rosy pink dress. "You should try this on."

You wrinkle your nose. "You know I'm not really into pink anymore, and I told you I wasn't here to try any on."

"Oh, come on, please. It might help me figure out what I want by seeing you in a few."

You sigh. "Fine, but find something else." There was a time when you were obsessed with everything pink, but these days, it has to be the right shade as your interests have changed. Usually a deep, dark shade.

Camille dashes away and comes back quickly with a strapless teal dress.

"Really?" you protest.

"Just try it on," she snaps and shoves the dress at you.

You huff as you slip into an unoccupied room.

"Wow, you look very mint-like." Camille bursts out laughing when you walk out awkwardly.

"Can I take it off now?"

"Sure, try this one next."

"Really? Look how delicate it is. I'll probably rip it trying it on," you complain as you take in the smoky gray chiffon sequined dress with a thin strap around the waist. You do like the coloration, but it just looks flimsy.

"You're just making excuses. Try it on." Camille shoves it into your hands before pushing you back into the changing room.

"Did you see the price tag on this?" You walk out with the tag in hand.

"I'm not supposed to worry about price. I've got plastic." Camille flashes a credit card you assume is from her father.

"Satisfied?"

"You look nice, but I don't think it's your style. However, I'm convinced I got the perfect one." Camille hands you a black dress.

"You know what, let me go find you one, and then we can try them on together."

"I love that idea."

You pull up on the gray dress so you don't trip on it, and you go out onto the floor, looking around for a few minutes before settling on a floor-length royal blue dress.

"I saw that one earlier, but thought the shade was too dark, but why not?" Camille grabs it and goes into the room next to the one you are using.

You look at yourself in the mirror with a groan. You feel self-conscious as you step out, holding together the thigh-high slit with your hand. "Cam, what's taking you so long?"

"Coming." Camille opens the door, stopping in her tracks. "Wow, you look amazing."

"Amazingly uncomfortable. Feel like some goth chick; it's so black."

"What do you think?" Camille does a twirl.

"Looks good on you." You're awed yourself.

"Really?"

"Yes. Suits you well."

"I thought so, too. Seems to make the brown in my eyes pop. Guess I was too quick to judge."

"Does that mean we're done now?" you ask with hope.

Camille laughs. "Yeah, guess so."

You are so relieved to take off the dress and put back on your comfortable clothing. You felt like someone completely different. You step out and wait for what seems like an eternity. "What's taking you so long this time?"

"Sorry, I'm just mesmerized by how I look. Why don't you go to the bookstore for a while and I'll meet you there?"

"Where did you get this dress?"

"Just hang it on the door. I'll take it back."

"You're not trying to get rid of me and thinking of doing something irrational, are you?"

"What?"

"Cam," you warn.

"No, I swear."

"You'd better not."

"Would you just go to the bookstore? The more time you spend without me, the less time I have to wait for you to browse every shelf."

"How is that fair?"

"Trust me, it's more torturous for me than this was for you," Camille groans.

You smile to yourself before heading to the used bookstore near the end of the mall. Camille hates accompanying you since you can spend countless hours searching high and low for any and all novels that catch your interest. You are glad to have a few minutes of peace without Camille nagging you to hurry up.

You glance over the latest bestsellers on the front display, but nothing interests you. You head around and start at the beginning of the alphabet, looking for anything that stands out that you haven't already seen before.

Every now and then, you glance up at the entrance, keeping a lookout for Camille before your back is turned. When you find yourself on the other side of the bookcase, you look up and see a familiar face in the mall lobby that makes you shudder.

Jomar.

You drop your eyes. What's he doing at the mall? Is he following you? You glance up again, only to find he's gone like he was never there. This time, you see Camille heading your way.

"What's wrong?" She searches your eyes.

"Nothing, why?" You pick out a random book from the shelf and pretend to read the text on the back.

"You're pale as a ghost."

"Where's the dress?" You change the subject.

"I took it out to the car. I wasn't going to lug it all around the bookstore."

"Oh, well, I'm done anyway." You place the book back on the shelf.

"Really? You didn't even get halfway."

"I don't want to find anything. I've got enough at home to read."

"Okay, I won't argue."

As you follow, a particular classic novel authored by Anne Rice catches your eye on an end shelf. You shake your head and keep walking. Only you feel on edge. Like someone is watching you. You focus on every single person's face that passes by, but don't find the one face you are looking for.

— ◯ —

Chapter 13

You jump when your cell phone rings and buzzes on the nightstand. It's just after nine o'clock on Sunday night. Your mother has a rule no calls after nine. Who would be calling you this late, and why?

You look at the display and freeze. "Cam?"

"Nad…." A sniffle. "Can I come over?"

"It's a school night." The words automatically pop out, as you know what your mother would say.

"I should have known it was a mistake coming over." She disconnects.

A mistake coming over…? You rush into the family room and open the front door. You see Camille, with a duffel bag, heading down the sidewalk from your home into the street. Quickly, you shove your feet into your gray UGGS by the door and run out after her.

"Cam, wait," you shout after her.

"Forget it," she tosses over her shoulder.

"Cam." You reach out and place your hand on her shoulder, only she shrugs it off and stops in place.

"My parents want to get a divorce." She drops her blue duffel bag before turning and sobbing into your left shoulder.

"What?" You're dumbstruck. The only thing you can do for Camille at the moment is comfort her. You hesitate before you wrap your arms around her and hold her tightly on the cold winter night.

"I'm getting snot all over you." Camille pushes back as she wipes at her face with her sleeve.

"It'll wash out. Why don't we get out of the cold?" You reach down to pick up the duffel.

Camille nods.

"What's going on?" your mother asks as you enter the front door.

"Can Cam stay the night?"

Your mother studies Camille, understanding something is up before answering, "Of course."

"Do you want some hot chocolate? I can make some while you change into your pajamas," you encourage.

"Yeah, that sounds nice," Camille agrees before walking down the hall and into the bathroom.

"What's going on?" your mother asks in a whisper.

"Her parents want a divorce."

"Oh, dear. I'd better call her mother and let her know she's with us."

You wait for the hot water to finish brewing in the coffee pot, then you prepare a mug of hot cocoa with mini marshmallows on top, the way Camille likes it, and head to your bedroom. You find Camille slipped under the blanket, hugging Leo with her face buried in the back of his head. Leo is purring with reassurance.

"Here you go." You walk forward.

Camille looks up and releases Leo before accepting the mug, but just stares at the contents inside. Leo snuggles up against her, continuing to purr. He knows what to do without being told. "My mom was putting the threatening letters in the mailbox."

"Why would she do that?" You go rigid.

Camille puts the mug on the nightstand. "She's been wanting my dad to retire for a while, and she thinks the latest case he's working on is dangerous."

"How did he find out?"

"He caught her. They had this huge fight, and he walked out claiming he wanted a divorce."

"What case is he working on?"

"I don't really know. I overheard something about blood going missing from the hospital."

"Blood? Why would someone steal blood?"

"I don't know." She shrugs. "I can't believe he wants to give up on their marriage just like that. They are high school sweethearts, for crying out loud." She bursts into tears again.

You sit down on the edge of the bed and embrace Camille in a tight hug, since you don't know what else to do.

"Is it wrong that I'm slightly mad?" she whispers.

"You're asking the wrong person, but I think it would be kind of normal."

"I've been so naïve to believe in fairy tale endings."

"What do you mean?"

"Love is supposed to always prevail," she pushes back.

"Just because they are giving up on each other doesn't mean you have to stop believing in happily ever after. Sometimes love just isn't enough, and people grow apart."

"But why?" she semi-whines.

"I don't know. Love isn't really my specialty."

Camille sinks lower into the bed and turns to her side with her back toward you, stroking Leo.

"Try to get some sleep," you encourage.

"I don't want to have to choose between them." Camille chokes back a sob.

"Don't. No parent should ever make their child choose."

Camille says nothing. Not knowing what else to say, you slip under the covers as well and turn off the bedside lamp. You are uncomfortable in these kinds of situations. You don't always know what the right thing to do or say is, or the wrong. You know it's going to be a long night, sensing Camille is most likely crying silent tears into the pillow. You hate knowing Camille is hurting, and there is nothing you can do about it.

At some point in the middle of the night, you manage to drift off, but you don't sleep soundly. Several different dreams that don't make sense flash through your mind, including one with a blue fire ring. You wake with a start when your alarm starts blaring off early in the morning. You groggily hit the snooze button and lie there completely drained as if you didn't get sleep at all. For a moment, you forget about Camille. When the fog lifts, and you remember, you reach over to the other side of the bed, only to find it empty.

"Cam?" You shoot upright, swing your feet to the side of the bed, and stand, your heart racing.

"In the bathroom," she mumbles before the faucet turns on.

You walk out of your room and peek into the bathroom, where you find Camille brushing her teeth.

"When did you get up?"

She shrugs before spitting out her toothpaste. "About ten minutes, I guess."

"Wow, never heard you." You stretch out your arms and aching back.

"Good. I was glad to seize my opportunity in the bathroom." She flashes a grin.

You hold your tongue. Camille seems in better spirits, and you don't want to say anything that would cause the memories of last night to resurface.

An aroma opens your senses, and you follow your nose into the kitchen and find your mother making eggs and pancakes. "Something smells delicious, but aren't you late for work?"

"I rearranged my shift so I could go in a little later this morning," your mother replies.

"Wow, breakfast hot off the stove. I could get used to this," Camille comments as she enters.

The car is eerily quiet, which is unusual for Camille, as your mother drives you both to school. Again, you can't help but feel uncomfortable. The first class can't come soon enough as you both walk into the building.

Camille gasps when approaching her locker. You look between Camille and what she is staring at before seeing Vince standing in the crowded hallway. Camille makes a dash for the girls' bathroom.

You narrow your eyes at Vince, wanting to walk over to him and demand some answers, but now is not the time. You hate being torn in two different directions. With a puff of air, you follow Camille.

"I'm sorry, I just wasn't prepared to see him," Camille sobs uncontrollably.

"It's okay." You rub her back.

"You should get to class before you're late. I've got to take care of my mascara." Camille grabs some paper towels and starts rubbing away the smeared dark lines.

"Are you sure?"

"Yes, go, I'll be fine."

You hesitate. Part of you wants to go, but part of you wants to stay. You're not sure what Camille needs right now, a friend or to be left alone. You know, if the roles were reversed, you would just want to be left alone.

"Go," Camille reassures.

With a sigh, you turn and leave Camille as the first bell rings.

The day goes dreadfully slowly. All you can think about is Camille and that you made a mistake. You text her a few times throughout the day, but she doesn't respond. She is quiet in history. You should have stayed with her, not left her alone in her misery.

When you walk into English and see Vince, you stop thinking about Camille for the first time. All the thoughts swirling around your mind rush back.

"I've got questions," you say as you approach his desk.

"I've got answers, but only if you ask the right ones." He meets your eyes.

"Don't play games with me. I'm not in the mood." You fold your arms.

"I'm not here to play games."

"Who are you?"

"Vinson Weber."

"What are you?" You inhale a deep breath before exhaling slowly. You're not sure if you really want to know. Until now, you hadn't realized how he speaks. How he acts. As if he is older than he appears, with a slight accent, he tries to cover over. He doesn't act like a typical teenage boy. Acts as if he is above their pettiness.

He sighs. "I'm afraid I can't answer that."

"Why not?" You pierce his eyes without blinking.

"I'm not at liberty to disclose, and you're not privileged to know. It's for your own well-being."

"What kind of answer is that?"

"One you have to accept."

"Why are you here?"

"To discuss *Romeo and Juliet*. I apologize that we are a bit behind."

You continue to stand there with your arms crossed.

He sighs, "Why I'm here has nothing to do with you or Camille; that's all I can give you."

"I think you should stay away from both of us."

His eyes drop as he nods once before the bell rings.

Chapter 14

Friday night is eerily calm. Calm before the storm. The forecast is expecting three to five inches of snow overnight and into Saturday morning. It's not a really big storm, but more snow accumulation than there has been so far for the winter season. Winter has been pretty mild, as more snow generally comes in February into March.

Camille has been trying to cope. It hurts you to know your friend is hurting inside, and you don't know what you can do to take her pain away. You don't want to push her if she isn't ready to talk, but you feel like a terrible person acting as if nothing is wrong. You don't want to trigger anything, so the only thing you know how to do is to be there, even if you don't talk that much.

You look out the door onto the back porch into the unknown with Leo in your arms. You rub your finger under his chin as he purrs with glee. His purr is serene.

You jerk when the landline phone rings. It's getting late. Your stomach twists in knots. You fear the worst – that something has happened to your mother. She's later than usual. You're uneasy about the fact that she's been working too many extra shifts lately.

"Hello?" You neglect to look at the caller ID.

"Nadine?"

"Yeah." You frown, confused at the male voice. It sounds familiar, but you can't quite pinpoint who it is.

"Is Camille with you?"

"No." Realization dawns that it's Camille's father.

"Do you know where she is?"

"No, she didn't mention anything when she picked me up after my shift. I assumed she went home."

"She's not there. She told her mother she was spending the weekend with me."

"Let me try her on her cell." You reach for your cell.

"Don't bother. Camille's cell is at her mother's place along with her car."

You should have known the first thing he would do was to try to track her. He is a police officer.

"Do you know a Vince?"

"Yes, why?" You are hesitant, not knowing where this is going.

"Do you have his number, by chance?"

"No, why?"

"She talks about him a lot."

"I think she might have his number in her cell. I could try contacting some girls from school."

"I'll look into reaching this 'Vince.' I appreciate you wanting to help, but I've got it handled. Sorry if I alarmed you. I'm sure there's nothing to worry about."

You hear the strain in his voice. It's unlike Camille to disappear without telling someone, especially you. You did drift apart slightly this week, whether you like to admit it or not. Camille is hurting inside, but you tried brushing it off, pretending she was okay. You were a fool. There were signs, but you ignored them. If something happens to her, you will never forgive yourself.

You make a beeline for the kitchen drawer by the sink and grab the old address book from your younger days. You have no idea if any of the numbers from your classmates when you were in elementary school are still in service, but you have to try something.

The first number you call is still in working service. However, it goes straight to an answering machine. The next number is disconnected, whereas the third just rings and rings.

You flip to the next page and pause.

Trevor Bennett.

The first and only guy you ever had a major crush on. It was innocent. He showed more maturity than the rest of the boys. You felt different whenever you were around him. A feeling you couldn't make sense of at the time. You shake your head and dial the number.

Disconnected.

You breathe a sigh of relief, glad, before flipping to the next few pages, but the numbers don't pan out either before you pause again.

Lindsey Conway.

Someone you once considered a friend. That was before you went to your very first school dance and discovered who Lindsey ended up with.

Trevor.

Lindsey knew you had a huge crush on him. It wasn't much of a secret; everyone knew. You believed even Trevor did. You didn't really hide it well and waited patiently to be asked by him to the dance, but he never did. You didn't even want to go to the stupid dance, but Lindsey insisted, and you secretly hoped that just maybe you'd end up dancing with Trevor.

Only Lindsey did. She knew how much you liked Trevor and had to know it would hurt you, but Lindsey accepted when he walked over and asked. To make matters worse, you found out Lindsey had made a deal with Gregory. Simply get you to the dance, and he would have Trevor dance at least once with her. You had no clue Lindsey had had a crush on Trevor as well.

Hurt and humiliated, you left early and cried so hard that night into the morning. The last time you ever allowed yourself to cry. Gregory had sought his revenge, which was the last time you were ever going to give him or anyone else the satisfaction. The next day, as you walked into school while everyone whispered and laughed, you headed straight for Trevor, told him about how you felt, and asked if he ever had any feelings for you. When he told you that he didn't feel the same way, you told him you were glad it was addressed before walking away with your head held high.

As for Lindsey, your friendship faded as you kept your distance from her and focused on school studies. You kept your distance from everyone so as to never be disappointed again…until Camille came along.

You hold your breath when the line rings, and you hope no one answers.

"Hello?"

"Hello, uh, Lindsey?"

"Yes, who's this?"

"It's, umm, Nadine."

"Nadine?" You hear the surprise in Lindsey's voice.

"I'm calling to see if, by chance, you might know where Camille might be. She's not at home, and her parents are worried."

"Umm, no, I have no idea." You pick up on a hint of hesitation.

You are about to question further when you hear a beep signaling another call coming through. "Okay, well, thanks, got to go."

"Nadine, it's Tom again."

"Did you find her?"

"No, and no answer from Vince."

"Nothing on my end either, sorry."

"Don't be. I'm going to head up to the cabin to see if she's there. If you hear from her, please let me know, but I might be out of service."

"Okay, you'll be the first to know."

"And Nadine."

"Yeah?"

"Promise me you'll stay home and not try looking for her yourself."

You swallow the lump in your throat. "Okay, promise."

He disconnects.

You have mixed emotions. You're worried, and yet now starting to get mad. Camille never pulled a stunt like this, and you just made a promise to a cop that you might not be able to keep.

With steely determination, you redial the last number.

"You know something, Lindsey, and you're going to tell me right now," you demand.

She sighs. "I can't. If Camille's father finds out—"

"He won't," you cut her off.

"If it gets out that I told you…"

"No one will find out. Now tell me," you state with pointed words.

She sighs again. "There's a party going on at Greg's place."

"Thank you for the information." You hover over the end call button. "Nadine?"

You pause before placing the phone back to your ear. "Yeah?"

"I'm truly sorry for everything."

You let dead air hang between you, uncertain how to respond. "I'm sorry, too, but I'm glad you're happy." You disconnect. You meant what you said since she's still going strong with Trevor.

You pace. Greg's place is on the other side of town. The only transportation you have is your two feet. You suspect alcohol is involved. If Camille is drunk, there is no way you will be able to walk her home, especially in a snowstorm. There is only one other option. Walk over to Camille's place and hope you can grab the car keys and drive off without being seen.

You slip on your boots and rush out the door, dismissing the time to grab your jacket since you have your vest over your sweater. Light snow has already started, but it's too warm to stick to the roads yet.

You hustle the few blocks over to Camille's place and discover the house is dark. The only car in the driveway is Camille's Charger. You walk up the front walkway before pausing to reach down and grab the small cast-iron turtle in the flower bed. You slide the shell to the side and reach in for the hidden key. You let yourself in using your phone as a flashlight. You find Camille's set of keys hanging on the wall next to the coat rack and grab them.

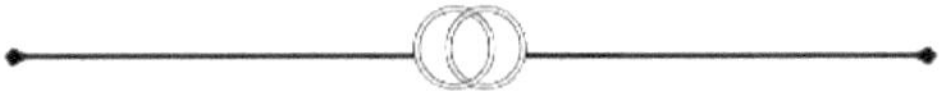

The snow is light and steady during the whole drive. You stick to the back roads. In a matter of minutes, you see a bunch of cars lined up on the street beside Greg's house with a vibrating bass coming from inside. You see some classmates hanging out on the front porch.

"Oh, uh, who told the party crasher?" Dillon mocks as you march up the steps.

"Where's Camille?"

"Who?" He takes a swig from his beer bottle in mock jest.

"Guess I will have to find her myself." You head toward the open doorway.

"Invitation only." Dillon blocks your path.

"Step out of the way."

"And what are you going to do if I don't?" he slurs while his two buddies chuckle.

Without hesitation, you knock the bottle of beer from his hand.

"Hey!" he yells, rushing after it as it spills all over the porch.

You waste no time as you hurry inside before he has time to react. Music blares. You look all around to see your classmates acting like fools. You push your way through the crowded rooms, looking high and low for Camille.

"Chug, chug, chug," you hear chanting from the kitchen. It's a slow go, but you manage to weave your way into the kitchen, where you see Camille downing a big red cup of, you presume, beer.

"Camille!"

"Nadine," she slurs with delight. "Come join me."

"I think you've had enough." You snatch the cup from her hand.

"I don't recall inviting you. Who told you?" Greg spits out.

"Doesn't matter. Party's over."

"It's over when I say it is." He gets in your face.

You stand your ground while holding your breath. If he decides to get physical, you're not sure if you'd know how to defend yourself.

"What's going on here?"

Chapter 15

You look over to see Greg's father standing in the entryway of the kitchen. Everyone in the kitchen freezes, staring at the adult while the ones behind slowly creep toward the front door. At some point, someone turned off the music.

"Dad?" Greg looks surprised.

"I asked you a question, Gregory."

"I thought you wouldn't be back until tomorrow."

Your focus shifts back to Greg. He's deathly pale with wide eyes.

"Looks like you assumed wrong."

"Dad, I can explain."

"I think I've seen enough." Greg's father shifts his gaze to the room around them and demands, "I want everyone out, now!"

"I think I'm going to be sick," Camille announces before running through the open sliding glass door onto the back deck and hurling over the side. You follow. When Camille finishes, you drape her left arm over your shoulder and escort her back through the kitchen.

You can feel the tension in the room. Greg stands like a statue, his eyes filled with dread. You switch your focus to his father, who stands there with furious eyes locked on his son.

No one had to be told twice. Everyone has already fled. You want nothing more than to leave as well, but something doesn't feel right. You don't owe Greg anything. He deserves the punishment he gets, but you can't pretend that something more serious might happen.

You lead Camille to the couch and guide her down. She is out of it and has no idea what is going on.

"Dad, I'm sorry."

"What were you going to do if the cops showed up?"

You appear just in time to see Greg's father backhand him across the left cheek.

"I, I don't know, Dad. I said I was sorry." Greg presses a hand to his cheek in shock.

"If you were sorry, you wouldn't have done it in the first place." He raises his hand again.

"Stop," you utter before flinching.

Greg's father whips his head in your direction, his face red. "I told you to get out!"

You jerk back half a step. "You're angry."

"You're damn right that I'm angry!"

"You're not thinking logically."

"I'm thinking perfectly well." He turns like a raging bull at his son. "I work hard to put a roof over your head, clothing on your back, and food in your belly, and this is the thanks I get? You're selfish. A selfish brat who doesn't do anything to help out and spends all my money!" he screams, looming over Greg.

"Please, Mr. Pierce, calm down." You shift forward, keeping your distance.

"Who do you think you are, missy?" He shoves Greg hard before turning his attention back to you.

"I'm not a bystander," you state.

"You're a fool, just like my son."

"I can help clean up." You change the subject while you position yourself at an angle to insert yourself between them if you need to.

"No, it's his mess. He'll clean it up, all on his own, all night if he has to!"

"Okay, maybe he should start now?"

"Fine."

You both redirect your attention to Greg. He stands up against the counter with his back toward you both. Abruptly, he spins with a butcher knife in his hand. He raises the knife high in the air and moves toward his father.

You react without thinking and rush forward, pushing Greg's father out of the way. You freeze with wide eyes, seeing the blade aiming down at you before you close them tightly, turning your head, and moving your right arm up to shield your face, waiting for the impact. You dread the searing pain to surely follow.

"Gregory Ray Pierce!" Mr. Pierce cries out.

Only pain doesn't come. Instead, you hear fabric rip. You peek over your arm.

"Release the knife," you hear Vince's voice say. The knife clacks against the white and gray linoleum floor.

You notice a huge gash in Vince's left shoulder blade around the torn baby blue shirt he wears. To your horror, you watch as the ripped skin instantly begins to repair itself.

"You will not remember this encounter. Your father came home early and grounded you for the rest of the year. You will wait here until your father tells you to go to your room."

"What are you doing to my son?" Mr. Pierce demands.

Vince is on him like a speeding bullet. An impossible speed.

"You will not remember this encounter. You came home, discovered your son threw a party, kicked everyone out, and grounded him for the rest of the year. Tell him to go to his room."

"Gregory Pierce, go to your room." He points.

You watch Greg obey without a word.

"Cam's in the car," you hear Vince utter. Before you have a chance to look over at him, you discover he's vanished.

"I thought I told everyone to leave." You turn to Mr. Pierce as he points. "Get out of my house."

Without a word, you slip out of the kitchen and make your way to the front door. When you reach the car, you find Camille in the passenger seat, all buckled up and passed out.

The snow is coming down harder. A layer has built up on the road, making it slick. You drive slowly but can feel the tires slip every now and then, especially around turns.

A million thoughts are screaming below the surface, but you keep them at bay, focusing on the road ahead of you. You have to get Camille home safely before you can even start processing what just happened tonight.

You're relieved when you see the lights are still off at Camille's house. You don't want to face her parents. Don't want to face anyone right now. It's taking all your strength just to keep it together.

"Cam, wake up." You shake her shoulder.

Camille moans as she stirs. With persistence, you manage to get her to her feet and help her inside, letting her crash on the couch. There is no way you are going to be able to get her up a flight of stairs, so you let her sleep on her side.

You pace the living room, trying to figure out how to contact her parents without letting them know it's from you. You promised not to go out after Camille. Finally, you come up with a solution as you rush up the stairs and into Camille's room, and find her phone. You pull up Camille's father's number first and then her mother's number, and leave them both a text message.

Camille's home and safe.

Violent shivers rake your body when you step outside, as your adrenaline has run its course. Only now do you realize you're without a jacket. You cross your arms and walk down the road in the direction of your home. The night seems endless as you put one foot in front of the other while the wind whips up, swirling the snow around. You stop in your tracks when you notice a figure appear in the veil of snow in front of you. You know who it is as he closes the gap.

Vince.

"You asked me once before what I am. I couldn't answer you before, but I can answer you now. I'm a vampire." He stops before you.

Your racing heart skips a beat. It can't be true. This is reality, not folklore. A nightmare you just didn't wake up from yet.

"I'm not here to hurt you." He takes a step forward.

You swallow hard. "Just drain me dry of my blood, right?"

"No." He shakes his head before moving in swiftly and placing a firm grip on your upper arms, staring directly into your eyes. "Nothing significant happened tonight. I am not a vampire. There is nothing suspicious about me. You will continue to dislike me because I am rude and arrogant."

He just threw your own words back in your face. Had that been something else Camille told him? Or had he overheard it? "Get off of me!" you shout, kneeing him between the legs, only to realize that was a mistake and wince.

His frown overshadows his grimace. "You still remember?"

"Doesn't just magically go away." You twist out of his grasp and fall onto the snow-covered ground.

"What all did you have to eat today?"

"What?" You pant, flabbergasted.

"Would make the difference why it didn't work."

"Why? What didn't work?"

"Compulsion."

You stiffen before your face contorts from shock to anger as you lurch to your feet and take a swing. You are prepared to fight tooth and nail for your life.

"I wouldn't." He is quick to catch your right wrist inches from his face.

"Don't touch me." You reel back as if his touch burns you. With fury, you swing your left arm, which he catches as well. Infuriated, you stomp down on his right foot and again learn it's a mistake. It's like stomping down on a concrete floor. No impact. Now you're starting to realize why he's been preventing you from punching him. You can only imagine what your hand would feel like afterward.

"Calm down."

"Calm down? Calm down? Don't tell me to calm down!" you scream in his face.

"You should go home."

"Don't tell me what to do."

"We'll talk later." He removes his jacket and places it over your shoulders before fading away.

You look all around, but he's gone. You divert your attention to the jacket on your shoulders. Despite wanting to shrug it off, you pull it tighter. Your sweater does not repel the snow, and your arms are soaked and cold. You are mildly disappointed that there is no body heat to absorb.

Chapter 16

You bury your face into Leo. You can't sleep. You can't get warm. You hate crying, but you've reached your breaking point. Once the tears spill over, you can't get back in control. The image of Greg coming at you with the knife keeps replaying in your head. The fact that Vince confirmed your fears that he is indeed a vampire terrifies you. Deep down, subconsciously, you suspected. Only you refused to believe it was true. Your mind tried thinking up logical explanations, but nothing ever added up. The dark bruise you received just by bumping into his rock-hard exterior, Tommy's lapse in memory, the dent in your mother's Jeep, and blood going missing from the hospital.

He couldn't erase your memory. You don't know what's worse, being in the dark or knowing. Why is he even going to school in the first place? Whatever reason he has, it can't be a good one. The way he talked; it was as if you were an innocent party who was not supposed to be involved.

"Nadine, dear, don't you need to be getting ready for work?" your mother says as she pops her head into your room.

"My stomach doesn't feel so good," you groan, keeping your back to her.

You hear her enter the room before she places a hand against your forehead. "You don't seem to be running a fever. What did you have to eat last night?"

"Asparagus quiche."

"Hmm. Want me to call you off work?"

"I hate to make them short."

"They will figure it out. Don't you worry about that."

"Okay." You nod.

You listen as your mother leaves the room. You feel guilty, but you just don't have the strength to pretend everything is okay. To face anyone today.

She's gone for several minutes before returning. "Here are some crackers and a soda. Get some rest. I have to go in this morning."

"But you worked a double shift yesterday." You start to shift in bed, but stop yourself.

"It's only for a few hours. They are a bit short-staffed this morning. Call me if you get worse, okay?"

"Okay."

Ten minutes later, you hear her walk out the door before the Jeep purrs to life and leaves. You let out a breath, relieved. You have never faked being sick before, and you don't like how it feels. It actually makes you sick to your stomach. Plus, you most likely look terrible after a night of crying. At least you prevented your mother from seeing how you look. Being vulnerable is one thing, but letting someone see your vulnerability is another that you don't take lightly. You don't like showing weakness.

You rip back the covers and swing your feet to the floor. Usually, you don't mind having the house to yourself. You like the quiet, but today, it seems too quiet.

You grab your gray cardigan and slip it over your red and black flannel pajamas, still feeling cold as you make your way to the bathroom. Staring into the mirror, you see your cheeks are still a bit puffy and red against your ghostly complexion. You turn on the faucet and wash your face. When you finish, you head into the kitchen, turn on the radio, and stand there with uncertainty. You don't feel hungry. Don't feel like cooking. Don't feel like reading. You don't really know what to feel.

Leo rubs up against your leg with his back arched. You reach down and grab him. You hold him tightly while he purrs. "What would I do without you?"

He meows before butting his head into yours. You can't resist smiling. Even in the darkest of days, Leo can shed light and warm your inside. He always knows when you're feeling down.

Without warning, Leo stops purring and becomes tense. He sniffs the air. A low growl rumbles in the back of his throat. You freeze when you hear a knock on the front door.

Your eyes dart to the radio playing. You're not sure if it's loud enough for whoever is outside to hear. You know for a fact you don't want to answer the door, and you hope they go away.

"Nadine, I know you are home."

Vince.

How does he know where you live? This can't be happening. This is supposed to be your safe place. You thought everything would be okay if you just stayed home.

You hear the door creak open. Was it not locked? Leo scrambles out of your arms and runs out of the kitchen. Alarmed, you hurry after him before coming to a halt at the entryway of the family room. You see Leo in Vince's hands, held out away from his face, as Leo snarls and hisses, swatting the air with his paws. You have never seen him act like that before. So vicious. So primal. In a matter of seconds, he relaxes and becomes mellow again. Meows once as Vince sets him on the faux-wood vinyl flooring.

"I didn't invite you in." You gasp with wide eyes when you realize he's standing in your house.

He cocks his head to the side. "Were you reading up on vampires?"

"No." You cross your arms and stare, perplexed at how Leo is now rubbing up against his leg again, purring.

"I think you were."

"Get out of my house," you demand, pointing as he smirks.

"We need to talk."

"I don't give you my consent."

He tosses his head back and laughs. "Vampires don't exactly ask for permission."

"Which is wrong."

"You surprise me, even when you're scared."

"What did you do to my cat?"

"I let him look into my eyes, into my soul, to see I mean no harm."

"You mean forced him."

"Nadine." He takes a step forward.

You back away before scrambling into the kitchen and opening the cupboard to the spices. You find what you're looking for and quickly unscrew the cap.

"I'm not here to hurt you." You hear his voice closing the gap behind you. You spin and toss the full contents of garlic powder in his face. He turns his head and coughs, but nothing else happens. "Nadine."

He takes a step forward again. You make a beeline to the drawer next to the sink and pull it open, fumbling around the junk until you locate what you are searching for. You whirl and spray the can of mace directly into his eyes. You don't know what to expect. It's the only weapon you have. Only nothing can prepare you for the sight that follows. Crimson tears stream down his face. He seems just as shocked when he wipes the sticky substance from his cheek.

"Enough of this charade." He grabs your upper right arm and leads you to the far side counter, where he pauses. Your eyes go wide when you see him pull out the largest knife from the five-piece wood block set. "Everything you've read or think you know about vampires is a lie." He releases your arm, turns your hand out, and places the handle of the knife in your palm before aiming the blade directly at his stomach. "My greatest weakness would be a knife into my stomach. My life force would drain out too vastly for me to heal, allowing you to escape or inflict a fatal wound."

Why would he tell you that? It couldn't be that easy. It had to be a trick. Yet, he stands there with his arms up in surrender, waiting for you to make a move. Your eyes drop as the realization sets in that you are holding a large knife. The image of Greg flashes through your mind. Your hand begins to tremble. Vampire or no vampire, just the thought of plunging the sharp blade into someone's flesh makes you sick.

The knife drops against the tile floor as you rush to the kitchen sink. You cup your hands around the sides of your neck, holding your hair back, and vomit what little you have left in your stomach. Seeing a small piece of asparagus in the sink makes you vomit some more. When you're done, you turn on the faucet and let the water wash down the remnants in the sink before you cup your hands to rinse your mouth from the sour taste. You stand for a few minutes more, hovering to ensure you are finished. Slowly, you rise, holding onto the sink for support. You feel weak. You're no match against a vampire. You have no idea what to expect.

"I'm so sorry. I didn't even think about the ordeal you went through last night." He moves forward with an outstretched hand.

"Stay back," you demand, jerking away.

He stops and puts his hand down. You study him. He seems modest.

"Why don't you sit." He grabs a chair and places it in front of you.

"I'm fine standing," you reject, even though your legs feel like they might go out from under you at any minute.

He sighs.

You're overwhelmed. Have mixed emotions. He's a vampire, and vampires are supposed to be dangerous. Yet, he saved your life last night, kindly gave the jacket off his back when you were in need, and even told you his weakness. Your eyes waver. "I don't want to be compelled."

"It's for your own good," he whispers.

"I won't tell anyone. They wouldn't believe me anyway."

"It's forbidden for a human to know of my kind's existence. It will be better for you. It will give you peace of mind." Leo jumps up on the counter next to Vince, who reaches out and gently strokes the cat's head.

"Why are you here? Why high school?"

"I'm searching for someone."

"Who would you be searching for in high school?"

"There is a prophecy that the monarch of vampires will meet his doom to the one marked with the Dragon's Eye."

"Dragon, what?" You blink, bewildered.

"Dragon's Eye."

"What happens when you find the one who is marked?"

"I'm to take them to Vladimir."

You shudder involuntarily at just the mention of the name. "Why couldn't you compel me last night? What happens if you can't erase my memory?"

"Asparagus prevents vampires from compelling humans. Once it's out of your system, I will compel you."

"Why asparagus?"

"I have no idea," he says with a shrug as you frown.

You look away. "How much are you planning on taking away?"

"Just your suspicions and facts regarding me, including last night, nothing more."

"So, what are you waiting for?" Your eyes meet his.

His sigh is deep. "I can't compel you until after twenty-four hours of you consuming asparagus. In the meantime, I need your cooperation. You can't tell anyone. Not Camille. Not your mother."

You nod once.

"I'll be back tonight." He turns, but stops. "And Nadine, please don't do anything foolish."

Chapter 17

He's gone. You stand in the kitchen alone, with the exception of Leo, who is watching you from his perch on the counter.

"Traitor," you mumble.

You're startled when you hear your cell phone ring in your bedroom. So much has happened in the last several hours that you had completely forgotten about Camille. You walk forward on shaky legs before holding a hand against the counter and then the wall toward your room. You see the display showing on your outdated Motorola that Camille is calling before it goes to voicemail. You sit on your bed, staring at the phone on your nightstand. Should you call her back? You're not even sure if you can keep your composure. Why would she even be calling this early?

The phone rings again. You inhale before answering.

"Nad? Oh, good, you answered."

"What's up?"

"I'm grounded."

"You called me at seven thirty in the morning just to tell me you're grounded?" You frown.

"Yeah. Aren't you going to ask me why?"

You know why, but Camille doesn't know that you know. "Why are you grounded?"

"I went to a party."

"A party?"

"There was drinking involved."

"Camille…" Your voice is laced with disapproval.

"Save the lecture. My dad already gave me one, and I've got a headache to prove it."

"I'm sure he did. Did he break it up?"

"No, which brings me to why I'm calling before you start work. I kind of don't remember what happened last night. It's all foggy, but I could have sworn you were there."

"At a party?"

"You're right, forget it. Anyway, afraid I won't be able to give you a ride."

"Don't worry about it. I got it covered."

"Vince was there."

You freeze. How would she know that?

"Well, I think he was. I think he was the one who took me home. I have this fuzzy image of him carrying me." She pauses with a deep intake of breath and releases a sigh. "Someone sent my parents each a text message from my phone that I was home safe. They didn't get it right away since they were out of reception. They were together in the same car, heading up to the cabin. Can you believe that?" she rambles on.

"I'm sure they were worried about you."

"My dad stayed the night."

"Cam…." Your tone issues a warning.

"Yes, I know, don't get my hopes up," Camille mutters, using her best impersonation of you.

"How much did you have to drink?"

"I, I don't remember."

You can tell she isn't being truthful.

"Well, I'll let you go now. My head is spinning." She hangs up.

You exhale the breath you didn't realize you were holding. You made it through the call without Camille asking any questions. You're not good at lying. You have no idea when Vince will be back. Since Camille is grounded, it will be easy to avoid her for the rest of the day. However, your mother is a different story. For now, all you have are your own invading thoughts.

You curl up into a ball on your bed and pull the covers up over your head. You hate to admit it, but he is right about one thing. It would settle your mind if you didn't have it looming over your every thought. You don't want your mind to be tampered with, but you also don't want to live life feeling the need to always be looking over your shoulder, wondering if every stranger could actually be a vampire. He isn't here for you. He never did anything to harm you, at least that you know of. He walked among you peacefully. Unless…

You throw off the covers and reach for your phone. You bring up a search engine and enter "Dragon's Eye" in the field. A bunch of pictures depicting what a dragon's eye looks like appear. You scroll through them until one stands out to you, a symbol. You study the upside-down triangle with a 'Y' inside it. Something about the symbol looks familiar.

Your eyes go wide. You jump to your feet, forgetting you're weak, and you fall to the floor. You pick yourself up and slowly make your way to the bathroom. You pull your hair back to the left and look at the birthmark behind your right ear. It's not as distinctive as the image of the symbol online, but it's close enough. Too close for comfort.

Your heart sinks to your stomach.

You find your way back into the kitchen, casually peering outside and seeing no movement. You have to regain strength despite your stomach doing somersaults. The only thing you can think of that you can handle is some toast. You reach into the refrigerator for the bread, and pause as your eyes find the leftover asparagus quiche. Every fiber in your mind fires warnings, but you dismiss them and reach under the cellophane wrap, pulling out a piece of asparagus and eat it. Your stomach churns as you focus on keeping it down.

You drink some water, taking it easy. You have no idea how much asparagus should be in your system to avoid having your memory erased. You're not sure if you can even pull off faking it if the two small pieces you managed to choke down aren't enough.

Only an hour has lapsed. You haven't regained your full strength, but you can't stand pacing around the house for another second. Your mind is your own worst enemy. For the first time in your life, you have the urge to go outside and run. Run to take your mind off everything. Run to get out of the house. Run to feel alive.

Running is a lot harder when there is snow on the ground. Some roads are shoveled while others wait for a plow to go through in the neighborhood. You are out of breath shortly when you start, but you focus on one step in front of the other and not on things that go bump in the night.

When you finally find your way back home, you shovel the driveway before making a pot of minestrone soup. You are thankful your mother didn't press you much when she came home from work and went to bed after checking on you. With nothing left to do, you grab the keys to the Jeep and go to the only place that helps you feel at peace.

You breathe in the fresh pine air at the quarry. You don't want to be at home when Vince returns. Don't want him there with your mother in the house.

The temperature drops as the sunlight fades. Only you don't feel the cold. All you feel is numb as you lean against the hood of the Jeep with your hands in your jacket pocket and collar popped.

You angle your head to the side, focusing when you hear snow crunching. The moment you have been dreading has arrived.

"You weren't trying to hide from me, now, were you?" Vince asks from a distance to your left.

"How many are there?" You ignore his question.

"Over a thousand. There are rules."

"How many are in town?"

"Just me."

"How much blood do you need to survive?" You watch as the last rays of sunset fade.

"A human's body is mainly made up of water. The same goes for a vampire. The amount of water a human must drink to stay hydrated is the same amount of blood a vampire must consume to stay strong."

"Why are you cold?"

"The temperature of my body regulates to the type of blood I drink."

"Meaning?" You turn to face him for the first time with a frown.

"Fresh blood helps to keep a vampire's body temperature manageable."

"So, blood from a blood bank does not?"

"Correct." He nods.

You don't know what's worse; stealing blood from a human being or stealing donated blood from a hospital. However, the knowledge actually surprises you. For the first time, you don't see him as a blood-sucking monster. "Would a vampire die without blood?"

"Eventually, yes, but unlike humans, vampires can survive longer without an adequate amount of blood. Vampires deteriorate a lot slower. However, the thirst for blood would eventually activate the instinct to survive."

You turn back to see the last bit of light swallowed up by the dark as a cold breeze begins to blow. Vince answered all your questions without hesitation, but why wouldn't he, since he's going to make you forget anyway?

"Do you have any more questions?"

"I...." You bow your head, thinking, but you are just stalling the inevitable. "I guess not."

"I promise it won't hurt."

You nod as he closes the gap.

You feel his cold finger slip under your chin, lifting your head until your eyes meet his pair of blue ones.

"I am not a vampire. There is nothing suspicious about the temperature of my skin, the strength of my build, or Tommy's actions when facing Greg. There was never a dent in your mother's Jeep. You never followed me. You did not go to Greg's party. No knife was aimed at you. Nothing to be wary of. You dislike me because I'm rude and arrogant. You will get into the Jeep and go home."

He's gone like a hurricane wind.

You blink before you climb into the driver's seat, fire up the engine, and head in the direction he commanded, home. He said it wouldn't hurt. He's right, it didn't hurt because he didn't take your memories away. You still remember everything.

Part 2

EDGE OF DARKNESS

⎯⎯⎯⎯⎯ ◯ ⎯⎯⎯⎯⎯

Chapter 18

You jump from the edge of your bed when you hear the honk of a horn outside. You have been dreading the day ahead. The horn sounds off again. Is Camille here or someone else?

You walk to the front door and peek out to see a cop car at the end of the driveway. At first, you are alarmed, but soon you realize it's Camille's father.

"Good morning, Nadine."

"Good morning, Mr. Epler," you reply, closing the back door on the passenger side.

"I'm so sorry, Nad. I forgot to call you last night. I couldn't text you since my cell was confiscated." Camille glares at her father with a sour attitude.

"It's fine," you shrug off.

You drift off into your own world while Camille's father makes small talk. You assume you answer questions he asks, but you don't remember anything. All you can think about is how to survive the day without Vince becoming the wiser.

"What's going on with you?" Camille asks as soon as her father drives off.

"What do you mean?"

"You seem…distracted."

"I'm fine," you say with a fake smile.

"I smell rats." You both turn at the sound of Greg's voice.

You take a step back as the flashback of him coming at you with the knife invades your mind. You hardly got sleep over the weekend, and when you did drift off, the violent image of him coming woke you up over and over again. You've been feeling apprehensive about your first encounter with him.

"What are you talking about?" Camille asks.

"Couldn't keep your mouth shut, could you?" he directs at Camille before focusing on you. "And I bet you told my father, didn't you?"

Camille turns to you with confusion. You just shake your head numbly.

"Don't be a sore loser because your father busted you," Camille snaps back. "C'mon, Nad." You let her pull you along. However, you take a peek over your shoulder and see Greg sneering.

"Better watch your backs," he shouts.

"Nadine, what's wrong with you?" She cuts into your footpath.

"Nothing," you whisper in a weak voice.

"It's not like you not to retort."

"I've got to take care of something before class. I'll see you later," you say and dash off.

You suspect Camille will follow, but are relieved when she doesn't. You knew it was going to be hard facing him when you remember everything, and Greg has no recollection at all. You know what he's capable of when he's pushed over the edge. Getting caught in the crosshairs is something you don't ever want to face again.

You stand over the toilet, holding your stomach, shaking, and swallowing as the bell rings. You wait a few minutes more before ducking out into an empty hallway and speed-walking to your first class.

Before the end of the next few classes, you ask to use the restroom. You don't care about being late to every single class. As long as you avoid Greg and Vince, that's all that matters. The only place where you will run into any problems is in gym class. Every nerve in your body begs you to skip, but if you do, you risk tipping Vince off.

You follow a group of girls onto the gymnasium floor and stick close to them, keeping a neutral expression while avoiding eye contact with any of the guys over at their section. You move your low ponytail to the right in a subconscious movement to ensure it covers your birthmark.

You stretch your muscles out before the whistle blows, signaling everyone to run laps. At once, you run, keeping your head low. You focus on your breathing. Focus on the rhythm of your feet hitting the linoleum floor. All you want to do is make it through gym class and avoid a scene.

You hear footsteps closing in. You have no idea who is behind you. You pick up your pace without realizing it, trying to stay as far ahead as possible. Only the person passes on your left. It's no one of importance, but there are still several more footsteps behind you. You try to tune them out and refocus on breathing. You're already starting to feel winded.

You see the blue mat appear before slamming against it. Lucky for you, it was positioned along the side of the gym and cushioned your fall. You have no idea what just happened. One minute, you were running, and the next, you were lying on the blue mat. You lift your head and see Greg running away with his head over his shoulder, looking at you with a smug grin. He must have tripped you.

"Are you okay?" You turn your head and see Vince offering a hand.

Your first instinct is to recoil, but you stop yourself as you try to think how you would have handled this before you knew what he was. He's supposed to be rude and arrogant, not polite and humble, offering his assistance. Besides, you'd be fuming mad at the situation and want no help from anyone, especially him.

"I'm fine." You put some attitude behind the words, decline his hand, push up to your feet, and sprint onward.

Somehow, you manage to block everything out and get through the rest of the class.

You practice inhaling and letting it slowly escape as you change in the girls' locker room. You are only halfway through school. One school day never felt so long in your life before. You wish you didn't have lunch period with Camille. You just want to be alone in the empty auditorium. A time out to decompress.

As you wait for the bell to ring, you can't stand listening to the girls gossip one minute longer. With purpose, you slip out of the locker room and head down to the equipment room. Normally, you despise seeing the treadmills, weights, and other exercise equipment. The stench of everyone's sweat sickens you, but there is something you feel the urge to do. Release built-up tension.

You place your bag on the bench before approaching the punching bag. Balling your hands into fists by your sides, you visualize Greg coming at you with the knife, and you punch out with your right hand. You shake your hand out, unprepared for how hard the punching bag is. Only, you don't allow that to stop you as you punch it again and again.

The bell rings.

You ignore the desire to be obedient. You refocus your mind onto everything that ever made you angry so that when you see the image of Greg coming at you with that knife, you won't freeze. You will be prepared to face him and punch and punch and punch to defend yourself.

The bag moves all over the place along with your hair, which is down and not tied back. You pivot, following the bag until it slams against you.

You temporarily lose your balance before reaching out and grabbing it to stabilize it and yourself. You rest your head against it, hair plastered against your sweaty face and neck while you gasp for air. You look down at your right knuckle, which stings, and you see you've torn the skin as blood seeps out.

"They make gloves for that, you know."

You jump and whirl to see Vince leaning against the doorway. You look down at the blood before tucking your hair back behind your ears. How stupid could you have been? Now, you have a vampire standing before you with the scent of fresh blood in the air.

"Do they?" you manage to retort as you walk over to the bench and reach for your bag.

"Or tape to wrap around your hands to protect them." He grabs a paper towel from the dispenser.

"What are you doing here?" You slip the strap over your shoulder, watching him intently while calculating your chance of skating past him through the open doorway.

"I was wondering the same thing about you." He dampens the paper towel and adds some soap before slowly approaching.

"I asked first." You inch back and to the left, gripping the strap with your right hand, the blood held away from him.

"Did you?"

You fight against the urge to hurl your bag with force against him and try to escape. Only you know it's fruitless, as you won't get far when he's faster.

"Let me see." He flicks his eyes to your hand.

You pull back, and at once regret it. You're not doing a good job of selling your unawareness. You've never been a good liar.

"You want to talk about Friday night?"

"What?" You exhale a deep breath. "I mean, oh, why do you ask? Nothing relevant happened."

"I know you still know."

Your racing heart skips a beat. "How?"

"The beating of your heart betrays you."

You sigh, defeated.

"Let me see your hand." He extends his, but keeps a distance from you.

"Doesn't the smell bother you?"

"Do you guzzle water when you're not thirsty?"

You are still hesitant.

"I don't forcefully take blood from someone unless I'm given permission."

Are all vampires like that? Or just him?

Slowly, you step forward, release the strap, and extend your hand into his outstretched one. Gradually, he lowers his other hand with the wet paper towel.

"This might sting a little," he warns before placing the paper towel over your hand with a gentle touch.

You wince.

"You know," he says as his eyes lift to yours, "not talking about it makes it worse."

"Are you a therapist now?" You yank your hand back.

"Far from it."

"What does it matter, since you're going to compel me anyway?"

"Maybe this time I won't compel Friday night from your mind."

"Why wouldn't you?" you ask, perplexed.

"Why did you consume more asparagus?"

You feel your heart kick up again, and this time, it's not from running laps. You reach up and make sure your hair is covering your right ear before you decide against the action. Realizing what you just did, you stare at Vince with wide eyes.

Without warning, he grabs your right upper arm with an iron grip and reaches up to push back your hair.

"Don't," you plead in a whisper.

You see him stiffen. Time stands still. You don't dare breathe as you watch him in your peripheral vision, waiting for him to make his next move.

In the blink of an eye, he releases his hold and vanishes.

Chapter 19

Camille stands with her hands on her hips when you close your locker. "So, are you going to clear things up on what's going on with you today?"

"I'm just having an off day." You shrug.

"I may have had one too many drinks Friday night, but I'm sober enough to know that you're lying."

"I'm sorry, Cam." You pause, dropping your head. "It's not something I want to talk about."

"Did I do something wrong? We tell each other everything."

You sigh. "You just have to trust me…"

"Ouch!" Camille's shrill yell cuts you off.

You look up to see Camille rubbing her shoulder before looking beyond to see Greg smirking as he walks onward.

"What was that for?" Camille complains.

"I don't know. Let's go." You put a hand around her back and usher her along with you.

"Let's go?" She steps aside.

"What?" You meet her creamy coffee-brown eyes.

"You're not going to jump down his throat?"

"He's not worth my time," you dismiss.

"Not worth your time? What has gotten into you?"

"Cam, just stop, okay?" You whip around.

"You know you can talk to me, right?"

"I know." You choke on the sob in the back of your throat. You want so badly to be able to talk about everything you are going through right now, but you can't. Not if it means getting Camille involved and putting her at risk. If anything were to happen to her because of you, you would never be able to forgive yourself. You can't do that to her. She has her own problems right now. She can't help you anyway.

You hear a horn blaring and look up to see Camille's father's cop car waiting.

"Ugh, he's taking this humiliation thing a little too far," Camille groans.

You are thankful for the change of subject.

"You scared him. You scared me."

"I scared you?"

You bite your lip. "He called me looking for you."

"Oh."

You can see in her eyes that she wants to question you further, but she doesn't as she opens the passenger door. You are quick to slide into the back seat.

"How was your day, ladies?" Tom looks back.

"Dad, really?"

"It's a simple question, Camille." He rotates forward.

"It was fine," she huffs.

"Nadine?" Her father's pale, topaz-blue eyes glance at you in the rearview mirror.

"Fine, thanks for asking." Your smile is polite.

The rest of the drive is silent. You feel the tension in the car and are glad when you're able to retreat when he drops you off at the front door.

Vince isn't in school the next day, the day after that, or the following day. It's as if he disappeared without a trace, and frankly, you have no idea how to feel about it.

"Just when he started acknowledging me, now Vince just up and disappears, again. I hope nothing is seriously wrong." Camille sighs as she slips her iPhone into her back jeans pocket. "I've been texting him all week."

"How would I know?" you're too quick to answer.

Camille closes her locker. "What aren't you telling me?"

"About what?" Your eyes shift back and forth, studying her.

"Nad, you've been acting weird all week."

"No, I haven't."

"What's bothering you? You've been unusually quiet."

"I'm tired." You wave a hand.

"Why are you tired?"

Before you can think of an answer, Camille's books go flying out from under her left arm.

"Hey!" Camille turns to face Greg.

"Hey, what?" he mocks.

"What's your problem?"

"You." He gets in Camille's face.

Camille takes a step back.

"Wimp," he taunts before diverting his eyes to you with a sneer.

You stand frozen as a statue.

"I'll take that." Greg scoops up Camille's geometry homework from the floor.

"Hey, I need that. Nadine?" Camille whines, looking over at you for reinforcement, while students in the hallway just stare at the scene.

Only you can't find the strength to move as the image of him with the knife replays in your mind. You know what he is capable of. You saw it firsthand.

"Give it back." Camille tries to grab her homework with determination from Greg's hand.

"No." He shoves Camille away.

You gasp as Camille bangs up against the lockers. The image in your mind changes. You're no longer the victim. He wasn't aiming for you. He was aiming for his father. "She's not your father."

Everyone's attention snaps in your direction, including Greg's, as he grumbles, "What did you say?"

"You prey on the weak to feel superior because it gives you the control you don't have at home. You have no right to hurt others because you can't stand up to him." You step closer.

"What do you know about my home life? My father?" A vein bulges on Greg's forehead. His face turns red with rage as he approaches.

"You're becoming just like him."

"You don't even know him!" he yells in your face.

You should be terrified at how close he is to you and fear being hit, shoved, or targeted by him. Only you're angry. Angry that he has been intimidating you because he found a crack in your exterior. Angrier that he put a hand on Camille. Without thinking of the consequences, you squeeze your right hand, reel back your arm, and connect with his nose.

The small crowd that forms gasps, including Camille.

"My nose! I think you broke my nose!" Greg screams.

You stand there stunned at what you just did as blood gushes out of his nose. "Don't ever touch Camille again. Do I make myself clear?"

Greg whimpers as the bell rings. Everyone scrambles away, including Greg, who leaves Camille's homework behind.

"Where did you learn how to do that?" Camille's jaw drops.

"I didn't." You look at your right knuckle and shake off the feeling. Punching a bag and punching flesh and bone are completely different. Yet both hurt. You feel your stomach churn.

"What was that talk about his father?" Camille presses.

Realization hits that you let slip something you knew that you shouldn't have known. How are you going to talk your way out of this?

"Would Nadine Drexel please come to the office," the loudspeaker crackles to life.

You freeze. You have no idea what fate awaits you. Your mother is going to be pissed. Would you be expelled or just suspended, and if just suspended, for how long? You've always been a model student who never got in trouble, and who worked hard to earn good grades. Now, that doesn't matter. One bad thing could ruin your reputation. One bad move could alter the course. Everyone will remember that one bad thing you did instead of all the good.

Sensing your apprehension, Camille pulls you into a hug. "I have your six."

You hug her tightly before pulling back. "Thanks, but I have to take responsibility for my own actions."

Everything is a bit foggy afterward. The only thing you can recall from your encounter with Principal Johnson is that you are being suspended, as there is a zero-violence policy. You cringe when he announces he's going to call your mother to come and pick you up, when you know she's at work.

"You punched another student?" your mother asks in a calm tone while sitting behind the wheel.

"I'm sorry, Mom," is all you can manage.

"I thought I taught you better than that."

You stay silent.

"You're grounded."

You nod.

"What has gotten into you this past week?"

You look over. You feel like an open book when it comes to your mother. She can always sense when something is up, even if she doesn't know for sure. You expect her to spout off some more. However, she seems to be handling it well, too well. "I don't know." You shrug.

You are completely alone in this. You won't risk the lives of the two people who mean the most to you. They can't know. They can never know.

Chapter 20

You slip into the passenger seat of your mother's Jeep in the bank parking lot and click your seat belt into place. You say nothing. You still feel the shame of disappointing her. The look on her face is neutral and hard to read. The events of yesterday still linger fresh in the air as you watch town traffic out the window.

You frown when your mother goes sailing past the road that takes you home. You wonder where your mother is going, but you don't dare ask.

You keep quiet as you continue to watch out the window, as the miles fly by, for any clues as to your mother's destination. You have no idea until she pulls into the large parking lot.

"I thought you worked tonight. Why are we at the mall?" You look over and study her.

"I have the day off."

"You have off on a Saturday?"

"I took off."

"Why?" You raise both eyebrows.

"Because I wanted to take my daughter shopping for a prom dress."

Your mouth hangs open. "But I'm not going to prom."

"I won't allow it."

"Did Camille say something to you?"

"No. Nadine, prom only happens once in your life. I don't want you to regret not going."

"You can't afford to get me a dress."

"I've set enough money aside from the extra shifts I've been picking up."

"That's why you've been working so much?"

She nods.

"But I'm grounded."

"I never specified for how long." She shrugs. "Besides, I think being suspended is punishment enough."

"I might not even be allowed...."

"Don't you worry about that," she cuts you off.

"What does that mean?" You jerk your head.

"I may not know the reason you did it, but I know that Gregory Pierce had it coming, and so does Principal Johnson."

You are flabbergasted. Your mother has gone completely one-eighty from last night. Everyone knows Greg deserves much more than what he got, but that still doesn't make it right.

"Enough talk. What's past is past. Let's go dress shopping," your mother says as she opens her door.

You climb out and follow. Prom dress shopping. Again. You already did this with Camille. There was nothing that caught your eye. You're not even interested in going. Your stomach does flips. You can't even remember the last time you wore a fancy dress.

Every dress that your mother insists you try on makes you feel insecure. Either there is too much cleavage showing, arm skin, leg skin, or open back. There is nothing you are interested in. You also feel like a completely different person.

"How about this one?" Your mother shows up with a simple yet elegant red dress.

"Sure," you sigh as you take it and go back into the dressing room. Of all the dresses you've tried on, this one is different. There is no big slit halfway up the leg, no spaghetti straps, and no open back. When you look at yourself in the mirror, you still look like someone you don't recognize, but you don't feel as exposed. The ruby red dress is long, down to the floor, but is closed. Though there are no sleeves, the pearl-like mesh is thicker, covering your shoulders. The back isn't as open and forms a diamond shape. The chiffon straps give the dress a little something extra, as well as the thin chain belt. Simple, yet sophisticated.

"Wow, Nadine, you look beautiful." You hear the catch in her mother's voice and see her eyes glaze over.

"Mom, it's just a dress. You don't have to cry."

"I'm not." She turns and wipes at her eyes. "I just got dust in them. Do you like it?"

"It's the only one not so revealing."

"You can try on something else if you want."

"No, this one will do."

"Great, it suits you. Now, all we have to do is find a pair of shoes to go with it."

"We're going shoe shopping too?" you moan.

"Sweetie, you can't have a fancy dress and wear boots."

"Why not?"

"Nadine," she says in her tone.

"Fine." You slip back into the changing room. What has come over her?

Finding the perfect pair of shoes is even more exhausting than trying on dresses. You absolutely do not want to have heels, but your mother convinces you otherwise, as heels are necessary to avoid tripping over the dress all night. It will give height so that the dress is just above the floor.

You settle for a pair of red block-heel pumps. A nice thick heel instead of a toothpick – one that you most likely would end up breaking your neck on. The heels are higher than the low-heeled boots you normally wear, so you will have to learn how to walk in them. That is if you even make it to prom.

You can't exactly tell your mother not to waste the money without having to explain yourself. Besides, it has been a long time since you've had a mother-daughter day between both of your busy schedules. It feels nice. You embrace the moment in what it feels like to be totally human.

Afterward, you both do a little window shopping and, of course, don't leave without visiting the bookstore. Just like Camille, your mother hates when you browse all the aisles. An easy place that you get lost in.

"*Interview with the Vampire*." Your mother narrows her eyes at the book you select.

"Thought I'd try something different." You shrug.

For a few hours, your spirit is lifted, and you almost forget about all your worries. Only as you sit in the Jeep, looking out the passenger side window, do the invading thoughts resurface.

"You should call Camille," your mother encourages when you enter the house.

"I thought I was still grounded."

"Yes, but if I have to hear the phone ring one more time, I'm going to lose my mind. Does she not realize we have caller ID?" she states right before the landline rings.

You smirk. The phone has been ringing every hour since you got home from being suspended yesterday. "Hello?"

"Nadine?" Camille shrieks with dismay.

"Yeah."

"Finally! I've been trying to reach you."

"Well, I'm kind of grounded, but since you keep calling, my mother let me answer."

"Does your home phone have caller ID?"

"Yeah."

"Oh, sorry. So, you're grounded?"

"And suspended."

"You're suspended?"

"That hasn't made its way around school yet?" You are genuinely surprised.

"No. I'm so sorry, Nadine."

"Don't be; the fault is mine."

"What am I supposed to do without you?"

"You'll be fine."

"I can't believe you're suspended. Did you tell Principal Johnson everything?"

"Doesn't matter. The school has a zero-tolerance policy toward violence. I'm just glad I was suspended and not expelled."

"This is all my fault."

"Cam, stop. Nothing is your fault."

"You get punished and that jerk gets not even a reprimand."

"Well, to be fair, he did get punched in the face." You half smile to yourself.

"I can't believe you punched him. The look on his face." Camille starts to giggle, which prompts you to start to chuckle a little yourself. Thinking back to Greg's expression, one of sheer shock, you embrace the moment now that you are not reeling in the shock of it. It was a long time coming, and what he deserved after years of torment and bullying. What you did was wrong on so many levels, and yet, it also felt exhilarating.

"I've got something to tell you that you're probably not going to believe."

"What?" Camille's voice turns to concern.

"My mom took me prom dress shopping today."

"What? Does that mean?" she shrieks.

"Yeah, guess so. I'm going to prom." You pull the phone away from your ear as Camille screams with ecstasy. "Are you done yet?"

"You'd better not be joking."

"Why would I joke?"

"Oh, my goodness, I'm so excited," Camille squeals again.

"Okay, would you stop before you make me go deaf?"

"Everything is becoming perfect again. My parents aren't getting a divorce, and you are going to prom."

"Your parents aren't getting a divorce now?"

"No. They talked it out and came to a compromise. Besides, neither one ever filed."

"When did this happen?"

"Last night. My dad has been staying at the house all week, and they finally sat down with me and told me."

"That's wonderful," you pitch with happiness in your voice as you push away the reservations that fire in the back of your mind.

"Now, all we need are dates for the prom."

"We don't need dates. We have each other."

"Yeah, but I'd feel more special dancing with a guy to my favorite slow song."

"It's overrated."

"I was hoping Vince might be that guy, but it's like he dropped off the face of the Earth again."

You say nothing.

"Well, I'd better hang up before my dad comes down on me for being on the phone. I'm still semi-grounded."

"Goodbye, I'll see you…." You stop.

"See you when I see you," Camille finishes before hanging up.

Chapter 21

Your mother bursts through the bedroom door. "Nadine, you're going to be late for school."

"Umm, Mom, I'm suspended, remember?" You cringe as the words escape your mouth.

"Oh, right, sorry," she replies in a somber tone. "Well, go back to bed. And stay home. I'll see you tonight."

Lying on your back, you listen to the birds chirping outside. The sun is shining bright through the window. Leo gets some much-needed attention from your gentle strokes. The day is alive, yet you feel dull inside.

You have no idea what you're going to spend the day doing. This isn't a vacation, so doing anything pleasurable is off the agenda. Reaching over and sliding open the nightstand drawer, you grab the string you have for Leo and let it dangle in front of his nose. He swats at it on full alert. Although he has toy mice and balls to play with, at his leisure, his favorite toy is a simple string. He acts like a kitten despite being twelve years old.

A knock on the door immediately seizes your attention. "Who would be knocking at...8:22 in the morning?" You don't expect a response from the cat. However, he jumps down and sprints from your room.

You swing your legs to the floor, grab your cardigan, and approach with caution. Leo rubs at the front door. You've never seen him do that before when someone comes knocking on the door. You scoop him up before opening the front door and freeze in place.

Vince.

"May I come in?" he asks.

"Depends, are you here to take me?" You place a hand on your hip.

"No." He shakes his head.

"Compel me?" Your eyes narrow.

"No, things have changed."

"Why are you here?"

"It's good to see the fire in your eyes is back." He half smiles.

"I'm angry at you. You turn my world upside down, and then you just leave me hanging for days, not knowing what to expect."

"I'm truly sorry, Nadine." You hear the sincerity in his voice.

"Apology not accepted." You slam the door in his face. You hug Leo tightly and lean against the door. With a deep sigh, you reopen it. "What chance do I have against a vampire when I'm an ordinary human?"

"That's why I'm here."

"How am I supposed to trust you?"

"What have I ever done to make you *not* trust me?"

The image of him pointing a knife at his stomach and leaving it in your hands crosses your mind. "Why would you disobey an order?"

"I don't believe in his ways. I haven't for a very long time."

"It's just a birthmark. It means nothing."

"Not to him. Not if he gets wind of it."

"I need a cup of coffee." You release Leo and turn away.

"Am I invited in?"

"Really, Vince?" You look over your shoulder and see him kneeling outside the doorway, petting Leo, who is rolling on his back and exposing his belly. "Yes, close the door on the way in."

You continue into the kitchen, open the cupboard, remove a bag of breakfast blend coffee, and set it on the counter before grabbing the decanter and filling it with water from the faucet.

"Do you drink coffee?"

"No."

"Noted." You dump half the water in the sink. You add coffee grounds to the filter, add a dash of cinnamon, and turn the pot on. "How did you know I wasn't in school?" You place the bag back into the cupboard.

"Camille told me."

"You saw her?"

He nods.

"How did that go?"

"As you might expect it."

You smirk to yourself as you open the opposite cupboard and imagine how Camille must be going out of her mind not being able to talk to you about him. You grab a mug, walk over to the refrigerator, pour some cream into the base, grab a spoon on the way back, and fill the cup with what's already brewed. "So, where did this prophecy originate?" You sit down at the kitchen table with your coffee.

"From a powerful witch named Immilla."

"Witches exist?" You look at him wide-eyed, standing in the entryway.

"Not anymore."

"How's that possible?" You frown.

"It's a long story."

You take a sip. The coffee is bitter even with the cream mixed in, and it turns your stomach. However, you know there's more than one reason your stomach is doing somersaults. "It's not like I have anywhere to go."

"I'm sorry you got suspended. If I had been there…"

"You would have what? Broken his nose? I'm not some damsel who needs a knight in shining armor on a white horse, Vince."

"Noted." He squares his jaw.

"So, the prophecy?"

"I should start at the beginning. A time when there were two types of magic: light magic and dark magic."

You raise your eyebrows with skepticism.

"A treaty was put into place after the fall of a powerful sorcerer named Maximilian. Witches were to pledge the type of magic they would represent. No witch could represent both, as a truce, in order to keep balance."

"You can sit," you interrupt when he pauses, nodding over the top of the mug. You are still feeling a bit guarded as you watch him take a seat across from you. But if he was going to do anything, he would have by now.

"When Immilla pledged to dark magic, her father was not happy. He knew she would be a threat to him, so he cast a spell for her to fall in love with a mortal, Vladimir."

"How was she a threat to her father?"

"He was a witch of dark magic who was siphoning magic from other witches. She was a threat to discovering his deceit, so by making her fall in love with a human, she would have to forfeit magic altogether."

"So, what goes wrong?"

"While living in her home near the Carpathian Mountains, Vladimir was severely wounded by a wolf. Even though she closed herself off from magic, she was still connected to it. It was in her blood, and she was still strong enough to use it to heal his wounds."

"So, she didn't turn him into a vampire?"

"No, her father did. He was a member of the witches' council. It was forbidden for a human to know that witches existed. Vladimir was sentenced to death."

"Why did her father turn him?"

"He brought him back to life when he found out she was with child."

You take another sip of coffee.

"Only, he wasn't the same, and the spell she was under was broken when his soul was disconnected briefly from his body. She knew something wasn't right. She left to cleanse herself and found answers by tasting her own blood. Blood reveals everything about a person to a witch. She found out she had been manipulated by her father and tricked into loving Vladimir."

You raise your eyebrows with continued skepticism. Part of your mind wants to believe this is just some made-up story, but the other part reminds you that you are sitting in the kitchen with a vampire that shouldn't exist.

"She wanted revenge, but her magic was limited. The council was linked to her magic, so she couldn't use it without them knowing. Only she found a way around it. Placed her blood into an object and was able to use it without them knowing. Located the wolf. Discovered he wanted revenge against Vladimir for killing his mate. Left the wolf to do just that and protect the village from the monster he had become. Left to find Serene, her sister, and found their communication had been cut off for a long time. She wanted her own revenge. The only thing stopping her was her desire to protect her child."

You continue to listen, keeping your chilled hands warm by wrapping them around the hot mug.

"She isolated herself on an island. Met a local fisherman who helped take care of her. Taught her what true love was, and helped her to find trust in people again. She became involved with the community and hung up her magic."

"So, what changed?"

"Witch-hunts were on the rise again. She left that world behind, but she was still part of it. It was in her blood. She watched her father from afar. Discovered her father's true intent. When a witch dies or pledges to light magic, their dark magic is released back into the universe. Her father had been collecting that power. She was the only one who knew and the only one who could stop him."

"How could she stop him? Wouldn't he be more powerful?"

"Yes."

Your coffee is lukewarm, so you take a bigger sip despite it still being bitter.

"She watched multiple scenarios of the future. None of them came without sacrifice. She found out Vladimir was still alive and working with her father. The only thing Vladimir had to fear was witches. He was immortal otherwise. Not only did she want to take down her father, but she wanted the use of magic to be forgotten. To her, power changed perspective. Power was an addiction. Power was poison to everyone's wellbeing."

"How do you know she felt that way?" You shake your head, puzzled.

"From her journal."

"So, how did she defeat her father?"

"With light magic. It was falsely believed dark magic was more powerful than light magic when, in reality, it was the other way around. Dark magic is cognitive. Light magic is reflective."

You raise your eyebrows again in skepticism. This is all too much for you to comprehend.

"She gathered drops of blood from every bloodline of witches, binding their souls to hers. When her father attacked them and burned them with witch-fire, their magic filtered into her. They would then rise from the ashes and be reborn without magic."

"I'm sorry, but this is a lot to take in." You massage your temples. "How is she able to defeat her father when he possesses so much dark magic?"

"His thirst for power overshadowed his love for her. Choosing to kill her destroyed the use of magic for everyone."

"Oh." You realize she tricked him. A sacrifice. This is still way over your head. More than you asked for. "Okay, so how do I fit into all of this?"

"When Vladimir killed her sister, Serene, she told him what his future held if he chose the wrong path. The prophecy was one of the last things she wrote about."

"He killed her sister?"

He nods.

You swallow the lump in your throat. "And how was the prophecy written?"

He clears his throat. "For I saw Vladimir's other path written clearly in the stars on the night sky. He would meet his doom and burn at the hands of the one marked by the Dragon's Eye."

A glacier chill runs up the length of your spine. You stand abruptly and walk over to the kitchen sink, dump the rest of the coffee, and hover. "This isn't my fight," you whisper.

"Not when you're human."

"Absolutely not." You whirl with daggers in your eyes, dropping the mug. It cracks. How dare he even suggest it?

"I suspected you'd feel that way," he sighs.

"Don't ever again suggest I turn into a vampire. Don't ever try again to compel me. And under no circumstances will you ever take a drop of my blood. I don't care if your life depends on it."

"I accept your terms," he complies with no hesitation.

The fire in your eyes diminishes as you narrow them.

He stands slowly. "I'm the only one who knows the truth, and I intend on keeping it that way. After graduation, you will never have to see me again, and you can go on living a normal life. As long as you keep your hair down, like you usually do, to conceal your mark, everything will be fine."

You watch him walk away.

Chapter 22

You pace the front door, eagerly waiting for your ride to arrive for school. You hated staying home from school. It dragged. Running has become your therapy. When you couldn't stand the noise in your head, you went out to run around the block. It has become your new obsession. A distraction you needed, focusing on your breathing and tuning into the rhythm of your pounding feet. A way to release pent-up energy.

"You got Roger back." You slip into the passenger seat of Camille's car.

"I'm so glad. It was brutal having my dad take me in."

"It's so good to see you."

"Likewise." Camille leans in and pulls you into a hug.

A hug has never felt so good before. "So, what have I missed?"

"Nothing much." Camille puts the car into drive. "I'm so glad Vince was back to give me some company. I don't know how I would have survived all alone."

"Anything I should know?" You arch an eyebrow as Camille drives.

"He had a family emergency."

"Oh."

You both sit in silence as your attention drifts to the sights outside the window.

"It's so hard to be patient," Camille whines.

"What do you mean?" You look back over.

"You know, for him to ask me out on a second date."

"Oh." You laugh once in the back of your throat before making a jest. "Well, you could always ask him."

"Are you crazy?" Camille tosses her head over to you.

You shrug with a smirk of amusement. Camille is a traditionalist. She'd wait until the end of time before asking a guy out whom she's interested in.

When you step out of the car, you're met with so much noise. The squeaky brakes from the buses. Tons of students chattering that blurs all together. Car horns from impatient parents. You hate to admit it, but in a way, you have missed this.

"Hello, ladies." Vince guides over.

"Hi, Vince," Camille exclaims as she closes her car door.

"Hello." You close the door as well with a polite smile.

"Welcome back."

"Thanks?" You join Camille at the back of the car.

"Vince, I'm glad you're here. I, uh…" She giggles half-heartedly with flushed cheeks. "…wanted to ask you something. Are you doing anything Friday night?"

You stare at Camille with your mouth semi-parted.

"I don't have any plans. Do you want to do something after school?"

"Yes," she bursts with enthusiasm.

The first bell rings.

"We can discuss later." He nods once and meets your eyes for a beat of a second.

"Absolutely." Camille tries to contain her excitement as he departs.

"Aren't you still grounded?" You fold your arms.

"Yeah." Camille drops her head.

"I don't think your dad will agree to let you out for a date."

"I'll think of something. I still have time." She waves a hand as she advances. You follow in her wake before going your separate ways.

You feel tense when you walk into your first period. Half the students won't make eye contact, while the others fist pump the air.

You're overloaded with all the assignments you have to make up as you sit in the auditorium debating which one to work on first during lunch. By the time the bell rings, you've hardly made a dent.

"I've got the perfect alibi," Camille says as she waltzes over to your desk in history.

"Better not involve me." You look up from scribbling.

"Come on, Nad, you've got to help a girl out. It's a win-win for both of us."

You drop your head with a sigh and tap your pen against your notebook paper. "What do you want me to do?"

"Come over Friday night for a sleepover."

"You think your dad will go for that?" Your eyebrows pinch together.

"Yes, he agreed to let us go to Lexton after school today." Camille grins.

"Really?" You perk up. It's been weeks since the two of you have been there, and you suddenly crave a bagel and coffee. Something of normalcy.

"I am a genius." She smacks a hand against her chest.

"Don't get your hopes up. I still have to ask my mom."

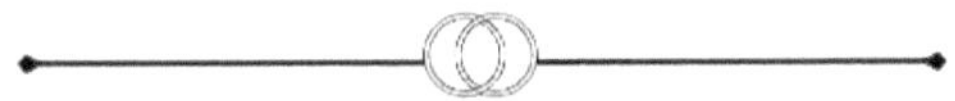

The bell rings. The class goes by at warp speed. When it ends, you dread going to your last class, English. You are so far behind in your reading assignments.

"All right, class, you should be nearly finished with your plays. Today, you are to discuss the scene you will be reenacting and start practicing," Mrs. Robbins announces.

"Guess we have a lot of catching up to do." Vince sits down across from you.

"How exactly does a relationship work between, you know?" You stare him down with slits.

He looks away and prolongs an exhale.

"Don't hurt my best friend."

"That's not my intention." He catches your eyes.

"Stringing her along is going to hurt her."

"If I said no, wouldn't that have hurt her as well?"

You open your mouth to say something, and stop.

"I know you are never going to trust me, but I promise I won't let anything happen to her."

"Don't make a promise that's outside of your control."

"Do you want me to cancel?"

"No." You look away. You know it would devastate Camille.

"So, any chance your mind has changed on the balcony scene?"

You scowl from your peripheral.

"Guess not," he chuckles.

"Only in your dreams. Well…." You lean forward and lower your voice. "That is, if you even sleep."

"I do not, which is now unfortunate." He smirks.

You roll your eyes. "I'm open to suggestions."

"Obviously, you will play Juliet."

"Why? I could play Juliet's nurse," you challenge.

"Okay." He opens his book, turning to a page that's dogeared. "Or I could reenact Friar Lawrence during Act 4, Scene 1 when he gives Juliet the vial."

You stare at the bent page with a twitch before opening your own copy and flipping through the pages. "I haven't even gotten to that part." You scan through it quickly and look up. "I guess that could work."

"Did we just come to an agreement?" He tilts his head.

"Don't get used to it." Your nose crinkles.

"I'll try not to." He half grins.

Despite yourself, you actually feel a bit relaxed in his presence. It's an odd feeling when you shouldn't feel calm at all.

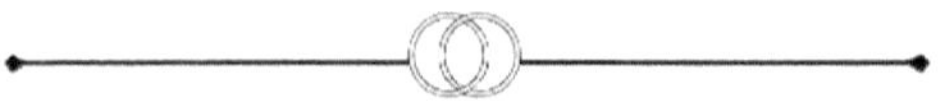

You are more than happy when the school day comes to an end, and eager to get your hands back onto something normal at the café.

"It feels like it's been forever," Camille comments as she sits down at an empty table with her mug and bagel.

"I know, I've missed being here." You take a deep whiff, take in the chatter and the scream of the steam. It's nice to embrace the small things.

"So, how much did you get slammed with?"

You groan from your blissful state.

"That bad?"

"Yes." You take an aggressive bite from your cinnamon bagel, minus the raisins.

"So, I was thinking."

"Never a good thing," you tease after swallowing.

"Hey. Anyway, so, I was thinking the perfect excuse to tell my dad when you come over…"

"If," you interrupt.

"When," Camille states adamantly.

You roll your eyes.

"We can tell him we are going to have a romance movie binge in my room. That way, he leaves us alone, and then I can sneak out."

"You're making me an accomplice."

"A date is not a crime."

You sip your espresso.

She sighs, planting her cheek against her knuckles. "I have no idea what I'm going to wear."

"You've got, like, four days to figure it out."

"That's not enough time."

"You're impossible." You shake your head.

You walk out with a giddy Camille arm-in-arm. You know the next four days are going to be obnoxious, but you wouldn't have it any other way. As long as you can move on with a normal life and try to forget everything else.

"Oh no." Camille unhooks her arm.

"What?" You look at Camille and follow her line of sight. Her back driver's side tire is flat. "We should go back inside." You tug at her arm, feeling a negative vibe.

"Do you girls need some assistance?" a male's voice calls out.

You look to your right and freeze.

Jomar.

It takes all your willpower not to reach up and make sure your hair covers your birthmark.

"Do you know how to change a tire?" Camille asks, stepping forward.

"Well, hello, beautiful."

Camille blushes.

"I do know how to change a tire. Do you have a spare?"

"Yeah, in the trunk." Camille walks to the back and pops it.

"Name's Jomar, and you are?"

"Camille."

"And it's Nadine, right?" He looks over at you with a smug grin.

"You know each other?" Camille looks back and forth.

"You remember me from the bank?" you ask.

"I never forget a helpful face," he says with a wry smile

You're on edge the entire time as he changes the tire. What is he doing here? You had forgotten all about him, but that same creepy feeling resurfaces in his presence.

"There you go, all fixed." He kicks the donut.

"Thank you so much," Camille sincerely exclaims.

"It was my pleasure."

"Is there anything I can do in return?"

"It's on the house for two pretty ladies."

Camille blushes again with a slight giggle.

"Have a good night." He walks away, stuffing his hands into his pockets.

"Why didn't I ask for his number?" Camille gasps once you're both in the car.

"That quickly you forget about Vince?"

"I'm joking," Camille laughs with a wave. "Hey, are you okay? You were pretty quiet the whole time."

"Yeah, I'm just eager to get home and tackle all my homework. I have so much to do." You glance at your phone. "Can I borrow your phone? My battery is almost dead."

"Sure." Camille hands hers over.

You open Camille's contact list and find Vince's number. You send a text letting him know it's from you, providing your own number, and asking him to call you in ten minutes. Once the text shows it's sent, you delete it from the history.

Chapter 23

You wave as Camille pulls away before you turn and pull your phone from your vest pocket, glancing at the display.

"Nadine, what's wrong?"

You look up and see Vince appear from behind the shadow of the evergreen shrub next to the house. "I asked you to call me, not show up on my doorstep."

"I was in the area." He shrugs.

"What do you mean you were in the area?" You slip your phone back into your pocket.

"I've been staying at the foreclosed house a street over."

"How long have you been staying there?" You cross your arms.

"A while."

You stare him down.

"Since I got here."

A lot of pieces fall into place you've been avoiding asking.

"What's Jomar doing in town?"

"He's here already?" He stands up straighter.

"And just happened to be around when Camille had a flat."

"You intrigued him when you waltzed over to the table at Franz. I wish you hadn't done that. He comes at the end of every month to check in with me."

"Why is he checking in with you?" You let your arms unfold.

"I'm here as more of a punishment for reading Immilla's journal."

"Why didn't you tell me about him?"

"It was one fewer thing for you to overanalyze."

"How do you know I tend to overanalyze?" You plant a hand on your hip.

"I tend to pay attention to things that capture my interest."

"I'm not sure what to say to that." You push your hair back behind your ear.

"That would be a first." He grins.

"I'm really not that interesting."

"You're different."

"Why, because of my stupid birthmark?" You graze it.

"No, you're not afraid to speak your mind or stand out from the crowd, and you're more observant than most."

"Well, guess I can't really argue with that." You half smile, knowing the words express truth.

"Did I just receive a compliment from Nadine Drexel?"

"Don't get used to it." You strut past him.

"Don't worry about Jomar. His specialty is intimidation. Once I meet with him tomorrow night, he should be gone until next month." The sound of his voice slowly fades.

"You know, I don't think I ever thanked you." You pause after stepping up on the small square porch step.

"For what?"

"Saving my life." You turn to meet his blue eyes.

"You're welcome." A bright smile appears, lighting up his eyes.

"You'd better go. My mom will be home any minute."

You hate how he's able to peg you as if you're an open book. Despite yourself, you do overanalyze the situation. You tried to diminish your inner thoughts by going for a run. Only when you got back, you ended up lightly packing three bags. Sleep does not come easily as you toss and turn all night.

You're still dwelling on it all morning during classes.

"I have to point out that you are in better control with your running." Vince jogs up beside you.

"I've been practicing, but something tells me you already know that." You're able to talk without being out of breath.

"You know where to find me if you ever want some company." He winks.

"I'll think about it, although it would give you less of an opportunity to stalk." You lightly jab an elbow in his side.

"I prefer to observe."

After finishing your laps, you're ushered to the equipment room, where the teachers instruct you to complete different strength-building exercises.

"I know what you should work on," Vince comments as everyone gets dismissed to go their separate ways.

"Oh, I can't wait to hear this." You glare before making your way to the weights.

"Balance." He nudges your right shoulder and causes you to stumble over your feet.

"Seriously?" You pick up a medicine ball and throw it at his head, but he catches it with ease.

"Careful, she bites." Greg circles from a distance.

"I know, but I bite harder," Vince mocks.

You snort with laughter at the irony. Only you understand, as Greg wrinkles his nose in disgust.

"I should teach you how to properly jab." Vince directs his attention back to you.

You raise an eyebrow before your eyes shift over to Greg. The color has drained from his face. He's totally mortified. You grab a pair of boxing gloves and slip them on. "Okay, show me."

You mimic his form, throwing a few air punches before attacking the punching bag he holds onto. So much easier to tackle when it's not moving all over the place. You are really getting into it until the bell rings. You lose track of time, and only now realize your muscles feel sore while you change.

"You know." You meet Vince at the entrance of the cafeteria after class. "I wouldn't mind learning more moves."

"How about tomorrow night?"

You're caught off guard. "Oh."

"Be an opportunity to start practicing our lines."

Your frame relaxes. "Yeah, guess we do need to start that. Okay, but after six."

"I'll be there."

"I still can't get the look on Greg's face out of my mind. It was priceless." You pull out a chair and set your bag on it, sharing a laugh with Vince.

"Did I miss something?"

You freeze as you look across the table at Camille.

"Since when did the two of you start speaking on friendly terms?" Her eyes shift between you and Vince.

"Well, umm." You hesitate.

"Since I agreed to go on a second date with you," Vince answers smoothly.

"Oh."

"I've got to go for now, but I'll see you two later." Vince smiles before walking away.

"Okay, bye." Camille watches with hungry eyes as he saunters off.

"So, figured out what you're wearing yet?" you ask.

"No. Why didn't you tell me about Vince? You two seem like you've been friends for more than like a day."

"Well, we do have that assignment in English, so I guess I've been gradually getting to know him. Besides, other than you, he's the only one who doesn't treat me any differently since I've come back."

"So, do you still think he's a serial killer?" Camille smirks.

"I'm still trying to figure him out." You turn away.

You're glad you are able to avoid talking to Camille about Vince for the rest of the day.

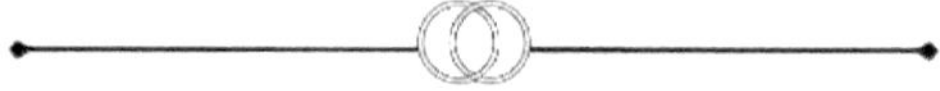

When you glance up from your homework and see it's a little after five, you close your textbook and walk into the kitchen. You grab the ingredients you need for the stir-fry you have planned.

Ten minutes later, your mother walks in through the door. "Smells heavenly in here. You are a natural. You sure would make a good chef."

"And slave away in the kitchen all day? No, thank you." You stir the cut-up steak, onions, and peppers in the pan before stirring the pot of boiling rice.

After your mother changes, she sits down at the kitchen table across from you with her plate.

"I'm heading out at six for about an hour when Vince swings by."

"Isn't Vince the guy Camille is dating?" your mother asks, cocking her head.

"Yes. We're just going to practice our lines for our English assignment."

"That's fine, as long as Camille is aware," she warns, casually sipping her iced tea.

You swallow hard. Your mother is an expert at making you feel guilty with just a tone and a few choice words. Only it's in Camille's best interest not to know. The fewer the questions, the better. "Mom, nothing is going on. We're just working on our assignment. Camille is my best friend. I would never hurt her like that."

"Good because I know I taught you better than that."

You look at the display on your phone and see a text from Vince announcing his arrival. You retreat immediately.

"So, where are we going?" you ask as you buckle your seat belt.

"You'll find out when we get there." He pulls off.

"Really? You're keeping me in the dark?"

He flashes a grin. "Just sit back and enjoy the ride."

Unable to stand the silence, you reach over to turn on the radio and adjust the channels until you settle on an old country station.

"You like country?"

"I like authentic and empowering. Can't stand all that auto-tune junk with a catchy tune they force down your throat."

"Have to agree with you there."

You sit in silence some more with only the radio as background noise. You can't help but think how you have willingly isolated yourself with a vampire. Only, at times, you forget what he is. He doesn't act like the bloodthirsty monsters you read about in books or see on the screen. He's completely different from them.

"Why are we here?" You scrunch up your nose when he pulls into the school parking lot.

"This is where we're going to practice."

"The school has an alarm system."

"Yes, and I have the code."

"And how did you acquire this code?" You fold your arms against your chest and give him a stern look.

"If you're wondering if I had to compel someone, the answer is no."

"So, the janitor just gave you, a student, the code."

"There are other ways, you know."

"You know what? I probably don't want to know." You open the door and step out, letting Vince lead you into the dark gymnasium. He flicks on the lights which glow to life.

"First things first. Let's warm up by working on your balance."

"What is with you and balance?"

"Having good balance is the first step." He nudges you slightly.

"Really?" you snap with annoyance as you stumble over your feet again.

"You must always expect the unexpected."

"I agreed for you to teach me defensive moves, not push me around."

"Why don't you stand on your right foot for a minute?"

You blink. "Only if you stand back."

When he moves away, you lift your left leg and hold your foot while balancing. You keep your eyes trained on him.

"Now, when the bridegroom in the morning comes...."

"What?" You lose your concentration and drop your leg, completely baffled.

Vince states with a smug smile, "You didn't keep your focus."

"You distracted me. What was that anyway?"

"You didn't recognize it? I thought we were also here to practice our lines. Guess we have a lot of work to do."

"Listen, I've had enough of this balancing act." You point a finger in his face, taking a step forward.

Without warning, Vince grabs your arm and spins you toward him in a hold. You gasp, unprepared and a little panicked, before, in a state of fury, you pull back your elbow with force, hoping to knock the wind out of him, but instead cry out in protest. In a matter of seconds, Vince releases his hold, and you find yourself tumbling down onto the mat.

"Maintaining your balance is an important ingredient to have in a fight. You will not have time to react if your focus is on keeping standing. Something so simple makes a big difference."

"It would be fairer if you weren't a statue," you grumble as you rub your elbow.

"I'm sorry," he says and kneels with concern, hesitating to reach out to you, "but your opponent will not show you the privilege of being fair. You up for practicing on your balance again?"

"You think I'm going to give up that easily?" You stare him directly in the eyes before extending your hand. "Care to give me a hand? It's the least you can do since you knocked me down."

He nods with a smile as he offers up his own. As you slip yours into his, you quickly tighten your grip, and put everything you have into yanking. Only he doesn't topple over onto the mat, as you had pictured in your mind. Instead, you find yourself yanked toward him face-to-face. You push back against his shoulders and stare into his blue eyes. Being so close to him unnerves you.

"No matter how many times you try to knock me down, you're not physically capable. So, you should stop before you hurt yourself." He tucks a lock of hair behind your ear.

"Underestimating a determined lady will be your downfall." You push away.

"I'll make sure to watch my back," he chuckles.

"So, are you going to show me anything useful tonight other than how to maintain my balance?" You gloss over the uncomfortable moment.

"Come with me." He leads you out of the gymnasium, down the hallway, and into the equipment room.

"Now, this is more like it." You grab a pair of gloves, slip them on, and jab the bag as hard as you can. You have a lot of pent-up energy to shake off.

"Not bad, but your form still needs work," Vince comments.

"Where would you like to start?"

Without warning, the punching bag swings your way and knocks you to the ground.

"Balance."

Chapter 24

Camille flaunts a pair of skinny black jeans and a shimmery royal blue V-neck sweater. "How do I look?"

"Good, like everything else you've tried on," you comment.

"But I want to look perfect."

"It's a date, not a wedding, Cam."

Camille's phone pings. She rushes over and grabs it. "He's here." She looks up in a panic.

"Relax." You watch Camille run over to the mirror, check her hair before grabbing her brush, brush hastily, and then pin her sides back. She grabs her hairspray and sprays it all over. You cough as the aroma invades your nose.

"Earrings or no earrings?" Camille turns abruptly.

"No earrings." You shrug. Only your best friend doesn't listen as she opens her jewelry box. "Are you going to make him wait all night?"

"I know, I know." Camille clips on a pair of round sapphire stud earrings. She pauses to look at herself one last time. "I guess this will have to do." She twirls. "Are you sure you'll be okay for an hour?"

"Yes, now would you go?"

"Thank you." Camille runs over and gives you a hug.

"Have fun." You watch Camille stuff her feet into her black ankle suede boots before slipping on her plaid jacket. She heads over to the window and opens it. You both lean out and wave at Vince, who is standing next to the red maple tree, before Camille climbs out of the window.

"Be careful," you hiss while holding your breath.

"You worry too much." Camille eases herself down slowly.

You hold your breath the entire time Camille descends. You stifle a gasp when she jumps down and stumbles, only to be caught by Vince, and you breathe a sigh of relief. You can't help but wonder if Camille was deliberate. You wave goodbye and close the window, keeping the night air out and the cozy air in.

You let *The Notebook* play loudly in the background. Camille's father hates seeing her cry, so binge-watching Nicholas Sparks romance movies is the perfect way to keep her dad from checking in. You're not fond of the movie, so open your book of *Romeo and Juliet*, and start mentally going over your lines. You have a week left to get them down.

You're glad for a break. Vince has been working your arm muscles hard for the last couple of days. Muscles you've been building up that you had not been aware of. You're sore and tired, but also feel stronger at the same time. It's a good feeling. You're also trying to make sense of how you feel in his company. You've never been friends with some guy before. You are completely new to it.

When the credits begin rolling, you stand and stretch before changing to a different movie. Since Camille isn't here to have a say, you pick the one you actually like, *The Longest Ride*. You sit Indian-style on Camille's bed with the bucket of popcorn and watch as the movie starts. You're not a fan of romance movies because they're predictable. When Camille dragged you to the theater to watch it for the first time, you found yourself intrigued. A week later, you picked up the novel and enjoyed it even more after getting through all the boring, sappy romance parts in the beginning.

Halfway through the movie, your cell goes off, announcing her return.

"Everything go okay here?" Camille asks as she climbs through the window.

"Just like you planned." You release her arm.

Camille waves goodbye to Vince before closing the window.

"So, how did it go?"

"Okay." Camille shrugs as she walks over to her dresser.

"Just okay?" Your head tilts.

"Yeah." She removes her earrings.

"Where did you go?" You sit down on the bed.

"The Red Palm."

"Oh, fancy."

You watch Camille grab her blue plaid pajamas before heading into the bathroom. When she comes back out, she dumps her clothing in the hamper before picking up a pillow, hugging it, and sitting next to you on the bed.

"I was hoping for a kiss tonight, but nothing," she says sourly.

"Maybe he wants to take things slowly," you encourage.

"He seems different."

"Different? Different how?" You perk up.

"I don't know. Distracted."

You don't know what to say. You're not sure if Vince is being deliberate or truly is distracted. You know it's in Camille's best interest, but it doesn't make things easier, and you don't like seeing her this way. You reach behind Camille, grab the other pillow, and smack her in the head.

"Did you just?"

You smack her again.

"Pillow fight!" Camille screams as she jumps to her feet on the bed, fighting back and laughing hysterically.

"What's going on?" The bedroom door opens, and Camille's father barges in.

"Nothing." You both drop the pillows.

"A bit old for that, don't you think? You two better pick up every single kernel," he sternly states, eyeing the popcorn that's spilled on the bed and floor before he closes the door.

"I can't believe you started it." Camille grabs the bowl and scoops a bunch of popcorn from the bed with a laugh.

"It's been so long since we've gotten into trouble." You kneel to pick up what's on the floor.

"Remember that time when we were home alone, and we couldn't stop laughing for no reason just by looking at each other?"

"Oh, I remember," you laugh heartily. "As if it were yesterday. I still can't believe I spit juice out everywhere over the kitchen floor."

"That was great." Tears are brimming at the corner of her eyes as she laughs with you.

You both fall silent as you continue to pick up popcorn. When you look over, you pause and note she's changed into a somber mood. "What's wrong?"

"We're going to drift apart after graduation, aren't we?"

"What? No. Why would you say that?"

"Everyone does. We'll probably end up going our separate paths."

"Don't think about the future. Focus on the present. Live one day at a time."

She jerks her head before joining you on the floor.

The truth is you have no idea what is going to happen after graduation. The road you take will probably be different from Camille's, but she doesn't need to hear that. Vince said he would disappear and that you were supposed to live a normal life. Only you don't have a plan. You're just going to take it day by day. "Did you ever submit your college applications?"

"I've decided to go to community college for now."

Your hand pauses in midair. "Is your dad happy about that?"

"No, but it gets him off my case for now."

"I hope you're not holding back because of me."

"I was thinking of maybe doing some traveling before I get tied down with more school."

"Where?"

"I don't know, anywhere but here. You should come with me."

You hesitate. You would love to explore the world with Camille, but you have to be realistic. You have responsibilities here, unlike Camille, and deep down in the recesses of your mind, you have concerns about endangering her. Putting Camille at risk is the last thing you want to do. Going separate paths would be in her best interest.

"Can I ask you a question?" Camille sits back down on the bed.

"Of course. What is it?" You set the bowl on the nightstand and join her.

"Is there something going on between you and Vince?"

"What?" you choke out.

"Do you have feelings for him?"

"No, why on Earth would you think that?"

"You couldn't stand him before, and suddenly, the two of you have become friends."

You sigh. "After I was suspended, he, I don't know, helped me come to terms with it. It's complicated." That's an understatement. It's the best you can do without going into too much detail. You feel sick to your stomach.

"Why didn't you talk to me?"

"I didn't want to talk about it." You look away. "I thought I could deal with it on my own."

"I'm so sorry." Camille pulls you into an embrace.

"It's okay," you say, patting her on the back.

"No, it's not. I'm a horrible friend to think for a moment…"

"Cam, you're not a horrible friend – you're my best friend. You were going through some stuff, too. You know that through thick and thin, I'll always have your six. No guy will ever change that." You pull her back in and squeeze tightly.

Your attention gets captured by the movie still playing in the background, as Ira says to Sophia, *"Love requires sacrifice, always."*

Chapter 25

"Bring your knee up and strike out with the ball of your foot." Vince demonstrates.

"Like this?"

"Yes, very good. Now try it with force."

You bring your knee up and kick out into thin air.

He slowly approaches. "Jab, right cross, left hook, right hook."

You follow his command, punching into the focus pad on his right hand, only your enthusiasm isn't there.

"Front kick."

You kick but lose your footing and dance a little until you gain your ground again. "Yes, I know I still need to work on my balance," you huff.

"I've taught you well."

"Don't let it go to your head."

"Oh, I wouldn't dare." He resumes a neutral expression with a glint in his eyes.

You look down.

"Penny for your thoughts?" His tone switches to a grave one.

You inhale through your nose and let it ease out of your mouth before lifting your eyes to his. "I appreciate everything you've taught me, really I do, but I think it would be in both our best interests if this is our last time."

"Why?" You hear the confusion in his voice.

You rip the Velcro off both your gloves. "You're leaving after graduation."

"Have I done something wrong?"

You turn and walk away to avoid seeing the hurt as you pull off both gloves. "You're a vampire, Vince."

"I see."

"I'd like to go home." You grab your gray sweatshirt and pull it over your head.

"Did something happen?"

"Now, Vince." You pierce his eyes with annoyance.

"There's something I'd like you to have first."

"What?" You fold your arms.

"Mace is not an effective weapon, but this…." He pulls out a knife from his back pocket, pushes a button on the side, and a blade flips open. "This is more effective, and I'd like you to carry it with you at all times."

"A switchblade? Absolutely not!" You crinkle your nose, appalled.

"It would give you peace of mind. Nadine, you placed a packed bag in my car. The last thing I want is for you to always be paranoid."

"It was just a precaution. I'm over it." You shrug.

"Knowing what you know, you're always going to be on edge, especially when you come across people you don't know."

"I'd be expelled if caught carrying it at school or worse, fired if found out at work," you protest.

"You're just making excuses."

"I'm not taking it," you state firmly.

"Why do you have to be so stubborn?"

"I'm human."

You see the flash of hurt in his eyes.

"Fine," he caves. "I'll put it in your bag in my car in case you change your mind."

"That I can agree with." You start to walk past him.

He catches your arm. "If you were in danger, I would tell you."

You pull away and whisper, "But you're not always going to be here."

The drive home is silent. You are itching to get out of the car, away from him. You know you hurt him. You had no other choice. It had to be done.

You close the front door and sink to the floor in the pitch-black house. You jump when something wet brushes against your hand.

Leo.

You grab him and hold him tightly. "I don't know why you love me when I'm a horrible person," you mumble in his ear. He meows low before butting his head into yours.

As each day follows, you face them all the same, with a fake smile. You bottle up everything and put on a show to the world that everything is okay.

"How come you're not hanging with Vince anymore?" Camille asks before forking her spinach salad.

"Our English assignment is over." You shrug and try to block the memory. Being next to him, rattling off a bunch of lines, was completely awkward. Neither one of you made small talk. You went up to perform and walked away as strangers.

"How did that go?"

"We passed." You sip your diet tea.

You continue to run. You run in the morning. You run at night. Oftentimes, you find yourself pausing at the foreclosed home. You want to apologize. Just because he's a vampire doesn't mean you had to be so cruel. Only because he is a vampire, you move on. It's in your best interest. You can't remain friends.

You perform a search on asparagus for days, and find yourself frustrated. You read over the biology, history, and uses; however, nothing jumps out at you as to why it would have an effect on vampires and compulsion. When you dig a little deeper, you find one thing that captures your interest under the order of *asparagales*. It lists several genera forming trees, including *Dracaena*. Curious, you discover that in Romanized Ancient Greek form, it means "female dragon." Upon further research, *Dracaena cinnabari* and *Dracaena draco* are known, when cut down, to secrete a reddish resin referred to as dragon's blood.

You're overloaded with information, but still do not understand what it could mean or if it means anything at all. You want to ask Vince, but feel like it's something you should keep to yourself. You don't feel threatened by him. However, you can't be sure if he can be completely trusted. There's a possibility he could turn on you if his life depended on it. He doesn't owe you anything.

"What took you so long?" You pause mid-step in the hallway when you hear Greg's voice.

"I…" comes paired with a squeaky voice.

"Don't ever keep me waiting again, you hear?"

Silence.

You peer around, tightening your hands into fists when you see Tommy cornered by Greg. Before you waltz over, you think better of the situation and take a deep breath before reacting.

"Here's my geometry homework for tomorrow." Greg shoves a bunch of papers into Tommy's chest.

You take a step forward but stop when you hear Tommy mumble, "I'm not going to do it."

"What did you just say to me?"

"I'm not going to do your homework anymore." Tommy raises his voice a little with a bit of confidence.

"You think you can say no to me?" Greg grabs a fistful of Tommy's shirt, letting his homework fall to the floor.

"Yeah, I just did." Tommy rips himself out of Greg's grasp.

"How dare you?"

"Do your own homework."

Greg stares at him, assessing the situation.

"You heard him," you voice.

Greg looks over his shoulder before glancing back at Tommy. You imagine if Greg had a tail, it would be tucked between his legs as he reaches down for his homework and walks off without a word.

"Hey, Greg," you call out.

"What?" he asks distastefully.

"I'm sorry I punched you in the nose."

Greg's forehead wrinkles, but he says nothing before he disappears around the corner.

"How did it feel?" You approach Tommy.

"Terrifying."

"Yet, you stood up to him anyway."

"Does it get easier?"

"That depends on you."

"How long did it take for you to become fearless?"

You study him. "I'm not fearless. I've just learned how *not* to be paralyzed by fear, just like you did today."

"I still wanted to run and hide."

"What stopped you?"

"Your voice inside my head."

So, perhaps Vince didn't interfere this time. "Well, that's a good start. I'll tell you a secret. I've learned over the years that when there is something worth fighting for, you are invincible."

Your own words of advice ring inside your head. The thought of being destined to defeat an old vampire just doesn't make sense. He is nothing to you. There is nothing worth fighting him for. So, why are you marked by the Dragon's Eye?

Chapter 26

You stare at yourself in the bathroom mirror, feeling like a stranger. Breathtaking. You are completely transformed. Ready to take on the world. Camille applied some blush to your cheeks, mascara to your eyelashes, and nude eye shadow after you insisted on a natural color. Camille also French-braided your hair. You requested to have it braided to the right, but Camille disliked the idea. You find some of Camille's foundation stashed in her bathroom and apply some on your birthmark. Your recently painted ruby red fingernails match your dress perfectly as you open the door and walk out.

"Can you close me up?" you ask, turning your back and pulling your hair to the side. You wait and wait, but Camille doesn't say or do anything. "Cam?" You turn to face her.

Camille stares transfixed.

"What's wrong?" You look down.

"Wow, you look…." Camille trails off. "Different."

"Different how? In a bad way?"

"Definitely in a good way. You're stunning!" Camille turns you and buttons the clasp on the lace top.

"You don't look so bad yourself." You take in her royal blue dress, makeup, and curled hair with sides pulled back and bound in a blue rhinestone floral hair barrette.

"Girls, you're going to be late," Camille's father shouts from downstairs.

"All dressed up and no dates," Camille sighs.

"Excuse me, you're my date."

Camille cringes.

"Yeah, that sounds weird," you laugh.

"We're going to knock all those guys out of their socks."

"That's the spirit." You thrust a fist and head for the stairs.

"You girls look absolutely beautiful," Mom says, blinking back tears.

"I must get some pictures," Camille's mother exclaims.

"First things first." Camille's dad appears with two boxes.

"Dad," Camille gasps.

"It's not proper for ladies to go to prom without a corsage." He holds out the blue first to Camille, and then the matching red one for you.

"You're the best dad ever." Camille throws herself against him.

"Now, don't mess up your makeup before I get pictures," Camille's mom states.

"Mom," Camille moans.

Once several hundred pictures, it seems, are taken, you head out to Camille's father's cop car.

"I can't wait to see everyone's face." Camille grins excitedly.

When Camille's father pulls into the parking lot, he flicks on his lights and siren before stopping. You cover your ears as everyone outside stares. First, he opens the door for Camille and then you. You blush under your blush. You hate being the center of attention and feel insecure, especially when you're all dressed up.

You hike up your dress and walk forward slowly. You're still not used to the heels, but you have better balance in them with your stronger and more toned legs.

When you enter the gymnasium, the music is blasting away in dim lighting. Blue and white streamers hang from the ceiling, with a silver light projecting from a disco ball in the center.

"Let's dance!" Camille shouts, grabbing your arm after a picture is snapped of the two of you on the way in.

You feel awkward and stiff, trying to follow Camille's lead as she grooves to the beat. You look around the dance floor, taking in all your classmates. They are all enjoying themselves, paying you no mind.

"Who knew dancing could be so exhausting?" Camille makes a beeline for the refreshment table.

"Don't drink that." You snatch the cup of punch from Camille's hand.

"What, you think it's spiked?" She quirks an eyebrow.

"That's what usually happens during these types of events."

"Oh, come on, Nad, live a little." Camille snatches it back and gulps half of the punch down.

"Cam."

"Who cares if it's spiked. It makes things more interesting. You could loosen up some. Besides, can you really trust the water is actually water?" She nods at the cups of water.

"Who would spike water?"

"You never know."

"You two look like a million dollars."

You turn and see Vince standing there wearing a black tuxedo, open, with a white shirt lacking a bowtie. You had no idea he was going to come. You haven't talked to him since that night, and don't see much of him at school. He's been keeping his distance like you asked.

"Vince, you look very handsome," Camille beams, looking him up and down.

"Thank you. You're royally beautiful yourself."

Camille blushes with a giggle.

"You two having fun?" he continues.

"Of course, although I'd be having more fun if I could drink the punch." Camille glares at you.

"Allow me." He holds out his hand.

Camille hands over her cup, and with a slight bite to her lower lip, watches him take a sip.

"It's not spiked." He hands it back to her.

"Well, that's a bummer," Camille pouts.

You say nothing. You know he didn't take a sip. He probably already knew it wasn't tampered with.

"My favorite song," Camille gasps as the first chords of *Perfect* start to play.

"Well then, may I have this dance?" Vince offers his hand.

"Yes," Camille shrieks before handing over her cup and clutch to you. "Hold these, please."

You know Camille probably wants to save the cup for life since it has Vince's DNA on it. As you watch, you suddenly feel out of place as your eyes sweep the dance floor. Everyone seems to be with someone and happy. You have no idea what to do with yourself and are not accustomed to feeling like this. You gulp down the rest of the punch.

As the song ends, the DJ broadcasts for everyone to gather on the floor, and he loops the first beat of the next song he intends to play.

"Come on." Camille rushes over and grabs your hand, dragging you back out onto the floor.

"Let's get the party started." The DJ pumps his fist as he lets the electric slide blare.

"Yes!" Camille shouts.

Everyone forms a line, getting into sync. You look around the dance floor while pathetically trying to mimic everyone else, and find Vince is nowhere in sight. Where did he go?

The next dance, everyone does the YMCA. You are exhausted and more than thrilled when the DJ decides to slow it down once more. Dancing is definitely not your thing. You feel as if everyone is watching you, even if they're not. It's going to be a long night if Camille keeps dragging you out onto the dance floor. You like dancing in the comfort of your own home.

"Where are you going?" Camille calls after you.

"Just need a little air." You walk out into the hallway, leaving the loud music behind with Camille at your heels.

"Are you okay?"

"Yeah, you know me and crowds," you wave off.

You embrace the cool air as you step outside the school. The sky is overcast with dark clouds. Rain is in the forecast for tonight.

"It's freezing out here." Camille holds her arms together.

"You can go back in."

"I'm not leaving you."

You inhale deeply and embrace the wide-open space. Being in a crowded place for too long makes it hard to breathe sometimes. You just need a chance to catch your breath and release the tension. "Okay, we can go back."

"Are you sure?" Camille asks, shaking like a leaf.

"Yes." You smile.

Camille doesn't ask twice.

You're greeted with another up-tempo song as you walk back in.

"Where's my cup of punch?" Camille asks with wide eyes.

"I tossed it."

"But I wanted to keep it," she whines.

"Camille, it's a cup."

"But…"

"Get another cup."

"Did someone want more punch?" Vince appears, extending his hand with a red cup.

"Life saver." Camille takes it.

The song fades out, pausing briefly, and piano chords begin to play shortly after.

"I'd be honored if you would agree to a dance." Vince turns his attention to you.

"I don't dance well." You shake your head.

"You danced just fine earlier," he protests.

"Nadine, stop making excuses." Camille bumps you with her hip, causing you to stumble forward in your heels. Vince is quick to steady you in his arms.

"Seems you still need to work on your balance," he mocks.

You glare at him, annoyed. "Fine. Let's get this over with."

He takes your hand and leads you out onto the dance floor. "Your arms go here." He pulls your right arm up and lets it fall onto his shoulder. You mirror with your left arm. When he steps closer, you tense. He's close. Too close. "Don't get testy when I place my hands on your hips."

You stiffen when he places his hands cautiously on either side of your waist. When you take in the dance floor, every couple who is dancing is positioned the same way.

"Relax and just sway with the music." He shifts his feet.

Your eyes instantly drop to his feet, watching his every move. You also want a reason to avoid making eye contact with him.

"Don't look at my feet." He slips a finger under your chin and guides your head up.

You feel your heart pick up speed. You hate the fact that he can probably hear. Every fiber in your body screams for you to bolt, but you stay firmly in place.

"I'm surprised they are playing a Richard Marx song," you break the silence.

"I requested it."

You don't know what to say.

"I'm sorry," you exclaim, jumping back and looking down after stepping on his foot.

"Nadine, you don't have to be sorry. No harm done."

You lock eyes with his blue ones, knowing there are multiple meanings coded in his words.

"Red suits you." He steers the conversation elsewhere, closing the gap and leading you back into the dance.

"You clean up pretty well yourself."

"You know, when you're not overthinking it, you're a pretty good dancer."

"Don't expect another dance from me tonight. This is the only one you get."

Vince is about to respond before something catches his attention over your shoulder. You feel him stiffen. Alarm is written all over his face.

Chapter 27

"What's wrong?" You study him before you start to shift your head to follow Vince's line of sight. Without warning, he moves you to the left.

"Keep your eyes on me," he says in a low tone.

"Okay," you whisper back.

"You need to get out of sight."

You swallow hard and nod in agreement. You recognize the seriousness in Vince's tone. You don't have to see to know who exactly has Vince concerned.

Jomar.

"I'm going to make a move. When I do, I need you to react accordingly."

You feel his hand slip from your waist and fondle your bottom, and you don't have to act offended. The move infuriates you as you remind yourself it's only an act.

"How dare you! Take your hands off me." You push away from him and storm off.

You set your sights on Camille with rage, fighting against the urge to look in the direction Vince was focused on. As you close the gap, you notice Camille's expression looks mad.

"You lied to me." Camille turns on her heel.

"Cam, wait." You rush after her, slightly panicked, and try dodging around the crowded floor to keep up, but she walks with purpose. "Cam," you call out when you are both out of the gymnasium.

"You said nothing was going on between you and Vince."

"It's not what you think."

"Didn't look like that to me."

"Cam, I need you to come with me."

"No." She turns and hastens away.

"Cam, no!" You hurry after her, stepping outside to find the first drops of rain are starting to fall. You are full-blown panicked now. You have to get to Camille and get her away. Running in heels is difficult, and yet, Camille seems to run flawlessly. Faster than you can.

You come to a halt when you spy Vince's Impala in the parking lot. You know where he keeps the key hidden, and you make a beeline for it. You grab the key above the driver's side front tire. You hurry back and pop open the trunk. As soon as you grab what you need from your bag, you hop into the car and take off.

"Get in the car." You screech to a stop next to Camille as the fat raindrops pick up.

"Why do you have a key to Vince's car?"

"I'll explain later, but right now, we need to get out of here."

"I'm not going anywhere with you."

"Why would two pretty ladies be arguing on a night like this?"

You whip your head to the unfamiliar male standing to the right, dressed in dark attire. Instinctively, you position yourself in front of Camille. "You friends with Jomar?"

He tilts his head. "How do you know Jomar?"

"Why are you here?"

Like a streak of lightning, he closes the distance and firmly grasps your neck as Camille screams. "I ask the questions here."

You flick open the switchblade and stab him in the stomach before yanking it back. His eyes go wide as he looks down to see blood seeping out. Slowly, he releases his hold and staggers back before he falls to his knees, holding his stomach.

"Nadine?" Camille cries out.

"Get in the car, now!" you dictate. Processing your actions can come later.

Camille doesn't argue as she scrambles to the open driver's side door and hops over into the passenger seat. "What's going on?" Fear laces her voice. You have her attention.

"Not now." You close the door, put the car in drive, and lurch forward. You slam on the brakes, two car lengths away from the vampire you just impaled, and take in the scene before you. It's two against one. Vince is outnumbered in front of the school with his arms pinned back and Jomar punching him in the face.

"Do you have mace in there?" Your eyes drop to her clutch.

"Yeah."

"I need it."

"Okay." Camille shakily opens her clutch and hands it over. You stuff it down the front of your dress.

"Put your seat belt on."

"Nadine, you're scaring me."

"Put it on!"

Camille yelps before reaching back and strapping it across. You gasp and stomp down on the gas as Jomar slashes an ancient-looking blade across Vince's stomach. You know you're being reckless, but you can't leave him behind. He saved your life. Time to repay the debt.

Jomar redirects his attention as you close in. You spin the wheel to avoid a head-on collision with him, and you slam the side of the car into him. His body sails through the air and slams into a parked vehicle. You waste no time as you jump out and spray the other vampire, holding Vince, directly in the eyes with the mace. He backs away as you wrap an arm around Vince and help him over to the car. You open the back door and shove him in. When you close the door, you only take a step before something grabs the back of your braided hair.

"What did she do to you, Seth?"

You twist and see Jomar's shocked expression before spraying him in the face. His hold loosens enough for you to tear away, and you quickly slip back into the driver's seat and step on the gas, fishtailing on the wet pavement. You speed off, closing the door. You don't look back. You focus on the path before you.

"Why did you do that? You shouldn't have done that," Vince says between labored breaths.

"Save your strength." You glance in the rearview mirror briefly before looking at the road behind you.

"You don't realize what you've done."

"Do you have a stash of blood at your place?"

"You can't be anywhere near there."

The rain is now fully torrential. You grip the steering wheel so hard that your knuckles turn white, and you have no idea where to go or the consequences of your actions. You veer in the opposite direction of town and head toward the interstate.

"I have a stash in the trunk with the spare tire."

You know he has limited time. Every second you drive, he loses blood, but you're also risking the other vampires catching up. You look all around and see nothing suspicious before you pull off the side of the road.

You pop the trunk and step out into the pouring rain, lifting the back cover to reveal the spare tire and a black insulated cooler tote that holds four blood bags. You stare transfixed at them, rain dripping from your nose. Reality is starting to set in.

You shake off the trance, grab the cooler, and open the back door. You're horrified at the sight. Vince's white shirt is stained red as it continues to ooze out despite him keeping pressure on the wound. He takes the bag you offer and rips into it, draining the contents with hunger. You swallow hard. You know what he is, but he's never fed in front of you before. Despite the blood loss, he manages to stay in control.

"Is that a bag of blood? Why are you drinking blood?" Camille asks with hysteria in her voice. You ignore her as you slip back behind the wheel.

"He's a vampire," you blurt out.

"He's a what?" Camille shrieks, petrified.

"He's not going to hurt you."

"A vampire?" She claws at your arm.

You sigh. "Calm down."

Camille starts to scream. "He's trying to kill me."

You look over and see Vince gripping the back of Camille's neck before she slumps over, unconscious. You glance back at him.

"What did you do to her?"

"She was going into shock. I just knocked her out for a bit."

You reach the interstate and head north.

"Why did you come back for me? I told you to leave."

"Everything happened so fast. When I saw…" You pause. "I just couldn't leave you behind."

"You should have. He was just trying to get me to talk. Wanted me to go on a binge."

You meet his eyes in the rearview mirror. "I wasn't going to stand by and watch."

"You can never go back."

"My mother." You lift your foot from the gas pedal. "Leo."

"It's already too late."

"What if it's not? I can warn her." A car goes sailing by, blaring its horn, the driver unhappy with how slow you're going.

"They will be able to trace the call. Where is your phone?"

"At home."

"Camille's phone?"

You reach over and pry the clutch from Camille's hand before tossing it back. You hear Vince open the window to toss the phone.

"Where do you want me to go?"

"I don't know." He sighs, leaning back in the seat.

"I know a place."

"Where?"

"Camille's family has a cabin about an hour away."

"Okay, but we can't stay there for long. I'll need to rebuild my strength and get some supplies."

You don't have to ask how he intends to restore his strength. There are only two options. And you're not fond of either one.

Chapter 28

Camille stirs in the passenger seat. She looks out the window at first, before around the interior of the car, and then over in your direction. "Where are we going?"

"The cabin," you answer.

"Why?"

You flick your eyes into the rearview mirror long enough for Camille to look back.

"Vince?"

"How are you feeling?" he asks with a friendly smile.

Camille's eyes go wide before she reaches for the door handle. "Stop the car!"

"Cam." You touch her leg.

"Vampire! He's a vampire! Nadine, how are you not freaking out?" She keeps trying the locked handle.

You meet Camille's eyes. She's terrified. There's nothing you can do or say to ease her mind right now while Vince is around. You look at Vince in the mirror and nod. He instantly grips Camille's pressure point in her neck and knocks her back out. A discussion you had earlier in case Camille came out of it before you reached the cabin.

Vince carries Camille inside after you park. He puts her in her room while you look for a change of dry clothes. You're ready to remove the pasted wet dress.

You find Vince a change of clothing, as well, from Camille's parents' room before heading into the bathroom. You look at yourself in the bathroom mirror. You are pale under the streaked makeup. You wash your face clean before jumping into the shower. You stand there as hot water cascades all over you, only you're still shaking. You grab a bar of soap, lather suds into the palm of your hand, and just keep scrubbing. No amount of soap is going to make you feel clean.

You find the motivation to turn off the water and step out as you towel-dry yourself. There's no brush or comb that you can find, so you just finger-comb through your wet hair.

"What if I can't get through to her?" You walk into the living room dressed in comfortable clothing. Jeans, a black long-sleeve tee, and a forest green vest that was buried in Camille's dresser drawer you forgot you had left behind. At least you feel more like yourself.

"She's been through a lot tonight." Vince is standing by the radio, adjusting the dial. Camille's father's jeans and white tee fit loosely on him.

"The last thing I wanted to do was get her dragged into the middle of all of this." You sit on the couch, prop up your feet, and stuff your hands into your vest pockets.

"It's not your fault. If it's anyone's fault, it's mine."

"It's not your fault either. Where do we go from here?"

He sighs as he walks over and sits down in the chair opposite you, "The safest place for you is to stay off the grid. They can monitor every camera they desire and track facial recognition."

"Is this how I'm going to have to live for the rest of my life?"

He falls silent. The only sound comes from the music playing on the radio. His silence is your answer. This was not the plan. Everything shifted after that split-second decision you made. If you had the chance to do it over again, knowing what it would cost you, would you make the same decision?

"You know, I never got to finish my dance," Vince interrupts your thoughts.

You meet his eyes before looking at the radio and focusing on the song that just started playing. It's a slow piano melody. The same song you were dancing to at prom. Prom seems so long ago, and it's been less than two hours.

"Seriously? You want to dance at a time like this?"

"Why not? You can still live life enjoying the simple things." He stands, extending his hand.

You fold your arms against your chest.

"I won't take no for an answer."

"I'm not moving."

"I believe you agreed to a dance and did not fulfill that agreement."

"Seriously?" You scowl.

"We've got all night." He smirks.

"Fine." You breathe in deeply and release it just as vastly before placing your hand in his.

"Ouch, my foot."

You push back. "I told you I wasn't good at this."

A wicked smile spreads across his face. "Do you really think a vampire, such as I, could feel an ounce of pain from a mere human, such as you, stepping on his foot?"

"Then why did you holler?" You don't have the desire to play along.

"To see if you cared."

"Of course I care." You lock eyes with him. The beating of your heart picks up speed. "I'm actually feeling pretty tired." You step away.

"But the song hasn't finished yet. Here." He yanks you back, hooks his arm around your waist, lifts you slightly, and places your feet on top of his.

"Vince." You stiffen with an edge in your voice as you stare at his chest.

"Now you don't have to worry about stepping on them." He moves with the music.

You feel uncomfortable. You want to run, but there is nowhere safe for you to run right now. Despite yourself, you allow yourself to relax a little as he hums. You close your eyes and rest your forehead against his chest. You listen to the words of the song as you shift your head. Your eyes flick open shortly after when you register that he has no heartbeat. When the song ends, you step down off his feet. "Thank you for the dance."

"No, thank you." You see the glint in his eyes as, inch-by-inch, he slowly leans toward you.

"No." You turn your head. Before he has a chance to say anything, you walk toward the front door and slip out onto the porch. You hear the creaking of the wood planks as he follows. "Nothing can ever happen between us."

"Why? Because I'm a monster?" He bites out with bitterness.

You frown and meet his blue eyes. "You're not a monster, not to me."

"Then why push me away?"

"You're forbidden fruit, Vince."

"Seems pretty clear Camille wants nothing to do with me."

"It doesn't matter if you are with her. I'm sorry if you thought otherwise, but we will always be just friends." You walk past him back into the cabin.

He doesn't follow as you go to the other bedroom and close the door behind you. You wait for Leo to rub up against you, but soon you remember you will never see him again. You cover your face with your hands and slide down to the floor, fighting back the tears that threaten to surface. How can you go on living like this? You are in way over your head.

You can't stand the silence. You can't stand feeling alone. You have to remain strong. With a deep breath, you open the door and tiptoe over to Camille's room. She's sleeping on her back.

You climb into the bed and curl up next to her. You try to shut off your mind. You're exhausted, yet your brain keeps firing away. It would have been easier if Camille had not gotten involved. Her life is ruined because of you, and you still have to convince her that Vince means her no harm. Where do you go from here?

Shadows of darkness have you surrounded. It's hard to see much of anything past your nose. You reach out and feel the bumpy grooves of rough bark. You feel alone in the woods. Without warning, a breeze whips up your hair as it whistles by your ear. A dark figure materializes before you. Your first instinct is to step back, but there is a desire deep within that overrules the impulse. So, you stand there at a standstill. Are they a friend or foe?

The only sound is the drumming of your heartbeat before streaks of lightning spider above in the night sky. The dark form is still obstructed by shades of black and gray. No clear image. The figure is one with the night. Blending in perfectly well. Suddenly, a crack of thunder startles you before the earth begins shaking. You find yourself unsteady, trying to stay upright. All at once, your feet leave the ground. You feel a sense of security as you gaze into olive-green eyes.

A car door slams. You tear away from your dream state. Tires crunch against the gravel pathway. You spring out of bed, hurry into the living area, throw open the door, and watch as Vince drives away. Where is he going in the middle of the night? Is he coming back? You refuse to stress about it as you close the door. When you reach the bedroom, Camille is awake.

"Where is he?" She frantically looks around.

"He's gone."

"I have to call my parents."

"You can't." You block the doorway.

"Why?"

"I'm being hunted."

Camille takes a step back. "Because you stabbed that guy?"

"No," you sigh. "It's a long story. How about I tell you over a cup of coffee?"

"Wait, are you a vampire, too?" She reels back.

"No, I'm still human."

"How are you not freaking out about Vince?"

"Trust me, I did at first, but I wouldn't be alive if it weren't for him."

"Where is he?"

"He went for supplies." You hope.

Camille instantly relaxes. "Okay, coffee."

You close the gap and wrap your arms around Camille, hugging her tightly. "I'm so sorry you got involved in this."

"What exactly am I involved in?" Camille tenses, standing like a statue.

"Come, I'll tell you everything." You grab her hand and lead her to the kitchen.

While Camille slides into a chair at the kitchen table, you rummage through cupboards, looking for coffee grounds and filters. When you turn back to face Camille, you find an empty chair. You look toward the open living area and see the front door wide open. You shout her name and run after her.

You pause as everything is swallowed by the darkness of the night. Quickly, you run back into the kitchen and find a flashlight before stuffing your feet into Camille's mother's hiking boots, which are only one size larger than yours.

You study the ground, following Camille's footprints in the damp earth. She couldn't have gotten far. You stop and listen closely. When a branch snaps, you instantly run in that direction.

"Camille!" The flashlight beam catches her.

"I'm not going back," Camille yells over her shoulder.

You pick up your pace, ignoring the shrubs and branches you brush up against. The area is thick before thinning out as you close the gap and reach out for Camille's arm.

"Get off me!" She yanks her arm from your grasp.

"He can make you forget."

"What?" Camille turns before stumbling onto the ground.

"Are you okay?"

"No, Nadine, I'm not okay." She starts to sob.

"I know you're scared." You kneel beside her. "I am, too. But we can get through this together. You know you can trust me, right?"

You whip your head when you hear a snap. Camille claws into your arm as you turn off the flashlight. Something else is lurking in the woods, or someone else.

Chapter 29

The night is still. There's not even a breeze. Yet, you feel a wind tickle your face as something whizzes by too close for comfort.

"Well, hello there."

Camille screams as you flip on the light and find a tall, beefy guy with brown hair standing off to the left.

"Now, what would possess two pretty ladies to be out in the woods in the middle of the night and all alone?"

"That's none of your concern. We were just leaving, so goodbye," you bite back, tugging a whimpering Camille along as you step away from the guy. You know you are both in trouble. Big trouble.

"Well, aren't you a spitfire?" He is quick to shift into your path, standing much closer.

"Stay back." You drop the flashlight, remove your switchblade from your outer pocket, and whip it open, pointing it directly at his stomach.

Camille's shriek pierces the night as something rips her away from your grip. When you turn toward the sound of her hysterical crying, all you can make out is a tall, slender, dark figure holding Camille hostage.

"Let her go." You take a step forward, tightening your grip on the handle.

A horrendous scream erupts from Camille's mouth. You can't see well enough in the dark, but you don't need to see to know the vampire is sucking Camille's blood.

"No!" you shout as you charge forward.

In a flash, your wrist gets twisted up and the switchblade is yanked from your hold. You spin and slam hard against a firm body. The slender frame tenses as his hot breath breathes on the back of your neck. You smell his coppery breath, laced with a hint of some kind of spice. It makes your stomach queasy. You try to squirm out of his hold, but you're no match for a hungry vampire.

"Hey, I found them first, mind sharing?" the other vampire complains.

"Maybe you should learn not to play with your food so you don't easily lose it, Glenn," a deep, robotic voice utters by your ear.

"It's called having some fun, Marc. You shouldn't always take everything so seriously."

"I see no point in prolonging the inevitable when we have a job to do."

"You didn't even bother looking for the mark before you fed."

Your heart leaps into your throat. They're here looking for you. It was a mistake coming. You should have known better. You have a small circle, which would have made it too easy for Jomar to figure out where you went for safety. Did your mother suffer? Did Camille's mother and father suffer?

"There's no need. Unfortunately, this is the one we're here for."

You fall forward and land on your hands and knees between the two vampires.

"What? How do you know that?" Glenn asks.

You are half wondering that yourself but waste no time jumping back to your feet and taking off blindly through the woods. In the back of your mind, you know you don't stand a chance of outrunning them, but that's not going to stop you from trying. Adrenaline pumps through your veins as you press through shrubs and low-hanging branches. You hate yourself for leaving Camille behind, but there's nothing you can do for her now. You can't even think about it. Not yet. You have to live to fight another day first.

You smash against something hard and thick that wasn't there a second ago. You stand there in a daze. Everything is dark and in shadows.

"Did you really think you could outrun me?" Glenn's voice mocks as he inhales deeply. "You smell very appetizing."

You back away, only to be stopped by a thick tree. The vampire closes the gap with one long stride, places his right hand around your neck, and squeezes slowly. You hear the pulsating blood flow increase through your temples. You are at his mercy and feel helpless, but you won't give him the satisfaction of showing fear. You pierce his dark eyes with hatred before spitting in his face.

"You little…." He tightens his grip.

You choke, desperate to suck air in. Suddenly, his hold releases as he cries out in pain.

"I told you to find her, not torment her," Marc's deep voice growls as you gasp for air.

"My wrist, I think you broke my wrist!" Glenn hollers in agonizing pain.

"I will be reporting you for disobeying a direct order." Marc stands over him.

"Just wait until…."

"I'd think twice before issuing a threat," Marc slices him off. "As for you…." He redirects his attention. "We shall see what you're made of, but until then, time to sleep." He applies pressure to your carotid artery. You fight hard against unconsciousness. With your back against the tree, there is nowhere for you to escape. It's a battle you are never going to win.

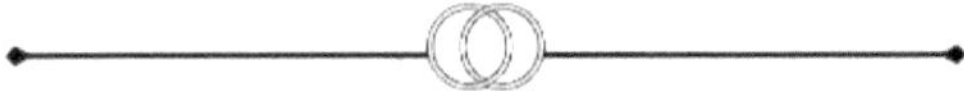

When your eyes open, light burns them. It takes several minutes for your eyes to adjust to the light before you become aware of a musty stench invading your nostrils. You push yourself up from a spring bed and take in the room. The cream-colored paint on the wall is severely chipped and stained, with loose plaster hanging. You involuntarily shiver when you note deep scratch marks dug into the wall next to the bed, along with some words.

I want to die.

You jump out of the bed, realizing the sheets are stained pinkish, before you notice restraints at the foot and bottom of the bed. You feel instantly sick and cover your mouth. You scurry over to the small single window, only to be met with disappointment. You are four stories up. Enough time has elapsed for the sun to slowly start rising. How are you going to get out of this?

You jolt when you hear several footsteps marching closer. You look around in a panic, searching for anything you can use as a weapon, and come up short. The end is nearly upon you.

The door creaks open before Seth, the vampire you sprayed in the eyes with mace, walks in, along with the vampire you impaled with your switchblade, an unfamiliar one, and a sneering Jomar. You ignore him as you study the unfamiliar vampire. He is tall and slender. You watch as he removes some sort of brown stick from his side pocket and places it between his teeth. Is he the one called Marc from the woods? You didn't get a good look at his face in the dark. You take in his physique from top to bottom. He wears a dark gray turtleneck beneath a black blazer, black jeans, and black leather boots. Has a five-o'clock shadow along his jawline. His dark hair hangs right above his downcast eyes as if he's bored. Your eyes narrow with hatred.

A high-pitched scream refocuses your attention. What is going on outside the room? You don't think you really want to know. One last vampire walks through the door before it's slammed shut. He is chubby and appears older than the rest. It's difficult to make him out as he wears a silver armored suit from head to toe with only his eyes visible.

Vladimir.

"So, I've wasted all this time believing you were the one I'm supposed to meet my doom to?" he mocks, approaching slowly and cupping his hands behind his back.

"A misunderstanding." You moisten your lips. "You have nothing to fear from me."

"Ain't that the truth? The very first and oldest vampire in existence meant to cower to a mere human?"

"Clearly, I'm not the one foretold in the prophecy. So, you can just let me go and live a boring human life. I'll forget this ever happened." You try charming him with a smile. Your only option is to try to talk your way out.

"And let you miss out on the surprise I have for you?" He inches closer.

"I'm okay with that." You shudder at his dark, stone-cold cobalt eyes. They twinkle with delight.

Without a word, he removes his armored gauntlet and pokes you hard on the shoulder. "Ah, she does not burn me." He turns and shares a laugh with the others.

"How dare you touch me," you state through clenched teeth, balling your hands into fists by your sides.

He whirls on you so fast, you never see it coming before pain explodes against your cheek. The force of the blow causes your feet to leave the floor as your body sails through the air before slamming up against the wall, head first. For a moment, the room is completely black.

"Prisoners don't tell me what to do," his voice booms in your ear of your pounding head. "Now, I must prepare for your execution."

You hear the thundering footsteps pounding in your head as they leave. The room spins as you try to regain focus. You press an ice-cold hand against your throbbing cheek. Time is running out for you. You are surrounded by nothing but vampires and have no protection from them. The end is dangerously close. You don't know where you even are. The only escape is four stories below. Better than whatever execution they have planned. You doubt it will be swift.

You push up from the floor and walk your hands slowly up against the wall. The room still spins, but you set your focus on the window. All you have to do is make it over there before they come back. You take a few shaky steps and fall back to the floor. Shaking off the dizziness, you opt for crawling. You have no idea how far away the window is. The image keeps blurring in and out. You feel out with your hands, hoping you will make it in time.

The door swings open with a smack. You don't even hear the footsteps as your head still throbs. You hold your composure, sitting back against the wall, knowing you're defeated, but you won't give them the satisfaction of showing fear on your face.

"Pathetic," you hear Jomar's scorn.

Your vision continues to go in and out. You have an intense headache that is growing hotter. You keep your eyes directed to the floor to avoid the bright light.

"Come to take me to my execution?" you mock sourly with a slur as his odd-sounding footsteps stop in front of you.

"You'll be begging for death before it finds you. You failed to kill Brice. He enjoyed snacking on one of your classmates," he says with a sneer. "Would you like to hear how your mother begged...."

There's an unexpected crack before Jomar collapses to the floor, unmoving. Your eyes jerk to the hazy figure. You were unaware Jomar had company.

"I'll give you two choices: One, I can take you to your execution, or two, you can come with me and escape," the deep robotic voice from the vampire in the turtleneck says, confirming he is indeed Marc.

Chapter 30

You stare at his blurred face, bewildered. What sort of sick trick is this? You don't trust Marc. Despise him even. Why would he break you out when he was the one who brought you here in the first place?

"What choice would you like?" he inquires.

"Why?" the thought materializes.

"Now is not the time for explanations," he dismisses.

Do you really have a choice? There's no way you're getting out of this place on your own. You're in the vampires' lair. By default, you're going to have to go with him and figure out later how to get away.

"Escape," you lower your eyes and whisper.

Just when you distinguish the sharp sound you hear is glass shattering, you tense as you're scooped off the floor. You're not fond of how close you are to him in his arms. You pick up on the scent of a spice. Oddly, it has a calming effect on your firing senses. Against the dizziness, you catch his eyes. He has pale olive-green ones. They're vacant, and yet, something about them unnerves you.

"May want to hold on tight," he warns, briefly meeting your gaze before looking away.

You follow his line of sight and find yourself looking out the window. Your heart slams up against your chest. Is he going to jump out the window? You had not realized what his version of escaping entailed.

You grab his turtleneck in a death grip and tuck your head against his chest before he makes the jump. You close your eyes tightly as you feel the air whoosh past while freefalling. The motion comes to an abrupt halt. You dare to open your eyes. You are suspended a few feet from the ground. Just as you capture the sight, the world becomes disoriented. The fast motion, mixed with your dizziness, makes your stomach churn. You close your eyes once more and fight to keep down the bile, trying to focus on something besides the momentum of his super-speed. You fight against being swallowed by complete darkness. You have no idea what his motive is. At least your odds are better against one vampire versus a thousand. The first opportunity you get, you will try to get away. If you can muster up the strength.

You start to squirm as the motion becomes too much, and you pound on his chest. You're going to be sick. You can't hold back the bile buildup in your throat any longer. When you open your eyes, you look away from him just in time as vomit erupts.

Gently, he sets your feet on the ground. You feel weak, and your legs are shaky, but he holds onto your torso to keep you upright.

"Are you done?" he asks.

You fail to respond as you hover over the area.

"We have to keep moving."

"I don't think I can go your speed anymore."

"It's the only way." He scoops you up once more.

He speeds off before you can argue. You fight against the nausea. You have no idea where he's going or how long you have to endure the rhythm.

Fire blazes your closed eyes. You split them open to see the sun's rays shining brightly between sparse trees. It bothers you immensely as you shut them tightly and lean into him.

"Can you swim?" The vibration of his voice is loud in your ears.

"Yeah." You frown, looking up before you become aware of a roaring sound. Rushing water.

"We need to swim underneath the waterfall."

You look out at the fast-moving, cascading water. Your head already feels underwater. "You can't be serious."

He neglects to answer. He doesn't stop moving as he steps off the bank into the water. He advances slowly and steadily toward the waterfall. Each step he takes descends him deeper until the water laps above his knees. Slowly, he dips you in. It's freezing to the touch as you gasp and shiver. You find yourself standing on uneven ground. If he weren't supporting your waist, you would probably fall from all the uncontrollable shaking.

"When I tell you, take a deep breath. It's not far." He pulls you along until you are close enough to feel the spray.

You take a few short breaths between your clattering teeth before he signals. You manage a deep breath and duck beneath the surface with him. The flowing waterfall pounds on top of your head despite being under the water, which does not help your immense headache.

He guides you along and positions you at a narrow crevice before urging you to swim through first. It's completely dark, and you have no idea where you are going. You fight against panicking for air. You just keep swimming forward until you feel a hand on your foot stopping you. You tread water until he guides you to swim up. When you break the surface, you inhale with unsteady breaths and close into yourself.

"Hold on here." He guides your hands onto something hard, cool, and damp.

While you hold onto the rocky edge, you hear water dripping beside you. You can't see anything. There is no light anywhere. Just darkness. Even though it's good for your headache, you have this looming thought of confinement. You fight against hysteria.

You jar when he lifts you from the water's edge. You continue to shiver uncontrollably now on the cave floor. You pull into yourself and rub your saturated arms. It does little.

"Wait here."

You don't even have the strength to ask where he's going. You zip your vest, stuff your hands into your pockets, and kneel to conserve body heat. It's eerily quiet, with the exception of water dripping from you and from inside the cave. The sense of being completely alone alarms you. It's pitch-black. You can't even see your nose. If something were to attack you, you'd never see it coming. How long is Marc going to be gone?

You involuntarily jerk when you hear a snap.

"It's just me," you hear Marc's rich voice say.

You have a sense of relief mixed with annoyance as you digest his words. "You can see in the dark?"

"Yes."

A spark catches your eye. It's followed by a few more before Marc has a small flame going. You watch, memorized, as he moves the flame to a larger pile of wood. The cave illuminates. You felt so closed in, faced only with the dark. Now you can see the interior of the cave. It spans only about fifteen feet wide and ten feet long.

You huddle closer to the fire, reach out with your hands, and absorb the warmth, grateful. It registers later that you are looking at a fire pit surrounded by rocks. No way this is natural or the first fire burned in it.

"How did you know this was here?"

"I made it." He steps far back.

"Why?"

"For the solitude. No one knows about this place, so you are safe here for the time being." He leans up against the slick rock wall as far away as he can go.

"Okay, well, you've helped me to escape, so your services are no longer needed or wanted."

"You're not out of the woods yet."

"I can take care of myself."

"Can you?" he provokes.

"I'm perfectly capable." You shoot up to your feet. The cave room spins. You realize too late you've made a critical error with the fast movement and feel yourself falling.

"You should get some rest." He appears, catching you.

"Don't tell me what to do." You push away from him, wince at the sharp pain in your head, and place a hand against your forehead.

"It was merely a suggestion." He walks away.

"Did you kill my friend?" You drop your hand.

He pauses mid-step before resuming without looking back. "Yes."

"I hate you."

"Good," he utters in his robotic voice and slips through a narrow entryway camouflaged with the rocks.

You're glad he's out of sight. You hate being anywhere near him. You want to jump back into the water and swim away while you have the chance, but you know something is seriously wrong. You just have to endure being in his presence a little longer until your head stops pounding. Right now, the only thing you can do is close your eyes and hope this is all just a nightmare you have yet to wake up from.

You curl back into a ball on your side, next to the fire. Despite the heat radiating from the flames, you still feel cold to the bone. You fight against tears that threaten to surface as you think about Camille. How you failed her. She had her whole life ahead of her, and it's gone because of you. You think about your mother and how you failed her, too.

You wonder about Vince. You hate that the last encounter you had with him was an unpleasant one. Will you ever see him again? All this madness over some stupid birthmark. You are no one special. What is there even left worth fighting for? Nothing and no one. Maybe you should have just stayed and let yourself be executed.

Darkness seeps its way back into your vision. You don't want to surrender to it again, but you don't want to be lost in all your somber thoughts, either. Your head still aches. At least, in sleep, you won't feel all the pain.

Your eyes snap open. You had almost completely drifted off, but something put you on alert. You listen keenly. Soggy footsteps walk away from you. You turn toward the fire and stretch your neck out past the flames. You catch the backside of Marc before he disappears. What has he been doing? And why did he come close to you?

You reach up and feel around your neck for any bite wounds. You sit up. When you feel nothing on your neck, you start checking your wrists and arms. You come up short and stare back over the fire, perplexed. What was he doing here?

You look around until your eyes zero in on a stump makeshift cup with a deep hole in the center, placed to the left of you. Cautiously, you pick it up and look down into it. It's filled with water.

You bring it up to your nose and sniff it. The only thing you can detect is a musty, earthy smell from the wet wood. Awareness enters your mind of how sandpaper-like your lips and tongue feel. Your energy is depleted. You debate whether to drink the water. In the end, you are too exhausted to think it through, and you sip it. You feel the cold liquid travel down to your hollow belly. It demands more. Other than the woody taste, you don't distinguish anything else mixed in the water. You gulp the rest down and instantly feel a bit rejuvenated.

You settle back down and close your eyes. This time, it doesn't take long before you succumb to sleep.

Chapter 31

When your eyes flick open, you find that the embers are burning low. The light inside is dim. You blink the sleep away several times and wait for the fogginess to clear from your mind. You bolt upright. A tall figure lingers across from you in the shadows.

"Relax."

The voice sounds familiar as recollection strikes.

Marc.

"Why are you still here?" you demand.

"You're still not out of harm's way." He pushes off from the rock wall and heads over to the water.

"I told you I can take care of myself."

He says nothing as he steps off the ledge and into the water with a splash. You frown. You don't know what to make of him, but you don't take time to dwell on it as you sit up straight and feel the effects of sleeping on a cave floor. You stretch your neck all around before noticing the wooden cup is refilled with fresh water. You're instantly annoyed. You want to refuse to drink it, but it's a necessity. You have no idea when you will have another chance to revive yourself.

You gulp the water and shudder at the chill spreading throughout your entire body. The fire is still warm but doesn't provide as much heat. You're now aware of how cold and damp of a place you're in.

You stand and cross your arms against your chest, hovering as close to the fire as possible without getting burned. Your eyes survey the interior. There is nothing remarkable here. No cave paintings. No tunnels to explore. It's just rocks upon more rocks. You jolt at the sound of the surface water breaking.

"It's clear." Marc pulls himself out before approaching the fire and stomping it out, putting you into complete darkness again. Your heartbeat picks up the pace. You are not afraid of the dark, but this is too dark. He gave you no time to object.

You instinctively pull away when his hand brushes your arm, and you stumble to find your footing. You are ready to put up a fight, but when you look around, you can't see anything. You have nowhere to go in complete blackness. You breathe rapidly.

"You want to get out of here or stay in the dark?"

You follow the direction of his voice, but everything's so dark, you can't even see his figure. You sigh, dropping your head as your breathing slows. You tense when his hand gently closes around your left upper arm. This time, you don't put up a fight. This time, you let him lead you through the dark.

"Jump."

You gasp, realizing where he has led you. The water's edge. You don't want to get back into the freezing water. You're already cold.

"The sun is out. You'll warm up," he reassures as if he can read your mind. "Now jump."

You push off and slam into icy daggers. It takes your breath away. The shivers immediately begin as you tread water.

"Deep breath."

He gives you no time to protest. No time to think anything through. He just takes charge. Once again, he guides you through the crevice and under the waterfall before you break the surface. Sunlight greets you. You are quick to drop your head and shield your eyes with your arm. You peek over your arm and squint at the light before touching your forehead. Your pounding headache isn't pounding anymore. You have no headache at all. You close your eyes, tilt your head, and embrace the warmth as it helps to chase away the shaking.

You hear Marc strut past you, and you watch as he heads for shore. You cross your arms and follow. You stumble a few times along the way but manage to keep upright. You walk onto the luscious grass as Marc removes his blazer and wrings out the excess water. You mimic by squeezing the water out of your hair and moving down to your shirt. You stop and sneak a glance. He's not paying you any attention while he bunches up the bottom of his shirt. You see a white line, about an inch long, protruding from the skin of his side.

You make a mad dash and slip into the tree line. The forest is already becoming thick with new life as you push through thorny vines that snag your clothing. You don't care, and you keep pushing on. Without warning, your feet leave the forest floor.

"Put me down!" you shout in his face and squirm.

"Where exactly do you think you're going?" His hold remains firm.

"Away from you!"

"You won't last an hour on your own."

"I'm capable of lasting longer than you think. Now, let go!" You pierce his eyes with fury.

"If you insist." He drops his hand from under your legs.

You gasp as your legs buckle beneath you and you fall to your butt on the ground.

"You did that on purpose!" You lurch to your feet and point a finger in his face.

"I only did what you asked." He doesn't blink.

You release a loud huff before storming off.

"I'm curious. Do you have any idea where you're going?" he calls after you.

You ignore him and continue walking.

"You should know you are walking straight into the hands of the enemy." You pause before steering right. "I advise against that direction as well."

"Is there a direction you do approve of, Mr. Know-It-All?" You ball your hands into fists with annoyance.

"North."

You turn and glare. Without a compass, you have no idea which way true north is, and he knows it as he nods to the left. Your eyes dart beyond him. Calculating it, you realize the trail leads toward the waterfall, which also means it would incline significantly. You stifle back a laugh before continuing in the opposite direction.

"There's nothing for you that way."

"And what exactly is there for me north?" You whirl back.

"A safe place for you."

"You expect me to believe you?"

"You can believe what you want, but you asked me to help you escape, so that's what I'm doing."

You study him intently. You hate admitting even to yourself that your chance of survival is far less than likely on your own. You have no idea where you are or where the enemy lies. Your hearing and sight aren't as keen as his or any other vampire's. You're the prey, and they are the hunters. You would be a fool to walk blindly into the unknown when every corner could be met with a deadly consequence. Like it or not, you're stuck with him.

"Fine, but I'll walk on my own two feet." You stomp with purpose, past him and through brush and branches. You look for a clearer path. Only the path gets denser and rockier as you hold onto trees to keep you steady.

It's quiet. Too quiet. You don't want to look back, but the sensation to do just that nags. Casually, you toss your head over your shoulder and sneak a peek before swiveling all around, only to discover you are alone. You vaguely wonder where he went, but at the same time, you're glad to be rid of him. You suspect he's still somewhere close. It's clear he has an agenda. Wherever he wants to take you, you hope it's not too long a journey. The sooner you can be rid of him, the better.

You're exhausted trekking uphill and finally crest the top of the slope that runs parallel to the distant waterfall. You are still close enough to hear the soothing sound of rushing water. You sink to the ground. You're no longer cold and wet. Now you are hot and sweaty with your long sleeves rolled back.

You were half expecting to be greeted by his snarky attitude and blank face, but he is still nowhere to be found. You sigh heavily. Not only are you tired, but you're also thirsty and hungry. You don't know how long it's been since the last time you ate anything. You feel depleted. Running on fumes now that you're not running on adrenaline, and you just exerted a lot of energy.

You push back up to your feet. Refuse to give up. You're out in the wilderness and can't hunt for anything, but you can at least scrounge for something edible. You're near a water source. Surely, there has to be something nearby you can nibble on.

You sweep your eyes over the green landscape. You're really not an expert on which plants are edible and which are poisonous. You never had to worry about how to survive out in the wild. Even when you went camping, you had packed resources.

Your eyes land on a holly bush. You resist a smirk as you approach slowly before plucking a berry off. You examine the cherry red berry, contemplating.

"I advise you not to eat that." Marc's voice materializes several feet from your front left.

"I knew it! I knew you were lurking around here somewhere." You throw the berry to the ground.

"Aren't you perceptive?" He reveals himself. "Hungry?"

"No." Your stomach growls.

"Follow me," he beckons.

You want to refuse, but your feet end up betraying you. You step over a fallen tree, across the tree line, toward the water. You note a small fire burning with two small fish skinned and skewered on a stick, cooking. The stump cup sits on the ground, filled with water once more. He picks up the stick and hands it over.

"How do I know you didn't poison them?" You stand unmoving.

"You don't." He half shrugs.

You scowl for countless seconds until your stomach growls loudly again. You pluck the stick from his outstretched hand and sit on the log by the fire, inspecting every inch. You eye him warily. His back is towards you as he stands by the water's edge with a brown stick rolling between his teeth.

You tear off a small chunk, sniff it, admire the contents some more, and then plop it into your mouth. Your mouth waters at the delicacy of the meal. You don't detect a foul taste, so you quickly devour the first fish. You marvel in bliss before moving on to the second one. You eat every last bite down to the bone. You have no idea when you might get another meal. You reach down, grab the cup, and drain the contents. The small meal is enough to satisfy you, for now.

"Finished?" He appears like clockwork the second you're done.

"Obviously, you already know, or you wouldn't be in my face."

He stomps down on the burning embers, kicks away the stones, and pushes a bunch of dirt onto the area as if there had never been a fire. He picks up the sticks the fish were skewered on, breaks them into two, and tosses them into the water. "Time to go."

You place the cup back on the ground, stand, and put your hands on your hips. "Why are you helping me?"

"You asked me to."

"Why are you still helping me?" you rephrase.

"As long as you remain alive, fear will keep him at bay," he states in his monotone.

"From what?"

"Have you ever heard of Vlad the Impaler?"

"Huh?" The corner of your lips pulls up.

"How about Dracula?"

A half laugh manages to escape. "Who hasn't?"

"It's rumored Dracula was inspired by Vlad III, also known as Vlad the Impaler."

"And why is this relevant?"

"Vladimir believes he's a descendant of Vlad the Impaler, who had the reputation of impaling his enemies." His slender nose crinkles ever so slightly. "The sadistic things he did inspired Vladimir to be ruthless and despicable. His reign needs to end."

Despite the warmth of the sun, a chill runs up the course of your spine. You don't even want to imagine the horrendous things Vladimir has done over time. What was he planning for you? You doubt a simple death in front of a live audience. "I'm just a nobody. I just happen to have an odd birthmark that resembles the symbol from some prophecy. I'm not destined to do anything. I'm only human."

"I'm not here to convince you otherwise. What I do know is, since the prophecy was written, no one has ever found anyone bearing the mark until now."

You look away.

"We need to move." He swiftly sweeps you off your feet before you're the wiser.

"Put me down," you state through clenched teeth.

"Not this time." He doesn't blink as his dull eyes penetrate yours. "We've already wasted enough of our head start."

Your glare wavers. "Fine, but let's get a few things straightened out." You narrow your eyes. "First, my blood is my blood. You will not take a drop of it."

"And?" he presses, still without blinking.

"Don't ever try to manipulate my mind. Are we clear?"

"What makes you think you are in a position to make demands?" His head tilts.

"I'm the chosen one. Obviously, you need me for something."

"I have no desire to do either one, chosen one," he counters with a blink before sprinting off at a high rate of speed.

Chapter 32

Everything is a blur. No telling which way is up or down, or even sideways. Everything collides in chaos. You can't even tell if the sun is still up or the moon. You try to focus on the songbirds, but it's just a bunch of jumbled whistling.

"Are you ever going to put me down?" you complain when you can't take it anymore.

You don't get a response or a break in the fast momentum. You have never experienced motion sickness before, but you sure can relate to the feeling of it now. The only thing you can do is close your eyes and focus on not bringing the fish you ate back up.

You have no idea how long it's been when he finally slows. You peek an eye open and can see the trees and sky plainly. "Finally."

"You weren't enjoying the view?"

"What view? It was all distorted. Would you put me down now?"

"Whatever the chosen one wants," he mocks, dropping his arm.

You gasp as your feet drop to the ground. You're not quite prepared to bear your own weight. You reach out and grab onto the closest thing to steady yourself.

Marc.

You find yourself clinging to his forearm in a death grip. When you realize what you're holding onto, you stumble back.

"Jerk." You throw a jab at his face.

"That won't end well for you." He catches your wrist delicately.

You storm off before walking directly into a spider web. You claw at your face, grumbling with annoyance, and stop dead. You just put on a show for Marc. You look over, and for the first time, you see a minor expression cross his face, a smirk. With that smirk, a dimple slightly caves in on his left cheek. Before you have a chance to say anything, he slips away.

You mutter under your breath and march in the complete opposite direction. You pause at a thick bush and look around the whole area, listening keenly. You step behind the bush and take care of business before you continue.

The trees become sparse and thin out. You stop at the edge when you see an open valley with your mouth slightly open. A majestic sight of many colors ranging from buttercup yellow to carrot orange to lilac purple to, of course, shamrock green. Everything around you stops as you take in the open, tranquil, and inviting space. With or without you, time does not stand still. It moves on. The sun is low, magnifying the sky with pink and orange hues, like a fire lighting up the sky. Several hours must have elapsed.

"What's wrong?" Marc's voice whispers parallel to you.

You are transported back to reality. You crane your neck, prepared to spout off, but hold back. You see genuine concern masked behind his eyes.

"Nothing." You flick your eyes back to the landscape. An untamed land.

"I found you something to eat." He resumes a robotic tone.

You look back at him. The regard in his eyes has glazed over. He nods before turning. You follow without argument. A large chunk of meat is cooking over a small fire. It's bigger than the two fish combined. You're not sure if you want to know what animal it belonged to. The shape isn't complete, so there's no way of knowing unless you ask. You're not a big meat-eater. You're not completely vegan or vegetarian, either. You have mixed feelings. You feel guilty some poor animal's life had to end in order for you to survive.

"This needs a few more minutes." He turns the meat to cook on the other side. "In the meantime, you can start on the chicory."

Your gaze follows his toward a stump with some purple flower petals lying on top. "You want me to eat flowers?"

"They're edible."

"Or poisonous."

"Makes perfect sense to save your life just to poison you." He walks off.

You stare after him. You're sarcastic yourself. A way to say what's on your mind, in a joking manner, that others are none the wiser of, when most of the time, it's truth. You're not accustomed to someone giving back a taste of your own medicine.

You grab a petal and continue to stand. It feels good to be on your feet. You inspect the petal. You remember reading somewhere that dandelions are edible plants, but you never tried them, even though they sprout up in your back yard. Beggars can't be choosers. An all-meat diet isn't going to provide you with some of the vitamins and minerals that plants can.

You take a nibble off the petal. You are surprised at the taste. A bit nutty along with woody. After a minute, you take another bite.

"So, what's north?" You fall in line with him, biting into a second petal.

"You'll find out when you get there." He stands up straight from leaning against a tree.

"Why can't you tell me now?"

"When you need to know, I'll tell you," he dismisses. "The meat should be ready." He retreats to the fire and removes the stick.

"So, how far do we have to go?" you press.

"Miles."

You inhale deeply and let it release just as fast before grabbing the stick. He's a hard egg to crack. Annoyed, you walk back to the open field and lean against a medium-width tree. You still don't understand why he is continuing to help you. Don't know why he is being so mysterious about where he's taking you. There's a part of you that whispers he poses no threat, but you still can't trust him fully. He's hiding something from you – something you most likely won't like, which is why he is keeping it from you. What does he have planned? You know nothing about him. The only thing you know for sure is that he killed your best friend without hesitation. Something you can never forgive him for or forget. Only you're going to have to try a different tactic. Find a way to get him to slip up.

"There's about an hour of daylight left. You want to stand and eat or walk for a bit?"

"What do you think?" You give him the side-eye.

"Walk it is, then." He gestures with his left hand, offering you to take the lead.

You walk gradually, keeping to the tree line, tearing off pieces of meat. Your mouth salivates. You have no idea what you're eating, but it's good. Supposedly, everything tastes like chicken, so you just focus on that, even though you know there is no way this is chicken you're eating. The only thing that matters is it will sustain your needs mixed with the chicory.

He trails you. It feels nice to be able to walk on your own instead of being carried. You absolutely hate it. Hate being that close to him. Forced to wear his scent on you. Being on edge the whole time. You still have no clue where you are. Obviously, not close to civilization.

Your mind wanders to Vince. If only you could tell him you were okay. Hope he isn't foolish enough to try to come after you. He would be outnumbered. He wouldn't exactly be welcomed back with open arms. You hate that you hurt him. Hate being put into that position in the first place. You wonder if you'll ever see him again.

You pause when you spy a doe grazing with her fawn. You don't want to make a noise that will spook them from their meal, so you settle on watching them as you finish what remains of your meal. You notice how guarded the mother is as she lifts her head, surveying all directions as her fawn happily munches away without a care.

The doe whips her head and stares directly at you. Her tail swishes in rapid succession before she flees with her fawn closely beside her.

"It was my presence she sensed, not yours," Marc utters.

You turn and meet his dull green eyes. How did he know what you were thinking? He knows nothing about you, yet it's as if he can read you.

"I'm done." You hand him the stick.

He takes it and buries it.

Light fades with every step you take. It's starting to get harder to see even ground to place your feet on now that you are on thicker terrain. You're not ready to stop walking. Not ready to be carried in his arms again. You know your time has pretty much expired. You're honestly shocked you had this long. You've been trying to think of something casual to ask, but you're also guarded. Getting to know him is the last thing you want to do. It's easier not to peel back layers. Only you have no idea how long you are going to be stuck with him. You are growing impatient and want answers sooner, not later.

Chapter 33

Your eyes open to a navy-blue sky. You hear the wind whistling through the trees and see the trees above swaying. They are moving, but you're not. Awareness enters your foggy mind that you are no longer in Marc's arms. You push yourself up and something falls from your upper body.

Marc's blazer.

You stare at it. A moment of numbness overtakes you until you feel a drop in your body temperature. With a sigh, you slip it on. You pat the ground with your hands, feeling little needles on the forest floor. The trees above you must be pines.

You stand, realizing you're on elevated ground. The large boulder behind you reduces the wind blowing against you.

Where are you? And where is Marc?

He ran for hours and hours in the dark. You hadn't been tired when he first started, but there was nothing for you to do while he ran at full speed. Eventually, you nodded off, regaining consciousness a few times to no change…until now.

You manage to take a few steps before tripping over rocky, uneven ground. Blinded by the night, you retreat to the boulder and sit with your arms wrapped around your knees. You are going to have to wait for Marc to come back or for daylight. Whichever comes first.

"Good, you're awake."

You tilt your head at the sound of his voice, which has a little pep, and see the outline of his form surface on the rock above you.

"Come with me." He extends a hand.

"Are you going to throw me off a cliff?" you quip with unease.

"Yes, that's exactly what I've got planned for you," he mocks.

"You're aggravating." You stand and cross your arms against your chest.

"You're not exactly a peach yourself."

Your mouth drops. The nerve of him! "If I'm such a burden, then leave. No one is making you stay."

He sighs as he jumps down. "I'm not going to throw you off a cliff."

You believe him despite not wanting to. There's an earnestness in his tone. It's hard to admit, but you didn't really doubt him in the first place.

"Fine." You relax your arms and roll your eyes.

A gasp escapes as he lifts you and leaps higher upon the large rocks. You know you're at a high altitude, but you're shocked to see you are near the peak of a mountain.

"You're not afraid of heights, are you?"

"A bit late to ask that, don't you think?" You glare.

"I won't let you fall." You feel his eyes on you despite it being hard to truly see them in the dark.

"No, I'm not afraid of heights." You look away.

"Good." He sets you down on the end of a rock that's not too close to the edge of the mountaintop. There's a smooth rock surface right below your feet.

The wind is stronger now that you are out in the open, and it carries a chill. You have no idea why he brought you up here.

"Here, drink this." He hands you a cup formed out of a rock, warm to the touch.

"What is it?"

"Pine needle tea."

"How do you know how to make tea from pine needles?"

"Just something I picked up along the way." He shrugs. "And no, it's not poisonous. It will provide you with some antioxidants." He moves away.

You bring the cup to your nose and sniff. All you smell is a crisp, spicy aroma. You take a small sip. It tastes bitter, but it warms your insides, so you take another and peer over the cup at his backside. He's staring out into the bleak night. Why did he bring you up here? You divert your gaze and watch for several minutes until an orange glow bursts forth from below the skyline.

Sunrise.

"Even on the darkest of nights, the sun still rises," he utters softly.

You watch, captivated. You've never had a chance to witness with your own eyes the first rays of sunlight in the early morning dawn, unobstructed.

Time stands still while inch by inch, the sun ascends. In this moment, all that matters is watching a new dawn rise. All your worries take a back seat, a time out. You feel free. Able to embrace the wonder of it all as warmth cuts against the cool night air.

"Hungry?"

You look down to your left. When did he leave? You never saw him move, and he was in your line of sight. You nod and slide down the rock. He leads you to a rock with a deep hole cut into the center, filled with, you presume, mushroom soup, along with a wooden spoon. You pick it up from ground level and take a cautious bite. It's not lukewarm but not burning hot, either.

"So, your name is Marc?" you ask his back before taking another bite.

"Yes." He turns to face you with an arched eyebrow and pockets a brown stick.

"Is that your given name or a shortened version of something else?" You slurp from the spoon.

"Marcus."

You take another bite. "Marcus?"

"Why do you want to know?"

"I don't." You shrug. "Just filling the awkward silence, I guess."

"Calderon, and I prefer Marc."

You wait several beats as silence fills the void before he turns away again and removes the brown stick from his pocket. "Would you like to know my name?"

"If you feel it's essential for me to know, by all means."

A flash of anger crosses you at his callousness. You stab the soup with your wooden spoon. "It's Nadine. Nadine Drexel, and I prefer Nadine." You jerk your head up. You shouldn't be forthright, but that's what he probably expected from you.

He tosses a glance with arched eyebrows and creased lines on his forehead, surprised you actually answered.

You can't help but smirk a little. "So, how do you know how to do all this?" You raise the cup of soup.

"Boy Scouts." He slips the brown stick back into his pocket once more, leans up against the tree to face you, and crosses his arms.

"The Boy Scouts taught you how to make pine needle tea?" That seems a bit sophisticated.

"My one counselor did. He taught me a great deal of things."

You say nothing as you see a faraway glance in his eyes. To a time when life was less complicated. A time of innocence.

When you finish your soup, you notice the shape of the inside of the bowl is a bit jagged, almost as if a fist punched through it.

"So, you want to climb down this mountain or take the scenic route?"

"Umm." You glance at the difficult terrain. Without proper gear, you're not equipped to climb down. Only you're not sure you are fond of the other choice.

"It will be over before you know it." He scoops you up before you hang suspended in the air.

He doesn't give you a chance to utter another word as he springs to some high rocks until you are overlooking the edge of the mountaintop. Then he jumps. You may not have a fear of heights, but tumbling down a mountain makes you a bit anxious. You close your eyes tightly and lean into him.

"We're down."

You open one eye and see green at his feet before popping your other eye open and tilting your head back. You are indeed on ground level from the mountain. You stiffen when you realize your right arm is wrapped around his neck, your left hand is clasped tightly around his shirt, and your head is buried in the crook of his neck. Too close for comfort. Way too close.

"Are you trying to give me a heart attack?" You shove away from him and shake out your hand, which has gone numb.

"Guess it didn't work," he taunts.

"Release me," you demand.

"Whatever the lady wants."

You remember what to expect just before he removes his arm. You brace for impact and land upright on your feet without the need for stability. "Ha. Didn't drop me this time, did you?"

"Appears you've learned how to stand upright on your own two feet."

"You're antagonizing me." You pivot away, take a step, and smash into something soft. When you lift your foot, you discover that you stepped into a pile of clumped pellet scat.

You whirl on him and hesitate. There it is again, a smirk on his face. With that partial grin, a small amount of lightness appears in his olive-green eyes. Something you sense he hasn't been able to feel in a long time. You're not really amused it's at your expense.

With a snort, you rip his blazer off and fling it at his face before walking away with purpose. You have no idea if you are heading in the right direction, but you don't care, and he doesn't say another word. As you continue down the heavily trampled path, you comprehend that you're on a game trail. You should be concerned about predators, but you do have the most dangerous predator tailing you. One whiff of Marc would send all the other predators and prey running.

You listen to the morning songs of the birds. They are happy and thriving with life. You feel at peace here. Just you and nature. There is no rushing against time. Upholding commitments. The only thing to do here is survive to see another day.

"There's a mulberry tree to your left." His voice startles you from your trance.

You survey the area. Generally, it all looks the same. You have no idea how long you've been walking, but from the position of the sun in the sky, you can tell it's been a few hours. Your legs feel achy. It's been a while since you've had an opportunity to do some extensive walking. It feels liberating.

"You can fill up on some dark berries until I return."

"Where are you going?" You frown.

He doesn't respond as he disappears into the foliage.

"Really?"

You sigh before stepping over to the bush and examining the color of the berries. Most are a light shade of color, but there are some that are deeper purplish-black. Considering it is early in the season, it makes sense not too many would be ripe.

You pull off a berry and pop it into your mouth. You've never eaten a mulberry before. It resembles a blackberry and has a mixed taste of sweetness and tartness.

Chapter 34

You've eaten a small handful when you hear a rustling coming from the game trail ahead. A part of you thinks it's odd Marc somehow got ahead of you, but you dismiss it as you grab another berry. You stop mid-chew when you hear heavy breathing.

"Seriously?" you grumble to yourself after swallowing.

You crane your neck around the tree limbs and freeze when you see a black bear heading in your direction on the prowl for food. You're standing at his food source.

Slowly, you begin to back away. Oblivious, the bear has not picked up Marc's scent, which means Marc isn't close by. You are on your own. You have to remain calm.

The small steps you take backward do not account for the large steps the bear takes forward. He's closing in on you as his nose seeks out the aroma of the berries. So far, it seems he hasn't picked up on your scent yet.

A twig snaps under your foot. You stand perfectly still. The bear turns his attention to you and lets out three short growls. You startled him. Now, he's assessing the situation, just as you are. He rears up on his hind legs to tower over you and lets out an angry roar.

"Marc!" you yelp before sprinting off.

You panic. You know running is probably the worst thing you can do, but that doesn't stop you from flight mode. No way you're equipped to fight off a bear.

You feel the earth vibrate beneath you. The bear is in pursuit of you. Even though you know there is no way you are going to outrun him, you put on a burst of speed anyway. Your right ankle twists on something loose before you collapse. You twist around and see the bear charging. You feel his hot breath blow against your face as his huge paw rises. He is nearly on top of you. You have no time to react. The irony. To be hunted by vampires but killed by a bear.

The bear halts. There's a shift in his body language. He huffs with alarm before he retreats. You recognize the same emotion mirrored in your own eyes. Fear.

He looked above you before running off. You tip back your head and see Marc standing there with dilated eyes and teeth lengthened with a bit of blood streaked down from his lower lip. He looks horrifying.

"Can't leave you alone for five minutes without trouble finding you," he taunts, resuming his normal expression as he wipes the blood away.

"Was that some kind of sick joke?" Anger blazes behind your eyes.

"I wouldn't do that." He frowns.

"You expect me to believe you?"

"I don't expect anything." His sigh has despondency in it.

He sounds sincere. Irritated, you lurch to your feet. You wince at the sharp pain in your right ankle when you put pressure on it.

"You're hurt?" He goes on alert.

"I'm fine." You wave him off, take a step, and wince again.

"Let me look." In a flash, he lifts you, places you on a log, and begins examining your ankle.

"You don't need to do that." You sharply inhale when he touches the tender side.

"It's not broken. Can you wiggle your toes?"

You wiggle your toes in your shoe to humor him. You sense he won't stop fussing until you convince him otherwise. "Yeah."

"How about moving in a circular motion?"

You move it up and down, and then in a circle. "See? It's fine. I just need to walk it off."

"It could be sprained. It's better to keep weight off it." He picks you back up.

"Of course," you sigh, unamused.

You fold your hands in your lap with your head bowed. It takes you a minute to realize he is walking at a human pace and not his typical warp speed. Confused, you glance up. His eyes are focused on the path ahead, but there appears to be something more beyond them. Is he upset?

"Do you ever rest?" you break the silence.

His eyes briefly flick down. "Vampires don't need rest unless severely wounded."

"How long can you go without blood?"

"Don't worry about that. I promised not to take a drop of your unappealing blood."

"That's not why I was asking." You shake your head.

He locks eyes with you.

You break the contact, feeling unnerved again. "How long have you been a vampire?" You gloss over the uncomfortable moment.

"What's with all the questions?" he snaps.

Obviously, you touched on a sore subject. For a fleeting second, you saw something beyond Marc's empty eyes. Pain. A history he wants to leave in the past. You find you can empathize with that.

"I don't want to become a vampire," you confess in a whisper.

He stops. "Who said you had to become a vampire?" he asks, a bit prickly.

You look up, shocked.

"Nowhere in the prophecy does it state you'd have to turn in order to defeat him."

"Bet it doesn't say how I would either," you fire back.

He doesn't answer as he moves on.

"So, where exactly are we, anyway?"

"Monongahela National Forest."

You shudder. He has to have run hundreds of miles by now. Yet, you're closer to home than you like knowing, even if it is a state away. Was Vladimir's lair close to your back yard? Why did Vince never tell you? Did you really have to ask that question? He obviously was sparing you from the anxiety.

Gently, Marc sets you down on a stump. Lost in thought, you're unaware that the sunlight has faded between the gaps in the trees. Unaware of the dark clouds gathering. Now, you feel a shift in the atmosphere. The temperature has dropped, and you can smell moisture in the air. A storm is coming.

"What are you doing?" You look up and see Marc snapping off some long, thick branches in a tree and letting them drop to the ground.

"Making you a shelter before the storm hits."

"Is there anything I can do to help?" You grimace at the slight twinge in your ankle.

"Stay off your ankle." He meets your eyes with bafflement.

"What?" You cock your head to the side.

"Nothing." He jumps down.

Why has offering to help mystified him? Of course, you don't possess the same strength he does, but there must be something you can do to help.

You gauge the area. There are some low-hanging thin branches splayed out with an abundance of leaves. They could make a roof. You take it slowly, walking over to them, twisting, and bending them until they snap off.

"What are you doing? I thought I told you to stay off your ankle."

"I'm helping," you insist, reaching for another branch.

"I don't need those."

"And I'm not an invalid, so stop treating me like I am," you hit back.

He grumbles before lashing out at the closest thing to him.

"Be careful. Those have thorns," you declare.

"I told you, I have no desire to take an ounce of your blood." He rips away the thorny brush with force.

"You don't have to get mad at me."

He sighs. "I'm not mad at you."

"You don't have to be mad at yourself either."

"My wounds heal quickly. Remember, I am a vampire." He's quick to change the subject.

"So, how do you replenish yourself when we're in the middle of nowhere?"

He pauses a beat. "Animal blood."

"How does that work?"

He doesn't answer, as one-by-one, he thrusts the thick branches into the ground next to a thick-based tree, constructing the shelter in the form of a triangle. Next, he gathers some dead leaves, dried grass, and moss, tossing them on the outside of the structure before laying lush shrubs over the material. Just as he is finishing the final touches, the wind whips up, along with the first fat drops of rain.

"It's done. You can wait out the storm in there." Marc nods.

You approach slowly and hesitate when you find yourself next to him. You are at a loss for words. You duck under and press your back against the base of the tree, wrapping your arms around your legs. You wait for him to follow, but only hear feet shifting away. "Where are you going?" You crawl back to the front.

He fails to answer.

Frustrated, you tail him. "You don't have to stay out here and get wet. There's plenty of room for both of us."

He jolts as the brown stick between his lips drops. "I'm fine here. Now go back before you get drenched."

"Not without you."

"You need the extra room to elevate that ankle." He points.

"Would you quit blaming yourself for that? My ankle's fine." A low rumble of thunder overhead.

"I left you alone for too long." He shakes his head.

"You got there in time. I wasn't seriously hurt. All I did was overextend my ankle. Nothing permanent." You study him.

"Would you please go back to the shelter?" His eyes beg as the rain picks up.

"Only if you come with me."

His eyes drop, and he shakes his head again.

You walk forward, reach down, and pick up the brown stick. "Why do you chew on cinnamon sticks?"

He looks at your hand and partially shrugs. "Habit."

"Like a stress reliever?"

His eyes are drawn to yours. A clap of thunder startles you. The storm is intensifying. "Please, go back to the shelter."

You look at the sky. "Was that loud to your ears?"

"No. I can control how much my hearing is amplified. Right now, it's about the same as yours. Now, would you please go before you get soaked?"

"Why are you being so stubborn?" You step closer.

"Why are you?" He glares back.

"Where are you taking me? I have the right to know." The rain picks up. The leaves are thoroughly drenched now and spilling water down to the forest floor.

"You'll find out soon enough." He stalks away.

"What did he do to you?" The trees sway above as you follow.

"Isn't it obvious?" he barks over his shoulder.

"How did he break you?"

"Get back into the shelter," he threatens with his grisly face. He wants to scare you. Only you're not intimidated.

You hear a loud crack. It didn't sound like thunder. You hardly have a chance to comprehend a large tree limb, at least the thickness of both your thighs, dropping at a high rate of speed aimed right at you. Your mind screams, but nothing escapes your lips. You know you should be running; however, your legs stand frozen. There isn't time. Your life is flashing right before your eyes in slow motion.

The world spins wildly as your back is plastered against concrete from the strong arms around your waist. A reverberating snap echoes merely inches from you. Only the limb does not crush you. You gasp as a heavy breath exhales next to your ear.

"You are more than I bargained for," he whispers.

Your eyes widen as you twist your head. "Marc, oh, my gosh, are you okay?"

"A tree branch harm a vampire?" He releases you.

"Oh, right." You drop your head, taking in the scene. It was a clean break. Meant for you.

"Now, would you go back to the shelter like I asked?" He points with authority.

You nod without further argument. Somehow, you manage to maintain your composure, even though you are trembling inside. You've faced vampires. You've faced a bear. But you've never felt so close to the brink of death.

You curl up into a ball on your side and just stare without really seeing. You thought you were going to die. You didn't want to die. You've barely had a chance to live. Even if you haven't figured your life out, you always assumed you would have plenty of time. Now, you hardly have time to plan for a future when it's all up in the air.

Chapter 35

You hear some rustling, but you're not motivated to go check it out. Shortly afterward, a hole opens from the side. You realize he's breaking down the shelter.

"The worst of the storm is over. We can move on," Marc states as he finishes breaking down the structure.

You say nothing as you stand and wait for him to finish. You glance around the area. Several medium and small branches are scattered over the forest floor. The largest snapped cleanly in half.

"Let's go."

You comply, following at a slow pace, stepping carefully.

"You're unusually quiet." He falls in line with you.

"I'm tired."

"Want me to take over?"

You nod.

Without a word, he has you in his arms, and the world becomes a blur. You close your eyes tightly to avoid seeing his. It's taking every ounce of strength you have not to fall apart.

The momentum of his speed relaxes you for a change. You could swear at one point, he splashes through water. Only you don't care. You keep your eyes shut.

At some point, you drift off. When you open your eyes, darkness swallows you. In a panic, you start to thrash around, afraid that, somehow, you've gone blind.

"Relax." His grip tightens on you.

The fog lifts from your mind as you realize it's twilight. You managed to sleep the rest of the day away.

He sits you down between two large exposed roots of an old-growth tree. Before he leaves, he places his blazer around your shoulders. You hear him in the immediate area. He brings back materials before starting a fire. Light illuminates.

You pull his blazer tight before wrapping your arms around your knees. He walks out of sight, but you hear him nearby, as well as a trickle from a nearby water source before some splashing. Several minutes pass before he returns, handing over a stump cup of water before placing a fish over the fire. You watch it cook. You're not really in the mood to eat.

"We can't stay here for long, so eat up. He walks away.

As soon as you finish what you can stomach, he puts out the fire and moves on into the night. You're glad it's dark. Glad you don't have to see his eyes. Glad the world is nothing but a blur.

The first thing you notice when you reawaken is that everything is still. You're lying in a bed of soft moss on the forest floor. Birds sing happily with a new dawn before a raspy caw invades. You push up, look around, and feel alone.

"Marc?" you call softly.

"Over here," his voice calls from your left, where he is concealed by a tree.

You rise to your feet and walk toward where his voice came from, and frown when you catch sight of him. He's leaning against a tree with his cinnamon stick in his mouth.

"What's going on?" You wrap his blazer tightly against you and cross your arms. You're not sure why you feel cold.

"We're close."

"To what?"

He drops the cinnamon stick and marches forward.

You stare at the stick with a frown before you follow. You feel uneasy and feed off his anxiety. Something has him agitated. Now more than ever, you dislike not knowing what he's keeping from you. You want to demand answers. You hate blindly following into the unknown.

The eastern sunrise makes the morning sky a kaleidoscope of warm colors as you approach an open field. The sunrise is just as vivid on ground level as it was up on the mountain. Only you dread what's to come next. The morning is alive, but you're muddled inside.

Marc turns just outside the tree line. His posture is stiff as he walks at a snail's pace. He keeps a watchful eye on the trees. What would frighten him?

"Release the girl."

A strong-built guy with broad shoulders appears from behind a tree about thirty yards down the line. He has slicked-back platinum hair, wears an odd, off-white, skin-tight suit, and has a scar over his left eye.

You eye him suspiciously, sticking close behind Marc. You assume whoever this guy is, he's the reason for Marc's apprehensive behavior.

"I come in peace," Marc declares, tipping up his hands low at his sides.

You grimace.

"With a human as your prisoner?" the guy's voice booms.

"She needs sanctuary."

"Release her then, unharmed."

"Go to him," Marc whispers without removing his eyes from the stranger.

"Who is he?" you ask in a whisper.

"Your protection."

"How exactly can he protect me?"

"He's more than what he seems."

"I will not ask kindly again," the guy rumbles with authority.

"What do you mean by that?"

Marc sighs. "He's a wolf."

"A wolf?" You reel your head back as you note the guy's huge biceps. He reminds you of some extremely athletic dude who spends his time at the gym as a sport. "Do you mean a werewolf?"

"Did you think all monsters only existed in fairy tales?"

You take a moment to process, scanning your memory on anything you know about werewolves from folklore. The stories always marked vampires and werewolves as enemies. All the myths about vampires were untrue, and yet seeds were buried within. Vince told you Immilla sought out the wolf who wanted revenge against Vladimir. Are you now facing that creature?

"What happens to you when I go?" you mutter.

"You'll be safe. Now go."

"This is your last chance," the man-wolf warns.

"I want your word no harm shall come to him once I leave his side." You step in line with Marc, a fire within rekindled.

"What are you doing?" Marc whispers, confounded.

"Well, this is an interesting turn of events." The man-wolf tilts his head.

"Your word." You fold your arms against your chest.

"Never have I witnessed a human coming to the defense of a vampire, unless…."

"Unless what?"

"He compelled you," he states simply.

"He didn't compel me," you protest.

"How can you be so sure?" He plants doubt.

You divert your gaze and ponder. You don't know Marc well. His alluring green eyes could make you do anything he wanted without you having a clue. That is the purpose of compulsion.

"I'm not being forced to do anything against my will." You're not going to allow this man-wolf to mess with your mind for one second. The only thing Marc has to gain is to keep your mouth shut from asking too many questions.

"You sound so certain, but I must confirm that with my own eyes."

"He can tell if I'm under compulsion just by looking into my eyes?" you whisper with a frown. You didn't see that one coming.

"I've heard stories but never saw it in the flesh," Marc answers.

"I won't leave his side until I have your word."

"And I can't give you my word until I see for myself. Seems we are at an impasse." The man-wolf tilts his head again.

"Then let us both leave unharmed."

"I can't allow that."

"Yes, you can. Just pretend you never saw us."

"You are an innocent. I make it my mission to protect the defenseless against vile and selfish creatures such as him." He inches closer.

"And how do I know I'll be protected in your hands, or should I say paws?" you fire back, positioning yourself in front of Marc.

"Offending him is not going to help," Marc mumbles.

"We do not feed on human blood."

"Then how about we come up with a compromise?" You sense the situation is about to unravel.

"I'm listening." The man-wolf raises a hand and strokes his chin with curiosity.

"I'll meet you halfway only when the members of your pack shows themselves."

His eyebrows pinch, seemingly impressed. "Very well," he whistles through his teeth.

One by one, seven men appear from the forest and stand in line behind him in the form of a 'V.'

"How do I know that's all of them?" you challenge.

"You don't, but he does." The man-wolf nods.

You angle your head so you can see Marc out of the corner of your eye for confirmation. He nods once. You search his eyes, looking for a sign not to go. There isn't one. You are at a stalemate. "You first." You meet the leader's eyes.

"Cautious. I respect that. Seems I underestimated you." He takes two long strides forward.

"You wouldn't be the first," you retort before whispering back at a slight angle, "I don't like this."

"Being outnumbered, there's no other option."

Chapter 36

You bite your lip before taking a hesitant step. Your mind is firing a mile a minute. There are too many scenarios that could go wrong. You might be safe with the wolves, but Marc clearly isn't. He is their natural enemy. Even though he is strong and fast, you have no idea what werewolves are truly capable of. These werewolves. You can only hope that the man-wolf keeps his word, and that you can come up with a compromise with Marc.

The man-wolf is the first to close half the distance. Your eyes are trained fiercely beyond him to each member of his pack. You honestly expected more. Any slight twitch or movement from any of them will make you retreat.

You stop four feet away, just out of arm's length. With a deep breath, he takes a step forward, his eyes bearing into yours. On guard, you monitor him closely while you try to keep tabs on any trouble from the others. You know you don't stand a chance against any of them. They may look human despite the odd skin-tight material in different shades, but you are now the wiser.

"You're not compelled," he says, shocked at the discovery.

"Just like I told you."

"You should be scared of him, but you're scared *for* him," he states in disbelief.

You swallow hard, shifting a foot back.

"But I cannot allow you to be in his company anymore." He swiftly reaches out and grabs your left arm with an iron grip.

"No!" you scream and try to pull back.

The next second plays out in slow motion as the pack reacts just as hastily. Four surround you and the leader in a protective circle. Two have shifted into wolves, and the other two stay as men while a pair of others have Marc pinned against a tree. The last pack member moves closer in his dark-brown pelt wolf form. Marc fails to fight back.

"Please, don't hurt him!" you plead, facing the leader.

"He's a soulless killer. He must be eliminated."

"A soulless killer wouldn't have saved my life," you fire back.

You see his eyes falter. "He's the enemy. He can't be trusted."

"I trust him," you declare.

He studies you, muddled. "I'm sorry, but I canb't." His eyes shift with a nod.

"No!" you yell, wrestling against his hold. You manage to rip yourself out of the blazer, escaping his loose grasp on the bunched-up sleeve.

"Stop her," he commands.

At once, the older guy standing at the head reacts, grabbing your arms with both hands. You fight hard, but the cause is hopeless. You lock eyes woefully with Marc. He still refuses to put up a fight, as if accepting his fate.

"I bear the Dragon's Eye mark." You pull your hair back to showcase, realizing you have one card left to play. "And if you want my cooperation, you will release him, now!"

Your eyes blaze into the older man before following his gaze to the leader with a nod of validation. What happens next is his move.

"You were protecting her?" the leader inquires with his dark-brown eyes cast upon Marc.

"Yes," Marc confirms.

"Interesting."

"Yes, there are a lot of interesting things. Now let him go," you snap.

His eyes shift to yours before to each of his men, and then he flicks his hand. You watch as the two men remove their hands from Marc and step away. The one in wolf form, however, pulls back his lip with disapproval.

"Caden," the leader warns with authority.

You tear from the older man's hold and sprint over. The dark-brown wolf cuts off your path and stares you down. You come to a halt, staring right back. He curls his lip with a low warning growl. You think about your next play and step to the left before tearing off in the opposite direction. The wolf, Caden, falls for your ploy and jumps toward the left, providing you enough time to pass him and insert yourself between him and Marc.

"Back off," you command as your eyes pierce his with intense fury, with your own lip curled.

He snorts with disgust before sauntering off.

"Impressive," the leader utters.

You ignore him as you survey the rest of them. They keep their distance. Slowly, you face Marc. "I guess this is where we part ways."

"That should make you happy. You finally get rid of me."

"What will you do now?"

"There's no need to concern yourself about me." He lifts his hand but drops it.

You look away to nothing in particular. "Thank you."

"For what?"

A deep-throated growl redirects your attention. The dark-brown wolf stalks the tree line. Another growl comes from your left, from a tawny wolf. Swiftly, Marc scoops you up and closes the gap to the leader, who is the only one still in human form. No one has to tell you what the cause of the alarm is: Vampires.

"Take her to safety," Marc says, holding you out to the man-wolf.

He shakes his head. "It's too close. They'll be able to pick up her scent. You take her for now. We'll distract them and come looking for her after."

Marc nods. A silent agreement passes between the two.

"Hang on." Marc glances at you as the leader shifts into his own white wolf form and howls.

You grab onto his shirt and lean your head against his chest before he takes off.

The world is a blur. Yet, you're lost as you try to process the events that just transpired and what they could mean. The more miles he runs, the more steam rises from your collar from your ireful thoughts.

"You're mad?"

His stride slows, and you glare at him through seething eyes. "You were going to leave me with a bunch of werewolves?"

"The only haven for you," he explains, setting you down gently.

"If I don't want to become a vampire, what made you think I'd want to become a wolf?"

He heaves a sigh. "That's not why I took you there."

"You knew you were risking your life, didn't you?"

"Why would you defend me?" he counters.

"You don't even know me."

"You're supposed to hate me," he states at the same time.

"Why would you do that?" You talk over him.

"I wasn't going to allow the same thing to happen to you that happened to me," Marc argues.

You soften. "You spared my life. It's only right that I spare yours."

He turns away. "There's one thing the wolf got right."

"Yeah, what's that?"

"You shouldn't trust a soulless monster."

"True monsters show no remorse."

You reach out and lightly touch his forearm. He yanks it back as if the touch burns him, and he moves away. "Did you forget I killed your friend?"

"No, I did not." You moisten your lips.

"Well, it seems like you have. That's something you should never forget," he advises before strutting away.

You sigh and look to the forest floor as your temper rises once more. "Don't you walk…."

He cuts you off, rushing back over and clamping a hand over your mouth before placing a finger against his lips. His eyes dart around the surrounding area before he grabs your upper arm and drags you to a nearby balsam fir. He moves some branches aside before nudging you. You're not keen on having to conceal yourself among the base of the tree, surrounded by an overpowering pine aroma, but you suspect that it will best mask your scent.

Your heartbeat kicks into overdrive. Concerned the fast rhythm will give away your location, you inhale deeply through your nose and exhale slowly out of your mouth. You close your eyes and focus on your breathing. Distant voices filter into your eardrums. You lower your head and try to peer between the needles of the fir. Whoever's approaching is not in the immediate vicinity, but their voices are slowly becoming more audible.

You close your eyes again and hold your breath. One voice is higher in pitch. The other is lower. They're becoming clearer, and one sounds familiar.

Chapter 37

You inhale sharply, snap your eyes open, and shove your way out of the pine branches into the open when you see his back.

"Vince!" you shout with joy as you run toward him.

"Nadine?" He whirls in disbelief.

You launch yourself into his arms and seek comfort. He squeezes tightly as if he will never let you go. You never thought you would see him again.

"Nad?"

Your eyes go wide as you tilt your head to the right. It isn't possible. How could it be?

"Camille?" You push back from Vince. "You turned her?"

"No." He shakes his head.

"I did." You turn toward the sound of Marc's robotic voice standing out in the open.

"He's the one who killed me!" Camille gasps.

"I'll show him no mercy." Vince gently moves you toward Camille.

You stand there, numb, staring at Marc, unable to find words.

Vince closes the gap and takes a swing, only Marc calmly sidesteps out of the way. With anger, Vince whirls and takes another swing, missing again before he hurtles into Marc and slams him onto the ground. He punches him again and again and again.

"Vince, don't!" You step forward.

"He deserves what he gets." Camille places a hand on your arm.

"He saved my life."

"He took mine."

The splintering of wood redirects your attention to see Vince shoved a distance away, crashing into a tree and bringing down several branches with him. As soon as his feet touch the ground, he charges back after Marc with a bellow.

"Vince, stop!" you shout.

Camille blocks your path.

"If you're not going to help me, stay out of my way." You duck around her and rush over.

You pause as Marc drops to his knees just as Vince bridges the gap. Vince strikes the ground like a bolt of lightning tumbling over his head.

"Stop!" you command as Vince hops back to his feet.

Only, he ignores you. He has tunnel vision. The only thing he has his mind and eyes set on is Marc as he stalks closer.

"Enough!" you shout, intercepting Vince.

"Get out of the way!" His eyes never waver as his arm lashes out.

You feel the breath knocked out of you as you hit the ground hard. You feel dazed.

"Nadine!" Camille exclaims and rushes to your side.

You try to remember how to breathe oxygen into your lungs. You manage to take a breath before you lift your head. You see Marc's stunned look before it changes to anger as Vince advances once more. Marc bends his knees and lowers his top half slightly before picking Vince off the ground, tossing him into the air, and slamming him down. Vince kicks out hard, and then he's on top of Marc. They begin to wrestle.

"Are you okay?" Camille asks frantically.

"I'm fine." You start to push yourself up.

"Maybe you should lie back down."

You ignore her as you look around the surrounding area. There has to be something you can do to get their full attention. To get them to stop. Your eyes land on a thick covering of brush. Brush with thorns. You waste no time rising to your feet, even though your body is sore and protesting.

"What are you doing?" Camille calls after you.

You don't respond. As soon as you get your body in sync with your mind, you rush over. When you get there, you pause. What you are planning to do is a huge risk, but it's the only solution at present to get Vince and Marc to stop fighting.

With a deep breath, you reach out, grasp the thorny vine in your right hand, and squeeze tightly. You bite your lip as the thorns rip your skin, and you watch the three puncture wounds seeping crimson on your hand.

You hold your hand up high, allowing the breeze to carry the scent of your blood. At once, Vince and Marc are at a standstill, with their attention directed onto you.

"What have you done?" Vince growls from on top of Marc.

"It was the only way to get you to stop," you bite out.

"Nadine." Camille's deep, shaky voice is one you have never heard before.

You look over and see Camille's horrendous face. A face you do not recognize. You know the risk you are exposing yourself to, but forget that Camille is new to being a vampire…an extremely thirsty one. Your friend is gone. In her place, an animal that lusts for blood. Your blood. Your mind screams for you to run. However, you just stand frozen as Camille races toward you lightning-fast. An impossible speed. There is no time to react. Just as she's on top of you, something collides with Camille as a body materializes, shielding you.

"Fight the urge. Don't think about the blood. Think about your friend, Camille." Vince wrestles with her as she squirms underneath.

"Get off me!" she shrieks.

"Not until you relax."

"Blood. I want blood."

"Cam?" You peer over Marc's shoulder.

"Stay back." He blocks your view.

"You're letting the blood have control. Fight the urge. Do not let it control you. I know you can do this," Vince urges.

Camille continues to wrestle.

"Focus. Look at me. Breathe. Remember what I taught you."

Camille continues to grapple a moment longer, until her eyes find Vince's blue gaze. Slowly, her body begins to relax. Her fangs are the last to turn back to normal. Camille gasps. "I almost killed her."

"But you didn't," Vince reassures.

"Only because you stopped me." She sniffs.

"Cam, it's okay." You step to the left of Marc, who quickly shoots up his arm.

"No, it's not okay." She sobs uncontrollably, and red tears stream down her face.

You feel helpless. You want to console your friend, but you're the problem in the first place. Instead, you watch as Vince gathers Camille into his arms, holding her tightly. The relationship has shifted. Camille doesn't loathe him anymore. The transition must have been hard on her, and the only person she had to lean on was Vince. Guilt rips through you.

"This is all your fault." Vince narrows his eyes with hatred onto Marc.

"Enough." You duck under Marc's arm. "He's not the only one responsible here."

"How can you stand to be in his presence after what he did to her?" His eyes flick down. "If you only knew all the other vile stuff he's done as Vladimir's right-hand man, you'd be repulsed."

"I wouldn't be standing here if it weren't for him."

"Don't be a fool, Nadine. You can't trust him."

"He's not the one who slammed me to the ground in a fit of rage." You fold your arms against your chest.

Vince opens his mouth to retort before closing it again as the realization sets in. He looks away, mortified.

You approach, kneel next to him, and place your left hand on his shoulder. "Like it or not, you are both on the same side when it concerns me."

Vince glares at Marc with disgust before softening his eyes. "Did I hurt you?"

"No." You shake your head once.

"Nadine, I'm so sorry." Camille pushes back from Vince.

"I know, I'm okay." You reach toward her.

Without warning, Camille jumps to her feet and backs up against a tree. You frown before looking down at your right hand. The aroma of fresh blood lingers in the air and was near Camille.

"Let's take care of this." Vince rips off the cuff of his sleeve and wraps the white material around your palm.

You have no words. You want to just give Camille a simple hug, but she looks like a cornered animal. One wrong move could set her off. You never had to tread lightly around her before. Now you have to.

"I'm going to help her overcome it. I promise you." He grasps your shoulders.

You fake a smile.

"I thought I lost you." Vince cups the side of your face with his left hand.

"I know." You eye his hand. It feels tepid.

"Don't mean to interrupt, but you all need to get out of here right now," Marc utters.

Vince's eyes narrow with revulsion at Marc before his posture stiffens.

"Not without you." You turn to Marc after interpreting his words.

"You don't need me anymore."

"Please, don't go," you whisper.

"Let him." Vince sweeps you possessively into his arms. "If he wants to help, he can be our decoy."

You don't feel right in his arms. It feels wrong. When he turns away, you look over his shoulder and seek out Marc. You plead with your eyes before he becomes too far away. There is no time to talk it out or make sense of anything. Now, he's just a distant memory.

"Why are we stopping?" Camille asks.

"We can't outrun them forever; they'll just follow the scent trail." Vince sets you down. "Crawl into that log."

"Really?" You raise your eyebrows.

"I need to go get a set of wheels."

"You're leaving?" Camille exclaims with alarm in her eyes.

"Five minutes tops. If I'm not back, go without me."

"I don't like this." Camille's eyes bulge at you.

"Vince, wait," you start.

"There's no time. Now crawl in," Vince snaps, pointing before taking off. You pass a look to Camille.

"You heard him." She nods.

You heave a sigh as you kneel and pull yourself inside the fallen rotten log. It smells of decay. Several bugs crawl hurriedly away from you. You're not amused. Five minutes is going to seem like an eternity.

"I think I hear someone coming," Camille whispers after three minutes.

"Cam," you whisper, panicked, but it's too late. She's already gone.

You are alone. Normally, you'd embrace the solitude, but now you are afraid of it. You can't see anything. What if someone finds you before Vince or Camille comes back? Where did Camille go? What if she gets hurt? You are terrified, not knowing what to do, and feeling completely useless.

A branch snaps at approaching footsteps. You clamp a hand over your mouth and hold your breath. You are completely defenseless. Seconds slowly tick by as you wait and listen.

"Got you." A hand fastens down on your ankle and yanks you out of the log.

A gurgled scream escapes your throat as you try to hold onto anything inside the log, but all you get is rotten wood embedded underneath your nails before you're pulled out into the sunlight. You kick with your other foot.

"Feisty one, aren't you?" the blonde vampire chuckles.

"Take your hands off me." You twist and turn to no avail.

He only chuckles.

Where is Vince? Where is Camille?

You still when a whistle, like a speeding bullet, zips past. The vampire's smirk wanes as he slowly looks down and sees blood oozing rapidly from his pierced stomach. Revelation enters his eyes as he turns to face his opponent.

"Traitor," he spits.

"Loyalist."

You gasp when you hear the snap of the vampire's neck before his body sags to the ground. The only one left standing is Marc. Seeing the viciousness from him should horrify you.

"You okay?" He drops to a knee in front of you.

"I thought you left."

"You asked me to stay. I will until you no longer want me to."

You realize his brutality doesn't disturb you. He doesn't kill for pleasure.

"Nadine." Vince bursts forward, coming to a dead stop. He takes in the scene, bouncing his eyes from you to Marc, to the dead vampire, and back to Marc with a bit of jealousy.

"Nadine." Camille rushes onto the scene, taking it all in as well before curling her lip up at Marc's presence.

"I'm okay," you quickly reassure.

"Let's go." Vince turns on his heels.

You don't understand why you feel a pang of guilt as Marc secures you in his arms and falls into line after Vince.

Chapter 38

There's a negative charge in the silver Corolla as Vince accelerates past civilization onto a highway. A place that now feels so foreign to you. It has been only a couple of days, yet it feels like a lifetime since you saw the hustle and bustle of traffic and other human beings.

You should envy them, but you don't. You don't want to be back in reality any more than you want to be hunted by a sadistic vampire. You just want peace. A simple lifestyle where the only thing you have to worry about is yourself and not have a fate bearing on your shoulders. You are no superhero nor do you want to be. Even though you might stand up to face a fire head-on, you're not the kind of person who willingly runs into each one you happen to come across. You like to avoid fires altogether if you can.

You glance over to Marc beside you in the back seat. He avoids looking anywhere but outside the window. Meanwhile, you catch Vince darting daggers into the driver's side mirror every now and then at Marc. As for Camille, she sits quietly in the passenger seat, staring out of her window.

No one speaks. No music plays. The only background noise is the tires on the asphalt, picking up stones every now and then before kicking them out of the treads.

You settle for looking back out your window and watching as miles and miles zip by for hours on end. There are times when your eyelids grow heavy, but you deny yourself sleep. How can you? Where do you all go from here?

Headlights begin to blind you as sunlight fades by the minute. You turn your head and find your neck is stiff. You tilt your head from side to side, listening to your bones crack at the movement. Your eyes briefly lock with Vince's in the rearview mirror. You lower your eyes and go back to staring out the window.

You perk up when the car drifts into a turning lane. You study Vince, trying to decipher his intentions. Your mind is alive as you watch the remote darkness pass by. You gather you're somewhere in upper Pennsylvania near New York from the signs on the highway.

"Where are we going?" Camille breaks the silence.

"Hopefully, someplace where we can stretch our legs," Vince answers.

He drives for a little while longer before he kills the lights and turns off the main road onto a single lane, passing a sign next to a mailbox that reads Foreclosure. A bit back from the road is a rustic-looking log house with a long porch that hasn't seen good days in a while.

Vince pulls the car around the back of the house and parks the car in the woods out of sight from the road. No one dares to make the first move.

"I'll keep watch," Marc utters before slipping out the door.

There isn't much light from the half-moon hidden by trees as you watch his dark figure disappear. You want to go with him. You don't know what to say or how to act around Vince and Camille.

"Let's go inside." Vince pushes his door open.

You follow suit along with Camille. You find you have to lean on the car as your legs are inflexible from being immobile.

"You okay?" Vince magically appears beside you.

"I'm fine, just got to get the…" You stop yourself before saying the rest of what comes to mind first. Mentioning the word "blood" in he company of a vampire might not be the smartest idea.

"Here, lean on me." He slips an arm around your waist.

Your first instinct is to push him away, but you decide against it and just comply, walking with him to the back door and up the steps of the deck. The tension you feel around him is still very much present, and you're not entirely sure why.

The door creaks open once Vince breaks the lock. The interior is pitch-black, and you can't see anything. Ice creeps up the length of your spine.

"Wait here." Vince leaves you standing at the back entrance.

You hear him rummaging through drawers until he finds what he is looking for. A flashlight. After he turns it on, you see what a mess the place is.

"Here you go." He hands it over. "Cam, go see if you can find some candles to light.

She leaves the kitchen without a word to go on her search.

"Let's see if we can find you something to eat. You must be famished."

You want to argue, but you don't have the strength. In truth, you are hungry. Starving, actually. You can't recall the last time you did eat something. You didn't have to worry about that when you were in the wilderness with Marc. Pure adrenaline was what was keeping you going, and it has now faded dramatically.

When Vince opens the refrigerator door, no light illuminates, and a foul stench instantly fills the room. Obviously, the electricity was turned off, and there is probably nothing edible left in the refrigerator. Vince closes the door and proceeds to look through the cupboards. The first one he opens holds glassware. The next is stacked with bowls and china. The third contains spices and items for baking. Finally, he finds a cupboard with canned foods.

"Here's a can of tuna." He sets it down on the counter. "There's a bunch of soup, beans, vegetables, and fruit."

"Tuna's fine." You snag it off the counter. You open the nearest drawer in search of a manual can opener, and have to open a few more before you find one. Once you remove the lid, you grab a chunk between your fingers and pop it into your mouth. You crinkle your nose. It's not fresh from the water or cooked over a fire, but it's the fuel your body needs to recharge.

"I found some candles." Camille returns and sets them on the kitchen table. She strikes a match and lights all four of them.

You switch the flashlight off and stick it in your back pocket. The candles provide the kitchen with enough light.

"I'm going to go keep watch on the front porch," Camille announces before she bolts.

You chew on another piece of tuna in awkward silence.

"You should get some rest."

"Don't tell me what to do." Your eyes blaze.

He throws his hands up in surrender. "You must be exhausted. I'm sure you've been through a lot in the last couple of days."

You sigh and deflect. "I'm sorry, Vince."

"Hey." He closes the gap in seconds, grabbing you gently by the shoulders. "You have nothing to be sorry about. If anyone should be sorry here, it's me. I never should have left."

"I don't blame you."

"I know you don't."

"Please, don't blame yourself."

He looks away.

You reach up and guide his head to face yours. "It's no one's fault. We will all get through this."

"Did he hurt you?"

It's your turn to look away as the memory surfaces of Vladimir hitting you so hard that it caused you to bash your head against the wall. You shudder at the memory. You can still feel the sting.

"I have to find a way to kill him." He begins to pace. "You deserve to live a normal life."

"You'll only get yourself killed. Besides, what exactly is there for me to go back to?"

He stops pacing.

"How did you know Camille wasn't…." You trail off, unable to say the word.

"When I found her, she was awake."

"How exactly does one get changed?"

"They would have to die with both vampire venom and some of their blood in their system."

You fade out processing the information and try to make sense of it.

"Absolutely not. I won't allow it," he bellows.

You jerk your head and comprehend his words. "Don't worry. I have no intention."

"Good."

"I think I will go lie down." You snag a candle, walk out of the kitchen, guide through the living area, and find a bedroom on the opposite side. There is a black-and-white striped comforter made on the bed. You set the candle down on the nightstand and curl up on your side, facing away from the open door.

There's so much on your mind. You're mentally spent. You have no idea what to do. No idea what to do to make things right. You have no idea how to face either one of your friends. They're wrapped up in this with you, whether you like it or not. You're tired, but you find your mind won't stop racing. You have so many questions. So many things to get to the bottom of. Only you are stuck on one question you can't stop thinking about, and only one person can answer it.

⊙

Chapter 39

You become keenly aware of floorboards shifting underfoot as steps approach. You want to pretend you are asleep, but you know Vince will probably see right through you.

"We should get going," he calls into the room.

It's still dark outside. You have no idea what time it is or, frankly, what day. The only thing that matters these days is living to see another one. You roll off the bed, grab the candle, and trail him. You see him grab a backpack that wasn't there before from the kitchen table .

"Here, found some water." He hands over a bottle of Deer Park.

You take the warm bottle from his hand and realize how thirsty you are. You twist open the cap and guzzle half the contents.

"Cam, we're leaving." He raises his voice slightly.

"What about Marc?" You wipe the drip from your chin.

Vince blows out the candles before strutting out the back door in long strides. You pick up your pace to try to keep up with him.

"Vince, we're not leaving without him."

He pops open the trunk and places the bag in before closing it.

"Vince!" you shout.

"I'm here."

You whip your head to the left and see Marc standing a short distance from the front of the car. You want to talk to him, but don't want an audience. A puff of air laced with annoyance redirects your attention. Camille glares at Marc before walking around the back of the car, as far away as possible from him, and slides into the passenger seat.

With a sigh, you walk opposite Vince to the rear passenger seat while Vince climbs into the driver's seat. As he starts the ignition, Marc slips into the seat next to you.

Everyone is silent once more as Vince drives. You notice the visor is down when the sun isn't even up yet. As you think back, you recall the visor was down the whole drive yesterday. The only logical reason you can come up with is that it helps block a good visual of Vince's face.

You hate this. Hate walking a tightrope. You can feel the negative vibe in the car again. You want to scream. This is not healthy for any of you. However, where do you start?

You rest your chin on your hand and stare out the window. The quiet is killing you inside. No one is happy. They're all here for you, but you're also the problem. You want to release them from their despair. You don't want anyone to have to take care of you. You used to be capable of doing that yourself. Only you can't be fully responsible anymore. You don't have keen senses. You don't have superhuman strength. You are a nobody and accept that as fact. You never fit into anyone's inner social circle, and you never cared to. You never liked being the center of attention. You liked to pick your battles. You were a loner. The opposite of the norm. Now, you have no idea who you are or who you will become.

You feel strange. Your stomach is a bit queasy. You take a sip of water, but that seems to make it worse. You lick your dry lips and just focus on tree after tree passing by. Only the motion seems to make you more nauseated. "Stop the car."

"Why?" Vince studies you in the rearview mirror.

"Just do it." You struggle to keep down what wants to come up.

He screeches the tires, pulling over to the shoulder. You fumble with the handle before shoving the door open. You don't make it very far from the car as you retch up nothing but sour liquid. The taste in your mouth is horrible. It makes you heave. You despise throwing up. Something you're glad you don't do often. However, it's happened more often lately, and it tends to take a lot out of you.

"Nadine, are you okay?" Vince appears, patting you on the back.

"Fine." You try waving him away, but more liquid comes up.

"What do you need me to do?"

You hear the panic in his voice, but don't have the strength to talk. There is nothing he can do. Hovering isn't helping matters. In fact, it's only making you feel worse. Your stomach still feels uneasy, but there really isn't anything left for you to bring up. You manage a few quick, short breaths before standing up tall.

"I'm okay." You smile weakly.

"It doesn't look like it."

"It's nothing, let's go."

You turn on shaky legs to the car. Camille is standing by the open door. You hope she doesn't say anything that will set Vince off. Camille knows you the best. It's not nothing. You are always the strong one and never show weakness.

When you climb back in, you can't even bring yourself to look in Marc's direction. You hear Vince and Camille's mumbled voices outside. You just want to move on and have them stop fretting about you.

Your door opens.

"Here are some crackers." Vince hands you a sleeve of saltines.

"I'm okay now, promise." You fake a wider smile.

"Okay." He hesitates, but says nothing more as he closes the door and climbs back into the driver's seat. He pulls back out onto the road.

You don't want to open the sleeve. Don't want to eat a cracker, but feel Vince's eyes on you. You start to pull apart the wrapper, only you have no strength. You lower it to your lap and avoid the rearview mirror. The dead weight of the crackers becomes light as a feather. You look down and see Marc's hand wrapped around the sleeve before you glance up. Your eyes dart to the mirror. Vince is not currently watching. You release your hold. Marc pulls the wrapper apart in half a second before handing the sleeve back to you.

"Thank you," you mouth and take back the sleeve. The wrapper makes an excessive amount of noise within the soundless car as you pull out a cracker. You munch on it and grimace. It's stale as your stomach rolls with the punches. You set the crackers aside.

The only thing you can do is try to get some sleep. Or at least pretend. At least that will get the focus off you. You tilt your head back and close your eyes. Your mind, though, just won't stop. Are you breathing steadily or unevenly? Is Vince still watching you? Is Camille? How long is he going to be driving? All day again? Where is he even going? Is there anywhere safe that the vampires won't find you?

Your eyes crack open as something brushes against your leg. You stare down at the hand on your left knee before looking over at Marc.

"Sleep," he mouths as though he senses your anxiety.

You close your eyes, breathe in slowly through your nose, and let it quietly back out. His simple touch quiets your mind. Restores strength. The tension built up inside seems to slowly ebb away. You allow yourself to relax against the seat.

When his hand starts to pull away, you quickly place your hand on top of his. You feel it tense. Slowly, you slip your fingers in between the top of his. After two pounding heartbeats, his hand relaxes before gripping the tips of your fingers.

There's a sense of security. A warmth spreads throughout your core. You can let go of your guard. Shut off your mind and let sleep invade you.

Chapter 40

The once smooth ride turns bumpy. You slowly blink your eyes open and see a landscape of trees. The car is no longer on the road. You are somewhere in the woods. Streaks of sun rays bear down through the gaps in the trees.

"Where are we going?" you ask.

"Hiding the car." Vince parks it facing a thick growth of trees.

Marc's hand slips from yours. You shudder as cold seeps back in, and your mind becomes wide awake.

"How are you feeling?" Vince leans around to face you.

Your stomach growls. "Hungry, actually."

"Let's see what we can find you." He opens his door.

Your eyebrows furrow as you try to decipher the meaning when your door opens. His hand extends toward you. You hesitate before taking it and slipping out. Once you're on your feet, he loops an arm around your waist.

"Cam, get the bag from the trunk," Vince commands.

You see a slight facial twitch from Camille before you're lifted off your feet. "I can walk," you protest.

"It's a bit of a hike. Just relax and enjoy the ride."

You are far from being relaxed. On edge even. You casually look over Vince's shoulder, only to find Marc is already gone. Cam refuses to even look your way as she grabs the bag from the trunk and slams it shut.

You look ahead and try to make sense of where in the world he's taking you. Soon, you see a break in the trees that leads to an open area. Beyond sits a dark blue house, darker than the sky. As dark as the depth of the sea.

He walks the long open field of grass. Grass high and wild. Grass that hasn't been maintained in a while. When he closes in on the house, he walks around to the side and tugs on the sliding glass door, letting himself in.

The first room is a small living area with a brown L-shaped sofa on one side and a television mounted on the wall on the other. He proceeds straight ahead into an open interior, where a small square dining table sits with four wooden chairs. To the right is a small foyer that leads to the front door. To the left are two separate rooms. One is a bedroom, and the other is a combined bathroom and laundry room.

Vince pulls out a light brown barstool from under the kitchen counter before setting you down. He advances into the kitchen area and opens the refrigerator.

"Allow me." You hop down and duck under his arm to view the contents. There is no electricity. However, the odor emitted doesn't smell rotten. There is a carton of expired milk. A liter of regular Coke half empty. A gallon of Arizona green tea is about three-fourths empty. Condiments on the door. Eggs and bread on one shelf. Some yogurt, cheese, and lunchmeat are on another shelf. A bunch of vegetables in the bottom drawer. Fruit in the drawer above the vegetables.

You grab the tea and set it on the counter behind you before pulling out the drawer of fruit. You grab an apple that has more good spots than brown before searching the drawers for a knife. When you find one, you cut off the brown spots before biting into what remains of the apple.

"Found some more food," Vince announces after opening the last cupboard by the kitchen window at the sink.

You step over and look at the contents. A container of natural peanut butter catches your eye. When you unscrew the lid, you find the seal still intact. You break the seal and dip your finger in. It tastes delightful. Your hungry belly begs for more.

"Well, good, she finally found something to eat. Now, what about us?" Camille plops the bag on the table.

"When's the last time either one of you…" You pause.

"Don't worry about us, we're fine," Vince intercepts.

Camille snorts.

Vince glares at her. "You're safe here." Vince grabs you by the shoulders.

"Yeah? For how long? Because it worked out so well the last time." Camille sneers.

"Camille," Vince snaps.

"What? Only stating the truth."

"It's different this time." He turns completely toward her.

"Yeah, how so?"

"You're letting your senses overpower you. Close your eyes and focus on silencing all the noise."

Camille narrows her eyes before flicking them toward you, back to Vince, and back to you again. With a sigh, she complies and closes them.

"Good, now deep breath in and release."

Camille follows his direction.

"Now open your eyes."

"I'm sorry." She hangs her head.

"Hey, it's okay. You just lost yourself there for a minute." He grasps her shoulders. "And despite the circumstances, you're doing very good."

"I am?"

"Yes, which is good because…." He sighs. "We need to recharge, too, so I need you to watch Nadine until I return. Can you do that?"

"You're leaving me alone with her again?" she pushes back, rattled.

"They don't know where we are, not this time. And you would never hurt her. I believe in you."

"You do?"

"Of course I do."

"Okay." Camille nods.

"I know it's what you don't want to hear." Vince redirects his attention. "But I won't be long, I promise. There's no way for them to trace us being here."

"You don't have to explain," you respond.

He nods before glancing back at Camille. You see his hesitation before he goes. Only he has no choice. They must be running on fumes and need blood, just as you need to replenish yourself with nourishment. Everyone is suffering. They can't keep running without taking care of themselves, too.

You now understand why Camille is acting so cold. How hard is it for her to be in the same room or car as you and not want to satisfy her hunger? It's hard for you to wrap your mind around the fact that Camille is no longer human. There is so much you want to say to Camille, but you don't know what the right words are. The atmosphere is charged with unease. One wrong move could set her off again. You will have to wait for the right time. You sense that now is not it.

"I'm a bit tired. I'm going to lie down until Vince returns," you say, making your exit.

Camille doesn't protest. You head toward the bedroom and close the door behind you. The bed is made. A comforter with club-shaped symbols in dark blue, nearly black, and outlined in white is neatly covering the bed with pillows on top. You sink onto the bed and curl up on your side with your back to the bedroom door. A blue drape, a close shade to the outside of the house, hangs from the window.

You have no idea how much time has passed since Vince left or since you locked yourself in the room. There is only one thing on your mind. An opportunity you have been longing for.

You swing your legs to the wooden floor. Slowly, you rise, taking care not to creak the floorboards as you tiptoe to the window. You pull the curtain back, unlock the window, and gently lift it. You wait several seconds, keenly listening, before you dare to slip out.

The distance is pretty far to the woods from the house, but completely grass-covered. You have no idea if grass makes noise enough for a vampire to hear. You hope Camille isn't paying any attention to you. You have no idea what she is doing in the first place. What exactly is there for a vampire to do in an empty house?

After several minutes of patiently waiting, you sprint for the trees. As soon as you pass the first tree, you stop to lean up against it and catch your breath. You pant heavily before getting your breath back under control. You feel the burn in your legs. A good burn. A spark of life.

You peer around the tree, looking for Camille, but she is nowhere in sight. You see no movement at all. You sigh and close your eyes as you lean against the tree. How did it come to this? Running away from your best friend because you are unable to talk to her?

With a deep breath, you move onward. You have no idea how far the woods stretch. No idea where to even start looking. All you know is you want to find Marc.

"Going somewhere?"

Chapter 41

You jerk to your right and see Marc leaning up against a tree with his arms crossed as if he was expecting you.

"Just, umm, needed some air."

He slightly snorts, pushing away from the tree. He knows you're not being honest but doesn't call you out on it.

"I have something that belongs to you." He reaches into his back pocket before closing the gap.

"My knife." You stare at the switchblade in his palm. "You've had it all this time?"

"Meant to give it back sooner." He shrugs. "I've cleaned it."

"Thank you," you say, accepting it. You study it as pieces of the puzzle start to fit together. A big piece connects.

"You can ask what's on your mind," he coaxes.

Your eyes drift upward. The question is on the tip of your tongue, but you pause.

"Why did you turn her?" you whisper.

He heaves a long sigh. "I don't know, honestly. I don't have a good answer for you. I was selfish. Saw an opportunity. There are no female vampires. If you failed, I knew that when she was discovered, chaos would ensue. I hadn't planned on breaking you out. Guess it was my way of being defiant."

"You want to kill him yourself?"

"Yes." A flicker of hatred burns in the depths of his eyes.

You take a moment to process his words. "Why are there no female vampires?"

"He knows how to control men, not females. After being cursed, he never trusted one again."

You're not amused by the irony of the curse. "What did he have planned for me?" You notice his eye twitch.

"It's best you don't know."

"Some kind of duel against him?"

"It doesn't matter; you're safe now."

"It does matter. I know how to fight with my words, but I don't know how to fight with my physique. Would you teach me?"

He stares at you, speechless.

"What?"

"What about Vince?"

"What about him?"

"You wouldn't prefer him to teach you?"

"I asked you, didn't I?"

"Why did you want me to stay?"

"What's with all the questions?" you ridicule his line.

"Follow me." He sighs as he heads deeper into the woods.

You repeat his question in your mind. Why did you want him to stay? You have every reason to want him to go. You theoretically don't need him anymore. You have Vince and Camille. Vince is fiercely protective of you. He would go to the ends of the Earth to keep you safe. He doesn't get along with Marc. If you thought killing your best friend was the worst thing Marc could do, turning Camille into a vampire is even crueler. You have every right to hate him. You want to hate him. Only you don't. You have no idea why.

"Pretend this is a sword." He tosses you a long, thick stick.

"Okay." You catch it, swivel it, and continue to trail him. The trees begin to thin out as you step into an open area near a rippling stream.

"Depending on the sword you use, you'll have a firmer grip with two hands. Your right hand would be placed at the top and your left below." He demonstrates.

You mimic.

"For now, do what comes naturally." He gets into a fighting stance.

You get into your own stance, keeping your eyes trained on him, stepping left when he shifts left. You half circle when the glare from the descending sun blinds you. You lift a hand to shield your eyes.

Marc pivots forward and knocks the stick from your hand. "Always be aware of your environment. Don't allow yourself to be backed into a corner. Your opponent will be quick to turn any disadvantages against you."

You nod before picking up your stick and moving out of the blinding sun. You keep your eyes trained on him. Ready for his next move. You circle once more. When the sun is just getting into your line of sight, you stop.

He jabs you in the side. "Don't stand still. It gives your opponent an opening for attacks."

You get into position again, focused. When your position is at a disadvantage from the sun, you change direction. He follows suit. When he strikes out, you block him. Your automatic response is to step back out of reach from his next counterattack.

"Good, but be mindful of a potential jab from your opponent." He demonstrates.

"Okay."

You stare intently, with each step mirrored. You wait for him to strike out, but he doesn't. You decide to make the first move. You lunge and stab out with your stick sword. He sidesteps out of the path and holds his against your neck.

"Stabbing movements should only be used when your opponent is vulnerable; otherwise, you open yourself up for an attack."

You push his stick away and get into position with more determination. He thrusts forward to your right, which you block, then to the left, then fakes back to the right before jabbing forward, touching your stomach with the end of his stick.

"Never remove your sword from the 'ready' position. Keep it perpendicular to the ground with your body at a forty-five-degree angle."

You huff with frustration. So much to be mindful of. So much to remember.

"It takes time and a lot of practice. Eventually, it will come as effortlessly as the air you breathe. Let's practice some of your swings."

You copy as he goes top to bottom, straight down before straight up from the bottom, diagonally down to the left and right, diagonally up from right to left, and then horizontal strikes.

"Block me," he urges.

You watch intently, reacting accordingly, blocking blow after blow, getting into the rhythm. He takes it slow at first, but then picks up speed. He strikes with the same four. Up, down, before side to side, becoming a sort of dance.

You quickly jump to the opposite side of his next attack. You stab forward only to be stopped by his stick sword. You are dumbfounded. You thought you could fool him.

"Nice try." He smirks.

"How did you know?"

"Your eyes betrayed you."

You yank your stick back. "Again."

You resume the dance. Nice and slow before the speed increases while you plot your next move. On the last side strike, you step in with a vertical attack. You stand face-to-face with Marc. Stare into his olive-green eyes. Catch a whiff of his faint cinnamon-laced breath. Time stands still. You don't move. You are captivated. Drawn to him. It's something you've never experienced before, and you don't know what to make of it.

You're pulled away with force as your feet leave the ground. You look over as Vince punches Marc in the face, and you gasp in shock.

"Stay away from her!" Vince screams.

Fury takes hold, and you pound on Vince's arm wrapped around your waist.

"What is your problem, Vince?" You shove his chest when he lets you down.

"He killed your best friend!" he screams in your face.

"You think I'm not fully aware of that?" you scream back.

"You sure don't act like it. If you knew all the other despicable things Marc's done, you wouldn't be able to stand the sight of him."

"What about you?" you bellow.

"What about me?"

"You've never done something you've regretted."

"I feel remorse. He doesn't." His angry eyes blaze beyond yours with slight waning.

You look over your shoulder and see blood streaming down Marc's nose. "Why are you bleeding?"

"You're coming with me." Vince grabs your arm.

"How dare you!" You rip free. "You don't own me."

"He killed my mentor. Tortured him first. Ripped out his eyes because he saw something he shouldn't have."

You stare at him, stunned. Cringe while visualizing the brutality.

"What about the girl he loved? Did he tell you how he killed her?"

"Vince, stop," you whisper.

"I'm just getting started," he shouts.

"Please." You beg with your eyes.

"Have you told her who you really are?" Marc counters.

$$\infty$$

Chapter 42

Vince storms away in silence. Without a word, Marc leaves the area as well. You stand deeply disturbed. It's all going south. You have no idea how to make it right. You can't. It's out of your control. You never had control in the first place.

"That was intense," Camille comments.

You jerk your head at the sound of her voice. She leans up against a tree with her arms crossed. You didn't even know she was in the vicinity. You need her support now more than ever. You can't put it off anymore.

"Cam, I'm so sorry. You were never supposed to get involved in all of this."

"Yeah, well, I did." She shrugs.

"It should have been me."

"Yeah, but it wasn't."

"Where do we go from here?" you murmur.

"I don't know," she sighs, looking away. "Everything's different now."

"It doesn't have to be."

"You can't fathom the willpower it takes not to want to satisfy this constant urge. Not unless…." She leaves the words hanging.

"I turn?" you finish for her with raised eyebrows.

"I don't know why you're stalling the inevitable." Her cream-coffee eyes meet yours.

"Do you even realize what you're asking of me?"

"It's your destiny." She stands tall. "Eventually, it's going to happen. You're the strongest person I know. If I can resist, you can, too."

"I don't fight without purpose." You shake your head.

"You'll never find purpose by hiding."

"Even if I did, what chance would I stand?" You hear the pitch rise in your voice.

"You're Nadine Drexel. You're capable of anything you put your mind to."

"I've stood at the edge of my dark side. Caught a glimpse of what I could become. It was someone I didn't recognize. Someone to be afraid of," you state in an even voice.

"You're not capable of evil." She shakes her head.

"Yes, I am. We all are."

"But you're not alone."

"I'm not turning." You ball your hands into fists before peeling off.

You're mad because it's clear whose side Camille is on. She knows you the best. How could she expect you to turn willingly? Her expectation is ludicrous. Your life will never be normal again, all because of some stupid superstition.

"You'll never be able to find happiness with him if you remain human," Camille calls out.

"What?" You spin back, bewildered.

"Maybe you're fooling yourself, but you don't fool me." Camille turns on her heel.

You stare after her until she disappears. Your eyes divert to the ground, processing. What is she talking about? You shake your head and stumble through the woods, having no idea where you are going. All you know is you want to be alone. Everything is unraveling with the fading light of the sun. It's all becoming too much. Pressure is building up in your chest. You try to ignore it and focus on one step in front of the other. As you trip over an exposed root, you catch yourself on a nearby tree. A sudden feeling overwhelms you: loneliness.

The feeling of being lonely and isolated is something you've never truly felt before. You used to crave alone time. To get away from the world and its expectations, closing into yourself. You find comfort in being alone. Suddenly, being alone is the last thing you want.

You don't want to be in Vince or Camille's presence. They only make things worse. Don't understand you. Add to the burden you already carry on your shoulders. There is only one person left you can turn to. One person who plagues you with guilt but also understands. The only one who comprehends why you resist. Marc.

He's hurting, too. You have no idea where he took off to or how far he may have gone. You don't know the distance of the woods. Part of your mind warns you about aimlessly wandering as darkness sets in. The other part ignores it completely. Camille's words replay in your head. Is there something more going on than just a simple alliance with Marc?

You take a deep breath and close your eyes, blocking out all the noise in your head and focusing on the quiet feeling of your surroundings. A chill is in the air, but there's a warmth a distance slightly to your right. You flick your eyes open and blindly follow your instincts. You think this is crazy. Only you have nothing to lose. It helps to calm your nerves already. One foot in front of the other, you traipse over roots and duck under branches.

The warmth grows stronger. The light has completely faded. There is no telling how deep you are embarking. You refuse to stop as your heart pounds through your temples. You freeze. The silhouette of his figure leans up against a tree. Your heart skips a beat. It's not possible. Has to be just a coincidence.

"Marc?" you whisper.

He whirls so fast with a frown. "How did you find me?"

"Are you okay?" You take a step forward.

"You came here to ask me if *I'm* okay?" You hear the bewilderment in his voice.

You nod slightly.

"You don't have to do that anymore around me." He takes a step.

"Do what?"

"Pretend." He continues to close the gap.

"Pretend what?" you whisper hoarsely.

"To be strong when you want to fall apart." He tucks a loose strand of hair behind your ear.

You bite your quivering lip as your eyes start to glisten. You've been fighting so hard not to surrender. Only your willpower has grown weak from all the weight you carry.

"Sometimes, you just need to let go of all the anguish. I'm here to pick up the pieces."

His arms slowly slip around you and pull you close. You let out a heartfelt sob from deep within as you submit against his chest. Once the dam breaks, you can't stop as tears pour down your face. You carry so much more weight on your shoulders than you realized. You cry for your mother. Cry for Leo. Cry for Camille. Cry for Vince. Cry for Marc. And you even cry for yourself.

All the pain and tension you've been carrying inside releases as it washes out of you. You feel relief instead of shame as he cradles you, stroking your hair gently. Being comforted is something you have always avoided. You didn't think you needed it, and you refused to let anyone see you weak. You did not expect to feel lighter and stronger for it in letting go.

"What about you?" You push back and look up.

"I've let my anguish out a while ago."

"Alone?"

He pulls you back in without answering. You slide your arms around his waist and hug him tightly. It feels good. It feels right.

"Her name was Mallory," he mumbles over your head.

"You don't have to feel obligated to explain yourself." You speak with renewed strength.

"I've never been able to talk about that day to anyone. I had to bury how I felt behind a mask in order to survive."

More tears begin streaming down your face.

"I didn't really know her as well as I thought I did. I don't think what I felt for her was love."

"You cared about her," you say.

"Only it wasn't enough for me to stop myself from draining her when she begged for mercy. A voice in the back of my mind pleaded for me to stop, but the monster I had become took full control."

You hear the agony in his voice.

"He set me up to fail." Anger replaces the pain on his face. "Compelled her to slit her wrist, knowing I wouldn't be able to resist the bloodlust."

You feel sick. How many souls have been tortured? How many sick games has Vladimir played over the centuries? He truly is a monster. "You want revenge for Mallory?"

"No, I wanted it mostly for myself. For turning me into something I never wanted to become. For taking away my choice."

You blink up at him. You have no words. You hate the thought that he had to endure so much on his own. How did he hang onto his humanity? How did he not lose himself? He's beautifully broken but still strong. Sometimes, when you have nothing else left, strong is all you have.

You squeeze back into him. You never want to let go. He warms the inside of your core. You know you are far from being truly safe with the threat of Vladimir still out there. Only you feel safe in his arms. Secure. You're not alone in this. You have someone you can lean on both mentally and physically. A sensation you have never known before. You only hope you can provide the same for him.

Chapter 43

For the first time in such a long time, you feel completely rested and relaxed as you open your eyes. There's a warmth from the inside out. A sense you've never experienced before. The darkness does not constrict you.

"How long have I been out?" You slide off his lap onto the ground and lean up against the thick-based tree beside him. You were snuggled up against his chest.

"A while."

You quirk an eyebrow in his direction, unamused.

"I wasn't really paying attention."

You shift closer and lean into him as he drapes an arm around your shoulders. A feeling of contentment. "What did you do while I slept?"

"I just listened."

"Well, that's kind of creepy." You crinkle your nose before a horrible thought crosses your mind. "Do I talk in my sleep?"

His whole chest vibrates with a chuckle. You have never heard him laugh before. You smile. Despite everything, you're happy. Truly happy. You don't want this moment to end. You want time to stand still. A new dawn not to rise.

You tilt your head back and look through the gaps between the treetops. You see nothing but darkness. You can't make out much among the thick tree cover.

"Where are you going?" he asks when you push up to your feet and stumble forward.

"I want to see the sky."

"Allow me." He scoops you into his arms.

A jolt courses through you as he takes off. His eyes are focused on the path ahead. You are becoming keenly aware of the intensity inside you. Something you were denying. There's been a spark from the moment he touched you that you tried to bury beneath hate. Hate was easy. Hate was distant. Only trying to distance yourself from him proved to be fruitless.

He steps out into the open. The night sky is clear. There are no lights to disorient the stars or clouds to cover them. There are so many of them glowing in the pitch-black sky. You embrace the carefree wonder of it all. A calming peace lost in the stars.

"Puts it in perspective – how small we are compared to the world. So many stories written in the stars," Marc softly says as he sets you down.

It's late in the season for Orion to be visible. The stories you've read about the constellation, you always believed to be just myth. If you didn't see it with your own eyes, it couldn't be true. Only now, things have changed. Your eyes are wide open. There is truth buried in myths. Truths that aren't easily accepted, due to ignorance and fear. Fear is the greatest enemy. Everything else is just pawns of fear. When it loses its hold, that's when you can be truly free and become limitless. No running. No hiding. No strings attached.

You reach out and lace your fingers in the spaces of his before curling them. A sturdy field of energy courses throughout your body. Before, whenever he touched you, you dismissed the odd sensation. Fought against what it meant. Like a moth drawn to a flame. Like metal resisting a magnetic pull. Both are against their fundamental nature. Both knew the danger. There had been an ongoing battle between your mind and your heart. One that had been emotionally draining. You don't resist it now. You embrace it.

He curls his fingers around yours. So much heat radiates from the simple touch despite his cool hand. You look up into his eyes as he looks down into yours. Your heart is drumming double time. You don't oppose the desire as you lean toward him, close your eyes, and rise to your toes.

"No." He places a hand on your shoulder. "You're upset."

You shake your head. "Not anymore."

"I won't take advantage of you." He releases your hand and turns away.

You reach out for it and place it on your chest. "Do you feel that? It only does that for you."

"I don't deserve you."

"You don't deserve to be alone either." His tremble vibrates into you.

"Yes, I do," he says, pulling away.

You follow him. "You wanted to know how I found you earlier? I found you by reaching out and sensing the heat that you've ignited within me since the moment we met. A fire I didn't understand. A fire I had never felt before. A fire I've been holding back. It guided me to you."

He stands unmoving with his back to you.

"You didn't feel that spark, too?" you implore in a whisper. You know he did, but he stands there like a statue without uttering a word.

You flash back to the moment he firmly held you against him. He stiffened. Caught off guard by the pulsating energy firing off when simply brushing up against you. A magnetic force fused. You sensed how on edge he was when carrying you in his arms. There was an instant attraction that overwhelmed you both.

Your mind dismissed it as lust. Your heart and your soul were captivated the moment you met. You were able to see who he was on the inside when his guard was down.

You sigh and turn away. Thought you knew what a crushed heart felt like, and never wanted to feel that again. Heat leaves your body as your heart fractures. Loneliness creeps in again.

The dimming flame inside explodes with lightning force when he pulls you into him and presses his cinnamon-scented lips to yours.

Fire.

Passion.

Desire.

He pulls back slightly. "I feel it, too."

You rise on your toes, hungry for more. A need.

He pulls back again. "I'm not really an expert at this."

"Neither am I. We can learn together." You slip your hands around his neck, pull him close, and deepen the kiss.

Your emotions are wild. On overload. Intoxicated by him. Forgetting how to breathe, you gasp for air. You never knew such intense feelings could be rejuvenating. Is this what everyone is searching for all their lives? A surrendering without question. The knowing of it being true. Of being right. Even if it didn't make sense. Even if it was complicated. Nothing mattered but the explosion of fireworks inside.

Your mind swirls with ecstasy as he pulls back. Instantly, you grasp what it means to be deprived.

"What's wrong?"

"It's too dangerous for you if it goes too far." His hands grasp your upper arms.

His voice is shaky. Conflict radiates from him. You allow your mind to clear as you try to understand what caused him to react this way. Your tongue tingles. The memory flashes, scraping your tongue against his exposed tooth.

"I trust you."

"I don't trust myself."

"I know the risks."

He shakes his head. "If I lose control...."

"You won't."

"I won't take that risk, not with you," he states while his body quakes.

"Hey, it's okay." You step closer, placing your palm on the side of his face, and stroke the short stubble with your thumb along his jawline. "We'll take it slow."

"Why don't you hate me anymore?" He grips your hand.

"A vampire is what you are, not who you are."

He kisses your palm. "I've been a shell of myself for so long, living in the dark. You make me feel alive again."

You press your lips lightly against his before taking his hand and leading him to the nearby rippling stream. You settle down in the long grass with the stars above your heads. You don't need to speak to enjoy his company. You both revel in the present. Embraced, sharing this moment of peace. A new dawn would come soon enough.

"He was my mentor, too."

You look over at him.

"Taught me how to wield a sword. Taught me how to disguise the emotion in my eyes. Taught me to never give up on hope."

You nestle into him and stroke his middle with your hand as he opens up.

"His name was Kumal. The only friend I had. The only person I could trust. He saw the true me. He was there since the beginning of it all."

You continue to listen to him, knowing that what comes next is going to be hard.

"I was the one tasked to torture him. He gave something to Vince behind Vladimir's back. Saw something he shouldn't have. If I hadn't done what I was supposed to, without remorse, to Vladimir's satisfaction, I would have met the same fate. I still wanted my own revenge. Now, I had another reason."

You pop up on your elbow. "You're not alone anymore with your demons."

"What did I do to deserve you?" He combs his fingers through your hair.

"Captivated my heart."

He pulls you in close, kissing slowly and softly.

You curl yourself against him. All the horror he had to endure angers you. All the horror that took place over the centuries fuels your fury. How many others were like him, struggling to live to see another day behind a mask? You're the one supposed to end it.

"What's this?" You slip your hand under his shirt and feel the imperfection on his lower abdomen that you recall seeing before.

"An old scar."

"Don't all scars heal when you're a vampire?" You study him.

"Not the ones you have before you become one."

"How did you get it?"

Marc clamps his hand over yours and moves it. "It doesn't matter."

"It matters to me." You push up on your elbow.

He sighs. "I had a disagreement with my brother. In his rage, he ended up stabbing me."

You look at him, horrified.

"I don't want to dwell on the past." He looks to the sky.

You hit a nerve. One he isn't fully ready to touch. "Why did you bleed after…" You trail off, not wanting to say it.

"Too much animal blood weakens a vampire after time."

"Oh, Marc."

"I promised you, not one drop." He looks back at you.

You straddle his hips and kiss him with passion. He leans into the kiss, sliding his hands up your back. He craves you as much as you crave him until he breaks free, tossing his head back, and focuses on deep, slow breaths before his elongated teeth return to normal length.

You snuggle into the crook of his neck. You don't want this time with him to end. Yet, you know time does not stand still.

"How many wolves are there?" you whisper.

◯

Chapter 44

His hand stills from stroking your hair, and his relaxed state becomes rigid. You know where his mind will go first. You'd be denying it if a part of you didn't want to do it on his behalf.

"Don't you go there. Not because of me," he whispers.

You look him directly in the eyes. "I don't want to run anymore."

His eyes glisten with crimson tears. You reach up and wipe away the one that brims over. "I won't allow you to be used as bait."

"The best defense is a good offense."

He pushes you to the side and stands.

"Not only does Vladimir fear me, but he also fears the wolves. Why else would you take me there?" You push up to your feet as well.

"They will never work alongside a vampire."

"I can be persuasive," you state with determination.

"Why do you have to be so stubborn?" He growls with irritation, pulls you close, and smashes his lips onto yours.

He takes your breath away. The world stops. You find it hard to concentrate on anything but the moment. This blissful moment in time that you never want to end.

"I won't…" You take a breath. "…let…" You struggle to want to break free. "…my mind…" You push back despite your body screaming for more. "…be influenced."

He sighs, defeated.

"We're stronger together," you pant. "We'll find a way to defeat him. He may have his vampire army, but I will have an army of wolves."

"Where would you like to start?"

"First, I need to speak with Vince and Camille and see where they stand."

"All right." He nods.

You turn away from the stream with purpose.

"Save your strength." He scoops you off your feet.

You smile at him. Welcome the warm feeling you get when you are in his arms. You don't have to pretend anymore that you don't relish it.

He pauses at the end of the tree line overlooking the yard. Light is creeping in on the midnight-blue sky. A caw from a waking bird overtakes the silence. You stare at the back of the blue house. It's a nice little house. You never pictured anything big or fancy. You always saw yourself somewhere rural. Away from the chaos. Away from all the noise. A peaceful life. One you could appreciate and enjoy.

"Whatever you need, I'm here for you." He squeezes your thigh slightly.

You look at him without a response. You don't know what to expect when you walk in with him, but you know it's not going to be pretty.

"Even if you want to pretend nothing happened, I understand."

You frown. "Why would you say that?"

"I know you care about Vince, too."

You blink. Not only have you been denying your feelings for Marc, but you are also denying what you feel for Vince. You take a moment to dissect it before reaching out and cradling Marc's face. "You're right, I do care about Vince, but it does not compare to what I feel for you."

You sweetly seal his lips with yours. He kisses you like he'll never kiss you again. You have to pull back, gasping for oxygen. He leaves you breathless.

"Together."

He sets you down and threads his fingers in between yours. You grip hard as you walk across the grass, hand-in-hand. Alone, you might not have summoned enough strength, but with him by your side, you have someone to fall back on. It's such a good feeling to have.

You take the lead as you slip through the sliding glass door. You think better of it and release his hand. Not because you want to, but because you know it's necessary for the time being.

"Finally," Vince utters from the dining room.

"I thought he was going to put a hole in the floor from all his pacing." Camille flips a page in a magazine she must have found somewhere, lounging on the couch. When her eyes drift up, she grows tense.

"What is he doing here? He's not welcome." Vince stomps into the living area.

"We need to talk, all of us." You take on a business tone.

"Not with him here."

"Dining table now, both of you." You fold your arms against your chest and stare Vince down.

"Sounds like we're in for a serious talk," Camille breaks the silence, popping up from the couch. "Come along, Vince."

You quietly watch as Camille grabs his forearm and tugs him to follow. You lean back into Marc for a second while their backs are turned, as they sit opposite each other at the small square dining room table and wait for you to make the next move. You really didn't expect their cooperation so soon.

"If you don't mind, I'm a bit parched before we begin." You slip past them into the kitchen and look through a few cupboards before finding a glass. You pour some of the green tea into the glass and take a couple of sips, keeping an eye on them from across the small kitchen island. Your eyes briefly dart toward Marc, who keeps his distance at the end of the living area from the dining room.

He nods once.

You inhale deeply and let it release slowly. "I'm not going to run anymore."

"What?" Vince lurches to his feet.

"You're going to turn?" Camille asks at the same time.

"What did you put in her head?" Vince shouts at Marc.

"Vinson, sit down," you demand forcefully, slamming the glass down.

He looks over at you in shock.

You shift your eyes to Camille. "To answer your question, no, the prophecy does not say I have to become a vampire."

"Where did that idea come from?" Vince glares at Marc. "You're delusional to believe his lies."

"That's quite enough, Vince," you state with authority, placing your hands down and leaning over the island.

"You'll never get close enough to him without manpower," Vince bites out with anger.

"Exactly why I need to align with the wolves."

"Wolves?" Camille perks.

"You know about the wolves?" Vince's anger slightly wanes.

"I've seen the wolves."

"You know where the wolves hide?" Vince shifts his focus to Marc.

"Only a general sense of their territory," Marc replies.

Vince looks back at you. Casually, you take another sip and avoid his eyes. You know what he's starting to piece together.

"What do you mean by wolves?" Camille inquires, lost.

"Werewolves," you supply.

She scoffs. "You've got to be kidding me."

"Cam." You pause and reach for your necklace before walking around the island. "I would never ask you to do something you didn't want to do. This isn't your fight. I understand if you want to leave."

"Where else am I supposed to go?" She half laughs.

"Wherever you desire."

"I'm a vampire, Nadine, or did you forget that?"

"You're in control, not it."

"What if you're wrong?"

"You resisted me."

"Only because Vince held me down."

"I believe in you, Cam." You reach out and place your hand on top of hers. "I know you are fully capable of maintaining control."

"What can I do?" Camille pulls back.

"I can't have your back like you have mine."

"I know the risks." Camille's face partially twitches.

You narrow your eyes at her.

"What if I don't want to stay?" Vince interrupts, scraping the chair on the floor as he stands.

"The offer stands for you, too, Vince." You redirect your attention.

"You're a fool if you think you don't need me."

"We all need to be able to work together efficiently. I'm not going to ask you to stay if you can't do that."

His mouth purses. His eyes study yours. His stare discomfits you. Your cheeks warm. Unable to bear it, you break eye contact with him, raise your glass, and freeze.

Someone is standing visually in the grass just outside the open glass door. Someone you recognize. Seth.

The glass in your hand slips from your hold, bounces off the edge of the table, and shatters on the floor. Reaction after reaction unfolds.

"Vince, no!" You reach out to him but miss as he dashes after Seth while pushing Marc out of his path. Your panicked eyes lock with Marc's.

"Stay here." He bolts after Vince.

"Marc!" you call after him.

The front door bursts open. You whip your head over to the sound and see Jomar enter. You quickly reach into your vest pocket and flip open your switchblade. Something pushes down on your arm. You rotate your head and meet Camille's blank eyes.

Chapter 45

Marc stands in front of you with his eyes wide. Your mind has a hole. You don't understand why he is looking at you like that. There's a heaviness in your right hand. Your eyes drop to the switchblade you hold. It's covered in blood. His blood. Your eyes drop further to his midriff. Blood gushes out as he presses a hand to it.

"No." You drop the knife and look back up.

"I'm sorry," Marc whispers as he sinks to his knees.

"No!" you wail, reaching out to catch him and falling to the floor with him. You sob uncontrollably. Place your left hand on top of his as blood oozes between his fingers. "Don't you dare give up on me." You tilt back your head and look him square in the eyes. "Take my blood."

"No."

"Marc, please," you beg him.

"I love you."

You weep, shaking your head. "Please, don't leave me."

"Never." He places his free hand upon your chest.

"Very, very touching." Jomar claps as he circles in.

"Don't touch her," Marc growls defensively.

Jomar throws his head back and laughs. "And what exactly are you going to do about it?"

You swiftly press your lips to Marc's for one last kiss before Jomar grabs a fistful of your hair and yanks you away.

"Hold onto her." Jomar shoves you backward.

You struggle before realizing you are being held by Camille. Your best friend betrayed you. The one person you thought would always have your back is the one responsible for stabbing it. When did she align with Jomar?

"Do whatever you want with me. Just let her go." Marc pierces Jomar's eyes with his own.

"Oh, I plan on it." He circles behind Marc. "You know I can't let her go."

Jomar kicks him in the chest, knocking him down.

"You have what you came for. Leave him alone." You take a step forward, but Camille keeps an iron hold on both your upper arms.

Jomar looks over at you with a grin. He reaches down, plucks the switchblade, and wipes the blood off onto his pants.

"How sweet that a pathetic and powerless human like you would think you could stand up to a dominant and powerful predator like me."

You scream in agony when searing white-hot pain shoots up your right forearm. He moved on you so fast. Cuts deeply into your flesh with your own weapon.

"No!" Marc shouts as he tries to push himself up, slips on the blood, and collapses back to the floor.

"Did you like her scream?" Jomar cynically chuckles as he circles again.

Marc lifts his head and looks at you with angst. You see the fear in his eyes. You tremble as you press tightly against your wound.

"I always knew something was off about you." You watch Jomar straddle over Marc. "Oh, how I was so right about you."

You struggle despite it being useless.

"But he never listened to me," he states bitterly before grabbing Marc's shirt, raising him slightly from the floor, and punching him in the face.

"Stop, please, stop!" you cry out.

"Oh, but it gives me great pleasure." Jomar punches Marc again with a derisive grin.

"Camille, make him stop, please, make him stop," you plead. You've never seen Camille's eyes look so cold. So heartless. So merciless. "I know you will never be able to forgive him. You have a right not to, but he doesn't deserve to be tortured."

Camille does not stir or blink an eye.

A loud crack fills the room. Marc stifles a groan. You watch as Jomar lifts his foot from Marc's broken ankle. You whimper. Being the one to inflict a fatal blow on someone you deeply care about is your worst nightmare. However, watching him being tortured and unable to defend himself is even more brutal. You never felt so human before. You can't do anything for him. Not even end his suffering.

"I'm going to kill you," you spit out vehemently. Hatred grips your well-being. Hatred boils your blood. You will have no peace until you have a chance to hurt him like he's hurting Marc. Hurting you. A feeling you have never felt so consuming before. A powerful malevolence.

"Oh, yeah?" He stalks closer to you. "When will that be?"

If only you could burn him with your stare.

"Is that supposed to frighten me?" he mocks.

He snatches your arm. You want your fury to singe his skin.

"Guess I didn't cut as deep as I thought." His finger presses hard into your clotted wound.

The jolt of searing pain surprises you, breaking your trance. You muffle a moan.

"There's nothing really special about you, is there? Your blood doesn't even burn me," he jests while inspecting his finger.

He's only fortunate your blood doesn't have that power.

"Nothing but a sweet delicacy." He sucks the blood from his finger.

You can't harm him physically, but you can disgrace him. Mess with his mind. You'll take the pain. You want him angry. Angry at you, so his temper is directed away from Marc. You spit in his face.

"Witch," he says before he backhands you.

The room spins. You feel a split second of pain, but your rage overshadows it. You blink to clear your vision before facing Jomar once more.

"Is that the best you can do?" he mocks.

"When I get my hands on you, you're going to wish you never became my enemy."

"Oh, I'm quivering with dripping fear."

"You can't even face me without having someone hold me back because you're a pussy."

His hand wraps around your neck and squeezes.

"Do it," you choke out.

You see the veins in his neck bulge. His face is red with fury and the desire to kill.

"You only wish I would." He releases abruptly.

You cough and gasp for oxygen. "Didn't even have the balls to do it."

His hand rises. You don't even flinch as you wait for the strike. Fear has vanished from your eyes. He no longer has that satisfaction. He can't kill you. You both know why.

A gurgled shout emanates from his throat. He looks down, shocked. He disregarded Marc, who managed to crawl over and sink his teeth into his ankle.

"Get off me." Jomar kicks Marc with force, in the ribs, with his other foot, and sends him across the room. Furious, he stomps over and kicks him again and again and again.

"No!" you holler.

You take a step forward, only Camille's hold is still firm.

"You always told me you'd have my six through thick and thin." You turn with angry eyes.

"You vowed that no guy would ever come between us," Camille counters.

"That's what this is all about? You're not the friend I thought you were." You reach up and yank off your necklace. "If you want your revenge, don't just stand there like a doormat!"

Camille becomes oblivious as she stares at the necklace on the hardwood floor.

"You could never do anything for yourself. Could never think for yourself. Always had to rely on me for everything," you continue to berate her.

"Don't listen to her. She's just trying to get in your head," Jomar barks after punching Marc in the face.

"Come on, Camille, get your hands dirty."

"Don't worry, that's the plan once I'm through with him." Jomar kicks Marc again.

"Do it! Kill him! And then you'd better kill me after because I will show you no mercy!" you scream at the top of your lungs.

"She'll kill him when I tell her to!" Jomar whirls and yells back.

Camille's eyes finally rise. First to Marc. Then to Jomar before shifting momentarily to meet your burning ones. She slightly casts hers down as if direct contact singes her eyes. They're not blank anymore.

"Camille, bring her to me." Jomar's voice is laced with concern.

Camille fiercely looks over at Jomar. "No."

Her hands are quick to grasp your neck before your world plummets into complete darkness.

Part 3

INTO THE DARKNESS

A lone wolf wanders dangerously close to vampire territory. The damp terrain carries the wolf's musky scent toward the guarded perimeter. At once, ten vampires break away in pursuit of the wolf.

A pair of yellow eyes peers through the dark and mist. A low growl emanates from the wolf before he takes off, sprinting away from its hunters.

The vampires are hot on its tail. The wolf zigzags between trees. The moist earth sprays up from the wolf's large paws. Only a foolish wolf would dare enter vampire ground alone and think it could escape.

A large square-built vampire at the head makes the launch. He envelops his arms around the wolf, rolls onto his back, and releases his hold. Enough momentum to knock the wolf off his paws while at the same time protecting himself from being bitten.

The wolf slams against a tree, momentarily stunned. The vampire is the first to stand. He surveys the area, only to discover that he stands alone. Where have his fellow vampires gone?

The light-tan and brown wolf stands. He locks eyes with the vampire. His lip curls back with a deep growl. He is prepared to fight.

The vampire pulls his dagger from the sheath on his belt. The vampire knows to avoid the wolf's teeth. A non-lethal bite will slowly heal. A lethal bite will end him.

A branch cracks and falls from above. As the vampire looks up, a shadow drops to the ground between him and the wolf. The vampire takes you in as you slowly rise to a standing position. You are dressed all in black with your hair pulled back short. A sleeveless leather black body suit is zipped up just above your cleavage and paired with knee-high black boots. A black double-buckle belt is wrapped around your waist, along with another that's silver. The only color on you.

The vampire retreats at once. Fear radiates from him. He knows he just ran headfirst into a trap. A mistake that many others before him also made and paid for with their lives.

He comes to an abrupt halt. You are standing in front of him. He doesn't know how you managed to outrun him and cut him off. He thought he could outrun you. Little does he know that you are faster than he could ever be.

"Who are you?" his voice thunders.

"Your worst nightmare." You unclasp the silver belt.

His eyes are drawn to it. It's a flexible metal. Something he has probably never seen before. You flick the sword-like weapon in a figure eight. He should run. He should fight. Only he stands frozen with fascination, like many before him.

You lash out with the flexible sword, striking him. He reaches up and touches his neck, feeling a sticky substance oozing. His blood.

You inhale deeply through your nose. "Don't you just love the smell of blood?"

"What are you?" he stutters.

If he wasn't afraid before, now he's terrified. He shouldn't be afraid of anything. Least of all, a female like you. He is supposed to be the top predator. The vilest and most evil thing in existence. He doesn't have to be told he is facing death itself.

You are on him like a bolt of lightning. No time for him to react. You pin him to the ground. Pin his thighs down with your knees. He thought he was strong. You are stronger.

You push his face to the side, away from you, holding it against the ground. Only he catches a glimpse of your horrendous face. A sinister demon.

You toy with him. Lick the dried blood off his neck. Breathe your hot breath heavily against his skin. Your razor-sharp teeth slice into the side of his flesh. You tear into layers of his skin. Rip a chunk off straight to his esophagus. You suck through it like a straw and drain him of his life force.

He tries to squirm out from under you, patting the ground near him in hopes of finding the dagger he dropped. He is at your mercy.

"No," he gurgles.

You pull back, blood dripping down your chin. His blood. You wipe the blood with your thumb and lick it clean before staring down at him. You unsheathe your own dagger from your hip sheath that's wrapped around the leather corset belt. You grab his jaw and position his head straight up with a firm grip before cutting into his forehead. He screeches in agony as you carve into him. A symbol he has seen on other bodies. Mark of the Dragon's Eye.

"We'll meet again in hell." You break his neck. He won't die. Not yet, since there's still blood in his system. His bone will mend slowly.

A small whine redirects your focus. You gaze into the small tan and brown wolf's yellow-green eyes.

"You know what to do." You stand and walk away.

The wolf approaches the dead vampire before transforming into a young man, grabbing the foot of the vampire, and dragging the body through the forest floor.

You stay at a distance. Listen with acute hearing to the events about to unfold. The young man-wolf will take the vampire to the others, who are wounded by wolf bites and surrounded by the rest of the pack that ambushed them one by one. You know by heart the speech to follow.

"Be warned, your way of life does not go without consequence. The mark of the dragon lives on. Evil does not prevail. You live today only because we choose to allow it. Not everyone is as fortunate. Take your own and report what you have seen. Let mercy be with your soul," Gabriel, the oldest, concludes.

This is the moment the wolves will part and make an opening for the vampires to escape. They will not pursue them. They are to go back and report yet again another ambush by the wolves.

Only you're going to change the formula. It's time for chaos to ensue. You race into action. Before the vampires take off at a run, when they're in an ideal position past the wolves, you cut them off at the head.

The nine vampires stand motionless. Each holds onto his slow-healing wolf bites. The venom from the bite weakens them.

"Tell me, how many does it take to deliver a message?" you ask.

You watch them exchange worried glances before panic has them splitting into different directions on the run. The one in the back releases his hold on the dead vampire, while the second drops to his knees and folds his hands together, closing his eyes.

"What are you doing?" Gabriel asks in his human form.

You do not answer as you rapidly launch your attack. You speed off to the right and are quick to puncture a wound in the first vampire's stomach, pausing to snap his neck before attacking the second one, then the third, and lastly, the fourth. Once you have slayed them all, you dart over to the left. You slay them all as well before you return to the last remaining vampire still on his knees.

"Please, don't kill me," he begs, keeping his head bowed.

You laugh scornfully above him.

"I'll do anything."

"I'm sure you would."

"I want you to end his sovereignty so I can free my brother."

You blink. "What's your name?"

"Terrence," he whispers hoarsely.

"Well, Terrence, I need you to hold very still." You grab hold of his short hair and yank his head back. You wipe the blood from your dagger onto his shirt as he groans before you place the tip of it against his forehead. He muffles a scream as you carve the Dragon's Eye symbol on his head. "You have a very important job to do," you whisper next to his ear. "Tell Vladimir exactly what you saw. Tell him a war is coming. So, he'd better be prepared."

You release him abruptly and stand back as he falls to his hands. You stuff your dagger back into its sheath.

"Should I still take the body back?" he whimpers.

"No. The symbol on your forehead will tell Vlad all he needs to know. Now, go before I change my mind."

He begins to crawl slowly forward on his hands and knees. When he passes you, he cranes his neck, watching your feet, waiting for you to change your mind. When you don't make a move, he continues to move forward, stops to wait a beat, and then slowly pushes up to his feet. He freezes at the sight of an angry, dark-brown wolf blocking his path.

"Step aside," you command.

The wolf whips his head toward you. He pulls back his lip and snarls with yellow eyes glowing at you.

You hear Gabriel's light footsteps approach behind you. Hear the low growl in the back of his human throat. It takes all your willpower not to retaliate as the dark-brown wolf's eyes shift beyond you. He snorts with contempt as he slowly moves away.

The vampire eyes the wolf suspiciously as he unsteadily limps in an arc away from the wolf while keeping a hand pressed to the bite wound on his upper leg. His gait is slow and sloppy. He does not stand a chance of outrunning the wolves or you. He knows, but he doesn't look back as he stiffly moves onward.

You see conflict in the wolf's eyes. He scans between the vampire and you, lowly growling. Only he refuses to let the vampire go. His muscles tense, ready to launch an attack. Before the wolf has a chance to make his move, he's knocked down.

Fury blazes in the dark-brown wolf's eyes when he recognizes who knocked him off his paws. He grasps the back of the small light-brown wolf's neck and flings him through the air. The dark-brown wolf takes a step forward, only to be intercepted by you.

"This isn't part of the plan, Nadia." He morphs into his human form, covered in a full skin-tight body suit that resembles his wolf pelt, and bites out.

"It is now."

"You've just jeopardized our operation."

"No, you did. By revealing a crack in our association." You turn from him and take a step.

"Don't walk away from me." He grabs your upper arm.

You slam your elbow into his torso, crouch slightly, reach back to grab a fistful of his hair, and yank him forcefully over your head to the ground.

"Don't touch me." You stand over him.

You don't flinch as he scrambles to his feet with a raised fist.

"Enough." Gabriel firmly grips Caden's hand.

"Lamont's not going to be happy about this." He spears your eyes with his own. "Just wait until I tell him."

"Is that supposed to scare me?"

His eyes seethe with hatred at you.

"Let's go," he calls to two of his buddies before shifting back into his wolf form. He takes off in the lead.

"Should I go after him?" The youngest appears next to you, eager to tail him.

"No, Cameron, let him go," you dismiss.

"Are you sure you still want to let him go?" Gabriel asks while watching the vampire stumble in the distance. "There's no turning back."

"Positive."

"Okay, then, let's go home."

Chapter 47

You are in no hurry to return. Gabriel takes off in wolf form with the other three wolves. You follow them at a slower speed before you slow to a snail's pace. Cameron follows you every step of the way.

The morning sunrays burst through gaps between the trees before you step out into the open. You shield your eyes as you head toward an eastern white pine. One that did not survive a storm many years ago. You slip between the branches that hide an opening to an underground cave.

The cave is completely dark as you descend. Neither one of you needs a light to see where you are going. You know the tunnel well, and your eyes can adjust to see somewhat in the dark. Enough to see any obstacles in the way. Enough to see rocks everywhere.

The narrow passage branches off to the left. You pause at the large rock wall. You push back on it with one hand as if it is as light as a feather. A dim light glows from the other side. The pathway is lit with a few flaming torches. Just enough not to be in complete darkness and to adjust your eyes to light so that when you step outside, sunlight does not blind you.

"How can you stand there and defend her? Has she brainwashed you?" Your ears tune in to Caden's shouting.

"Be mindful of whom you are speaking to," Lamont's deep voice calmly utters.

"Do you even realize the higher risk she's exposed us all to?"

"We've always been targets among the vampires."

"They will come at us with even more force now that she's revealed herself."

"Patience, Caden."

"How much more patience do I need? Every day, they grow in numbers to compensate for the ones they've lost. They outnumber us. We need to start turning more of our own kind."

"A war is not won based solely on numbers. We will all be ready to fight when she is."

"We all know she's ready. It's you that's holding her back," Caden snaps.

"Are you questioning my judgment?" Lamont challenges.

Noir emits a loud raspy call as she swoops down from her perch on the rock above, interrupting the conversation. Caden looks over his shoulder and locks eyes with you. The fury in them intensifies as the black crow lands on Lamont's shoulder. Without another word, Caden storms down one of the many labyrinths of the cave.

"Nadia, a word." Lamont turns down a different tunnel.

You ignore the whine from Cameron as you walk with your head held high past the low growls and toward the tunnel that leads to Lamont's private chamber. Water trickles from the cave wall, distorting any conversations to prying ears.

"My understanding is you executed nine vampires today and allowed one to escape." Lamont strokes Noir.

"That is accurate." You blink once.

"You have a plan?"

"A bit of chaos."

"I hope you are prepared for the consequences that are surely to follow. You're dismissed." He sighs with disappointment before waving his hand.

You leave his quarters and pause outside when you see Gabriel leaning against the rock wall. "Are we to practice afterward?"

"After the storm, old dog."

You breeze into your quarters. It's a small space, but you don't need a lot of room. You hop onto the protruding rock and look up at the small hole at the top of the cave ceiling. A beam of light shines down from above.

"Was he mad at you?" Cameron asks from across the distance in human form.

"Be quiet," you hiss while shaking your head.

You concentrate on adjusting your acute sense of hearing, pinpointing two specific voices and blocking out all the other noise.

"Others are growing restless and questioning your direction," You hear Gabriel state beyond the dripping.

"Has there been talk about taking action?" Lamont inquires.

"Not at present."

"Good."

"I can't guarantee that won't change now that circumstances have shifted. Plus, Caden crossed the line today."

"That does not concern me. They won't succeed, and I will deal with him accordingly."

"You, of all people, should know not to be so overconfident."

There is a pause while the water continues to drip.

"I'm starting to doubt if I can help her break through the barrier and overcome hate. Physically, I know she is capable, but her mentality is still questionable," Lamont admits.

"We've waited centuries for her to arrive. I think we can give her a little more time. She has a perceptive mind. One you've underestimated before."

"I'd give her all the time in the world if I didn't have a pack as my number one priority. I won't lead them into a losing battle."

"I know you won't. And neither will she. You can't make them respect her. She has to gain that for herself. Until then, we wait."

You hear Gabriel's retreating footsteps.

The pack considers you an intruder. A rival living among them. The soulless enemy they were taught to hate. They follow Lamont's orders. Are instructed to obey you when he is not present. They believe you are just as much of a monster as the rest of the vampires. You don't care to show them otherwise. You are a wildcard. No one knows how to control you. They are inferior to your power.

The ray of light dims. You amplify your hearing and pick up on a rumble of thunder in the distance. The storm has gained speed. You want to be there when it hits.

"Stay here," you command Cameron as you slip off the rock.

You move with purpose. You don't care who watches. You ignore the whispers. Don't care who reports to Lamont. You aligned with them, but you are a sheep in wolf's clothing. A very dangerous sheep at that. They know to keep their distance.

As you step outside, the wind soars viciously. The sky is black like your non-beating heart. The first drops of rain begin to fall. You welcome it as you walk out into the open, and a flash of lightning lights up the dark sky, followed by a clap of distant thunder. You close your eyes and tilt back your head, letting the rain beat against you. Hoping to be transported to a time anywhere but here. To try and feel a connection with the environment. Something you have become numb to.

The rain is not pleasurable. Your instinct is to listen to the rumbles of thunder on a low frequency. Lightning does not blind your low field of vision. You walk against the howling wind next to the tree line. Watch the branches sway and fight to remain standing.

You pause at the edge of the tree line. A particular spot you are known to spend some of your time at. A place none of the wolves comprehend.

You place a hand against the same yellow poplar tree in the groove you always touch when you come to the area. The only thing you feel is the rough bark. The trees are nothing but objects. Do nothing for you every time.

You step into the forest. You search the area with enhanced scent receptors. An overwhelming smell of petrichor invades. The one scent you are looking for does not reveal itself among the release of chemicals secreted by the wet, musky earth.

Your focus snaps to attention. Slowly, you turn. You perceive resentment in the yellow eyes of the wolf stalking you. A deep growl emanates from his throat.

Caden.

almly, you reach for your sheath and leisurely pull out your dagger. Caden lowers his head and keeps his burning eyes of hatred trained on you. He pulls back his lip, exposing his pearly white canines as he watches your every move.

"If you came here looking for a fight," you say, releasing your hold and letting the dagger drop, "you'll be disappointed."

Caden licks his lips with a snarl.

You turn your back to him. You wait for him to engage. You don't care if he does. He's wanted you dead since the beginning. You don't care if he follows through. You want him to.

A yelp emanates before a body slams up against a tree. You face back around.

"Cameron?"

He has never disobeyed you before. He's supposed to be inside, not sidestepping closer to your defense. He is the smallest wolf of them all. He does not normally engage in fights.

Caden lurches to his paws with anger. His focus is now on the light-brown wolf standing in his way.

"Cameron, leave," you command sternly.

He ignores you. His fur stands on end, with his tense body hunching lower to the ground. You try to reach out and grab him. Only you are too late. He hurls his body through the air and collides with Caden.

The fight is savage. Back and forth, they engage and disengage, aiming for a weak spot while the storm rages on. You can hear the sickening sound of flesh and fur being ripped apart as the wolves fight tooth and nail. You hear Cameron cry as Caden rips into his shoulder before he clamps his jaw onto Caden's right ear.

"Stop, both of you!" you shout, only to be drowned out by a deep rumble of thunder. Neither wolf complies as they continue to brawl.

Both rear up on their hind legs, jaws sparring while trying to push one another down. This is a brutal fight that shouldn't even have taken place. They are family. Family who may have different viewpoints, but fighting among themselves is prohibited. The only exception is to challenge the one in charge.

Caden picks up his right foreleg and slashes out with his back claws extending into Cameron's rear hindquarters. Cameron whines out in pain, distracted long enough for Caden to knock him to the ground.

You watch as Caden grasps the back of Cameron's neck, forcefully picks him up, and whips him through the air up against a tree. Disoriented, Cameron struggles to push back up onto his paws, but Caden is on him like lightning, clamping his jaws around his ruff and tossing him again.

You have had enough. Swiftly, you insert yourself between Cameron and an advancing Caden. Before you can speak a word, Caden hurls his massive body weight against you, shoving you to the ground. His hollow eyes tell you all you need to know. As his jaws widen, you instinctively bring up your arm to defend your vitals. His jaw clamps down onto your bare arm and breaks skin before releasing abruptly as he howls in pain.

You both redirect your attention to see Cameron has his razor-sharp teeth gripping Caden's left hind leg. Caden snaps at his muzzle. Cameron reacts too slowly, weak from the fight. Caden smacks him away and pursues. He stands over Cameron, baring his teeth, prepared to go for the jugular.

Caden howls in pain once more. When he whips his head over his shoulder, he freezes, disturbed. You have your own elongated teeth embedded in his right hind leg, with fury in your eyes.

"Enough!" Lamont's voice booms over the thunder.

You immediately retract your fangs and sit back on your knees against the soggy ground, watching Lamont angrily stroll over.

"Would someone like to tell me what's going on here?" Lamont demands, folding his arms against his chest.

"She bit me! Did you see that? She bit me! Attacked me. She can't be trusted. She must be terminated immediately," Caden rants as soon as he transforms into his human self.

"You also disobeyed an order."

"It was an act of self-defense," Caden protests.

"Not from what I saw."

"She's the enemy. Now, she's crossed the line." Caden glares momentarily at you with fury.

"You also crossed the line, Caden. Your disobedience leaves me no choice but to banish you."

"What?" A hint of fear flashes in his eyes. "Over her? I belong to this pack, not her. She's a vampire!"

"She's an ally to *my* pack. Now leave!" Lamont points.

Caden stares at Lamont's hand in disbelief, with his mouth partially open, realizing Lamont is serious.

"No." You rise to your feet.

"What?" Lamont glances over.

"There will be no banishment." Gasps and whispers erupt from the gathering members of the pack.

"That's not your call to make." Lamont drops his arm.

"I just did." You challenge him with your stare.

"I don't want your help," Caden spits with disgust.

"No one is making you stay," you clap back, but your eyes stay trained on Lamont with a slight head shake.

Caden falls silent.

"Gabriel, take him to isolation for now," Lamont backs down.

"You're going to follow orders from her now?" Caden retorts.

"Silence!" Lamont shouts.

Caden shrinks back from Lamont's piercing eyes as Gabriel grabs hold of his arm. Only he shrugs it off. "I know where to go."

Gabriel follows him closely as the pack begins to disperse from the scene.

"How's your arm?" Lamont flicks his eyes down. The bite mark is already being repaired. Only faint marks remain that are nearly dissolved.

"Don't pretend you care." You turn your back on him. Your eyes zero in on Molly, in wolf form, licking Cameron's wounds.

"Nadia." Lamont seizes your upper arm with force.

"Careful." You flash briefly at his hand on your arm before back up into his eyes. "You're getting personal."

He removes his hand. "Werewolf blood weakens vampires…"

"I'm not a normal vampire," you cut him off.

"You would tell me if you had some kind of reaction, right?"

"You'd be the first to know."

"Good." He inhales sharply. "Now, about Caden."

"There's nothing to discuss; he stays," you dismiss.

You see his jaw clench before he stalks away. You know Lamont, along with the other pack members who were present, can't fathom why you would want Caden to stay when he has had it in for you since day one. The only one bold enough to take you on. The only one you have to watch your back with. All he knows is how to shed enemy blood. You are a vampire and, therefore, his enemy. He wants you dead. He refuses to believe anything otherwise. It doesn't matter that you feed on vampires. It doesn't matter that you bear the mark. A vampire can never be trusted.

You hear a faint whine. Cameron is watching you.

"I told you to stay inside. I don't need you to fight for me, so next time, listen to my directive." You crinkle your nose before strolling back to the cave.

You sit upon your rock once more, listening to the slow dripping of water from outside cracks leaking in as you cut a deep line across your wrist and watch it heal simultaneously. You cut eight more times.

Lamont called an emergency meeting and is currently ranting about the importance of why they are all working together. The next one out of line will be permanently banished.

You narrow your range and hear Noir preening herself outside your chamber. You're annoyed. Reduced to being watched by a bird. You grew to tolerate Cameron, who was tasked with the job. He doesn't make it so obvious anymore. However, he is currently in the recovery chamber, recovering from the wounds he sustained in the fight.

You rest your head against the hard rock wall and glance at the tally of lines carved next to you. You don't have to count them to know what day it is.

For the first time in a long time, you finally felt something when Caden bit you. The venom from a wolf's bite is supposed to weaken a vampire. It did make your arm feel a bit numb at first, but it also made you feel like a fire was spreading through your veins. A sensation you wanted to feel all over.

The wound has since healed, along with the numbness. Much faster than what an ordinary vampire would have experienced. You feel much like your normal self. Fast and fierce. No setbacks.

You tilt your head back and examine the small opening above, which a sliver of light shines through. It's narrow. That's not going to stop you when this is the perfect opportunity. The only one watching you is the stupid bird. However, Noir is perched outside, not in, to watch your comings and goings.

Quietly, you rise and pull yourself up the slick surface. Inch by inch, you progress the long way upward. When you reach the narrow crevice, you make quick work as you shift your shoulder blades back and forth to widen the hole enough for you to be able to slip through.

At once, you hear the frantic, raspy caw from Noir as she flies into the chamber and begins to peck at your lower legs. You ignore her and continue to pull yourself up through the rocky outcrop.

When your hand touches solid ground, you heave yourself out. As soon as your feet hit the ground, you take off into the daylight. You run northeast, tuning in to your surroundings. You have a head start. The wolves are fast, but you are faster. Plus, you have the light of day on your side. Lamont won't risk a wolf sighting in a place where wolves should not exist.

Chapter 49

You peer at the back of the blue house from the trees. It still stands unoccupied exactly one year later. The betrayal still stings. The loss still splinters you into a million pieces. This is the last place you should ever come.

The sun is high in the clear blue sky, with not a single cloud to be seen. You inhale deeply and take a step from the shadows into direct sunlight, shielding your eyes. You walk in long strides across the grass, your focus completely on the house.

The sliding glass door had its lock replaced. You easily break the seal and slide it open, hesitating before stepping inside. You pick up on a faint chemical smell that was used to clean the hardwood floor. The floor where Marc's blood spilled. A human's eye would be inadequate to see the evidence that lingers, but a vampire can heighten its sight to see the bloodstain.

A sick feeling overcomes you, twisting like a knife into your blackened heart the way you twisted the knife into Marc under Jomar's compulsion. You were not prepared to feel that intense emotion as you see the image clearly in your mind.

You kneel on the floor and reach out to touch the spot. You want to feel that fire in your veins again. Want to feel that powerful electricity. Only you feel emptiness.

No fire.

Just cold.

Hollow.

"You wouldn't recognize the thing I've become if you were still here," you whisper softly. "I haven't been managing well." You pull your hand back, slowly rise, and stare. "Everything inside is shattered. I just want this pain to go away. I've lost myself. I hate what I've become, but you deserve justice."

When you reawoke, you were denied closure. There was no body to hold or to grieve over. Just ash inside the clothing he once wore. Marc was gone. You couldn't bring him back. He died because of you. Because your human mind could be manipulated.

Only you were not going down without a fight. One last kiss sealed the deal when you sliced your tongue on his exposed tooth. Licked his blood from your hand. A mixture of his blood and yours. A coppery taste. A sacrifice you were willing to make without batting an eye.

Only your sacrifice did not come easily. You were alone when you woke. The anguish you felt was overwhelming and magnified. You fought so hard against becoming the very thing you didn't want to become. The only one who understood why was gone. What would stop you from losing control?

In a moment of weakness, you staggered to your feet, plowed through the dining room table, and slammed against the refrigerator with enough force to leave an impression. You pulled drawers completely off their hinges until you found what you were looking for.

A large knife.

You grabbed the handle when your mind flashed to the bloody switchblade, reminding you of what you had done. You dropped the knife and sank to the kitchen floor, sobbing uncontrollably. Who would avenge Marc if you couldn't?

So much pain swelled within like a shaken bottle of soda, building a ton of pressure that wanted to explode. You wanted it out. Needed it out.

You grabbed the knife and cut a deep slit into your wrist. A fizz released, but the wound sealed too quickly for the pressure to completely burst forth.

Your mind shifted when you smelled your blood. Hunger racked you as you became keenly aware that your throat was as dry as a desert. Your nose knew where to take you. In a trance, your feet guided you to the foyer, where a blue plastic flip-top cooler sat on top of the extra freezer in the house. You mindlessly popped open the container and stared at the stash of blood bags. Slowly, you reached out and grabbed one. Every firing cell in your brain demanded the blood. You chucked it to the floor, overcoming the desire. You refused to drink from an innocent person who had donated in good faith.

In defiance, you raced back into the kitchen and plucked the knife from the floor. You cut deeply into your wrist and licked the blood that oozed before it closed back up. The monster inside you demanded more. Wanted you to go back and rip apart every single blood bag in the cooler. It was a tug of war with your own mind. What would stop you from taking innocent lives? You were alone. You had no one to help you. You had to stop yourself from being unleashed.

You took the knife and aimed it at your stomach. Your hand shook unsteadily with conflict. So many reasons you should. So many reasons you shouldn't.

You raised your hand while grinding your teeth.

"Are you sure that's what you want to do?"

You looked toward the dining room and saw a familiar face with a scar across his left eye standing there.

"You show up now?" Anger seized you as you charged him. He easily caught your wrist before knocking you off your feet and onto your back.

"I'm not your enemy." He stood over you with the knife that he had taken from your hand at his side.

"You're not my friend either." You grabbed his leg and yanked with force. You quickly rolled onto your stomach and pinned him down, taking aim, ready to throw a punch. Only an angry black bird, squawking frantically, flew into your face and slashed out with its claws. You batted the bird away from your face, realizing your mistake too late as you were flipped and pinned.

"Anger causes you to be irrational. Irrationality causes you to lose."

"Just kill me!" you screamed in his face.

"I'd prefer not to."

"Why? I'm a vampire now. That changes things."

"Yes, but we share a common goal."

"No, we don't."

"You cannot seek revenge alone."

"You want to make a bet?" You began to struggle against his restraint.

"If you leave now, in the condition you're in, emotionally unbalanced, you will fail. I can help you transition and maintain control." His hold was strong and true.

"You don't know what it's like."

"Werewolves share a transition of senses comparable to what vampires go through. I can help guide you."

"You expect me to trust you? Trust your mutts won't rebel?"

"You have to trust someone. They would not dare defy me. I am their pack leader. To defy me risks banishment. Without the safety of the pack, they have no protection from the vampires."

"He's not my number one priority," you stated in a hushed tone.

"I know," he whispered back.

You stopped struggling and narrowed your eyes on him. "And you're okay with that?"

"I'm not here to make you do anything you don't want to do."

You looked away, your eyes landing on the pile of ashes. You wanted to refuse. Only you were a novice. You had to learn what your strengths and weaknesses were. You couldn't do that on your own. Not until you knew what you were fully capable of.

"Release me."

"As long as this discussion continues rationally."

You met his eyes, blinked, and nodded once.

He released his hold immediately.

As you stood and brushed yourself off, you heard a squawk.

"Make sure to keep that thing away from me." You glared at the crow perched on top of the refrigerator.

"Her name is Noir." He raised his arm, prompting her to dive and land upon it.

"I don't care."

"A shame. Your personalities are quite similar."

"Let's get a few things straightened out here." You projected yourself in a business manner.

"I'm listening."

"We are not friends, now or ever. We are allies only. I don't care what happens to you or your pack or your stupid bird."

Noir took offense and yelled with displeasure.

You ignored her as you continued to speak. "You may be alpha, but you do not have authority over me. I will not tolerate you bossing me around, ever. Are we clear?"

"I understand completely, and as long as you pose no threat to my pack or use any means of your abilities against them, we can work together efficiently." He extended a hand.

"I can agree to that." You shook his hand once.

"Very good. By the way, I don't think we've ever been properly introduced. My name is Lamont."

"Let's skip the formalities." You stepped to your left and froze in place. The suppressed pain hit you like a ton of bricks as you held your stomach and crumpled to your knees.

"We can use the front door." He placed a hand on your shoulder.

"I refuse to let this subjugate me." You lurched to your feet, walked to the bedroom, and slammed the door.

"What are you doing?" he called from the other side.

You ignored him as you rummaged through all the items left behind. In the back of the closet, you found a black leather catsuit costume. You removed your self-defining clothing at once and slipped on the loose-fitting suit. Despising the feel of the long sleeves, you ripped them at the shoulder. You rummaged some more, finding a matching belt and some knee-high, thick-heeled boots, slipping them on before pulling back your hair and tying it up high.

You swung the door open and ripped it off the hinges. You advanced for the knife and swiftly chopped off your hair, leaving it pulled back short.

"Call me...Nadia."

Chapter 50

The front door bursts open with force. Footsteps pound against the floor. You wait patiently.

"What are you doing here?" Lamont demands, folding his arms against his chest.

"I don't answer to you, remember?"

"You do realize this is the worst place for you to come."

"I'm fully aware of that."

"Yet, you came anyway. It's a vulnerability for you and a liability to your mentality."

"I beg to differ."

"You're coming with me." He reaches for your arm. "You're forbidden to ever come back here."

You pull away just out of his reach. "How dare you treat me like a dog? I don't bow."

"How dare you bite a member of my pack? We had an agreement."

"Yes, we did. I also recall that you were supposed to keep them on a tight leash."

He sighs, deflecting. "Nothing good can come from this place. I want to see you overcome your hate, not be blinded by it."

"How touching," you ridicule.

The light breeze shifts, blowing in through the open glass door, along with a scent. A scent too close for comfort as Lamont's eyes shift, and a growl begins to rumble from his throat. Your eyes slightly rise as you twist your neck around. The intruder's blue eyes lock with yours for a split second before Lamont lunges in his cream-colored wolf form, just missing the intruder, who takes off. You stand there like a statue and inhale sharply. Your ears become acutely aware of the scene outside.

Lamont is hot on the intruder's heels, tearing up the grass with his huge paws, barely touching the ground. Both run lighting-fast across the open landscape. Just as the intruder reaches the trees, Lamont launches his immense body into the air, knocking against the intruder. Lamont is quick to gain his footing, tossing his head in the direction of his foe before initiating another attack. His jaws are open wide, prepared to clasp down onto flesh. Only Lamont snaps down on nothing but air as his quarry manages to roll out of the way in the nick of time.

"Stop!" You insert yourself between the intruder and Lamont, who ceases growling and stares up at you. "He's not an enemy."

In a matter of seconds, he shape-shifts back into his human form, studying you. "You know him?"

"Yes," you declare, shifting closer. "Go home to the pack. Your services are no longer needed here."

"I will return to the pack," he agrees.

You watch him obediently leave the vicinity. Once he is out of sight, you are reluctant to turn and face the vampire you know all too well. You close your eyes and inhale deeply to let your mind go to a calm state. A technique Lamont trained you on.

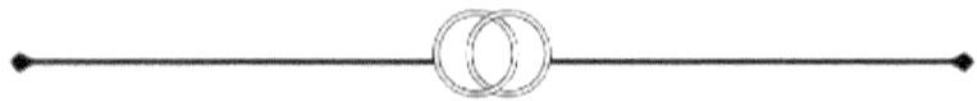

"I don't require oxygen," you stated with annoyance.

"I know you don't, but I also know it will do you no harm if you were to breathe it in," Lamont responded patiently.

Your human mind didn't need to remind you to breathe. It knew to do that on its own. Now, that part of you lies dormant. While your firing cells overwhelmed you, going in several different directions, you focused on one thing only.

Breathe.

Just as if you were human, it helped calm all the noise. You focused on the rhythm of breathing evenly. Your mind settled. Your mind did not have control.

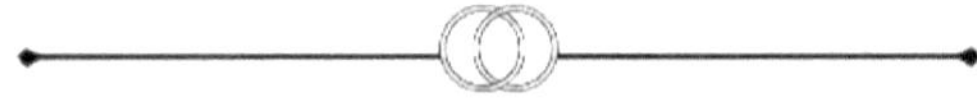

You turn slowly to face Vince. He's changed his appearance. Shaved off all his hair, and he's wearing a dark purple camouflage shirt with normal-colored camouflaged pants.

"Nadine?" he whispers in disbelief.

You are on him as fast as the speed of light, slamming him to the ground with blazing eyes. You press down on his chest with iron force, aiming your dagger at his stomach. "Who knows you're here?"

"No one," he answers.

"Why did you come back?"

"I...I don't know." He looks away.

You press the tip of your blade harder against him.

"I couldn't accept that you were gone...accept that the prophecy was wrong. I just wanted to find some kind of sign." His blue gaze meets your eyes.

"Where have you been all this time, Vinson?"

"Keeping a low profile."

"Coward!"

He jerks as if you slapped him, shocked by your insult. "How are you not dead? I saw Camille break your neck."

"Why did you let him come back alone?" you ask as your hands begin to shake.

"It was a trap. He was meant to. I tried to get away, please believe me, but Seth kept coming at me. By the time I got away, it was already too late."

"So, you just left?"

"I didn't know what to do. I would have been killed if I had been captured. Nadine, I truly am sorry. If I had known—"

"Nadine's dead. My name is Nadia."

His eyebrows crinkle. "But you don't like being called by that name."

"You shouldn't have come back here. You're fortunate that I spared your life. Leave and do the only thing you are good at, running and hiding." You abruptly release him, sheathing your dagger.

He rises to his feet. "I'm not going to leave your side ever again. Where you go, I go. I may not have been there for you when you turned, but I'm here now, and I can help you."

"I don't need your help." You get in his face and stare him directly in the eyes. "You will leave now."

"Okay, I'll leave." He turns and obeys.

You narrow your eyes as you watch him go. Despite your admission, you know him well enough to know that he would never do what you tell him. Never back down when it concerns you.

"Stop."

He frowns over his shoulder. "But you told me to leave."

"Forget what I told you to do."

"Okay."

You shoot off, covering the distance in the woods to the silver Toyota Camry that you had swiped to make the trip and parked just off the road in the trees. You slip into the driver's seat and turn on the engine while reaching out to close the door. As you yank the lever into reverse, he appears. You stomp down on the gas and fishtail backward onto the road. He rushes after the car and is able to yank the passenger side door open as you pause to shift into drive. He climbs in as you squeal the tires on the pavement. You grip the steering wheel.

"Where are you going?" he asks.

You ignore him, resisting the urge to speed.

"You should put your visor down," you advise, prompting him to reach for it.

You catch his wrist and squeeze hard. Understanding the cue, he pulls back.

"So, have you been with the wolves this whole time?"

You keep your focus trained on the road ahead without commentary.

"How did that happen?"

When it becomes evident that you're not going to answer any more of his questions, he sits back with a sigh and watches out his window.

You drive for hours in complete silence. The irony of it does not evade you. Memories flood your mind and stir things up inside as you drive the familiar highway in the night. You push them back and swallow hard. Fixate on even breathing. Fight for control.

"What are we doing here?" Vince articulates with apprehension when he recognizes where you're heading.

"Are you sure you still want to go where I go?"

"What do you expect to find here?"

You ignore him and keep driving. You navigate onto the town roads before you whip into the parking lot of the bank you used to work at and park directly in front of the outside camera.

"What are you doing? They will see us and come."

"Good." You flick off the headlights and turn on the interior lights to spotlight yourself.

"They will come in force. This is reckless."

"If you leave now, you might still have a chance." You stare down the red dot on the camera.

"You don't stand a chance on your own."

He has always been a thorn in your side. You should have known you weren't going to be able to shake him off easily. You flip the headlights back on, back out of the parking spot, and merge into the sparse midnight traffic. You travel down to the light and turn off the main road.

"Nothing good can come from this," he warns.

You remain mute as you park alongside the house that you once called home. Caution tape is strung across the door. It's uninhabited.

You open your door and slowly climb out before walking up to the white front gate. You pause before opening it. You didn't know your stomach could twist in knots like this as you push yourself down the path. Your hand lingers on the doorknob before twisting it and finding it unlocked. You let it swing open. The scent of death lingers. The coppery smell invades your nose. It's faint, but you can still decipher it, along with another scent that doesn't belong.

Bergamot.

As you step across the threshold, an assailant hurtles from the side toward your head.

Chapter 51

"Leo?"

You're quick to react, catching the orange tabby in midair after he propelled off the couch in the corner. He angrily growls and slashes out with his claws, but as soon as he hears your voice, he stills and stares directly into your eyes.

"How is that possible?" Vince asks from behind you in an astounded tone.

Leo retracts his elongated canines, twice the size, and meows softly. The house fills with his motor purring.

You stand stiffly, wrapping your mind around it. You have done so many horrific things, and yet when he looked into your eyes, into your soul, he still saw something good. "Take him," you say and pass him off to Vince.

You can't stand being in the same room with either one of them for one more second. You dash to your old bedroom and close the door, standing up against it.

Your breaths come in fast. Too fast. Aware, you direct your mind to slow them down. When you get your breathing back in order, you take in the room. It's a mess. Stuff with no value is scattered everywhere. Your mattress is flipped up against the wall. Clothes are in a heap on the floor. Your nightstand and dresser drawers are pulled out with all the contents scattered about. It angers you.

You waltz over and start to pick up what belongs to each dresser drawer, and you slide them back in place neatly. Any jewelry of value you had is gone. You lay down your mattress and smooth out all the wrinkles. The last thing you have left is your nightstand drawer. You put it back in place before picking up your hand lotion, lip balm, nail clippers, nail file, hair ties, phone charger, Leo's string, a notebook, some pens, old birthday cards, and some notes.

You pause when you pick up a note folded into a square with a frown face doodled on top. You rise from your kneeling position before sitting on the edge of the bed as you unfold the sheet of paper. The edges are frayed and clearly ripped from a notebook. Your fingers automatically start plucking at the edges. It was always one of your pet peeves. The blood in your stomach turns to ice when you see the note is written in Camille's handwriting. You stare at her name at the bottom of the note. You move your left hand up to your right, prepared to rip the letter to pieces, when your eyes catch sight of the words, *I'm sorry.*

Dear Nadine,

I'm sorry I wasn't a good friend and made you feel like I wasn't on your side. I don't do well with confrontations. I only laughed to cover my own anxiety. I was scared. Hurting you was never my intention. I hope you can forgive me and we can be friends again someday. I miss you.

—Camille

Your hand drops to your lap as the memory resurfaces.

You had not been friends with Camille for long. Your friendship was still fresh. You were both young but still old enough to have outgrown the playground, yet you both went anyway to the one across from Camille's house. You both claimed empty swings. Swung a little and wrapped chains while making small talk to get to know one another. Your likes and your dislikes.

A boy, a bit older, wearing baggy clothing, walked by the fence and made a rude remark as he passed by. A remark you happened to overhear.

"Why don't you come over here and say that to our faces, or are you a chicken?" you called out to him.

The boy scaled the fence and headed toward you. You stood your ground while Camille stood behind you at his approach. You had been slightly worried but refused to show it. You had not expected him to actually walk up to your face. If he got physical, you didn't know what you would do. If you had been alone, the outcome would have been different; however, you were not alone. You hadn't known Camille all that well yet, but you still had a primal instinct to defend her.

"Aren't you two a bit old to be on the swings?"

"I don't see a sign with an age limit."

He reached into his jeans pocket and threw a bunch of loose change at you. "Here's some change for you to buy a new life."

Camille started to giggle behind you. You couldn't believe she was laughing at his rude remark.

"I don't need a new life." You didn't move or blink an eye while standing your ground.

"You should reconsider. Yours is pretty pathetic." He walked away and hopped back over the fence.

You allowed yourself to relax when the danger passed. Your mind turned to anger, masking the hurt as you turned to Camille. "I thought we were friends. Why would you laugh?"

"I don't know. I'm sorry."

"I'm going home."

You had given Camille the silent treatment afterward. You don't recall when Camille passed the note. Don't remember ever reading it. You had your mind set on not forgiving her. Only, at some point, you did. Until now, you had completely forgotten the incident occurred.

You fold the note up twice, drop it into the drawer, and slam it shut. It means nothing to you. It only makes you realize that you made a huge mistake letting her back in. Giving her a second chance and putting your trust in her. Your fatal downfall.

"Nadine?" Vince knocks on the door.

You rip the door off its frame and slam him against the wall. "Stop calling me that."

"You'll always be Nadine to me."

"She's gone, and she's never coming back!"

"You can change your appearance. Change your name, but you can't change who you are inside."

"And who exactly do you think I am?"

"You're the girl who stands up for those who are too scared to stand up for themselves. You're the girl who doesn't back down even when she's afraid. You're the girl who will defend the people she cares about with everything she's got."

"I don't care about anyone anymore." You shake your head.

"Why did you defend me from that wolf? You could have killed me yourself, but you didn't. What held you back?"

You feel Leo rubbing up against your leg, purring. You release Vince abruptly and walk away. You walk mindlessly through the house and stop at the kitchen sink.

"Why are you holding back?" Gabriel asked you after a sparring match with swords in the training hall.

"What makes you think I'm holding back?" you asked as you both circled the area.

"Intuition."

"You're wrong, old dog."

"Prove it."

You lashed out with a jab that he blocked. Metal rattled against metal. You pushed him back, your swings fast and steady. He matched your pace until he found himself backed up against the rock wall. You brought down your sword, which he blocked just above his head. It was a stalemate. His arms shook as he held his own, summoning the strength to push you back and roll off to the side. When you brought your sword down, it scraped against a rock. You turned on him with anger and attacked again, coming at him with full force. You knocked the sword from his grasp and impaled him in the shoulder with yours. The smell of his blood stunned you as you pulled the blade out.

"Very good." He pressed a hand to his shoulder.

"I think we're done here." You retreated.

He was always pushing you. Pushing you hard. He knew you had more to give. Could be hurt in the process. Yet, that didn't stop him. He always provoked you.

You didn't want to hurt him. Didn't dwell on the fact when you did. He wasn't the one you wanted to hurt. He wasn't the one you wanted to kill. He was just a stand-in.

"Nadine, please reconsider," Vince pleads, jarring you from your memory.

You whirl around. "No one is making you stay."

"This is madness. You know it. He wouldn't want this."

You smack him across the face. "How dare you speak for him!"

"Don't let his death be for nothing." He rubs his jaw.

"I want you to leave. Now!" you bellow in his face.

"I'm not going anywhere."

"Leave!"

"No." He shakes his head.

You kick him hard and watch him smash through the wall into the dining room.

"I'm not leaving you alone in this." He stands.

"I'm not going to let anyone else suffer because of me." You clench your hands before realizing your own admission. You turn away sharply.

"Talk to me." He reaches out and places a hand on your shoulder.

"Don't touch me." You remove his hand, spin, pull his arm back, and slam him face-first to the floor with fire in your eyes.

"Without you, everyone will suffer."

You inhale deeply through your nose and stop. Your subconscious takes center stage as you become aware of a faint smell. Slowly, you crane your head to the right. An unknown force takes control. You open the cupboard and stare at the small containers of spices. Your eyes glide over each label until they land on the one that drew you in.

Cinnamon.

Slowly, you reach out and pick it up. You stare at the word on the label, frozen. Mindlessly, your hand begins to unscrew the top of the lid. When the lid is removed, an overwhelming scent of cinnamon fills the room.

You close your eyes and embrace the sensation that he is here in the room with you. You cannot see him. You cannot touch him. But you can feel his presence as fire burns through your core. All this time, you had grown numb to the pain. Buried all the feelings. Locked it all away, paralyzed, allowing only one thing to remain.

"Not because of me." Marc's words echo through your mind.

A light touch tickles your arm. You glance down and see Leo on the counter. He meows softly before stretching up to you and butting his head into yours. Love isn't something you can see. Love isn't something you can touch. Love is something felt by the heart and soul. You can shut love out. Drown in hate. Become broken beyond repair. Only, one spark can allow love to find its way back in. Help alleviate the ache you carry and restore the damage, even when you believed all hope was lost. Fuels that unexplained desire to defend the ones you care for, at whatever the cost, even if it hurts. It's the only thing worth fighting for.

Out of desperation, Marc declared his love for you. You had not been ready to understand how you truly felt – not when it was all so complicated and moved so fast. An impossible phenomenon. Now you understand clearly. You loved Marc, too. You'll always regret not saying those words back.

You turn back to Vince. "Let's get out of here."

Chapter 52

The gas tank is low. You stop at the closest gas station to fill it up, and wasting no time, you compel the attendant to program the system that you paid. As the tank fills, you pull out the hair tie in your short hair and let it fall choppily above your shoulders. Only the hair that falls into your eyes will be a distraction, so you gather the front and sides and pull them back, leaving only the back free. As soon as the tank is filled, you take off toward the highway.

"We shouldn't be on the highway. They'll be coming this way," Vince protests.

"I'm counting on it," you state evenly.

"You have a plan?"

"You'll see soon."

You drive into the night. Idle just above the speed limit. Cars are scattered on the road. You soon catch up to a tractor-trailer truck traveling in the left lane. You speed up until you are parallel with the truck, coasting for the time being until the trucker's left turn signal flashes. You gain speed and pop up ahead of the truck before it merges into the lane.

You note the dozens of headlights piercing the night ahead in the oncoming traffic lanes. As they near, you keep your eyes focused on the road straight ahead before black SUVs go sailing by.

"They made us," Vince announces with his neck stretched around.

You watch in the rearview mirror as the SUVs turn using the grass median. You have a short lead. You are going to keep them in the distance every second you can muster.

Timing it accordingly, you brake hard. The truck driver behind you slams on his brakes, burning rubber before the rig turns, crossing the line. You press hard on the accelerator. The truck has both sides blocked as you sail off into the distance. Many of the SUVs get caught up in the truck, but the rest quickly drive around.

You merge onto the exit ramp without slowing down. There is nothing but trees up ahead. When you come upon a ninety-degree right turn, you release the gas pedal and spin around. You keep control of the car flying down the winding road and see an SUV topple over onto its side, unable to make the hard turn.

You swerve left around the next sharp turn, eyeing a private drive ahead. You swing the car into the driveway, park the car along the trees, and shove open the door.

"Run."

Vince holds Leo and follows closely into the trees. You hear tires screeching to a stop shortly afterward, before a crash. The road whines some more as you dart across it back into a sea of trees. With no other choice, your pursuers have to follow on foot.

"Keep going." You catch a high branch and swing up into the trees.

"Nadine!" he calls out, slowing, but you are already gone. He picks up speed and continues reluctantly.

You climb higher into the branches before settling on one, listening and waiting. One by one, the other vampires whistle past in pursuit. There are over a dozen before the whistling lags. You get into position before torpedoing off the branch head-first, knocking into one of the vampires who was not expecting you. You twist your dagger into his stomach as you crash onto the ground with him. You rip it out swiftly before breaking his neck.

The vampire who brought up the rear comes to a halt. Before he has a chance to make a move, you swiftly silence him as well. You turn and follow the others.

You spur ahead and cut off four of them before picking them off. The trampling ahead turns course as the others become aware that you have gotten behind them. You dash off in the opposite direction. The other vampires are hot on your heels.

The trees ahead part. An opening presents itself. You run out into the middle before stopping abruptly in the center. You turn to face the vampires as they are quick to surround you. There are nine of them.

"It's over. There's nowhere for you to run," one of them dares to say.

You uncoil your urumi from around your waist and flick your wrist in a figure eight. You tune in to the environment around you, listening to every sound attentively.

"You think that's going to stop us?" another taunts.

A vampire from your right makes the first move. You lash out with your urumi and strike him in the face. He falls over backward. The next comes from behind. You slide to your knee, snap out, and trip him. One by one, they converge on you. You quickly whirl, whipping around your urumi, knocking out as many as you can. To your left, one jumps back before rushing you. You bring up your dagger and plunge it into his gut before jabbing your elbow into the chest of your next assailant. You fling your wrist forward, and your urumi cuts the side of your frontal attacker.

You release your grip on the urumi, toss your dagger to your right hand, and finish off the vampire directly in front of you before darting off and inflicting fatal blows on the others.

"Nadine!" Vince's voice cries out.

Blazing pain slices into your back. You turn and see that another vampire has emerged from the woods before Vince tackles him to the ground.

You reach back and pull out the blade before you are on the scene like a blaze of fury. You yank the vampire by the back of his shirt collar and shove him up against the tree before you tear into his flesh and drink deeply.

"No."

He struggles against you with diminished energy. When you finish, you break his neck.

"I thought I told you to keep going, Vinson." You glare at him.

"Did you just…?"

"Let's go." You pick up your dagger, sheath it, and charge back out to where you left your urumi, securing it around your waist before taking off with Vince closely following.

There is a small development of homes a quarter of a mile away. You find a parked van left running in the driveway and quickly slip in.

"You feed on vampire blood?"

"That's what you saw, isn't it?" You navigate to a main two-lane road.

"How is that possible?" He pets the top of Leo's head.

"Might have something to do with the fact that the first drop of blood I tasted was my own."

"You drank your own blood?" He's astounded.

You continue to drive.

"When did you know you could drink vampire blood?" he asks a few minutes later.

"When I picked up the overpowering scent of Seth's blood, you left behind wounded."

You were primal. The smell of blood was intoxicating – it was the only thing your mind heavily focused on. The hunger. Something you had never experienced before. It drove you mad. Instincts led you to the blood trail. When you found him in a weakened state, you devoured him. He wasn't the one you wanted, but he was a good stand-in. He curbed your agonizing hunger. The power you felt afterward was liberating. You were ready to hunt down Jomar right then and there. You didn't care who stood in your way or how many vampires you had to fight. You wanted his blood. All of it.

"How do you kill a monster? By creating a new one." You heard a sly remark.

Your dilated eyes fell upon the wolf in human form with a dark-brown skin-tight body suit.

"You dare insult me?" You shoved him back, not realizing your own strength as he went hurtling through the air. He crashed through several trees before landing.

"How dare you!" He jumped to his feet before morphing into his wolf form and charging.

"Stand down, Caden," Lamont cut him off.

In wolf form, he curled his lip, shifting his eyes from Lamont to you. The hatred in his eyes burns like an inferno.

"We must all come together if we are to accomplish our shared undertaking. A common goal. One that requires us to work together, which we shall. No one is to lay a hand or paw on her. Do I make myself clear?" Lamont held the attention of all who'd gathered on the scene.

"She should be terminated, and you know it," Caden declared, having shifted back to human form.

"Are you questioning my authority?"

"Tell your pet never to touch me again." He backed down.

"Move out." Lamont took the lead.

"You'll never get close enough to remove his armor," Vince utters, pulling you back to the present.

"You think my plan is to drain him bone-dry?" You glance his way with a raised eyebrow.

"What is your plan then?"

You meet him with bold silence.

"You can't go in there without one."

You snort. "Same old Vinson."

"What's that supposed to mean? And why do you keep calling me that?"

You don't engage.

"How many wolves are there?"

"Why do you want to know that?" You study him.

He hangs his head, avoiding your eyes. "I may have been staying off the grid this whole time, but I haven't given up the fight. I've been recruiting. Those who were broken, alone, and forgotten by society. Those who had nothing to live for. I provided them with a new purpose if they chose to join me."

Chapter 53

You stare straight ahead, processing his words. Trying to make sense of what they mean. Grasping the reality of it while focusing on trying to remain calm.

"You created your own army of vampires?" you manage to ask in a steady, even voice.

"I'm working on it, yes."

"That makes perfect sense." You sneer.

"They've been taught how to maintain their humanity," he clarifies.

"How many?" You grip the wheel.

He hesitates. "A few hundred."

"You teach them how to fight?"

"Most already had extensive training in that category, but yes, they are being trained to enhance their techniques. However, I don't have enough yet to go to battle."

"Numbers are not the sole factor in winning a war."

"You can't initiate one without a strategy."

You fall silent as the tires glide on the blacktop. You note headlights in the far distance behind. The remaining vampires are closing the gap. You figure that they most likely called in for reinforcements. You press harder on the accelerator as the mountain road loops around, providing some cover in the meantime.

"We have to find a place to throw them off our trail, or they will just keep coming for us," Vince declares.

You ignore him as you weave along the curvy road. The headlights behind are out of sight. A small parking area comes into view ahead to the right. The landscape is level. A trail.

You ease off the gas and swing the van into the parking lot, killing the lights. Without delay, you both leave the van's doors open as you race off for the trail. You have a short window, but there are only a few of them bringing up the rear.

You keep to the marked trail, making record time before it comes to an end, when you deviate into the thick forest. The thickness of the terrain slows you down.

"Head for the road. Don't stop or come back," you demand, nodding to your left before doubling back.

You reach the end of the trail, dagger in hand, and run full force into the vampire in the lead, thrusting him backward into the four behind him. The other two circle back as you somersault over your head, jab the nearest one, and chuck your dagger into the second.

The force of the blow has the vampire stagger back. You are quick on your feet, yanking the blade out and shoving him to the ground.

"Put down your blade. It's over. You're coming with us." The other four have you surrounded with their own daggers raised.

"If you insist." You let the dagger drop.

"Kick it over," the one in front of you orders, promting you to comply "Drink this."

He tosses a vial of blood, and you catch it in midair. The other vampires flinch at the motion. You train your eyes on the vampire in front of you as you unscrew the top and drink the contents. You groan, clenching your stomach, and drop to your knees.

"What the?" the vampire on your left exclaims before he screams. "Get it off!"

While they are momentarily distracted, you are quick to advance on the vampire to your right, rip the dagger from his hand, and impale him in the stomach before advancing to the lead vampire, slamming him up against a tree, and holding his arm away from you that holds his dagger.

"Go back to your vehicle. Report that I stole the other one and doubled back."

You release him and watch him take off back down the trail before you turn to assess the situation. Leo has the vampire he attacked on the run, while Vince has the vampire who was standing behind you indisposed.

"I thought I told you to head for the road," you scold.

"It's a good thing I came back. They nearly captured you."

"I had it under control."

"That's not what I saw."

"Why do you never listen?" you mumble with annoyance as you grab your dagger from the blades of grass and sheath it.

"I told you that I'm not leaving you again. I go where you go."

"One of these times, that's going to be a mistake."

"You're all that matters."

"Let's keep moving." You step past him.

"Leo," Vince calls out.

You take off to the end of the trail and back into the forest before stopping out by the highway that runs perpendicular, concealed by the trees, and wait. When a tractor-trailer truck roars by heading north, you match Vince's speed behind you before hopping in between the trailer and the cab, hitching a ride.

You feel his eyes on you. "What?"

"You drank a vial of werewolf blood, but you don't seem affected by it now."

"I never was."

"You're immune? How?"

"That I don't know." You lean out, allowing the wind to tickle your face as the landscape zips by.

Silence envelops you as you both stand on guard with every random passing vehicle, ready to act. Only ten minutes pass before a black SUV approaches from the opposite direction. You stand back against the cab, shoulder to shoulder with Vince, as the SUV sails by, followed by another. You weren't spotted.

The truck continues to head north at a steady speed. You relax a little, watching the road ahead. Leo purrs contentedly in Vince's arms as the vampire continuously strokes his head.

Fifteen minutes later, another set of black SUVs screams by.

"I don't like this," Vince voices.

"Relax."

"They're not going to stop."

"So little confidence."

You feel the truck shift speed. Both of you tip your heads out and see a town coming into view. You nod before jumping out into the oncoming lane and head for the grass next to a medical center. You run across a street behind a few businesses and homes before a grove of trees comes into sight. you keep to the trees until you pop out onto an open farm. You continue across the open field until it intersects a major highway. Seeing cover on the other side, you cross, vanishing among the trees.

"Why are we stopping?" Vince asks.

"I need to get my bearings." You slowly navigate left through an orchard up the lane and to the main house.

You break the door's lock and scan the interior of the house until you spot a laptop.

"It will have a camera," Vince whispers.

You ignore him as you lift it and let it boot up. You let it ping your current location, and you study the map. You are near the border of West Virginia. Northwest is Monongahela National Forest.

You close the laptop and head back to the orchard, slipping back into the trees. You race back the way you came before stopping and kneeling to watch the turnpike through the trees.

"We need to keep moving," Vince urges.

"Patience."

You hear engines revving from a distance as they speed down the road. You focus your eyes far into the distance, listening to the speed and doing mental calculations. The two vehicles are closing in. You take aim with your dagger, chuck it at the SUV in front, and blow out the tire just before the vehicle crests the turn in the road. The SUV loses control and rolls before crashing into the trees. The SUV behind abruptly stops.

As soon as the doors open, you are on them and disable the occupants. You speed off in their vehicle, leaving them in your dust to ponder what just happened.

"They'll be able to track the vehicle," Vince proclaims.

You roll your eyes and pick up speed as you steer the machine down the winding road. Once the road straightens, you push past the speed limit, knowing every second matters. You scream past the road you presume leads to the orchard.

No other SUVs are in sight yet. You ease off the gas as you take a sharp turn in the road, and then floor it once more. It takes nearly seven minutes until another pair of SUVs comes into sight. You step on the gas harder as they whiz by. Your eyes dart to the rearview mirror and see the brake lights flash on. You press on harder.

Three minutes later, you see the sign that welcomes you to West Virginia. You are closing in on your destination, but still have a distance to go. You are going to burn rubber with every mile you can until you have to ditch the SUV. The one thing on your side is that you'll have a lot of tree cover to escape to.

"Brace for impact," you announce after driving around a curve in the road and swerving the SUV over the line.

The vehicle careens into an open patch of woods. You hit the brakes, keeping the SUV steady as it bounces over uneven ground. A tire busts, along with the airbags, as you lean to the left before the vehicle comes to a stop. You hear the other SUVs fly past before the sound of tires screeching on the road fills your ears.

Wasting no time, you take off into the woods. You run and run and run without looking back. Run nonstop, keeping the lead. Intersecting the highway, crossing back over into the trees.

You know you can run faster, but hold back to maintain Vince's speed. The others are at bay. They are not gaining as you run miles and miles across the vast landscape.

You have no idea how much farther you will have to go or if you can even find it. You enhance your hearing by focusing on only one thing in particular: water.

There is running water far off to the left. Several far off in the distance ahead. One that is closer ahead, slightly to the right. You continue forward. You are still a bit of distance away. Hopping on hiking trails and game trails allows you to travel faster, but also allows your pursuers easier terrain to keep up.

"Pass me Leo." You slow down to match Vince's pace and secure the cat in your arms before speaking softly to him. "You won't like where we're going. Stay in the area. I'll come back for you."

Leo knocks his head against yours before you navigate to the right and head for the creek. You run through the water for a stretch before leaping out onto the bank. As the sound of the waterfall nears, you lightly squeeze Leo before lifting him toward the tree limbs. He grabs on and climbs higher.

You turn to Vince and place a finger upon your lips before slipping into the water slowly and quietly. He follows before you duck under the water and swim through the narrow opening under the waterfall. Being able to see it with your own eyes, you can fully grasp what Marc meant when he said he created it.

Chapter 54

Everything looks different now that you are able to see it without the light from a fire. It appears much smaller…and lonelier. How often did Marc come to this place? This was his only sanctuary. Yet, it still must have felt like a prison.

"So, this is the place Marc brought you?" Vince asks, taking it all in.

You whip your head around. "How do you know that?"

"He told me."

"When did the two of you have a civilized conversation?" you ask, narrowing your eyes.

"It wasn't really civil. You were asleep when we had it."

You fold your arms against your chest, and your eyes grow distant as you scan your memory. "What else did you talk about?"

"Umm…." He shifts uncomfortably.

"Tell me." You step forward and get into his face.

"Nadine, I don't want to tarnish your memory of him."

"When did that ever stop you?"

"It's different now."

"Why, because he's dead?"

Vince hesitates. "You won't like it."

"Stop stalling."

He sighs. "You had a severe concussion. The only way he knew how to help you was to give you his blood."

You blink once and turn away. "You always did underestimate my intelligence."

"You knew?"

"I suspected. Knew something was seriously wrong with me that wouldn't have been cured by sleep." You reach out and brush the rock wall Marc stood against. You recall the dagger words you threw at him.

"I didn't hate you. I hated what you did," you whisper.

You wanted to hate him. Said those words even though they didn't entirely ring true. Didn't feel right. Deep inside, you knew they were a lie. You hated yourself for the instant attraction. Hated that you could feel safe in his arms. Suspected his blood was mixed in the water. Knew you were in serious trouble that required medical assistance. His blood was the only fast way.

"I'm sorry," Vince whispers.

"Jomar compelled me to twist my own knife, the one you gave me, into Marc before he tortured us both. Allowing our pain to punish the other, knowing we were helpless to do anything to stop it. Sorry is not enough. Sorry will never be enough," you utter robotically.

Your eyes flick to the passage. You slip through the narrow opening and maneuver through it sideways. You hear steady dripping and stop by a small alcove where water pools before you continue.

Awareness enters your mind that some kind of energy calls to you. You have no pulse, yet your body pulsates with each step you take, almost like a sugar rush. What would make your body react that way?

The path ends, opening just a little, where you find a small pile of wood stacked in a semi-dry corner. Above the wood, in a crevice, lies a different-looking stick. One end has jagged edges as if it were broken in half. The light-brown surface is smooth. Two sections are carved into round, interlacing lines grooved on the non-carved section. The smoothed-out tip has a tinge of pinkish-red lines halfway down.

"Vince?" you call out.

"What?"

"Any idea what that is?" you ask, nodding.

His eyes follow yours. When he fails to respond, you look over at him. He stares intently with wide eyes.

"Vince?"

"How can that be here?" he asks in a whisper.

"What is it?"

"It belonged to my mother, but Vladimir broke it before throwing it into the fire."

"What did Kumal see that he wasn't supposed to?"

"I don't know. I never did find out. This doesn't even look burned. How would Marc come into possession of this?"

"Kumal mentored him, too."

He frowns. "I never saw them together."

"I'm sure there was a reason for that."

Vince drops his head. "He played his part well, didn't he?"

"He had to."

"How were you able to see past it?"

"It was the little things he did. The human side of him. To put value in my life over his own revenge even if it cost him."

He raises his head, only to hang it shamefully again.

"Who was Kumal?"

"My mother's true love. A father I wished I had." He pauses while his eyes spasm before covering over. "He was always there for me. The only one I could trust and be myself around."

You digest the information. The pieces are falling into place. A strategy is starting to form in your mind. One only you will be able to carry out. "How far is it to your vampires?"

"They're up north, at an abandoned corrections facility."

"You should take it. It belongs to you." You nod.

He hesitates before reaching out and picking up the stick. He turns it around in his hand before holding it out to you. "No, you should take it. I think she would want you to have it."

"Why don't you hold onto it for me, for now?" You turn away and slip back through the passageway.

You proceed past the fire pit to the edge.

"I don't think we are in the clear yet," Vince mumbles.

You walk off the edge into the water.

"Nadine." His voice carries annoyance as he follows.

You swim back through the passage, popping your head up against the rushing water of the falls, and stand flush against the rocks, quickly reaching for Vince to mimic.

"Stay here. I mean it this time," you whisper in his ear before piercing his blue eyes.

You slowly ascend the slick rocks left of the waterfall, pulling yourself up onto ground level. You sneak up behind the nearby vampire and shove him against a tree, covering his mouth with your hand.

"You will report that new orders have been received. All are to cease the mission and head back to home base. These orders are not to be questioned."

You disappear above him into the trees and watch as he sends the message on a disposable phone.

"Levi, what's going on? Who gave you these orders?" Another appears.

"I don't question orders, and neither should you."

One by one, the others gather around him and demand to know where the orders came from. After debating, they forgo the search for you and leave.

You leap from the tree, walk to the end of the cliff, and jump down over the waterfall. "They're gone. I bought us time."

"How did you do that?"

"I asked nicely." You turn and call out in an even voice, "Leo."

You see a ball of orange slink down from high in the trees, hop onto the ground, and run toward you immediately.

Now that you're not being chased, you can run a steady course. You don't waste time as you take off through the forest. You become aware Marc did not run a straight course to the wolves. He laid many false trails circling the forest.

"What is this place?" Vince asks as you stop before the fallen eastern white pine.

"The wolve's lair," you toss over your shoulder.

"This is it?"

You slip between the branches to the entrance of the cave.

"Wait, you're taking me in there?" He speaks with uneasiness.

"Would you rather wait outside?" You turn to face him.

"Are you sure you should even be showing me this place?"

"The only way to work together is to first build a truce."

"Umm, okay," he states with a hint of uncertainty.

You walk in silence down the tunnel. Sensing his apprehension, Leo climbs up onto your shoulder and jumps over to Vince, butting his head while purring.

When you push back on the rock wall, the scent of hundreds of wolves follows. When in human form, their natural scent is masked.

"Are you sure this is a good idea? There are too many of them for you to take on," Vince whispers sharply.

"Just stay behind me."

"This is a mistake. I shouldn't be here." You hear the edge in his voice.

You turn to him. "Do you trust me, Vince?"

"Of course I do," he states without hesitation.

"Then you need to trust that I have the situation under control, no matter what. You're to remain quiet with no sudden movements."

He swallows hard and jerks his head in agreement. He's afraid. A different type of fear you've never witnessed before. He has zero control over the outcome. He doesn't know how to handle it.

You walk down the lit tunnel. He follows very closely. You can hear muffled voices ahead from the narrow tunnel before it opens up, revealing the wide body of the cave. There are scattered groups of men and women engaging in social activities and sparring matches, as well as groups in wolf form.

Everything goes deathly quiet before the chaos begins. In union, all the men and women shift into their wolf form. Howling begins to echo within the cavern as the ground rumbles with growls. All eyes are cast upon the trespasser beyond you. A dozen approach hastily at once.

"Stand down!" you command as you back Vince up against the rock wall, spreading your arms, ready to fight and hunching over with dilated eyes and exposed fangs.

The advancing wolves freeze in place. You've never threatened them before. They glance around with uncertainty at one another.

"What's going on?" Lamont appears from the far opposite side. He stops in his tracks when he sees you, taking in your appearance as you resume a normal stance.

Chapter 55

A shrill caw pierces the cavern as Noir viciously launches toward you at a high rate of speed from Lamont's shoulder with outstretched talons. The bird screams in alarm and diverts when Leo jumps onto your shoulder, spitting, hissing, and swatting at the air.

"Why did you bring him here?" Lamont questions, crossing his arms.

In harmony, all heads turn to Lamont.

"Now, do you believe me?" The attention shifts to the other side, where Caden stands.

"Who let you out of isolation?" Lamont frowns.

"She's just exposed our lair. What happens to those who disobey an order?" Caden inquires.

"You will hold your tongue and go back to isolation." Lamont points angrily.

"She's just jeopardized the safety of the pack. We deserve to know her penalty for that."

"Silence!" Lamont declares.

"If you will not punish her, I will." Caden shifts into wolf form and charges. The others part to let him pass. His huge paws thunder off the rock floor as he closes in. His eyes burn with hatred.

Caden stops as Lamont's wolf form cuts him off. Caden's eyes shift from you and lock onto his leader. He does not bow. With fury, he launches an attack. Lamont mirrors and they crash against each other with jaws gnashing, pushing back with their forelegs just out of reach of vital areas. They shove back at the same time, dropping onto all fours, circling before launching again. Lamont is faster and sinks his teeth into Caden's nape. Caden yelps as Lamont slams him against the rock wall. Without pause, Lamont leaps on top of him, holding him down. He keeps his head low and bares his teeth with a deep-throated growl next to Caden's ear.

A whine escapes Caden before he licks at Lamont's muzzle, surrendering. Lamont leaps off Caden, walks the rest of the distance, and turns to face his pack with a snort before shifting back into human form.

"Need I remind you all, Nadia is an ally of this pack. She does not follow orders, nor would she risk your safety. We only prevail if we stand together as one. Some of you have lost sight of what we are fighting for." Lamont's eyes glide around the room to each and every member of his pack. "I know you all have questions, and they will soon be answered."

"I will answer your questions now," you say, falling in line with Lamont.

"Who is he?"

"Why did you bring him here?"

"Where have you been?"

"What is that thing?"

"How do we trust you?"

"Are we ever going to war?"

The questions fire in rapid succession, all drowning the cave in chaotic chatter. A snap echoes through the chamber, settling down all the babbling. You take command of the room with your arm raised and fingers against your palm from your snap.

"Earlier tonight, I had every intention of going to battle without you, alone," you begin and see Lamont stiffen from the corner of your eyes.

"What?"

"Why would you do that?"

"How could you?"

The chatter begins again. You spread your fingers to quiet the noise and wait for it to cease.

"I was wrong to make that choice for you." You lower your hand. "I wanted bloodshed. I was eager for it, but I did not have the right to make a decision on your behalf. I've been letting anger blind reason. I lost my purpose. Allowed a seed of hate to manifest and grow to become something I never wanted to. I've come to realize this war is not meant to be fought alone, as we all have something worth fighting for."

You pause to look over your shoulder and beckon Vince with a nod. Hesitantly, he approaches cautiously on your other side.

"Your fundamental nature is to oppose vampires. You fear what you don't understand. Tonight, that ends."

You pause until the whispers hush once more.

"This is Vince. My friend. An ally, and there are more like him, ready to stand with us and fight. It is time to let go of hate. The end will bring a new beginning: One that unites werewolves and vampires. A place for you both. The time for you all to decide what you are fighting for is upon you. We did not choose this life, but we can break these chains and make a better one. If you have something to fight for, stand with me. If you do not wish to fight, you have the freedom to stand down. The choice is yours."

You walk forward with purpose. Vince quickly falls in line behind you with discomfort as you walk past the pack, who are mostly in wolf form. All eyes are on you both. Low growls emanate from throats, but no one dares to make a move. Leo's claws bite into your shoulder as he growls back, watching intently. You hear Lamont's footsteps bring up the rear.

Vince releases a breath once you reach the other side of the chamber, away from the pack. You immediately follow the tunnel that leads to your quarters. You turn and face them both.

"Nadia, I'd like a word with you." Lamont side-eyes Vince. "In private."

"Whatever you wish to discuss with me, you can discuss in front of Vince." You fold your arms across your chest.

"What makes you think we can trust these vampires and that they will trust us?" Noir stares at Leo from Lamont's shoulder.

"Vince created them."

"That means nothing to me. The pack should not have been informed until the matter was discussed with me first."

"How do you expect your pack to put their trust in me when you question me yourself?" Your head tilts.

"I am responsible for their safety."

"I take responsibility as well."

Lamont pauses, shifting his eyes over to Vince. "You trust him?"

"With my life," you respond without hesitation.

"So, what's the plan?"

"I will accompany Vince and bring the vampires here."

"And if there is resistance among them?"

"I'll compel them." You blink.

"Compel?" Lamont and Vince inquire at the same time.

"Yes, I can compel vampires."

"Why have you never told me this?" Lamont asks with irritation.

"I only recently discovered I had the capability."

"Have you compelled me?" Vince queries.

"By accident, yes, only to make you leave at first. Since that incident, no." You uncross your arms.

"If you can compel vampires…." Vince trails off.

"You can compel Vladimir," Lamont finishes.

You nod.

"All right, go, bring these vampires here and take Cameron with you," Lamont orders before slipping out.

"Nadine," Vince starts.

"Stay here with Leo until I return." You reach up, grab Leo, and hand him over.

"You're going to leave me here alone?" Vince pipes up in an alarmed voice.

"Gabriel will give you some company," you utter, turning toward the entranceway as he is quick to appear.

"You sure do like to play with fire, don't you?" Gabriel comments.

You smirk.

"Nadine." Vince reaches out for your arm.

You stiffen at the touch before you shake him off and move out of reach. "Where's Cameron?"

"Still in the recovery chamber," Gabriel answers.

"He's still healing?" You frown.

"No, he's completely healed. As to why he's still there, well, you'd have to ask him. That is, if you can get him to talk."

You sigh.

"You did well," Gabriel utters softly with a light smile.

"What exactly do you think I did?"

"Challenged him."

"I think you are reading too much into things, old dog." You snort.

"He can't make the pack respect you. Only you can do that. He still has control, but you now have their attention."

"Would you keep an eye on him until I return?"

"I'd be honored to."

You slip past him into the tunnel, readjusting your hearing and tuning in.

"I can assure you, there is nothing to fear from me," Gabriel gently says. "That's an interesting cat."

"Leo belongs to Nadine."

"I see she left him to take care of you."

There's a moment of silence. "You accept my presence without question?" Vince asks.

"She would not risk bringing you here without reason."

"I don't think the rest of the pack feels that way."

"They will not touch you."

"How can you be so sure?"

"You didn't see the look on her face that she gave them when you walked in. She made it clear she would have ripped apart anyone who so much as tried to lay a hand or paw on you. She has never threatened the pack in that regard before."

"She never wanted to become a vampire. She shouldn't have had to go through the transition alone."

"She wasn't alone."

"I should have been there for her. I failed her. Failed her in so many ways. I wish I could go back and make everything right."

"You're here for her now. That's all that matters."

Chapter 56

You resume a normal human capacity of hearing as you continue your way to the recovery chamber. A single caw above diverts your attention. Noir sits perched on an outcrop before swooping. She yells at you while flapping her wings in your face and pecks the top of your head.

A ball of orange fur sails beyond your shoulder and makes contact with Noir, who caws erratically. You watch as Leo sinks his teeth into Noir's wing.

"Leo!" The cat lifts his head and meows with a flick of his tail, and you point. "Go back and stay with Vince."

Leo snorts, displeased, but complies. You watch as he saunters off until he is out of sight. You look down at Noir. She stands with her right wing held out at an odd angle. You kneel on the ground, remove your dagger, and cut into your hand, swiping at the pooled blood before it seals.

"Go on, drink." You offer the blade side up.

Noir cocks her head before lapping up the blood. Within seconds, the broken wing heals. She flaps her wing, assessing, before she turns and takes off down the tunnel in the direction of Lamont's quarters.

As you enter the recovery chamber, you find Cameron lying on his side on a smooth, long slab of rock. Despite his growth within the last year, right now, he looks as small as when you first met him.

You heard two sets of footsteps echoing in the cavern tunnel. Lamont hadn't been gone five minutes before returning with a young lad. He had a mop of dark hair that hid his eyes.

"Nadia, I'd like you to meet Cameron. Cameron, this Nadia." He turned to Cameron. "I would like for you to accompany Nadia for the time being."

"I don't need some kid babysitting me," you protested.

"I know you don't. Maybe he needs you."

"I doubt that."

"He will remain at your side until I tell him otherwise." Lamont nodded at Cameron before turning away, pausing at the entranceway, and added over his shoulder, "You might learn that the two of you have something in common."

"I'll only tolerate him in wolf form."

Cameron looked over at Lamont, who nodded before slipping back out. Without a word, Cameron complied, transforming into his light brown and tan pelt. His claws clicked against the rock as he walked over to the opposite side before lying down with his head across his paws.

You ignored him. Pretended he wasn't there as you paced the small quarters, trying to contain yourself. Your mind hurt. Was overwhelmed by the sensory overload. You had heard all the whispers when you first entered. The wolves didn't want you here. Didn't trust you. You didn't want to be at their home, either. You had lost everything. Fought against your evil nature. Now, all you wanted was to spill blood. A lot of it. Every single vampire you could get your hands on. Especially Jomar.

Cameron's head perked up with a low rumble.

"Quiet," you snapped.

He looked at you and went silent.

"Well, well, well, what do we have here?" You looked over and saw Caden with two other guys at his heels.

"Did you bring backup this time?" You folded your arms against your chest.

"Looks like all you have is a weak pup."

"Did you come here with a purpose or just to trash talk?"

"I'd advise you to watch that smart mouth around me."

"Or what?" you challenged.

"You'll regret it." His face twitched.

"I'm waiting," you mocked.

Angry, he changed into wolf form and charged. Cameron was quick to insert himself. There was no mistaking the surprise in Caden's yellow wolf eyes before he wrinkled his nose in disgust.

You stepped around Cameron, putting yourself within an inch of Caden's jaws.

"Do it." You met his eyes, egging him on.

Caden's growl rumbled deeper. His muscles tensed. You saw the conflict in his eyes. He wanted to attack. Wanted to so badly, but resisted, and he whipped around and walked away.

"I knew you wouldn't have the audacity to," you taunted.

"Do not misconstrue my hesitation as weakness. The moment you put the pack at risk, I'll be the one who enforces your punishment."

"I look forward to it."

"Let's go," he barked at the other two, stomping with aggravation.

"You should tell Lamont he threatened you." Cameron shifted back to human form.

"Did I say you could turn back?"

"He's a bully. He needs to be put in his place."

"I don't need you to defend me, I can take care of myself."

"I was just trying to help."

"I don't need your help. I don't need anyone's help. Now be a good dog and change back."

"He'll just keep rubbing salt in the wounds," Cameron uttered before shifting back.

Cameron was a thorn in your side that you couldn't shake off. He followed Lamont's orders and yours, for the most part, remaining a wolf in your presence. You got to know the wolf side of him. Shared a nonverbal language with him. He hardly spent time with the other wolves. Whenever he was around them, they shunned him anyway.

"Why are you still here?" you demand.

He doesn't stir or answer.

"I asked you a question."

"I didn't serve you well," he mumbles, barely audible.

"Serve? Are you a servant?"

He remains mute.

"If you had listened to me when I told you I didn't need your help, you wouldn't have ended up here."

"He was going to attack this time." He rolls over and meets your eyes with anger. They slightly falter as he takes in your new look.

"It was not your battle to fight."

"I wasn't going to stand by and do nothing."

Your head tilts up at the admission. "Why do you even care what happens to me? I haven't been nice to you."

He rolls completely over and sits cross-legged. "You don't do what you do because you enjoy it. You do it because you're in pain."

"How is that any different?"

"You still care."

"The only thing I care about is ending what destiny has in store for me. Now, I need you to stop sulking and come with me."

He perks up. "You need me for something?"

You don't respond as you walk back into the tunnel. You train your auditory sense and hear him following. When you reach the main body, whispers begin once more as all eyes are cast upon you. You tune them out and continue walking. They're not worth your time. A low growl comes from behind you.

"Keep moving," you hiss.

You don't care what the other wolves think about you. It's clear, though, Cameron is listening and not agreeing with what they say about you and him. Cameron snaps his jaws into thin air, whipping his head. Laughter taunts afterward.

"You think you can take us all on?" Paul steps forward. He's tall and plump with jet-black hair. The group behind him closes in.

Cameron snorts.

Metal against rock reverberates through the chamber. The men who have moved in toward Cameron jump back, redirecting their focus.

"You are all subordinate; therefore, you are all equals. Fighting amongst yourselves is pointless. To question me is to question your alpha. To ridicule Cameron is to ridicule your alpha. If you do not revere your alpha, you should not be here." You stare directly at Paul.

He drops his head and backs away into the men.

"Reacting only encourages more ignorance," you scold Cameron.

As you wrap your urumi back around your waist, your ears pick up on words that pique your interest. "We should tell her."

You zero in on Samuel, the voice you heard. He is standing with Quinn in the far corner with Helene close by. You scan the area all around.

"He told us not to tell anyone," Quinn dismisses.

"He made his choice. He's on his own," Helene inserts with a disapproving tone.

The crowd is quick to part as you advance toward them.

"I don't care what he said; I'm going to tell her." Samuel takes a step forward.

"Tell me what?" They jerk when they realize you are standing in front of them.

"None of your business," Quinn retorts.

"Caden left," Samuel answers.

"Like she's going to care."

You ignore his remark and keep your focus on Samuel. "Why did the two of you *not* go with him?"

"He didn't want us to."

You narrow your eyes. "When did he leave?"

"After your speech."

You turn away and strut for the tunnel that leads out.

"You're going after him?" Quinn asks, appalled.

"Yes," you answer over your shoulder.

"Why? You gave him a choice not to fight," Helene declares.

"Not to fight, yeah, but not to go out on his own. Without the pack, he is vulnerable."

Chapter 57

You race through the trees with Cameron trailing you, unable to keep up with your speed as you head toward the vampires. Other wolves wanted to follow, but you dismissed them. You ordered Samuel to inform Lamont and send Vince to gather his vampires. Told the others to prepare for the worst.

You pause on Caden's scent trail two miles out and listen.

"You know what happens to wolves who cross into our territory alone?" Several vampires have him surrounded.

"If you kill me now, your chance of getting your hands on the marked one goes with with me."

Caden speaks calmly, yet you pick up on the slight tremble in his voice.

"Why should we believe a word you say?"

"I want her dead."

"Why don't you do it yourself?"

"I've tried."

"Why come here?"

"I'd like to make a bargain."

The vampire laughs. "And just what is your request?"

"If we turn her over to you, you are to release the wolves you have imprisoned. We both then go our separate ways, peacefully."

"You expect us to trust you at only your word that no wolves will bother us again?"

"I'll be the one in charge. They would not defy their leader."

"Why don't you come with us, and we shall see what Vladimir decides."

You're too late to stop him. You're too far to intervene. They've doubled up on surveillance. You can't risk it. It's a delicate situation.

You look down at Cameron, who finally catches up. "There's nothing we can do right now. He's on his own."

He whines softly, flattening his ears before you turn back and walk at a clipped, somber pace. You know the news will devastate the pack. Many of them look up to Caden. You know he's just scared. He believes all vampires are soulless monsters and that his purpose is to defend and protect the innocent from them. He refuses to believe otherwise. He thinks Lamont grew weak, allowing you to stay with the pack. You can't blame Caden, especially when you haven't exactly proved that you aren't just as vicious as the rest of the vampires.

Cameron starts sniffing the air. You open your senses and smell a fire burning before you tune in to voices.

"Has everyone been out all night?" a girl asks in a honey-sweet, shy voice.

"Yeah," a boy chuckles. "I can't believe you decided to come after all. I'm glad you're here."

"I'm glad I'm here, too." You detect a smile in the girl's voice.

Cameron begins to growl.

"Keep moving. We're not here to insert ourselves into human affairs," you hiss as you continue forward.

Without warning, you find yourself knocked off your feet as Cameron dashes past your leg, bumping hard into you. He pauses to glance over his shoulder with a snort before disappearing.

"Cameron," you whisper sternly.

He ignores you. You sit there briefly on the ground, stunned. He is about to do something reckless. You have to stop him.

"Help!" the girl cries out.

As you stand, you hear an ear-piercing howl echo in the night. If you were mad before, now you're infuriated, putting on a burst of speed and then pausing at the scene. A girl, who appears your age, dressed in a black, button-up collared shirt and a long, black pleated skirt, is being tied up against a random post jutting from the ground. A small fire is burning nearby.

"That sounded like a wolf." The boy tying knots shudders.

"There are no wolves around here," the other boy declares as he releases the girl he was holding against the post. "It's just a dog."

"Please, let me go," the girl begs.

"I don't think so. Tell me something: Do you know what they did to witches back in the day?" the boy facing her asks.

"Please, don't do this." She struggles to break free.

"Burned them on a stake."

"I'm not a witch."

The two boys laugh hysterically.

"Pass me the gas," the lead boy orders with a nod.

The boy behind the girl reaches out for the gallon of gas sitting on the ground. He pulls his hand back immediately as Cameron reveals himself, snapping his jaws.

"Whoa!" the boy yells, backing away. "I told you it was a wolf."

With anger, the lead boy grabs a fistful of the girl's hair and yanks her head back.

"You're hurting me," she cries out.

Cameron snarls louder.

"Tell your mutt to leave," the lead boy demands.

"He doesn't belong to me." Tears stream down her face.

"Unhand her." You grip the boy's wrist with your own, standing by the glow of the fire.

"Who are you?" The boy meets your eyes with fury.

"Someone you don't want to mess with." You grip more tightly and twist slowly.

Feeling tension, the boy releases his grip on the girl's hair and pulls back, shaking out his hand when you release his.

"Why don't you mind your own business." He gets in your face.

"You should mind who you're talking to." Your upper teeth lengthen as your eyes dilate.

The boy's eyes glaze over with fear as it radiates from him. At once, he begins to back away and trips over his feet. The other boy doesn't hesitate to take off running first.

"Please, please, don't kill me," the boy pleads as he scrambles back from you.

"I'll consider it, only if...."

"I'll do anything!" he interrupts, desperate.

"Channel that anger of yours into helping others, not harming them. Grow into a man who does admirable things and not disgraceful." You take a small step forward as he continues to crawl back. "I'll be watching you, so you'd better work on it fast. Now, get out of my sight."

You don't have to tell him twice as he bolts from the area. You glare at Cameron. He snorts as he sits back and tilts his head.

"Don't give me that look," you huff.

"You, you're a vampire?" the girl asks incredulously.

"I can assure you I mean you no harm." You turn to the girl before approaching slowly to untie her hands.

"Thank you."

You pause, pulling out a knot before continuing, and say nothing.

"Here, you can have some of my blood." The girl offers out her right wrist once she's loose.

You stiffen. "Why would you offer your blood willingly?"

"It's the least I can do after what you did for me."

"I could drain you dry."

You lean closer, trying to intimidate her, but she doesn't flinch. "I know, but you won't."

You narrow your eyes, aware of her hazel ones slightly different from yours. "And what makes you so sure about that?"

"If you were hungry, you wouldn't have let those guys leave without quenching your thirst for blood."

"Well, aren't you perceptive?" You blink, unamused as you pull back.

"How long have you been a vampire? How many are there? Do you live around here?" the girl starts to ramble.

"I think you are a little too fixated on the matter," you snap with annoyance.

"Are you going to compel me to forget?" The girl inhales sharply.

"I think that would be in your best interest."

"You didn't compel anyone else."

"No one is going to believe those fools."

"What if I want to be a part of your world?" the girl whispers with a slight tremor of her lip.

"Trust me, it's not a world you want to live in." You step closer. "You will forget about me. Forget you snuck out late. Nothing significant happened tonight. You will go back home and go straight to bed."

You watch the girl turn away and obediently head home. There's something about her that struck a nerve. How could she want to be a vampire? How could anyone willingly want this curse?

"That felt liberating, didn't it?" Cameron asks in human form.

"You disobeyed me again."

"What's the point of having amplified abilities if we don't use them for the greater good and help those in need?"

"We cannot afford distractions right now."

"I think she admired you."

"This is why I only tolerate your presence in wolf form, so there is no chatter. Now help me put out this fire."

You spread apart the sticks as Cameron digs up dirt to cover the flames. As you stomp down on the embers, Cameron's head perks up. You listen keenly at once. A mob of vampires is heading in your direction, fast and with purpose.

You meet Cameron's yellow-green eyes. You nod as you both bolt in the direction the girl went, toward town. You run, with Cameron hot on your heels, continuing to listen before swinging up into a tree. You reach down and pull Cameron's human hand. The vampires are cruising by without detecting your presence, as they are focused on a mission.

"All the imprisoned wolves are with them. My brother is still alive?" Cameron whispers.

"You have another brother?"

He nods. "He was captured. I nearly was too when we were ambushed."

"How did you escape?"

"There was a vampire who attacked his own. He came out of nowhere when I was surrounded. Took them all out and let me go. I thought it was a ruse and spent a few days on my own before I went back to the pack."

All the comments you heard the pack make about him now make more sense. They belittle him every time he comes into their view. Refer to him as a scared pup. See him as a coward. Believe him to be some kind of vampire worshiper. Believe he should have been banished from the pack a long time ago. There's suspicion he will eventually betray them. They think he's a fool to believe for one second that there can be goodness in any vampire. You have had the urge to put them in their place on more than one occasion, but you bit your tongue because you didn't want to get involved. He meant nothing to you at the time.

You don't have to ask him to know who set him free.

"Let's show them what we're made of."

Chapter 58

The vampires surround the main entrance, as well as the other side exits, trapping all the wolves inside. They all wear armor and bear swords. Brice stands at the head with Caden. The sixteen captured wolves are muzzled and wear heavy chains around their necks. They are covered in filth and scars as ribs show.

"You have something that belongs to us," Brice proclaims. "If you hand over the one marked by the Dragon's Eye, we will release all that we took from you and go in peace."

Several hands reach for their swords as Lamont emerges slowly from the main entrance and stops a short distance from the fallen tree.

"First, I need a show of faith that your word is true," Lamont counters.

Brice shoves Caden forward. "Only when we have eyes on her."

Caden strolls forward, passing Lamont.

"Why are you doing this?" Lamont asks.

"It's what should have been done from the very beginning." Caden continues, disappearing beneath the limbs.

Lamont holds his gaze calmly on the vampires as they all wait.

"She's not here." Caden rushes out.

The vampires yank back on the chained werewolves, choking them.

"Where is she?" Brice demands.

"Here I am." You swing out from the trees to reveal yourself and land just above the entrance.

"Come down, it's over. We have the area surrounded," Brice demands.

"I see you've moved up in rank. I'm offended that Jomar didn't find it necessary to join us. I thought he'd be first in line."

"You'll see him soon enough. Come down from there, now."

"You have eyes on me. Release the wolves first."

"Only half, and when we have our hands on you, then we will release the rest."

"You have a deal." You nod once.

Brice turns his head down the line and nods.

The vampires yank the wolves to their hind legs, and in one fluid motion, break all their necks.

"No!" Caden shouts. "We had an agreement."

"Attack!" Brice commands.

You reach down, grab onto thick branches, and heave the dead tree toward the vampires, knocking down a good chunk of them. The cave entrance is completely open, and wolves, dressed in armor from head to hindquarters, burst forth. The wolves clash with the vampires.

You tilt your head back and howl into the night before jumping down into the action. You race toward Lamont and plow into an advancing vampire.

"Go." You part from him as he slips into the cave.

You pull the falchion harnessed to your back and break the blow aimed at you. You spin to the ground and kick out, swiping the vampire off his feet. Lamont bursts forth in wolf form with armor on his back, joining the battle before you race off.

Metal strikes against metal. Teeth crunch onto armor. The battle is evenly matched at the start. Then, one by one, vampires are thrown back through the air and knocked into trees or each other. Swords are quickly swept from their hands as different vampires in hunter green shirts and camouflage pants stand alongside wolves.

"Retreat!" Brice shouts.

The armored vampires comply.

Caden runs, in wolf form, away from it all. He has no leverage. He's lost it all. He's alone now. Has no idea where to go or what to do. All he knows is he has to run for his life. Run and not stop. Run right into the path of the thirty vampires stationed over one of the three side exits.

"Where do you think you're going? No wolf escapes." A vampire cuts off his path before he finds himself surrounded by five more. All swords are pointed at him as he growls.

Metal clangs against metal. In union, they all turn and see you standing with urumi in hand.

"Let's dance."

Five of them charge with swords held high. You snap out your urumi and rip three swords from the vampires' hands. You grab the handle of your sword from your back and block the blow from your left while kicking out with your right foot. You duck under your left arm while twisting around, kicking out with your left foot into the vampire's knees. You sprint to a nearby tree, push off, and land full force on a vampire reaching for his sword on the ground. You roll to the side and stand in time to block a frontal attack. Metal strikes the back of your right leg, bouncing off the armor concealed in your suit. You turn your head and smirk at the surprised vampire behind you who holds your urumi. Noir dives from the canopy of trees, screaming, and attacks the face of the vampire in front of you. He swats at her, leaving an opening as you kick him in the torso before turning completely around.

"That's not a toy to play with." You catch the urumi in one hand when he slashes out with it again, and you pull yourself in toward him, elbowing him in the throat. He begins to choke at once from the force. You open your hand and see that your blood stains the urumi from the cut that is now closed. A weight knocks into you, slamming you to the ground.

"I got her," the vampire announces.

His helmet is abruptly ripped off. He stares down at you with fear in his eyes before you reach up, grab the back of his head, pull him close, and sink your teeth into his flesh.

Once he is in a weak state, you push him off, roll onto your knees, and acknowledge Caden, who holds the helmet in his jaws. As you reach out for your sword, a foot steps down while a sword is pressed to your neck. Caden growls.

"I wouldn't if I were you."

You look up at the vampire. His eyes flick over your head. You turn your head slowly and see two other vampires with swords aimed at Caden's flanks.

"Ready to cooperate?" he asks.

A blur of fur slams against him. You tighten your hold on the handle of the sword and dive after the other two. You thrust up your sword, clanging it against the sword of the vampire to the left, and quickly grab hold of the other sword to your right. Caden launches on top of the vampire to the left, as you yank the sword from the vampire's hand before kicking out.

You whip your head at the sound of a wolf's cry. A dagger sticks out from Caden's side as he's shoved off the vampire. Noir flaps her wings frantically in the vampire's face as a distraction. In your peripheral, Cameron bounds toward the other vampire, from the one he knocked down, and in one big leap, grabs onto his helmet. The vampire tries to hold onto it, but Cameron is quicker and tears it off. He goes in for the kill, breaking the vampire's neck with his teeth.

You collide onto the ground, pushed down by the vampire, and drop both swords. You snap your head back, hitting true, move out your leg, entwine it, and roll until you are on top of the vampire. He reaches up to grab your neck, but you are first to break his.

You flip his helmet off before pushing up from him and narrow your focus onto Caden. You angle your head at Cameron. You sent him to find Vince and his vampires to bring them here as quickly as possible. Meanwhile, you were able to slip undetected down the unguarded crevice that led to your chamber. You worked together with Lamont to stall for time.

"Cameron, guard him."

You close the gap and stand by Caden's side. He lifts his head and whines before flopping it down. You kneel and yank out the dagger. Caden yelps. You stretch out your arm to his muzzle. He lifts his head once more.

"Take what you need."

He whines, confused.

"Go on." You nod.

He leans forward and whimpers at the movement, which causes a sharp pain to ripple through him. Slowly, he opens his jaws and applies gentle pressure on your arm until he breaks the barrier of your skin. He laps up the blood that oozes out onto your arm.

The vampire gasps as he awakens after the bone in his neck finishes repairing. Cameron growls in his face with his full weight pressed on top of him as the vampire feels around the surrounding area.

You zip over, push the vampire's face away from you, and feed. When he grows weak, Cameron hops off.

You lift your head, resume your natural features, and meet Cameron's eyes.

"I'm sorry I couldn't save your brother." Cameron sits back, hangs his head, and whines.

"I don't understand. I betrayed you," Caden says in human form.

"You didn't betray me. You betrayed the pack." You stand as you wipe the blood from your chin.

"I wasn't worth the risk. You should have left me to die. That's what I deserved."

"Despite our differences, you are still a member of this pack. I fight and defend my family."

"I don't think I'll be welcomed back after what I've done."

"Don't concern yourself with that. I'll take care of it. What matters now is what side you want to be on during the war."

Chapter 59

The sky is black. There is no moon. Wispy, thin clouds cover the stars. The darkest of nights. The air still. The forest whispers are quiet. Werewolves and vampires stand at a distance, sizing each other up. They fought together, and now they take a step back. They all share uncertainty. They are natural enemies. Where do they go from here?

A whistle in the night draws all their attention. You blend in with the dark. Scan the aftermath. Wolves lick wounds to heal. Vampires recharge from blood bags. Cameron and Caden bring up the rear in wolf form.

In unity, growls erupt from the wolves as their eyes lock on their traitor. Slowly, they advance. Cameron sidesteps over, hackles raised and head lowered. You move into their path.

"Regardless of his mistake, he is still your brother. You may find it hard to forgive him now, but he willingly stands on our side of the war to come."

All the wolves' ears perk up. Heads move side to side as energy radiates from them. Noir caws from above before swooping and landing on your shoulder. A significant moment that really gains their attention.

"Thank you for coming." You turn to the vampires and survey each one of them. "You don't know me, and I don't know you, yet you came anyway. For that, I am grateful."

You pause to gather your thoughts. All eyes are cast upon you. The attention does not deter you as it did once before. You do not know the vampires, but you know the wolves and consider them your family, even though you try to deny it. As long as the vampires fight to protect what you stand for, you will tolerate them.

"The time has come to make a decision on what you fight for. What I fight for is freedom from this plague of prejudice cast upon us that binds us all to the past. Tonight showed you that we can all work together for the greater good. We do not have to hide from one another. If you stand with me, I will lead you into a new dawn. A dawn in which the greater evil is eradicated. A future where we decide how to coexist. We do not have to be the monsters from fairy tales. We can do better. Stand for those who are unsteady on their feet. Stand for those on shaky ground. Evil will not prevail. Stand with me and walk into your future."

One by one, wolves step forward and bow their heads while vampires take a knee, showing you their respect.

"They brought the battle to us. We shall take the war to them."

Wolves toss their heads back and howl in harmony. Vampires thrust a fist in the air with a hoot. Noir flaps her wings and caws in approval.

You have them gather all the weapons from the training hall as you slip the last wolf armor over Gabriel's gray and black pelt. He crafted them all over the years. A narrow plate extends the length of his muzzle and widens past the head, and is shaped like a large saddle down his back, with two sets of straps around his middle with a metal plate covering his chest. He also crafted all the weapons and extra shields for training purposes that the vampires now hold. They wear chainmail armor, along with the Dragon Eye's symbol on their foreheads, drawn in blood.

You have all the gear you need. Your sword hangs securely on your back. Your suit is taut from the hidden armor strapped beneath, from your front down to your calves. The urumi is wrapped around your waist, along with a dagger secured on your hip. The only additions are metal wristlets covering your hands with four thick rings up to your knuckles, a metal band around your forehead, and chainmail armor sleeves to protect your arms. And a thirst for ancient vampire blood.

"Nadine." Vince approaches with a low voice, Leo perched on his shoulder. "You're rushing into this too fast."

"The time to strike is now, before they can prepare." Leo jumps onto your shoulder and purrs as you stroke a finger under his chin.

"You won't be able to get close enough to compel him. He will be holed up and throw everything he has against you to catch you off-guard."

"He won't succeed." You look him sternly in the eyes.

"At what cost?"

"It's a war, Vince. There will be casualties."

"I can't lose you again."

"If you let fear of loss hold you back, then you don't belong on the battlefield."

"Promise you will come back to me."

"You know that's a promise I can't make."

As he leans in toward you, you lean back. You see the fleeting hurt in his eyes.

"Hang onto Leo for me." You hand him back.

"You should take this, for luck." He pulls out the broken piece of his mother's crafted stick.

You hesitate as you stare. Your eyes glance up at him before glancing back down at the stick in his hand. You inhale quietly before reaching out and gently wrapping your fingers around it. It pulsates in your hand like a beating heart.

"There's something you should know about me."

"It will have to wait until after." You slip the stick into the side of your boot.

"But..."

"It's time," you cut him off.

You canter like thunder, tramping at a steady pace. Vampires and werewolves jog side-by-side. A slow run to conserve energy, yet faster than an Olympic runner.

You slow down before raising a fist in the air to halt. You look to your right at Lamont and Gabriel with a nod. Their muzzles turn inward, emitting a low woof. At once, Cameron and Caden tear up the grass, covering the last mile to the retreating vampires. Ten minutes later, the two lope back with a bunch of vampires hot on their heels. Alarmed, the vampires freeze. Their eyes travel a mile a minute before reverting.

You reach back and pull out your sword, charging forward. Noir flies above. Vince, along with his second in command, Darius, a tall, dark-skinned bodybuilder-looking guy, marches to your left as Lamont and Gabriel march to your right. The rest of the mass follows.

Small beams of light shoot up from the slowly rising sun, shattering the darkness. Orange and yellow hues begin to glow around the edges of the low clouds. The sky resembles the fury masked in your eyes. A burning fire.

You continue to march out into the wide-open lawn lateral to the front of a large sandstone asylum, where vampires quickly pour out of the front door to defend their castle.

Your eyes skim the front row, catching Brice, who aligns with the others. They wear their own armor. Wield swords and shields.

Active movement catches your eye as several vampires swing up to the roof. They stand in front of the clock tower with recurve bows and metal arrows.

Tension seeps into the ground. All stand at the ready. Ready to clash. Ready to strike. Ready to spill blood. Centuries have built upon this moment. An instant that defies them all. One they could never escape from. The only way it ends is for one to fall and one to rise above all.

Your eyes zero in on the back row as shoulders part. Each row separates, allowing an opening big enough to allow one to pass. Your eyes follow the movement like a sea parting, leaving a path.

The one who is approaching takes his time, confident the attack will wait for him. As if he has all the time in the world. As if they are waiting solely for him before they begin.

The repulsive stench violates your nose. Your stomach instantly churns. You do not have to see him to know who is making a grand entrance.

Jomar.

Chapter 60

You inhale violently at the sight of him. The muscles in your neck constrict. Your grip tightens on the handle of your sword. Your right eye twitches. The torture Marc endured from him flashes through your mind, as well as the horror you went through.

You hear Lamont grumble next to you as you take a step. You stop when you feel Vince's hand on the back of yours. You exhale slowly, relaxing your neck muscles. Jomar is not why you are here. You will not allow him to distract you.

"Nice outfit. It makes you look…serious. Is the bird supposed to scare me?" Jomar mocks.

Noir caws out three times from your shoulder.

"Ironic that Vladimir would leave you in charge when you failed him so miserably. Tell me something, how mad was he when you came back empty-handed?"

"You should know that Marc begged for me to terminate him. Cried like a fool while I watched him bleed out, suffering, before he disintegrated into ashes."

You suck in an immense amount of air before releasing it.

"The rising sun marks a new era." You redirect your focus to the vampires behind Jomar. "This is your last chance to surrender."

Jomar laughs disdainfully. "You're the one who should surrender."

"Those who do not wish to fight, I ask you to kneel." You ignore him.

Jomar glances to his left and then to his right. "Appears you have no takers."

"Pity." Your nose crinkles.

"This is your last chance to turn yourself in. If you do, we will let them all walk free."

You turn your head left. Vince and Darius meet your eyes with a slight nod. You turn your head right and encounter the same gesture from Lamont and Gabriel.

Lowering your sword, you slowly advance. The vampires across from you raise their swords higher as the vampires on the roof pull back on their bows and take aim.

After your third step, you stop.

"Never." You raise your left arm and snap your thumb against your middle finger.

Noir quickly flies from your left shoulder, cawing four times as vampires attack their own from different positions on the line. Ones you had compelled before sending them back while a mass of black ascends from the trees, swarming toward the vampires on the rooftop.

"Attack!" Jomar orders.

Several arrows manage to descend before the murder of crows attacks with flapping wings, knocking them off the rooftop. A line of shields, held by Vince's vampires, blocks arrows, rendering them ineffective.

The sides stampede toward each other, shields at the high from all the vampires, before they all collide. A power move in which the strongest is able to push back. Vampires are thrown back from each side. Openings allow the wolves to sneak in and lunge at the closest assailant. Sounds of metal clashing and metal crunching reverberate as they all go in hot and heavy. Wolves crack open helmets. Vampires stick the ends of their swords through throats to immobilize.

You zigzag through the crowd. Your eyes locate Jomar weaving his way behind his own for protection. You pursue him. Sensing your presence, he turns to block your overhead strike. He forces you back, quick to launch a counterattack that you step just out of reach from, with your stomach scrunched tightly. You flick your wrist downward, banging against his sword. His hand holds steady as both swords point away. He is able to react quicker, kicking his leg into your side and sending you flying back.

You crash into the back of another vampire. You roll off and raise your sword over your head as you push up on one knee. A sword comes crashing down, hitting yours. Before you have a chance to strike back, Lamont knocks over the vampire. He cracks the helmet in two with his jaws before delivering a fatal bite to the neck.

You swivel on your knee, scanning the area. Jomar is on the move, away from you. Gabriel actively shadows him. You take to your feet and follow.

Gabriel launches into the air just as Jomar drops to the ground on one knee, with his head tucked. You put on a burst of speed as Gabriel circles back without pause and takes another leap at him. Jomar rises as he thrusts his blade with precision into Gabriel's belly.

"No!" you shout.

Gabriel cries out as you plow into Jomar. You roll on the ground, fighting to get the upper hand. His helmet butts into the metal band wrapped around your head, knocking you back against the ground before he reaches out for a sword on the ground. You hit your hand against his wrist to stop him before he rams his head into yours once more.

His weight is forced off you. You watch as he hits the ground and runs away. You rotate your head and find Caden on the other side of you. You roll onto your side, push up from the ground with your hands, and freeze.

"Gabriel," you whisper as you crawl over.

He pants heavily. Blood gushes from his wound. It's already too late. The damage is irreversible as his body convulses. You nuzzle your forehead against the fur side of his as a crimson tear escapes, staining the side of your face.

"You can rest now."

His paw shifts weakly onto the back of your hand as his breathing slows. As he takes his last breath, the light dims from his eyes.

You heard someone enter, but pretended that you didn't hear them as you stared at nothing but rock. Gray slabs of rock that were dull like how you felt inside. Sat there like a statue, unfeeling because feeling anything hurt too much.

"You have the exact same look in your eyes she did when she found me."

Your eyes shifted toward the sound of the voice with a slight twitch, but quickly reverted.

"Betrayed. Angry. Malevolent."

Your nose crinkled.

"A thirst for vengeance."

You continued to look at the same spot on the rock across from you, trying to block the memories that wanted to resurface. You were not a weak and helpless human anymore. You were a powerful and deadly weapon now. All should fear you.

"You can alter everything about yourself, but you will never be able to change what's inside."

You bolted from the rock and slammed the guy up against the rock wall hard. You raised a fist, but hesitated after seeing him for the first time. He looked ancient and tired. Several wrinkles creased his forehead. His thinning hair was speckled gray, yet there were still several strands of healthy, prominent black mixed in. His eyes were pale yellow.

He grinned. "I see why you were chosen. You have the same spirit she did."

"Who are you comparing me to, old dog?" You settled for an insult.

"Why Immilla, of course."

Your arm dropped.

"Why don't you come with me."

Your legs automatically fell in line behind him as he moseyed into the tunnel before it split. He went to the left, which led deeper underground. The path narrowed a bit before widening and opening into a large area. Swords were mounted on the rock walls, chainmail armor piled below. Wolves in human and wolf form ceased practicing when they caught wind of you. You narrowed your eyes, daring them to continue staring. He walked on without acknowledging it.

He walked the outer ridge, slipping into a passage leading to a room with a large forge. Unfinished swords lay on a slab of smoothed surface rock. In a corner, scrap metal was heaped together. On the opposite wall hung different styles of swords.

He removed a medium-sized sword from the wall and tossed it. You snatched it from the air. You began to wave it around to get the feel of it. It felt natural in your hand. Not a burden. The desire to learn, desire to practice the art overcame you. A natural makeup.

"What's that?" You nodded at the coil of metal snaked to the right of the swords.

"It's called an urumi. It takes a great deal of practice to truly master it."

"You made everything?"

"I've had a lot of time on my hands." He smiled lightly.

"How much do you know about Immilla?"

"Everything. I am, after all, the original, what do they like to call it, werewolf."

"So, why aren't you in charge? Why didn't you seek your revenge for your mate?"

"I'm more of a loner. Although Lamont made the mistake of thinking that preferring solitude meant being ineffectual. His scar is a constant reminder otherwise. As to why I didn't seek revenge, well, I found it more sufficient to prey on his fear of me. To haunt him every day of his eternal life."

"You don't look at me the same way they do."

"They fear what they cannot control. Fear the unknown."

"And you're not afraid of me?"

"I've played my part. I do not fear death. It's an honor to be standing here before you."

"You don't even know me."

"I don't need to know you. I see in you that same courage she had. To stand even when you're knocked down."

"Courage..." Your laugh is fake. "Courage does not drive me. When you have nothing left to lose, you become invincible."

"On the contrary; you have everything to lose."

Chapter 61

Caden throws back his head and howls sorrowfully. Howls replicate across the field in brief mourning before turning into savageness from the wolves. The anger intensifies as they target vampires.

Gabriel trained you how to wield a sword. How to master the urumi. How to focus on training your body to work with you instead of against you. To put on a burst of speed yet not pass the mark. Most of your time was with Gabriel. He was patient with you. Spoke words of wisdom in small doses. You spent your life growing up without a father, and yet he was the father figure you didn't believe you ever needed. His praises meant everything to you, even if you didn't show it.

You knew he was tired. Had lived a long life building an army of wolves, learning human trades, and training them on every skill he could master. He was a wolf first. His soul belonged to the wild. He saved all the other wolves from being hunted down at times when they were being exterminated. One bite had the power to transform them into what he had become.

"You know what to do." You look at Caden. He takes off at the snap of your fingers.

You rise, wipe the blood from your cheek, and snatch your sword from the ground before taking off in the direction where Jomar was last seen. You moisten your lips before letting out a high-pitched whistle. One by one, nearby wolves break away from the fight and fall into line behind you. Another group darts toward the front door, along with Vince's vampires.

Jomar is long gone, but he left a trail of bergamot behind. The trail breaks off from the battle into the trees that lead to a hidden tunnel into the basement of the asylum. You hear a lot of movement ahead. So do the wolves as a dozen dart beyond you.

Screams echo through the tunnel. You stop and take in the scene as wolves target vampires in straitjackets feeding on frail human prisoners in blue scrubs. Sunken eyes. Rail-thin. Barely hanging on human beings with only enough blood for weak and starved vampires.

You snap your fingers. The wolves whip their heads in your direction in wonder.

"Let them go." You eye the wolves standing over the vampires and backing others up against the tunnel wall, including Terrence, who is in armor, shielding, you presume, his brother.

You continue forward, stepping around the sea of broken humans and vampires. You won't waste time with them. It will have to run its course. There is no erasing the horrors the humans have endured that will always haunt their minds. Death would bring them peace. If they manage to escape, they will be forever affected.

The wolves fall back in formation around you as you walk the rest of the length of the tunnel cautiously. It opens up to dozens upon dozens of jail cells. All the doors are open and unoccupied except one.

Two wolves head to the cell a vampire still inhabits. They stalk the vampire with deep, throaty growls and eyes trained.

Camille.

She doesn't even look up at the wolves from her seated position on the cold, hard ground. She also wears a cream-colored straitjacket with pants like the other vampires.

"Keep moving." You turn away.

"You're not going to kill me?" Camille whispers hoarsely.

You pause with your back to her. "I'm not here for you."

"You should be."

You circle back and see her dull eyes. "What you should do right now is leave. Leave before I snap my fingers and send my wolves after you."

You bring up your hand with your thumb and middle finger pressed together in the ready position. Only Camille does not move.

"I'll give you a six-second head start," you add.

Camille's eyes lift to yours with a little life revived in them. She takes in your appearance for the first time.

You flick your eyes to the tunnel exit. Camille slowly rises unsteadily to her feet. The wolves growl, watching her intently, ready to attack. Once Camille's feet leave the cell, she moves away, pulling herself along the bars in the opposite direction. She has minimal strength.

After six seconds, Camille has just reached the start of the tunnel. Only you drop your hand and do not snap your fingers, turning your back on her instead.

You hear some snorts from the wolves before they follow up the stairs to a gray door. You close your eyes, inhale, concentrate on the location of each vampire on the other side, and kick the door open. At once, four wolves torpedo through, attacking the first line of defense as you rush in before dropping to your knees, sliding across the floor, raising your sword above your head, and kicking out with your leg, dropping the vampire in the forefront. Before he has a chance to react, Samuel pounces on him, cracking his helmet, ripping it off, and snapping his neck with his teeth.

You are on your feet, instantly blocking another blow from your left while kicking out to your right before punching the vampire with your steel fist. You step back out of an attack while grabbing the handle of your sword with your other hand and striking down with force, knocking the sword from your attacker's hand. His eyes follow the sword before he jerks his head back toward you, and then he gets shoved to the ground from the side by a tawny wolf.

Your mind blocks out the fighting around you as your eyes fasten onto a vampire chained up by his hands in the middle of the fighting ring, known as the pit. In a trance, you gradually walk forward. You are in disbelief at what your eyes show you. If your heart were still beating, it would have skipped a beat or two.

Marc.

You look at him from top to bottom, back to top. He is strung up with only his toes able to touch the concrete ground. He wears dirty gray scrubs. His shirt is slightly raised above his midriff. His green eyes are dark.

"Nadine?" he whispers. "You're alive?"

"I thought you were dead," you whisper back.

"I thought you were, too."

"I'm so sorry." Your voice quivers.

"It's okay, baby."

You bring up your sword with both hands on the handle and block Jomar's blow from your right with fury in your eyes.

"When did you know?" Jomar pushes back on your sword before taking a step back.

"Marc never called me baby," you spit out, circling away from the clean-shaven imposter as you watch Jomar's every move. "But I knew the moment I saw he bore no scar on his side."

"You forgot that little detail, Lucas," Jomar grumbles with annoyance.

Lucas half laughs. "You'd think I would have remembered that, since I was the one who gave it to him."

Your eyes flick over to him for a split second in appallment. The second Jomar takes to slip behind Marc's twin brother and push him hard toward you as he kicks out, connecting.

You fall back, slamming against the concrete, managing to hang onto your sword with one hand and quickly roll right just in time as metal reverberates against concrete. You push up with your left arm while raising your right, just as Jomar's sword connects with yours, and you struggle to keep his back.

You fall forward as the push releases abruptly, and you hear a body slam farther away onto the floor. You sit back on your knees and look into Cameron's yellow-green eyes.

"He's mine."

You jump to your feet, twist, and charge toward Jomar, who also charges toward you. You toss the full contents of the open container of cinnamon you had tucked in your black belt into his face. He staggers back, turns his head, coughs, and gags on the powerful powder up his nose.

You hear Cameron's whine. You whip your head to the side and see the switchblade that once belonged to you sticking out of Cameron's shoulder before he rips out Lucas's throat viciously.

Intuitively, you duck and roll from the spot where you stood, pop back up to your feet, and place your second hand on your sword at the ready position.

"It's just you and me now." You face Jomar.

"I hate the smell of cinnamon." He circles.

"Good, I was counting on it."

You launch an attack. You go at him vigorously, the fury in you hot and heavy, with fast blows. He matches you, at first, before you are able to push him back as you continue to attack. A tug of war you are winning. A tug of war he knows he is losing. Your sword moves in closer and closer to him as he finds himself being backed into the ring.

Your swords collide above your heads in a deadlock. He sees the fire in your eyes. The thirst for vengeance. He musters up enough strength to thrust you back before tearing away. A mistake he realizes too late when he finds wolves blocking his path.

You slam your sword against the back of his weapon near his hand, breaking his hold. The blow from your sword to his midsection blasts him away, and he crashes into the side of the wall of the ring, falling to his hands and knees. You are on him lightning-fast, rolling him to his back, dropping on top of him, and pinning him.

"You'll never win." He spits in your face.

Cameron attacks from behind, cracking his helmet before ripping it off. As soon as the helmet is removed, you slice into his neck and suck his blood. He withers and squirms beneath you, but his power drains by the second.

He begins to laugh meekly. "And now, you just lost."

"What makes you think that?" You stop abruptly.

"I swallowed a vial of werewolf blood, and now it's inside you." He continues to chuckle.

"Well, then, I guess it's a good thing it does not affect me as it affects you."

"You're lying." The smirk disappears from his face.

"Am I?" You move swiftly, pushing down on his chest while removing your dagger, striking the floor next to his ear, and clipping it.

"You'll never beat Vladimir."

"Tell me something." You lower your lips to his other ear and whisper, "Have you ever had your bones crushed by the jaws of a wolf?"

His body involuntarily jerks before you stand and kick him out into the open. You snap your fingers, and the wolves attack from every side. The power of their jaws cracks his suit of armor open, like a can opener, before their teeth sink into his flesh and crunch bones in his arms and legs. He screams in agony.

As quickly as they attack, they cease when they hear the snap of your fingers once more. You approach slowly, looking down on him with the switchblade in your hand.

"The pain you feel will never compare to what you did to Marc. What you did to my mother. To Gabriel. To me. And every other life you destroyed with your brutality."

You sink onto him and begin to carve the mark on his forehead. He doesn't have the energy to fight back as he winces.

"Death is too merciful for you." You glare into his cold-hearted, dark-chocolate-brown eyes.

You snap his neck anyway and watch as he disintegrates into nothing but a pile of ash.

Chapter 62

You kneel back from Jomar's ashes. The switchblade drops from your hand. You close your eyes and focus on even breaths. You've visualized this moment every day since you woke, changed. The revenge you wanted for so long is simply over, just like that. You feel a slight weight lifted. Some of the pain is released. Justice has been served. Only it's not quite what you imagined. You're not totally free. You'll never be free.

A nose nuzzles your arm with a slight whine. You look over and see Cameron next to you before he licks at the tear that managed to streak down your face. You glance at his shoulder. His wound is licked clean and healed by one of the other wolves. You scan out to the others who stand waiting for your command. The vampires in the room have been overcome by them.

"It's time to finish this." You rise.

You slice an opening in the dome fence with your sword before hopping into the stadium rows of seats. When you crest the top, you burst forth into the main lobby. At once, the wolves take off and clear a path for you to the stairs as you amble forward through the battle hall. You keep your sword at the ready, blocking blows aimed at you and thrusting vampires back.

When you reach the stairs, Cameron shoots up them and knocks as many vampires as he can off balance. You step back as two vampires tumble down before bounding up. You block a frontal blow before quickly stepping away as the vampire loses his balance and falls the rest of the way.

Other wolves dart past you, up the stairs, as they help to clear the path to the fire escape stairwell. Once in the stairwell, the passageway is clear of vampires until you reach the last set of stairs.

You push the door open, and wolves flood the hallway, where more vampires lie in wait. You join the wolves in the ambush, taking out the vampires one by one until not one is left standing.

You drink more blood from a vampire to power up. When you finish, you lick the blood from your lips before it has a chance to run down your chin.

"Your services are no longer needed. Go back to the fight," you instruct the wolves.

In union, they bow to you before turning and leaving back down the way they came. All except Cameron, who sits down on his haunches.

"I must fight this one on my own," you declare.

He paws at your leg with a whine.

You drop to a knee. "You were such a dear friend to me, even when I didn't want one. When this is over, promise me you will live a life of your choosing."

He licks your face.

You stroke his pelt before placing your head against the metal over his.

"Go help the others." You stand and point firmly. "That's an order."

Cameron hangs his head and drags his paws. When he reaches the stairwell, he looks back at you. You flick your wrist with your finger still pointing. He throws back his head and releases an affectionate howl. When he finishes, he disappears down the stairs.

Alone, you turn your attention to the door that leads to the common room inside the clock tower. The heart of the asylum and Vladimir's sanctuary. He is the only one behind the door. You close your eyes, take in a deep breath, and release it slowly. You turn the handle and open the door.

"Jomar has failed me. I'm disappointed," Vladimir says by the vertical wooden shutters, watching the war below with his hands clasped behind his back.

"He'll never disappoint you again." You enter the room fully, letting the door swing closed behind you.

"Good." There is no empathy.

"Today, your reign ends."

At the same time, you both remove your sheathed swords, yours from your back and his from his waist, before you meet in the middle, matched with equal strength and loathing. You push away from each other and begin to circle.

"You're stronger than I expected, but you will not defeat me." He lashes out.

You block the attack as you fight back and forth, clashing swords, defending and fighting before you circle once more.

"Don't start a battle if you can't win the war." You strike first this time.

Up and down, side to side, high and low, you continue to combat an even match at lightning speed as you anticipate each other's moves. You jump as he takes a low swipe at your legs. When you counterattack, he blocks.

Vladimir seizes an opportunity, deceiving you as he steps back when you swing your sword and connect with air. Realizing the mistake, you arch your back and wait for the blow. The sword makes contact and bounces off rather than slicing through flesh. You thrust your sword upward and stand eye to eye with him. His cold blue eyes. Nothing but pure evil inside them.

"Aren't you clever, concealing a shield?" he gripes, ill-humored.

"Designed it myself."

"A shame we're on opposite sides; you'd make a great asset to me."

"A pity destiny had other plans."

The door bangs open.

"You're not supposed to be here, Vince," you growl out with irritation.

"Look who showed up, a father's greatest disappointment." He pushes away from you.

Your eyes never leave Vladimir, but they slightly bulge.

"Did my son, Vinson, never mention that little detail?"

"Don't let him get in your head," Vince asserts.

A smile spreads upon your face. They are both taken off-guard when you begin to laugh hysterically.

"What's so funny?" Vladimir's not amused.

"You honestly thought revealing that would weaken me? That I didn't know everything about the enemy before I went into battle with him?"

Vladimir bellows as he hurtles forward harder and faster than before. You block his every move, staying up to speed before he throws in a headbutt. The force of the blow flings you backward. Your sword, thrown from your hands, penetrates the wall.

As Vladimir hastens toward you with his sword aimed high, Vince intercepts, blocking the blow. You roll onto your stomach, stand, and yank your sword from the wall.

As you turn to face them, you watch as Vince hurtles across the room, momentarily distracted. You are quick to react as Vladimir bears down on you with his sword once more. You're backed up against the wall, a disadvantage, with nowhere to go as you hold your own. Before you have a chance to grasp his next move, he snatches the dagger from your sheath and jabs it deep into your side, twisting before yanking it out.

"Nadine!" Vince cries out.

"Looks like the prophecy got it wrong." Vladimir sneers.

"No!" Vince charges.

Vladimir lets you fall as he diverts his attention to his son.

Your sword clatters. You break your fall with one hand while pushing against your side with the other. The blood oozes between your fingers while it gushes from your side, along with your energy. You have to get back up. You have to find the strength.

You hear swords rebounding over and over again. Vince does not have the same strength you do. He is running on sheer adrenaline. With each stumble, he gives Vladimir an opening. He is no match for his father. He is not the weapon made to defeat him.

"I've been waiting for this moment. The moment when I could finally rid myself of you, a burden." Vladimir stands over Vince with a foot on his chest.

"It was a great pleasure to see the revulsion in your eyes," Vince offends.

Vladimir backhands him. "I'm going to enjoy making you suffer. No more lies will hold me back now. No one can save you." He brings the hilt of his sword down upon Vince's neck.

You hear Vince gag. You have to find the will to stand. You cannot fail. They are all counting on you. Every sacrifice that was made can't all be for nothing. They will all suffer if Vladimir continues to live and is set loose into the world with nothing to fear.

"I'm going to kill every last wolf, and when we drink in celebration, I will poison all who were tarnished by Kumal. And then the world shall be mine for the taking to inflict true fear." He grasps Vince by the neck and raises him.

Out of the corner of your eye, you see a glimmer. An outline starts to take shape as a flame spreads within your core. An electric charge. You hear a whisper. You did not come here for hate. You came here for what you loved. Love is not a weakness. Love is a strength.

Slowly, you rise to your feet. What little energy remains is what you focus on. You have just enough left to do what needs to be done.

"First, you will watch as I finish her," Vladimir scoffs and lets Vince drop before he turns away with his sword in hand.

The sinister smile on his face instantly plummets when he sees you standing five feet from him. Shock in his cold-hearted cobalt eyes. Caught off-guard. His mistake to assume you no longer posed a threat. One that he just realized he was dead wrong about. It'll cost him.

You flick your wrist, urumi in hand, with everything you have, and it connects with Vladimir's sword. It drops from his hold and bounces off the ground.

He overcomes his surprise as his face turns to sheer anger. He's quick to close the gap and grasp your neck, lifting your feet from the ground. "You're no match against me in your state."

"You think I'm weak." You choke hoarsely.

He squeezes tighter.

"But I'm strong enough to end you." You bring up your right hand, out from the top of your boot, and stab him in the eye with Immilla's broken wand, activated by your blood.

"No!" Vladimir shouts. "It burns."

The fire burns inside. His blackened eye burns to a crisp before he slowly disintegrates. His helmet slips off with a bunch of ash raining down.

The grip on your neck loosens as the rest of the armor caves in on itself. You feel yourself fall. You don't have the strength to support yourself.

"I got you." Vince slides across the floor on his knees and catches you in his arms before you hit the ground.

"It's over," you whisper.

"I'm sorry I never told you. I didn't know how."

You place a finger upon his lips.

He frees his one arm to remove his helmet and lowers his neck to you. "Take my blood."

"No." You place a hand on his chest.

"Please." He looks down at you.

"Stop the fighting," you whisper.

"You need blood."

"I'm not afraid." Your eyes grow heavy. You see a blue fire ring.

"Nadine, don't leave me, please. I need you." He shakes you.

"There's nothing for me here." Your eyes reopen.

"Yes, there is."

"What?"

"Me."

You shake your head ever so slightly.

"Nadine, I… I love you."

"Vince," you murmur and look away as a single tear of red streams down your face.

"We can finally be together." He wipes it away.

You meet his pleading blue eyes. He inches forward, closes his eyes, and presses his lips tenderly upon yours. You let him have his moment before you pull back and rest your forehead against his. There was no fire. No spark. He'll never let you go. You can't be the cause of another rift.

"I'm sorry," you mutter. "I'm not your Juliet."

You pull back and pierce yourself in the chest with the tip of the wand.

"No!" Vince wails in agony.

A searing inferno explodes within, consuming you from the inside out. The pain is more tolerable than the pain of a broken heart behind Vince's eyes. The last thing you will ever see as you fade into absolute darkness.

Epilogue

He stands among the ash and rubble where the clock tower once stood. Embers smoldered, and smoke lingered seemingly forever. All the horrors from the past were reduced to nothing. The only thing left was for new life to grow.

"She would be pleased by your decision," Lamont says, coming up alongside him.

"It should have been hers to make."

"She did, Vince, through you."

"When I thought I lost her the first time, I had a reason to fight. A purpose to carry on. How do I move on without her?"

"You take it one day at a time and find a new purpose. Someday, the memory of her will bring you joy instead of pain. You'll remember all the good instead of the sorrow."

"What if I become like him?"

"You won't."

"How can you be so sure?"

"You have your mother's heart, and unlike your father, you're not alone."

"She wasn't alone, either," he whispered.

"One thing I learned during my time with her was that she never did anything without a reason. Unfortunately, we may never know why, but I don't doubt she had a cause."

"Where do we go from here?"

"We'll figure that out together." Lamont extends his hand.

He accepts the truce and shakes hands with him. "If you don't mind, I'd like a few more minutes."

"Take all the time you need. I'll make sure everything stays in order," Lamont says before striding away.

The memory is still fresh in his mind. He scoops Leo up into his arms. The cat is the only link she has left behind, other than the memory he replays over and over again.

She was gone. Dissolved into a pile of ash. All that remained was the clothing she wore he still cradled in his arms. He couldn't understand why she would choose death over a life with him.

"Come back to me." He rocked back and forth, repeating over and over again.

He looked around the floor for his mother's broken wand, but it, too, dissipated into nothing. It did not burn when it was thrown into the fire, and yet, now it was destroyed. The last piece of his mother he had had.

He was alone. The war still raged on. They were victorious, and yet, there was no leader to declare victory. She wanted him to stop the fighting. He had to summon the strength to carry out her last request.

He punched through the wooden shutters before stepping out onto the rooftop. The war raged on below.

"Everyone shall stop," he boomed with authority.

He stood tall. He stood with determination. A fierceness that everyone below became attentive to. All eyes were on him. The power shifted into his hands.

He raised Vladimir's helmet high. "Your leader is no more. He has fallen."

He raised his other hand, opened his palm, and let the ashes of Vladimir be carried away in the light breeze.

"I am the son of Vladimir. From this moment forward, authority resides with me. Soldiers of Vladimir, lay down your swords. You will go through a period of reconditioning before a verdict is made. A new dawn has arrived. Vampires and werewolves will no longer be adversaries. We will unite and move forward with morality."

Music That Inspired

Part 1 Darkness Comes

"Miss Independent," by Kelly Clarkson

"Feel Invincible," by Skillet

"Perfect," by Ed Sheeran

"Right Here Waiting," by Richard Marx

Part 2 Edge of Darkness

"Dangerous Woman," by Ariana Grande

"Wrapped in Your Arms," by Fireflight

"Energize Me," by After Forever

"With You Til the End," by Tommee Profitt

Part 3 Into the Darkness

"Shot in the Dark," by Within Temptation

"Paralyzed," by NF (Tommee Profitt)

"If You Could," by Nemesea

"Fire and Ice," by Within Temptation

"Lost," by Within Temptation

"Faster," by Within Temptation

"Here I Am" (featuring Brooke), by Tommee Profitt

"Tomorrow We Fight" (featuring SVRCINA), by Tommee Profitt

"Together," by Lunatica

"Stairway to Heaven," by Within Temptation

"Cry with a Smile," by After Forever

"Sweet Curse," by ReVamp

If you enjoyed what you read, please post a good review online. Your input is greatly appreciated!

A SNEAK PEEK FROM

A Dance Between Light and Darkness

THE SECOND NOVEL IN THE DARK SERIES

Prologue

There's hunger in his eyes. The way he inspected her up and down made her skin crawl. She watched all day and into the night as the men rounded up the cattle and began the process of collecting the meat from their bones. As a group, they left. The opportunity she had been waiting for so she could sneak in and collect the spilled blood. She thought they had all left.

She studies him as he studies her. She never saw him before. He must be a new hand. Something she has come to learn about the farm is new hands come and go like clockwork. To most, it is a job. A means to make a living. The life they take is expendable. It is a highly demanding industry.

This one is different. He hung back to take pride in his handy work. To enjoy what it was like to take a life. To fulfill a primal evil that's inside him. An animal that curbed his appetite, but it would never be satisfactory for the killing need inside.

She dodges behind a carcass before pushing with enough strength to knock it into the next one that knocks into the next one, like a domino effect, until the one next to the man hits its mark.

She takes off in the opposite direction, her hair swishing behind her, before she slips on the blood and crashes onto the hard cement ground. He hoversd over her as he flips her onto her back. She knees him in the groin. His body tenses. Enough time for her to slip out from under him and start crawling away.

His hand grasps her right ankle. She kicks out with her left and misses. He pulls her back toward him. With anger, she bares her true facial features. He freezes. Freezes only a moment before he places a hand upon her neck with an iron grip and pulls out a pocketknife from his back pocket.

She is powerless. Despite being a sinister monster herself, the decision she made has weakened her. If she were at full strength, she would be able to overpower this wicked man. Only she is no stronger than who she was when she was a human.

He carves a line into the side of her face. She clenches her teeth, but refuses to scream. If this is the way she is supposed to go out, so be it. Knowing he faced a true monster, he'd never be satisfied again with just an animal carcass or human being.

His weight shifts off her with force before slamming into the carcass. She lifts her head in time to see him crumple onto the floor, unconscious.

She looks behind her. A tall, large, hooded being stands dressed in all black. She cannot see a face.

"My dear, why do you allow yourself to become so weak when you are meant to be powerful?" The voice is masculine.

"Who are you?"

"I am your new master." He removes some sort of rock medallion.

Her eyes follow as it goes back and forth and back and forth and back and forth.

"My dear, it is time to embrace what you are."

Acknowledgements

As you may know, it takes a village of support. I would not be where I am today without the encouragement of family, friends, and a network of connections I have made along the way in my author journey. My dream to one day become an author became a reality thanks to New Book Authors Publishing. They gave me the tools and assistance I needed to tackle independent publishing.

To my mom, thank you for always being my champion. Not all writers are fortunate to have an avid reader and advocate in their court so close to home. I am grateful for your editorial assistance and honest feedback. Unfortunately, no, I will not change certain aspects of the stories, as, like I have mentioned many times before, it had to happen.

I would like to give a shout-out to my friend Becca who reached out to me about attending a writers' group at our local library. By attending, I overcame the fear of reading out loud to a group of strangers who have now become family. As for the ladies and gentlemen at the writers' group, thank you for giving me a safe space to share my writings and helping to spread the word about my milestones.

As I enter a new phase in my author journey, I am grateful to Mikael for opening the doors of Warrington Publishing to authors like me who discovered the steep learning curve of self-publishing. I'm looking forward to building a successful and longevity author career together.

And lastly, I would like to thank YOU, the readers, for taking a chance on me and continuing to turn each page. Not only do I write for myself, but I write for you! Thank you for taking the time out of your busy lives to read my stories.

About the Author

Courtesy of JK Photography, LLC

Award-winning author M. C. Ryder has been composing stories, poems, and lyrics from the beginning of time when reading became a learned trait. The sky is the limit, but she enjoys exploring off the beaten path, both figuratively and literally. Resides in the Keystone State with a clowder of felines who rule the house. Enjoys long trail walks during the cozy tinge of Autumn, appreciates music with deep lyrical meaning, and relishes reading a variety of genres.

Website: www.mcryderauthor.com

 M. C. Ryder (page)
MCRyder0
mcryder0
mcryder0
mcryder0

www.ingramcontent.com/pod-product-compliance
Lightning Source LLC
Chambersburg PA
CBHW051435190726
48289CB00001B/202